MEPHIST

CATULLE MENDÈS (1841–1909) was a French man of letters and the protégé of Théophile Gautier, whose daughter, Judith, he married, though their relationship did not last long. In 1860 he founded *La Revue fantaisiste*, publishing such authors as Villiers de L'Isle-Adam and Charles Baudelaire. He gained the reputation as a sensualist after his 'Le Roman d'une Nuit,' which appeared in the same review in 1867, was condemned as immoral, and he was sentenced to a month's imprisonment and a fine of 500 francs for publishing it. He wrote voluminously—plays, poetry, essays, novels, and short stories. Friedrich Nietzsche dedicated his *Dionysian-Dithyrambs* to Mendès, celebrating him as "the greatest and first satyr alive today—not just today . . ."

BRIAN STABLEFORD has been publishing fiction and nonfiction for fifty years. His fiction includes a series of "tales of the biotech revolution" and a series of metaphysical fantasies featuring Edgar Poe's Auguste Dupin. He is presently researching a history of French *roman scientifique* from 1700-1939 for Black Coat Press, translating much of the relevant material into English for the first time, and also translates material from the Decadent and Symbolist Movements.

SNUGGLY BOOKS

CATULLE MENDÈS

MEPHISTOPHELA

TRANSLATED AND WITH AN INTRODUCTION BY
BRIAN STABLEFORD

THIS IS A SNUGGLY BOOK

ISBN: 978-1-64525-010-4

CONTENTS

INTRODUCTION

Méphistophéla, roman contemporain by Catulle Mendès (22 May 1841-8 February 1909), here translated as *Mephistophela*, was originally published as a feuilleton serial in the *Écho de Paris* in May-August1889 before being reprinted as a book by E. Dentu in 1890. It sold well, was reprinted several times over the next two decades, and has returned to print occasionally in more recent times; it was eventually recognized as a significant contribution to the Decadent Movement that extended from the early 1880s to the end of the century. It is, in fact, one of the archetypal novels of that Movement, and one of the most striking, precisely because it is such a discomfiting novel, whose deliberately controversial nature has been further enhanced as its surrounding social context has changed over time.

It is important to remember, while considering the novel, that it was an item of popular commercial fiction written for publication in a daily newspaper, and a deliberate exercise in melodrama. When a "definitive edition" appeared in 1903 the publisher added a brief preface—not written by the author— claiming that it is "a study of a very disquieting physical and psychic aberration" and "not a *roman galant* [erotic novel] but a formidable poem," but that is mere posturing. The novel is not, and was never intended to be, anything but a horror story. The judgments expressed by the narrative voice, and those attributed in the story to the physician Urbain Glaris, are artificial devices that do not reflect the true opinions of the author. They not only conflict with the attitudes adopted in other works by the author, but are also somewhat in conflict with the inherent rhetoric of the story on which they are supposedly commenting.

The plot of that story, seen as an ensemble, is a little unsteady in its pace, tone and focus, as is commonplace with much feuilleton fiction, written in short snatches for daily serialization and improvised as the author went along, under the pressure of maintaining dramatic tension and suspense at a consistently high level: a method of composition very hospitable to inconsistencies, diversions, changes of direction and contradictions. *Méphistophéla* is, however, a good deal more coherent than many *romans feuilletons*, and always retains a strong fundamental sense of direction. The real strength of the narrative, in any case, is not its plot but its inner tension: the disparity between what the narrative voice, in its more distanced moments, seems to be instructing the reader to think about its unfortunate heroine, and what identification with the character invites the reader to think when the narrative moves inside her consciousness to show events as she experiences and conceives them.

The narrative voice, when it is in its commentary mode, tells the reader that Baronne Sophor d'Hermelinge is a monster, and the story-line eventually obliges her (perhaps implausibly) to come to see herself as a monster too. The detail of her thoughts, feelings and ideas, however—Mendès often comes closer to his character's inner stream-of-consciousness in his dexterous shifts of viewpoint and reductions of narrative distance than is typical of narratives of the period—make it blatantly obvious that she is not. In fact, she is a victim, as thoroughly martyrized by her creator as any other heroine in the history of fiction, in spite of the enormous competition for that title established by the countless writers, male and female, who never tire of subjecting their heroines to the most awful mental tortures they can imagine.

The possible paradoxical effect of reading *Méphistophéla* was neatly summarized by the poet Renée Vivien (Pauline Tarn), who reported that it was the book that informed her of the possibility and reality of lesbian amour—a revelation for which she was very grateful—but that she hated the "bourgeois" attitude to that possibility and reality adopted by "the author." Several later critics have made similar judgments, interpreting the attitude adopted by the narrative voice toward Sophor as a general disapproval of lesbianism, although the preface does make it clear that Sophor is a special case, unique among lesbians by virtue of her demonic possession—whether that is construed literally or as a matter of insane delusion. On the other hand, even in the preface, the narrative voice regards commonplace lesbianism as an aberration requiring excuse, and that could easily be seen as good grounds for Renée Vivien's disapproval of the text, and the disapproval of many subsequent critics and readers.

The reader ought at least to consider the hypothesis, however, that much of what the narrative voice of the novel says is deliberately intended to provoke the reader to respond to its allegations that they are not merely wrong but wicked, and that at least some of its commentary is, in effect, an evil snigger, similar to the one that the story foists on the heroine as a mechanism of torture. In all probability, what the distanced narrative voice reflects is not the author's own opinion but something much more closely akin to the opinion of the hypothetical newspaper readers to whom the narrative is necessarily addressed: readers whom Catulle Mendès despised, while making every effort to appeal to them, in order better to undermine their prejudices while earning his living. In spite of superficial appearances, the novel is both clever and virtuous in using the logic of the story to contradict the commentary imposed on it. Anyone who doubts that intention merely has to compare the narrative voice's stupid praise for the supposed happiness inherent in meek conformity with social prejudice, and the consequent fatality of wanting to be extraordinary, with the example set by the author, who spent his entire life striving to be extraordinary, and manifesting an extreme and conspicuous disgust for bourgeois conformity.

＊

Catulle Mendès was born in Bordeaux, into a family of Portuguese Jewish extraction; when he came to Paris in 1859 in order to embark on a literary career he was taken under the wing of Théophile Gautier, whose salon was still an important nucleus of the fading Romantic Movement in that epoch. Times were difficult for writers because the stern censorship of newspapers and books introduced at the beginning of the Second Empire in 1852 was only beginning to ease slightly in 1859. It did not relent quickly enough for Mendés, whose short drama, "Roman de la nuit" [The Romance of the Night], published in his own periodical *La Revue fantaisiste*, in 1861, was prosecuted for obscenity; he was sentenced to a month's imprisonment and fined five hundred francs.

In spite of that setback, Mendes gradually began to build himself a successful career as a journalist, playwright and poet in the 1860s, and he was at the heart of the "Parnassian" Movement, launched with the anthology *Le Parnasse contemporain* (1866), which tried to reinvigorate the literary scene in the wake of Napoléon III's oppressions, when Romanticism was beginning to seem a trifle passé. The experience of his clash with the law was, however, salutary, demonstrating to him in no uncertain terms the danger, for a writer, of saying what one thought and doing what one wanted to do, if one hoped to be popular and safe. Mendès took the lesson to heart, and the narrative voice of much of his fiction thereafter is typically sly and ironic, and sometimes willfully deceptive and opaquely masked, as it is in *Méphistophéla*.

Mendès's relationship with Théophile Gautier is perhaps of some slight significance with regard to *Méphistophéla*, even though the novel was written long after the two had parted company. Gautier was very familiar with Heinrich Heine's poem *Der Doktor Faust* (1846) and had been instrumental in organizing an adaptation of it for the stage similar to his own Heine-inspired ballet *Giselle*. Heine's version of the Faust legend replaces the male tempter with a female demon named Mephistophela; Mendès would have known that and remembered it. In 1866, however, Mendès—whom Théophile Gautier knew to be a compulsive womanizer (albeit a less successful one than Sophor d'Hermelinge)—alienated the older writer by marrying his daughter, Judith (1845-1917).

Judith Gautier went on to become a writer of great ability herself. She noted wryly in her autobiography that her father had only ever given her two pieces of advice, both of which she had ignored to her cost: "Always wear a corset" and "Don't marry Catulle Mendès." The couple soon separated, and Mendès lived with the composer Augusta Holmes (1847-1903) between 1869 and 1886, although she would not marry him, even though they had three children together. He subsequently married the much younger poet Jeanne Mette (1867-1955) in 1897, but his most prolific period by far as a writer was in the interim between his relationships with Holmes and Mette, when he produced a veritable flood of works, including numerous novels and hundreds of short stories.

Mendès' short fiction, most of it wryly humorous, was almost all adapted for newspaper publication. Many of his stories are frothy erotic comedies, but he also became celebrated for his satirical *contes merveilleux*, which combine cynicism with sentimentality in a deftly distinctive fashion; they are reprinted in several collections, including *Les Oiseaux bleus* (1888; tr. as *Bluebirds*.) He produced occasional longer stories of a melodramatic nature, and, interestingly and innovatively, a large number of ultra-short stories only a few hundred words in lengths, written as "fillers" for newspapers, and for such periodicals as the *Revue populaire*, of which he was the editor in the early 1880s, and *La Vie populaire*, the literary supplement of *Le Petit Parisien*, to which he was a prolific contributor in the late 1880s. Much of his work in that unusual vein was collected in *Pour lire au bain* (1888; tr. *as For Reading in the Bath*), whose contents probably offer a more accurate account of his actual attitude to lesbian amour than *Méphistophéla*; the collection includes a futuristic fantasy in which lesbian marriage has become legal and commonplace.

Mendès' novels are mostly lightweight, and many have been more-or-less forgotten, but two of those that he composed under the influence of the Decadent Movement have retained a considerable reputation, the other being *Zo'har* (1886), an intense melodrama of incest, with occult overtones. In between *Zo'har* and *Méphistophéla* he completed a historical melodrama, parts of which dated back to 1870, *L'Homme tout nu* [The Stark Naked Man] (1887), which also features diabolism, in a more tongue-in-cheek vein. The Devil also features extravagantly in Mendès last, longest and most flamboyant novel, *Gog* (1896), which is very hard to find in the book version, although the serial version in *Le Journal* can be read on *gallica*. After 1898, however, when he produced his most famous verse plays, *Medée* and *La Reine Fiamette*, he devoted the bulk of his creative effort to work for the theater, frequently designing his work for musical accompaniment. His death in 1909, when his body was discovered in a railway tunnel, remained unexplained.

Mendès' influence—and especially the influence of *Méphistophéla*—on several of the most prominent members of the Decadent Movement was very considerable. Jean Lorrain, in particular, owed a great debt to him, especially to the example of his *contes merveilleux*, and Lorrain's novel "Coins de Byzance" (1902, with other works in *Le Vice Errant*; tr. as *Errant Vice*) features an account of a Russian family afflicted by a hereditary curse that is strongly reminiscent of the preliminary subplot of *Méphistophéla*. An earlier response to the character of Sophor is evident in *Les Demi-Sexes* (1897; tr. as "The Demi-Sexes" in *The Demi-Sexes and The Androgynes*) by Jean de La Vaudère, although the image of a predatory lesbian featured in that novel is not typical of the author's work, where such relationships

12

are commonplace, and almost always represented as rewarding and life-enhancing. La Vaudère also borrowed characters and an ambience from an erotic fantasy by Mendès and Rodolphe Darzens, *Les Belles du monde: Les Javanaises* (1889) in her Java-set novel *Trois Fleurs de volupté* (1899; tr. as "Three Flowers of Sensuality" in *Three Flowers and the King of Siam's Amazon*). On the other hand, Sophor is herself a trifle derivative of one of the earlier Decadent classics, Rachilde's *La Marquise de Sade* (1887; tr. as *The Marquise de Sade*), which surely played some part in suggesting the theme of his newspaper serial to Mendès.

✳

Lorrain, La Vaudère and Rachilde all shared with Mendès a strong interest in testing the boundaries of the unmentionable in contemporary fiction, and all four of them achieved some success in pushing back those boundaries. Aided by their initial success, those boundaries continued to be expanded, albeit slowly and with difficulty, but to such an extent that it is now difficult to appreciate how shocking the relevant works must have seemed at the time.

In placing lesbian amour in the foreground of the story, *Méphistophéla* deals forthrightly and intensively with a literary theme that had previously only been treated with delicacy and indecision, mostly in poetry. Charles Baudelaire had famously changed his mind about titling *Les Fleurs du mal*, *Les Lesbiennes*, and the poems suppressed from the first edition of 1857 included "Lesbos" and "Femmes damnées." Writers in the interim separating *Les Fleurs du Mal* from *Méphistophéla* were rarely as bold as Baudelaire, let alone more adventurous. Once the dam was broken, however, it did not take long for a flood to materialize. Four years after the publication of Mendès' novel, Pierre Louÿs' *Songs of Bilitis* launched a vogue that helped lesbian poets like Natalie Barney and Renée Vivien to begin publishing unapologetically Sapphic texts with fervent bravado. In a way, however, the most striking gesture of the narrative of *Méphistophéla* is not so much what it brings into the foreground of its story as what it conspicuously refrains from specifying there—the crucial element of Sophie's innocent sexuality that she needs to discover in order to become Sophor—thus calling acute attention to its continued forced diplomacy.

There can be few people nowadays who do not know what Sophie is so distressed by not knowing, until Magalo informs her—that the method by which lesbians routinely bring one another to orgasm is by manual or oral stimulation of the clitoris—but in 1889, all the relevant anatomical and mechanical elements were unmentionable in fiction for a mass audience, and female orgasm could only be discussed in oblique terms. The prevailing assumption at the time was not only that young women were not supposed to know about such things but—as the plot of *Méphistophéla* carefully emphasizes—even decent army officers like the appalling Baron Jean could also be assumed to be ignorant. The knowledge did exist, of course, and it was not unavailable, in spite of determined attempts at suppression. Several of the illicit best-sellers of the eighteenth century, most famously the works of the Marquis de Sade, had gone into great detail about the female orgasm and how to facilitate it, and the fact that those books were all still banned in 1890 could not prevent their clandestine circulation, aided by their notoriety.

It was also an item of popular folklore in nineteenth-century France—inevitably mentioned in Mendès' text—that the covert culture of female pupils secluded in convents and boarding schools routinely handed down the knowledge, and practiced such arts, and although Sophor permits herself a measure of skepticism, Jane de La Vaudère, who knew whereof she spoke, was in no doubt whatsoever that it was true. It is therefore very probable that a considerable fraction of the novel's initial audience knew exactly what the text was not saying, and were therefore well aware of the pointlessness of its continued unmentionability in print. In spite of that, however, the barrier was by no means easy to break down, even in France, let alone elsewhere (there was, of course, no possibility of *Méphistophéla* being translated into English in 1890, or during the greater part of the twentieth century.)

Given the importance of that hypothetical ignorance to the plot of the novel, and the crucial role that the secret, once disclosed to Sophor but not to the reader, plays in the unfolding of her brief triumph and long tragedy, it might seem odd to suggest that *Méphistophéla* is not fundamentally a novel "about lesbianism." In fact, however, as previously noted, it is essentially a horror story about demonic possession, about contrived and cruel damnation, devoid even of a Faustian pact, which merely employs obsessive lesbian desire as an instrument of damnation. As the prologue points out in its lavish description of the detail of contemporary Parisian moral decadence, lesbian amour was both commonplace and tolerated in Parisienne society, and what Sophor suffers from is something markedly different. It was, however, difficult in 1889 to take demonic possession literally in a *roman contemporain*, all the more so as Symbolism was then at the height of its fashionability, so there would have been a strong inclination then, as there is now, to regard the demonic possession as a representation of something else—and if not lesbianism, then what?

In fact, the text's vagueness on the subject of what Sophor actually does with her partners assists the suggestion that the real subtextual subject matter of the story is the desire to be extraordinary: to step outside the norms of socially sanctioned behavior. Sophor's lesbianism is merely a particular exemplar of that ambition. Catulle Mendès was no stranger to social prejudice, hostility and ostracism, not merely as a victim of then-rife anti-Semitism but as a "Bohemian" poet, a serial womanizer and—a particularly significant item in the Parisian literary community—the man who had broken Judith Gautier's heart. Obviously, he found it easy to insert his narrative voice into Sophor's imaginary consciousness, not only because, as a sex-addicted heterosexual male, he knew perfectly well what aspects of female bodies might fill her with lust, and was thus able to describe her temptations with real feeling, but because he also understood her determined pride in being different, and her defiant contempt for the small-mindedness of those who disapproved of her.

The most important point to be made about the evasions and deceptions of the novel is, however, the vitriolic sarcasm of its "message" that conformity is the only predestined road to happiness, with success guaranteed. Mendès could be sure that a fraction of his audience at least as large as the fraction who knew Magalo's secret would know that the assertion in question is utter balderdash, but that they also felt obliged not to mention the fact in polite society. He could be confident that some of them would able to guess that he meant the opposite of what he was saying in that regard, and that even if they could not, they would be capable of raising the objection that the vast majority of conformists actually lead lives of miserable desperation, which only differ from those that the extraordinary lead in being quieter.

On the other hand, even those readers of the *Écho de Paris* who knew that what the distanced narrative voice and some of the characters have to say about the inevitable happiness of conforming to social prejudice was rubbish might not have been sure that the author was being ironic, when he was being ironic, and to what extent; Mendès must have known that there was a danger that he might be taken at "his" word and classed as a craven advocate of conformism. There was, therefore, a measure of heroism in his taking the risk, and there is no doubt that the sections of the story in which a sophisticated reader is meant to take an implication opposite to the explicit statements of the narrative voice are the most challenging as well as the most interesting and the most artful.

In that respect, *Méphistophéla* and this translation nowadays have a much more hospitable context in which to work.

16

Everyone who is capable of thinking (many people are still incapable, but they are unlikely to pick up a book) not only knows that conformity does not engender happiness, and that wanting to be exceptional is not a bad thing, but also knows that it would be quite absurd to think that lesbian desire might be evidence of demonic possession, real or metaphorical, and that if such desire still seems to some people to be inherently "aberrant" or "unnatural" it is because the people to whom it seems so have a mistaken view of "normality" or "nature." The vast majority of modern readers will therefore have no difficulty in following the course of the narrative when it identifies closely with its misunderstood and ill-used heroine, and no difficulty with sympathizing with her, at least until the moment when the mysterious supernatural force of "ennui" forces her capitulation and seals her tragedy.

Ennui was, of course, the central motif and the great bugbear of the Decadent Movement, given legendary status by its chief precursor, Baudelaire. In that respect, too, the cultural context surrounding the novel has shifted. Those readers of the 1890s who had given up believing in the Devil but could still believe in Urbain Glaris' redefinition of Sin were very familiar with the notion of ennui and its most mordant variety, spleen. Modern readers are less familiar with it, although no less likely to believe in it for that. It would, however, require a very devout believer in its corrosive potency to swallow the idea that ennui could have the devastating effect that it is alleged in *Méphistophéla* to have on Sophor, or even on poor Magalo. At that point, if not before, the reader must surely be incited to revolt against the nasty insinuations of the narrative voice and the savage cruelty of the plot.

On the other hand, again, that revolt cannot lead the reader to think that Sophor's rebellion against social hostility, or Catulle Mendès' similar rebellion, could ever have been successful in any but a small personal measure: a matter of escape rather than victory. It could not have been otherwise in the 1890s, and it cannot be otherwise nowadays; conformity does not bring happiness, but it does always win the democratic battle for hearts and minds, virtually by definition. That is why Sophor's story is, essentially and inherently, a tragedy and a horror story. Such is life—and, of course, death, whether the latter occurs in a railway tunnel or elsewhere, explained or not.

✳

This translation was made from the copy of the Dentu edition reproduced on the Bibliothèque Nationale's *gallica* website. The layout of that edition is very dense, with paragraphs that often run on for several pages and no text breaks apart from the chapter breaks. It was probably set from the pages of the newspaper, where text beneath the feuilleton was very often cramped by copy-editors, in order to make maximum usage of the space. Working on the thesis that the layout is more likely to be the result of editorial decision than authorial intent, I have taken the liberty of introducing a few extra text breaks as well as numerous extra paragraph breaks, in order to assist readability.

—Brian Stableford

MEPHISTOPHELA

PROLOGUE

In the two-seater carriage, light on its high slender wheels, alongside a valet-groom dressed in a sky blue livery, Baronne Sophor d'Hermelinge, sheathed in white leather, which only covers to mid-thigh the swelling of a tight body-stocking, her upper body very straight in her gray jacket, with the reins pulled up toward her chin, is coming back from the Bois among the returning victorias and coupés. Between the toque that hides all her hair and the firm collar that grips her neck, her face, in the daylight, is pale, with round, iron-gray bloodshot eyes devoid of lashes and eyebrows. She is looking straight ahead; it seems that she cannot see anything, but that she has just witnessed a terrible spectacle. Her immobility is that of a stupefaction in which a residue of terror persists. Her features, which are certainly convulsed by fear, retain the distention of a grimace in the pale and dead peace in which they are fixed; also, the rectitude of her entire pose is a petrified frisson. One must remain thus after having contemplated Medusa. She provokes the idea of the aftermath of something horrible, of the minute that follows a sin—it is that minute, eternalized, that will be Hell—and she resembles the painted mummy of remorse.

She passes by; people sketch sudden gestures toward her; they follow her for a long time with their eyes. The whispers of an envious and scornful flattery escort her; that sound, "Baronne Sophor d'Hermelinge," accompanies her, envelops her, wrapping her like the bandages of a mummy; and in her funereal make-up, that long, pale, aristocratic name is like the trailing edge of a shroud.

21

But if, for a moment, she looks at those who are observing her, they no longer observe her, they talk about something else. Because they know her, because they sense that she is different even from those who resemble her, because something sinister, by virtue of being abnormal, distinguishes her, specializes her and isolates her, they experience, along with a desire to know everything, a fear of learning too much. Her mystery attracts and repels, lures curiosity and frightens it. In the tumult of Parisian life, she is often an occasion for silence; she inhibits laughter.

Certainly, the aberration that makes her illustrious is nothing henceforth but a mediocre and frequent anecdote. If the time has not yet come—the time predicted by the chaste and melancholy poet—in which the divorce of the enemy sexes will be accomplished in the south and the north, the west and the east; if, in the modern Heptapolis, enough wives and husbands, mistresses and faithful lovers, survive in the healthy observance of natural rules for divine punishment not to submerge as yet the abominations of sterile forbidden hymens beneath a torrential downpour of sulfur and bitumen, it is nevertheless true that the breath of woman often mingles with the breath of woman—and Paris will not linger in emotion long for so little.

It knows that the horror of being paid, or the disgust of paying, finally renders odious to the sad daughters of amour those on whom they live, or those who live on them, and exhorts them with reciprocal disinterest to feminine embraces that permit them the illusion of loving and being loved, while preserving them, strictly, from the possibility of a sincere abandonment in unworthy arms.

But the perfect scorn that accompanies sellers of joy, by reason of their profession, spares them one reprisal more.

Paris, in which candor would be as stupidly hypocritical as the simpering of a little girl on the part of a courtesan, knows that sometimes, when husbands are at the club, two young wives whom the dread of a lover's indiscretions or the peril of visibly adulterated loins advises against the excess of extreme flirtations, renew, less puerile but more chaste, in the scented penumbra of the boudoir, amid the hazards of gaping peignoirs, the languor of the old dormitory of the boarding school or the convent: the seductive, uncertain, tentative cajoleries of a wing unsettled, scarcely caressing, which no prayer or confession precedes, distractedly prolonged, heads hidden in lace, of the encounter, almost not strictly made, of a hand with a hand, to the extent of ascents that brush back the down of an arm or descents toward the unexpectedness of a hip; no kiss, except with a common accord not to see anything, an almost breathless mutism of gratitude and contained sighs; and then, after the lassitude of uncoupled arms dangling toward the carpet, not even a blush, the pink remorse of cheeks, remains of the sun, there is the resumed conversation, about the new play, or the ambassador's ball, or the form of the hat one will wear.

And Paris has indulgence for these occulted sins of silence and fragrant dusk, so scantly real by virtue of such short duration, suspected rather than averred, that even the culpable parties will forget, to the point of not rediscovering them in their memory on the mornings of stammering in the confessional of Saint Thomas Aquinas or Saint Philippe du Roule. Like the director of conscience, to whom one has not confessed everything, Paris, which is not unaware of anything, absolves.

For it no longer has the right to be equitable, a judge charged with crimes reduced to clemency by the fear of the ridicule that Lacenaire would incur in criticizing a thief of apples from the other side of a wall or the Marquis de Sade blushing at the impression of an embrace left in trampled wheat; comparable to a man who can see his internal corruption seething through every open pore in his skin, frightened of itself, and full of the shame, and also the pride, of being incomparable among damned cities, Paris contemplates its abjections and the hypocrisies of its last virtues, all the august, vile or absurd chimeras: the fatherland, pretext; art, commerce; the irony of the incense at the foot of statues and the speculation of prayer before altars; daughters sold by the father and mother—people practicing, admittedly, good housekeeping—destined for prostitution since the first rock of the cradle, which nevertheless resembles a refusal, methodically, with the patience implied by the choice of a career, as if after a resolution made in family council; the breasts of décolleté duchesses becoming sticky in brothels with the kisses reeking of sherry or port of drunken foreigners; more detestable, those virgin givers of their mouth and their throat and their entire naked body who, for the pride of an unwrinkled belly or to spare themselves the bother of a fetus cut into pieces and then thrown to the latrines, remain virgin in their obscene beds; and, in the offices of matrimonial notaries who are about to depart for Brussels or are returning from the Mazas, the name exchanged for money—not much money—misallied at a discount, as if the extreme descendants of illustrious families, peddlers of immemorial glory, were howling on the boulevards: "Get it while it's hot! Buy Rosbecque! Rocroy! Fontenoy! Latest edition!"

If it observes itself more profoundly, Paris sees its hideous, viler depths, like wounds one has on the feet: the odor of its outlying districts and suburbs, everything exhaled by the innumerable population, dirty and crossbred, of prostitutes and killers prowling from streetlight to streetlight in the ritornelle of dance-halls, and assembled by a whistle-blast that springs from the corner of a street on the intersections of the boulevard, in the sickening stink of brothels and abattoirs, and nocturnal brawls quivering with the glint of knives.

So profound and so irremediable, however, always sinking further, is the extinction of moral daylight on the heights, that Paris finally wonders whether it is not from the filthiest depths that in the future, long-awaited, a necessary light might rise: perhaps a conflagration, but a light nevertheless. There is, in the crapulous population, something akin to a frightful candor, something in the barbarity that resembles childhood; is there a commencement of dawn and spring in that gray swell, tinted pink here and there by murder? Who can tell? Might the future be ignited by the steel of blades?

In the meantime, Paris, which knows itself, no longer dares get angry because, in a boudoir, two similar friends, under the pressure of the same desire, two flowers of the same stem curbed by the same wind, cannot help transgressing an uncertain law, bringing together their perfumes of better roses. And it forgives, smiling. The smile is the supreme resource of those put off by the melodrama of maledictions; a resource, too, against the horror of oneself, the elegance of melancholy, the dandyism of despair and remorse.

Even for other mingled feminine mouths, Paris has complaisance. If, in the folly of nocturnal champagne, smitten beautiful women, hair and skirts flying, forget the difference between the permitted and the forbidden; well, what can you say about that? They are intoxicated by the happy intoxication of gleams in the eyes, intoxicated by the contact of bare arms and strawberries eaten with four lips for the amusement of desserts, and the odor of make-up that is no longer holding and running along the skin like the droplets of an artificial rut; and the sweat of waltzing together between the tables pushed toward the wall, the breasts of one leaning into the cleavage or touching the breasts of the other, envelops them in a moist exhalation of flesh in which it is pleasant to swoon.

Those Parisiennes, those pagans, are, unconsciously, the maenads of a triumph of Bacchus, in which the drunken god groups between his knees, in the chariot whose wheels are crushing enlaced couples without distracting them, nymphs drunk on ripe grapes, and enables them, in his embrace, to embrace one another. What there is of the frenzied in the ripping of their dresses, renders innocent the impudence of their nudity, just as, among the pell-mell of falls and abandonments on the carpets, on the sofas, on the disorder of torn underwear, broken crystal and porcelain, their laughter, which tangles black and red hair, their laughter, as resounding as the ring of bright metal, excuses the infamy of their kisses.

They are amorous madwomen! Amorous of whom, of what? Of everyone, everyone and everything. Descended from their frames in order to live the mythologies of the kiss, they are the faunesses and hamadryads of painters, mingling for their own pleasure and the pleasure of others, the snow and gold, or the living ebony-haired ivory of their bodies, which are indolent and are offered to one another. And Paris, that artist, a sort of Nero before the very city that the handsome tyrant-poet built on the ruins of burned Rome, loves the impetuous flesh of its white Corybants.

But Baronne Sophor d'Hermelinge does not resemble either the sad daughters of amour who demand from the female kiss a revenge for the virile insult, or the distracted socialites soon forgetful of the pleasure that they hardly had, or the extravagant beauties drinking lust from all the cups where it foams.

And people are astonished by her, and alarmed.

They are in the presence of a monster, who goes as far as perfection in monstrosity. She is devoid of weakness in evil; her sin never afflicts her conscience; she is irreproachable. "*Homo sum!*" cries Juvenal's Messalina, with reason, since it is males for whom she yearns in the brothel in Suburra. But the woman who virilizes herself definitively dehumanizes herself.

Imperturbable, haughty, authorized, one might say, Baronne Sophor d'Hermelinge, in her sinister fixity, in her pallor of a poorly-resuscitated corpse, is the pale empress of a macabre Lesbos.

From her attitude, from the abominable legend that follows her, the idea emerges of a continuous, methodical, unhurried crime, which resembles the exercise of a function, the accomplishment of a duty. It seems that she does not want her vice, that it is indifferent to her, even odious, but that it is obligatory, that she is submissive to it, as to an unbreakable law; that she has condemned herself to the forced labor of indecent pleasure. No arrest or termination is possible, she realizes her damnation without pause, upright, like a tombstone; nothing deters her or deflects her; she goes straight ahead.

Nowadays, when science is discovering verities parallel to the pretended lies of ancient magic and sorcery, in which experimentation is ceasing to belie ancient intuitions, when the professor in the midst of his demented patients is reminiscent of Urbain Grandier among his nuns, and one demonstrates hysteria by means that the demonologist Bodin used to prove possession, who can affirm that mysterious neuroses are anything, in reality—the names change but not the effects—other than the charms, curses and bewitchments practiced by sorcerers or empusas? And who knows whether the deliria of intoxications to which souls overloaded with anguish fatally surrender themselves are not the spasms and the frenetic tics of a demonic incarnation?

A master has written: "It is easy to grasp the rapport that exists between the satanic creations of poets and the living creatures that have consecrated themselves to stimulants. A man wants to be a god, but soon falls, by virtue of an uncontrollable law, lower than his true nature. His is a soul sold retail."[1] Perhaps there is more than a rapport; perhaps there is a perfect identity between the Fausts conquered by Mephistopheles and all the coveters of artificial paradises who request from the deceptive power of drugs the realization in humanity of the superhuman. They are thought to be drunk, but are possessed. Since celestial omnivirtue has its real presence in Bread and Wine, it might be that diabolical malice is consubstantial with opium, hashish and morphine, that a drinker of alcohol is drinking Satan, that an emetic is an exorcist.

If evil spirits can haunt a man and install themselves within him, it is a dismal demon, or demoness—for why should tempters not be one or other sex, the more brutal male and the more insidious female?—that possesses Baronne Sophor d'Hermelinge.

---

1 The quotation is from "Le Poëme du haschisch" (1858) by Charles Baudelaire, reprinted in *Les Paradis artificiels* (1860).

What is known about her is disconcerting by virtue of the measure, the precision and the clarity in her sin. She shows herself to be deliberately terrible. Morose in her frightful joys, she is perverse with gravity and perverted without tenderness, passion or charm; she does not seduce those whom an execrable norm constrains her to choose; she conquers them, takes them, curbs them with the certainty of a despotism; her gaze commands, the silence of her mouth orders; her cold covetousness is like an icy hook. Virgins have gone to her without her having made a sign to them to come, vanquished, and stupefied to be; beautiful young women, socialites or actresses, happy and joyful, turn their heads away in vain when she goes by, but soon follow her with the decision of the impossibility of resistance, their thought annulled and their eyes widened by vertigo. Prostitutes, whom she disdains to choose herself but has sent to her by procurers, like some lazy princely libertine, try to laugh and shrug their shoulders—they have seen many others!—as they climb the stairs of the house about which subtle and barbaric mysteries have been narrated to them, but shiver as they are about to enter, with sweat on their temples; they do go in, however, rapidly and furtively, closing their eyes, as one slides into a hole.

And all those who submit to her slowly clenched, tenacious and tyrannical caress remember it as an escaped prisoner recalls the cold wall, the chain and the carcan. Even in the abominable debauches that she sometimes deigns to confess in a curt and simple remark that forbids surprise, even in the extreme enragement of concupiscence, she contains herself, or, veritably calm, has no need to contain herself, as furious and cold as the torsion of a marble statue; and she shows her teeth in a slow and hard laugh.

One day, when a young maidservant—the story has been known and whispered for a long time—fled recklessly through the trees of the garden of a guinguette, people came running who, on penetrating into the arbor, saw Baronne Sophor d'Hermelinge standing against the table, impassive, not breathless, who looked at them, her eyes blank, very pale but with her habitual pallor, with a little moist rouge on her mouth.

However, amid the return of the victorias and the coupés, as she comes back from the Bois in her two-seater carriage, light on its slender wheels, even along the Champs-Élysées, where fiacres are more numerous and many bourgeois strollers are coming up and going down to the left and the right of the causeway, that murmur: "Baronne Sophor d'Hermelinge!" precedes or follows her; there is, around her a kind of outrageous triumph, the admiration that can be contained in scorn. Faustina, Isabeau and Lucrezia have known the glory of insult to that degree.

After having turned into the Rue Marboeuf, the carriage slows down in front of a vast town house with neither railings not garden, nothing but white stone, in which three high arches open, cold and devoid of sculptures; it turns into the widest of those pale tunnels, and stops. The Baronne gets down, one hand on the valet's elbow. Her movements are neat, measured and precise, reminiscent of what there would be of the static realized in a perfect automaton.

She goes up a staircase of marble steps between lush plants, only responds with a dismissive gesture to two chambermaids hastening along the landing of the first floor, lifts a curtain that falls back heavily behind her, traverses a drawing room, another drawing room and a bedroom—hard and bright luxury, white fabrics, very smooth, with steel roses, square furniture incrusted with tin, countless mirrors in which brutal pallors and precise forms are reflected infinitely—and arrives in a dressing room that is all raw alabaster and bare faience, spacious, devoid of frills and perfumes, in which the thousand objects of toilette, mat silver and new ivory, on the marble surfaces imitate parallel lines of arranged weapons, and regular complications of panoplies on the wall: something like the dressing-room of a Penthesilea.

It is the resource of the woman who has ceased to be, in accordance with one or other of her functions, a housekeeper or a tender coquette, differentiating herself as a warrior: Mademoiselle de Maupin—not the one of the divine novel—drawing her sword unceremoniously and killing, with a thrust in the belly, on the wedding night, the husband of the bride she loved.[1] By virtue of not remaining in the normal, the woman is constrained to the extreme; for her, there is no sojourn, even for an instant, between the banality scarcely surpassed and the beyond of excess. In masked balls, women in disguise show more impudence than men; everything that is usurped is exaggerated.

Scarcely having arrived in her dressing room, Sophor d'Hermelinge marches straight to a large mirror. Her face has not changed expression; so pale and devoid of movement, it still has the customary domineering fixity in which fear is immobilized. With a swiftly extended hand she picks up a powder-puff—being a Parisienne—and makes her pallor less ghostly. But she does not smile at her image, as young women do before a mirror. She does not admire herself, she observes herself.

Then, having taken off her hat and jacket, she turns round and lies down on a long, hard sofa devoid of cushions, with bronze ornaments, a sofa imprinted with the décor of tragedies in which the bad taste of leopard-skin abounds; her elbow in the back, her feet outside the ankle-boots whose heels she has removed with her toes, Baronne Sophor d'Hermelinge gives the appearance of dreaming.

Is she dreaming?

About her glory?

For, in the city in which one recognizes the habit of rarely being astonished, it is, after all, a glory to be a quotidian object

---

1 Before he turned it into an entirely fictitious novel, Théophile Gautier's *Mademoiselle de Maupin* (1835) started out as a brief "drama-documentary" about the opera singer Julie d'Aubigny (c1670-1707), who became Madame Maupin or "La Maupin" by virtue of a forced marriage; her life was sensationally scandalous, involving sexual relationships with both men and women, and involved numerous duels, which she usually won, being a fine swordswoman.

of surprise and alarm. Paris, with all its grandeurs and villainies, all its sciences of good and evil, only grants its curiosity infrequently, and one is worth something when one merits being considered with amazement there. To be exceptional in Gomorrah or Sodom would even have tickled the vanity of Heliogabalus or the divine Marquis.

Doubtless, she is dreaming, the frightful and bleak triumphatrix, of all that popularity around her, made of indignation and outrage, as tumultuous and dirty as an ocean of mud, and as grandiose. She knows that she is the distant and wanly luminous point where all maddened and unhinged attentions converge; she knows that no vice, between women, is realized on the benches of promenades or in the ditches of the suburbs, without being authorized by her example. She is the queen, not present but accepted, of the female Court of Miracles of evil; it is toward her, toward the erection, in a ruddy and dense shadow, of her sterilized femininity, that the universal odor of open female sexual parts rises like a strange incense.

And she has the pride of not being able to be calumniated. She has conceived and achieved more than people believe that she could have done. She has surpassed the hypotheses of solitudes and hysterias. She is, veritably, the perfect damned soul. And if it is by an evil spirit that she is possessed, the demon—or demoness—that has acquired her, has not been treacherous or miserly in the accomplishment of the pact, since to that rich and noble creature, who was and is beautiful, it has given in exchange for a soul consecrated to the uncertain inferno, all the indecent glory and undoubted pride of incomparable sin.

But while she is dreaming, her eyelids flutter spasmodically over the fixity of the pupils, as if sobbing, and in her round iron-gray eyes devoid of lashes or eyebrows, in which a transparency of emptiness was rounded a little while ago, in her widened eyes, shadows rise to the surface, and descend and rise again, like the clouds of mud that shift in stirred water.

Baronne d'Hermelinge has almost sat up; with her two hands behind her, clenching the bare wood of the sofa, she is considering something invisible in the throes of panic. Her gaze is that of Macbeth toward the armchair occupied by the spectral absence. Then, suddenly, with a desperate sideways movement of the head, she puts her palms over her ears, as if in order not to hear.

Hear what? There is no one except her in the room, nor any sound. What, then, has her hearing perceived? Is it in her ears that it is born, that it persists, that it is obstinate, the doubtless frightful sound?—for she is shivering from head to toe, spasmodically, and stammering words that implore pity. Rigid previously, her face, her forehead, her cheeks and her lips have become pale and livid, livid and earthen, relaxing and elongating, weakening in a cowardice, as if pasty and limply fluid; one might think her a mummy that is running to putrefaction.

Never has a human face expressed with a more perfect hideousness the discouragement of having lived, the confession of an irremediable agony. Oh, what self-disgust, what cancerous remorse can be residing in that woman, and eating her away, for her to resemble, before death, the cadaver of a creature buried alive that has just been exhumed, not yet a skeleton.

Two or three times she has extended one of her hands toward a chest of drawers placed not far from her; her gesture is that of a drowning person trying to take possession of a piece of wreckage, but she has not completed the gesture, as if in the inanity of all hope, as if in the certainty of the impossibility of salvation; she must know that even to attempt salvation will only exasperate the anguish of her disaster, since merely having the intention adds to the fear of her sinister face—yes, adds to the fear again.

However, suddenly changing her mind, with the long-combated decision of a starving man about to steal a loaf of bread, she leaps toward the chest of drawers, opens one of them, seizes a small gilded bottle and a nacre case, in which, when the lid is raised, a long, thin instrument of metal and crystal appears, which terminates in a needle—a Pravaz syringe—and the Baronne fills it with the morphine contained in the bottle. Then, her skirt lifted above the garter, she immediately finds on her skin, near the base of the thigh, the customary place, a gray and black callus as large as a sou, raised up, similar to the scaly ridges of a horse. The slightly puffy dry crust of that wound of sorts is hideous against the pale cream silk of the skin, amid the ruffles of batiste and valenciennes, alongside the pink ribbon that tightens the black stocking.

The hollow needle of the syringe, held between her thumb and the middle finger, has penetrated the flesh, enlarging the circle of the callus with a pin-prick; and by means of the light, adroit pressure of a single fingernail, that of the index finger, the liquid spreads under the dermis, insinuating itself, radiating like a warmth, reaching in the gliding descend the palms of the hands and the soles of the feet, and climbing again, squeezing the heart in passing with a familiar caress, which signifies: "You know, it's me," infiltrating all the way to the brain—the calm eyelids are no longer beating, the eyes, still wide open, are moistened by a liquid light—and enabling to blossom under the cranium a development of luminous and slow reveries, in which the bogged-down mind drifts, as if in the hammock of a sunlit siesta.

Then—for the regal and merciful poison pours out its largesse very rapidly into those accustomed to imploring it, like a god in haste to grant the prayers of his worshipers—there is an infinite bliss, without the reproach of any duty, a disdain for everything that is not the present moment, perhaps a minute, perhaps an eternity, the melting of all bitterness in a languorous mildness, the ignorance of yesterday and tomorrow, life arrested at the exquisite moment of forever, peace, forgetfulness, divine annihilation.

The face of Baronne Sophor d'Hermelinge—reminiscent of those singular faded, frayed flowers, relics of a dead spring, which, steeped in a mixture, resume the smiling splendor old former middays—opens and expands, blissfully radiant. For a long time, a very long time, as if not living, with the visible ecstasy of a deceased person dreaming of paradise, she remains in that delectable inertia . . .

But now she agitates, feebly at first, at the same time as an expression of discomfort deforms the calm of her smile; and her two hands, which rise up and beat the air, unconsciously desirous, one might think, like a sleeper, of driving away a fly, removing from the ears the importunity of a contact or a sound. Doubtless she does not succeed, for she agitates more violently, her limbs extended and then drawn back, and then opened wide; then, her head between her closed fists, she gets up with a single bound, and, her eyes bulging, her features contorting as if in demoniac or hysterical tics, with white foam on her lips, she starts running around the room.

As she flees—for, without quitting the room, she gives the impression of fleeing—she looks behind her, at the carpet, as if some invisible swarm of creatures were pursuing her, in order to bite her or crawl up her legs. That flight does not stop, going from one wall to the other, avoiding the mirrors; and now, Baronne Sophor d'Hermelinge utters the long howls of a beaten dog or a wolf baying at the moon.

Oh, what howls! And suddenly, in a more lacerating clamor that is followed by silence, she collapses, her forehead toward the fireplace. There, she writhes, rolling over twice, seizes the brass of the grate between her teeth and bites it, a more abundant drool on her lips.

Anyone who saw her would hesitate to bring her help, so hideous and formidable does she appear in that crisis; and during the rare calms, when the upheaval of her entire being is appeased, when the palpitation of her breast and abdomen relents, she has in her round, iron-gray, staring eyes, devoid of lashes or eyebrows, the bleak void of definitive despair.

BOOK ONE

I

That afternoon, in the vernal forest, it was raining and it was sunny, with the consequence that all the leaves of the birches, lindens and dangling willows, and also those of the tall plane trees along the avenue, were dotted with an innumerable downpour of golden droplets. Under a light wind, so light that one could not feel it, but only divine it by the sway of the more flexible branches, beads of rainwater, as round as pearls and as luminous as diamonds, also rained down on the vibration of heather in clearings in the wood, and on the blades of grass that, weighed down by water like eyelashes by tears, leaned over, each letting an empty drop vanish into the warm humidity of the soil.

In the sunlit space of the clearings, direct rays issued from ovals of azure between the fleecy clouds, like the gaze of blue eyes between white eyelids, enlarged, deployed in prismatic fans through the dense drizzle, fine to the extent of mingling with a moving mist, resembled the ladders of light emerging from extended rainbows, which, in images of sanctity, glide from beneath the throne of God the father, and along which the angels climb and descend. And between the clearings, in a bright mist, without any other sound than the patter of the rain—for the furtive birds had fallen silent temporarily—there was the immense freshness of verdure, the healthy exhalation of the earth and damp bark.

But, as the rain ceased—no longer anything but drips from the high branches to the low ones and from there to the undergrowth—everywhere at once, as if at daybreak, there was the thin chirping of thousands of little birds fluttering their wings among the trees, or hurling themselves, two by two, and sometimes an entire flock, across the sunlit avenue.

At the same time, from a thicket of vervain, quickly parted, laughter burst forth: vibrant, clear, joyful, repeated and multiple, as if all the good humor of adolescent trees and recent foliage were celebrating the return of good weather. Then, having crossed the ditch with a leap—flying, one might have thought—two young women, two girls, alighted on the pebbles of the broad avenue, still laughing, and started hopping around in the agitation of their skirts, their ribbons and all their frills, from which droplets scattered: the pretty shaking of wet warblers.

They were not country girls, but two demoiselles from the nearby town, out for a walk in the forest, not far from the large gilded gate, who, surprised by the downpour, had taken refuge under the branches in order that their beautiful clothes would not be spoiled. For they were very well-dressed, in similar costumes: floral dresses of light fabric, wide hats of white tulle, decorated with twigs and lilies of the valley, and which, as broad as umbrellas, set little moving shadows over their faces, in which the pink of the skin appeared.

Sisters? No, although one could have believed that they were twins, because each of them was seventeen; but there was no resemblance between them except for that of age. One, with brown hair, striped here and there by russet wisps, was small and almost thin, with the vigor of a sapling that will grow taller; the other was a pale blonde, already tall but as if weary of growing, and already a little plump in her angled slenderness: a strength next to a softness, with the equal exquisite charm of not yet being all that they would be. And their adolescence was in accordance with the puerile youth of nature, new in the renewal.

Without ceasing to laugh, the one who was blonde, Emmeline, noticed that her hair was damp with rain.

"Here, Sophie, look—look and feel!"

The other said: "Mine too; one might think that I'd been dipped in the water."

"I've got an idea."

"To dry our hair?"

"Yes, very amusing."

Emmeline took off her hat, which she went to suspend from a tree-branch, returned to the middle of the pathway, unfastened the heavy chignon that descended between her shoulders and let down the tresses of her long—very long and so abundantly light—hair, and started spinning round, spinning more rapidly, and more rapidly still, with the consequence that all her hair swung around her horizontally, so rapidly that she resembled a huge umbrella made of pale gold smoke. Then, abruptly, the child bent down, crouching, at the risk of soiling her dress on the gravel that was not yet dry, and, her hair covering every-thing, like a closed hayrick, she laughed underneath it.

Her friend had not failed to imitate her. Not as long, but thicker, with the roughness of a mane, her hair did not cede as readily to the rotational movement, and in order to disap-pear partly beneath the red and brown tumble, Sophie had to bend down as far as the ground; her face remained visible, as if through a rusty metal grille.

They imagined another amusement. They held one another by the hands, braced their upper bodies, the tip of their toes meeting, and while they spun again, but together, more reck-lessly, their hair extended behind their heads in two tapering radiations made of different flames, whirling without ever catching up with one another, like the two beams of a rotating lighthouse.

Finally, out of breath, unable to do any more, they threw themselves into one another's arms with the unconscious delight of possessing, in the young season, that exquisite and troubling thing, the amicable nubility of two virgins. One might have thought them two smitten naiads in an antique oaristys, and the fact that they were two bourgeois demoiselles in dresses of green and pink jaconas added a singular spice to their frenzy of forest-dwelling girls. But they did not know anything, and did not understand anything, except that they were quite content to have been soaked by the rain, to have shaken themselves, to have made their hair fly around them and to have embraced one another under the flight created by their mingled hair.

They embraced again, laughing more, mouth to mouth, skin touching skin, eyelashes palpitating under eyelashes; their joy was such that if they had lived a thousand years of uninterrupted ecstasies no memory would have remained to them of a delight equal to that of hugging one another, so ingenuously—for they were girls, after all—amid the melodious song of all the little birds, in the bright sunlight, which lit up more for holding them thus together, mingling and stirring laughter, in the tenderness of its caress.

Nothing matches the union of Paul and Virginie under the trees except that of a couple in which, for greater purity, there are two Virginies enlaced in a wood. The kiss of two girlish mouths not, strictly speaking, kissing, hearts beating breast against breast, almost not yet breasts, two breasts that sexuality does not know, in an enlacement so pure, compared with which, however, the rude bodily tussle of the nuptial night would be less gentle and less realizing of dreams. Puerile delights of senses that are only experimenting with differences! Sacred chastity, although already so amorous, amour before amour! Desire not conscious, not satisfied, redoubled in the impossibility, not even suspected, of its realization!

Virgin friends—those whom a perfect modesty does not permit to glimpse for a moment the ignominy of for-want-of-better—are the enchantment of poets, tender contemplators of young adolescence, O Erinnas, O Sapphos, and the fear of thinkers who, without having the right of a malediction—for to

38

curse those innocences . . . !—consider the end of human things and, after so many sterile tendernessses, the futility, for want of cadavers, of cemeteries.

✳

Those two children, Sophie and Emmeline, loved one another so tenderly. Since forever, they thought, since the beginning of life. Because Sophie' house, in Fontainebleau, was next door to Emmeline's—a door almost never closed was between the two gardens—they had played together when very small, tearing their skirts on the same thorns. In the evening, there were impatient calls from a mother at this window, and a mother at that one:

"Well, Emmeline, are you finally coming in?"

"Come on Sophie, it's bed-time."

After the re-entries, which Sophie—"a real tomboy," her mother said—resisted more, the two friends, in their bedrooms, did not go to sleep without having blown kisses and waving goodnight to one another through the window, and the following day, the games recommenced in the pathways of the two gardens. Whoever scolded Emmeline or Sophie would have made Sophie or Emmeline cry; but they were hardly ever scolded. People liked that amity between the two little girls, who swapped dolls, and ate desserts together in the little arbor, which they brought to one another after meals. When, after having saluted one another over the hedge, as befits honest neighbors, the two mothers chatted about local matters, it amused them suddenly to encounter in the parting of a rose-bush, the two tousled heads of Sophie and Emmeline, laughing in bursts; and behind the branches the children had their arms around one another's waist.

At the back of one of the gardens there was a kind of small house, a hut rather than a house, where the gardener left his implements—mattocks, spades, rakes—and where an old hammock had been forgotten, out of service, suspended from one wall to the other. If Sophie and Emmeline were not heard laughing, one was sure of finding them there, lying in the hammock, enlaced, mingling their arms and legs.

It was Sophie who had imagined that hiding place, and if anyone came to look for her for some lesson, she said: "In a while, we have plenty of time, we're playing little husband and wife." And she added with pride, shaking her hair: "And the little husband is me." But Emmeline looked embarrassed, as if she had been caught at fault; she hid behind Sophie's shoulder, afraid of being scolded.

Once—the children were then eight or nine years old—it happened that the two mothers had a disagreement, with regard to a servants' quarrel; both widows, both growing old, solitude had made them bad-tempered, prompt with acerbic repartee. Such arguments between neighbors, acrimonious at the start, often become enraged, precisely because of the inevitable encounters that exasperate the initial irritation. The door between the two gardens was shut and locked, with bolts added to the lock, and one morning, after breakfast, Sophie's mother signified to her rudely that she was forbidden henceforth to play with Emmeline; there would be no going back on that, it was decided.

At first, the child, who was raising a little silver cup to her lips at that moment, did not seem moved; doubtless she had not understood, as often happens when one receives the news of some unexpected disaster; but when the old lady had reiterated her order, Sophie went whiter than the tablecloth, and seized the cup between her teeth with such a powerful bite that it dented the silver, tipped her chair over with a bound against the back, and fell backwards head first on to the floor, while her feet caused the table to rock, shaking the crockery and glassware.

Motionless, her fists closed, her face contorted by a grimace, and very cold, she resembled an angry little corpse.

The physician, summoned in haste, found the girl, whom it had been difficult to undress, so stiff were her limbs, lying in bed in a room whose window did not overlook the garden but the street; it was there that Sophie would be lodged henceforth, in order that it would not be possible for her to communicate by means of signs, from one window to the other, with the neighbor's daughter. Amid the alarm of Madame Luberti and two domestics, the physician talked, somewhat at hazard, about an attack of nerves, of catalepsy.

"Perhaps growing pains . . . perhaps an influence of the stormy weather. The pulse is beating too feverishly, but the movements of the heart are almost regular; the crisis will finish in a natural sleep from which the child will soon wake, rested, placid and cured."

He scribbled a few lines and waited, considering under Madame Luberti's interrogative eye the invalid seemingly frozen in her motionless rigor, until the maidservant returned from the pharmacist. But he tried in vain to introduce the spoon into which he had poured the potion into Sophie's mouth; her teeth were clenched with a force entirely unexpected in a child.

"Let's see, let's see," he said—for he was a benevolent old man—"it's necessary to let nature take its course." If the crisis continued there would be grounds to summon doctors from Paris in consultation. But he was hopeful. It might be nothing.

Suddenly, toward evening, the rigidity of the little body, without relaxing, shuddered, and Sophie, her teeth chattering, started. Then, her limbs twisted, she rolled herself in her bed-clothes and then braced herself in an almost perfect semicircle, only touching the bed with her head and heels. And while the maidservants tried to maintain her, weeping with pity, and also with a little of the fear that one has before the gesticulations of someone possessed, with her face convulsed, she began to speak volubly:

"Emmeline . . . never again . . . dolls . . . in the garden . . . both of us . . . the hammock . . . little husband, little wife . . . never again . . ."

She also spoke about a noise: a buzzing, a kind of laughter, which made her feel ill; she often complained of hearing it, and blocked her ears with both hands; but she took her hands away very quickly, as if, with her ears blocked, she could hear it even more loudly, that laughter. Finally, toward daybreak, she dissolved in tears, with the suddenness of a ruptured sluice-gate, and after long sobs she seemed calmer—but she did not sleep.

That day and the following night, and the day after, she was no longer suffering, or at least did not seem to be. She lay there, her entire body abandoned in a slackness of chiffon, with neither a word nor a plaint, without a glimmer in her half-closed eyes. The crisis had certainly passed. The physician did not think it necessary to consult doctors from Paris. Sophie would gradually get better, recover her strength, and with a little healthy nourishment, some fresh air . . .

One night, a rather faint cry, a vague, distant plaint, traversed the silence of the chamber dolorously.

Madame Luberti, who was hardly asleep, lying near the bed among the cushions of a settee, sat up anxiously. It was Sophie who had cried out.

The mother leapt toward the bed-head in the gloom of the night-light.

"Sophie! Sophie! Let's see! Where are you? What's the matter? Answer!"

She was speaking in vain, groping in vain. There was no one there; the bed was empty. And she was alerted by a chill on her neck—the chill of the autumn night—to the open window. While her mother was half-asleep Sophie must have thrown herself into the street.

"Help!"

While Madame Luberti, leaning out of the window, from which the stout stem of a virgin vine descended, shouted: "Sophie! Sophie!" trying to discern a form on the sidewalk, the domestics came running, half-awake, in camisoles. They ran downstairs very rapidly, stumbling; it took quite a long time to unfasten the chains and draw the bolts of the entrance door. Once outside, they listened. No sound in the exceedingly dark night.

"A lamp! Hurry up! A lamp!"

The cook came back, carrying a lamp. They searched under the windows. Nothing, except broken branches. Perhaps Sophie had not thrown herself out; she had climbed down the vine-stocks of the climbing plant. But where had she gone?

Madame Luberti went to the nearby houses, called the neighbors, asking for help, imploring the closed shutters. Already, windows were opening here and there, from which heads were advancing in the pallor of night-caps.

"Well, what? What is it? What's happening? What do you want?"

But while the domestics explained things, heads against the windows, Madame Luberti did not reply; she had turned toward the large gilded iron gate that separated the street from her neighbor's garden; an idea had occurred to her by virtue of an instinct. She rang, took hold of the bell cord, pulled and pulled, ringing a carillon. In the darkness it was like the sound of a tocsin, all the more lamentable for being thin and cracked. All the houses in the area lit up, with comings and goings behind the curtains of people dressed in haste, and there was a sound of footsteps on the gravel of a pathway on the other side of the gate.

Emmeline's mother advanced, holding up a lamp and moving it from side to side in order to see into the shadows in front of her.

"Sophie must be in your house!" cried Madame Luberti.

On recognizing her enemy, the neighbor, furious at that nocturnal awakening, nearly turned back, but her daughter had followed her, dainty in her nudity, which was already filling out, under a mantle that did not cover her arms and legs.

"Maman! It's Sophie they're looking for! Oh, my God! Where can she be?"

And the gate was opened.

The servants and all the people who had emerged from the houses ran into the garden; everyone was running back and forth, interrogating one another, when Emmeline uttered a cry. There, under her own window, on the hard dry ground beneath a clump of bushes, she had just seen Sophie in a night-dress, lying down, resembling, in the pallor of the fabric, a half-buried cadaver. Dying of fear and joy, she let herself fall down alongside her friend.

Then, among the group of witnesses gathered in a semicircle, Sophie stirred slightly, extended her arms, and, although she had not opened her eyes, recognized Emmeline.

"Emmeline! Emmeline!" And she embraced her, clasping her against her little breast.

There was a great emotion among all the people present; nothing was more touching than the tenderness of those two little girls. It was easy to deduce what must have happened. In order to rejoin her comrade, the convalescent, with a bravery above her age, and the strength that fever gives, had slid down from her window along the virgin vine, and then, clinging to the bars of the gate, had climbed over it. That was extraordinary— such a high gate, with such menacing spikes! A cat would not have dared to make that ascent. Once in the garden she had gone—in a night-dress, on that autumn night, how cold she must have been!—toward Emmeline's window, on the ground floor; she had tried to climb up, her fingernails to the wall, had not been able to get very high, and had fallen on the hard ground, unconscious, after a cry.

Many people, because of that adventure, had tears in their eyes; the two mothers could not stand it; they were reconciled; and while the neighbors retired to their interrupted repose, the two children were carried to Sophie's bed, where, half fainted but smiling like ecstatic cherubim, they slept in one another's arms, opening one eye in order to see and closing it again, glad to have seen, and kissing one another with their fresh little lips. On the bed, so slender and semi-naked, clutching one another, with occasional vague starts, they were like two little birds al-most devoid of feathers, huddling together in the same nest.

Sophie's convalescence was rather slow, either because the crisis had been more serious than the doctor had thought, or because, by virtue of an instinctive tender cunning, the child took pleasure in prolonging it, in order to have Emmeline next to her as a little nurse, never weary of saying: "Are you feeling better? You aren't worse?" and was so lovely to see when she sugared tisanes and tasted them first. At night, they slept together; if they woke up, they told one another their dreams; and, curiously enough, they were always the same, those dreams: walks together in the forest, communal snacks at the garden table, dressing and undressing dolls and holding hands.

By day, Emmeline sitting beside the bed, and Sophie with her head on the pillow, they told one another stories, or played cards, or looked at the pictures in an album; they preferred telling one another stories, because they had no need to stop holding hands in order to talk. And how pretty they were, the one with her dark russet hair, mingled with phosphorescence, and her ivory whiteness, and the other more blonde, all young sun and young roses! When they leaned toward one another, their tresses mingled the shimmer of stormy shadows with the tender gold of dawn.

Finally, Sophie recovered completely. She even emerged from the crisis grown and strengthened, her bone structure and her young limbs seemingly solidified, with a joy in her eyes and a pride in danger vanquished. Except that she sometimes put her hands over her eyes with an abrupt alarm. It was truly singular; she could still hear, but more distant and vague, like an echo dying away, the little laughter of the nights of crisis. The astonished physician asked her whether, before being ill, she had perceived that kind of buzz, that tinnitus. She could not have said, exactly; she did not remember very well; yes, perhaps, when very small, she had heard it from time to time, but she was not sure. What did it matter? She was cured, entirely cured. There were the games of old in the gardens with the open door.

Nothing, henceforth, separated them. On the contrary, they were further united by a common education. They were not sent to a convent; Emmeline's mother and Sophie's mother, one very attached to religious proprieties, the other a rather eccentric individual with an obscure past, not devout and sometimes hazarding pleasantries in poor taste over dessert regarding sacred things, had fallen into accord on the point that it was necessary to keep the girls at home. The two little friends educated themselves from the same books, with the same masters, as people eat at the same table; their minds developed together. Ordinarily, it was Sophie, with a livelier mind, who did Emmeline's assignments.

And the preparatory exercises for their first communion arrived, which bore them away together in an ideal of holy images and incense.

As soon as the first lessons of the catechism they surrendered to the delights of belief and prayer, one with the languor of idle descent, the other with a fervent surge, Emmeline as one slides, Sophie as one leaps; if, in their pious dreams, they were not separated, it was because the latter drew the former. Destiny was already manifest in their early youth: Sophie would always be dominant, Emmeline always obedient.

From hour to hour, Sophie threw herself further forward into mysticism, prayers and passionate penances. She did not limit herself to the recommended books; she sought, she found, and she read with an increasing fervor, psalms, canticles and sacred prose. She learned, in the book of the ascetic, that Jesus Christ responds to the Beloved; she entered with Sainte Thérèse into the Castle of Souls. After fasts, which people tried in vain to prohibit, she knew ecstasies.

She died full of joy for the man who died full of pity. She followed him as in a marvelous forest where it is pleasant to be afraid, in the obscurity of parables. She loved him, because

46

he loved—and also because he did not love. The tenderness of Jesus spread over everyone, and was not reserved to anyone. He had pardoned the adulterous woman, he had accepted, on his feet, the perfumes of the Magdalen, but neither the wife nor the courtesan had deflected toward the earth his eyes full of the unique love of heaven, full of stars in their azure; he counseled virginities and virgin widowhoods, the solitude of beds. He was the enemy of weddings. She adored him for not having had a woman among his apostles, she adored him for having had a friend; he appeared to her as authorizing, as ordering, the separation of the male from the female; he divided humanity into unmarried sexes, and he did not prevent the hope that, in each group, couples, close to becoming angels, might fly toward paradise.

Those sentiments were not clear in her; she would have been very surprised if anyone had expressed them to her in precise terms. They were instinctive reveries, imminent thoughts; but she took pleasure in the blur of her strange fervors, and sank ever more deeply into them, with a vertiginous delight.

In the room that the two children had chosen in order to study their lessons, Sophie had placed on the mantelpiece, between two porcelain vases on which lilies were displayed, a large doll dressed in white satin; she had put a diadem of daisies and lilies of the valley on that image, and had decorated it with little girls' jewels, little necklaces of pearls, rings with a single sapphire, brooches of light gold; and since that doll was the virgin Mary, beneath her dainty silk shoes there was, with its lizard head in green gold and ruby eyes, an unrolled bracelet that signified the Serpent.

Thus, in their puerile religion, Sophie and Emmeline, without knowing it, imitated the infantile people who decorated idols; their doll resembled those figurines in rich garments, overladen with gold and precious stones, which emerge from their elegant tabernacles on ceremonial occasions and advance on two rails as far as the edge of the altar in Spanish churches.

Before the divine Virgin, they prayed for a long, long time on their knees, with Emmeline's head on Sophie's shoulder; and after the long litanies, when the evening twilight accumulated in the room the redness and the warmth of the pompous and melancholy setting sun, a languor invaded them, clutching one another tightly, feeling through the fabrics the warmth and heartbeats of life, and almost causing them to swoon, with a stir behind the forehead and a flight of all their being toward a single point, fainting; so weak that, no longer praying, their unfastened hands beating the air, they fell backwards. They remained motionless, not speaking, their eyes half-closed, scarcely alive by virtue of the occasional flutter of their eyelids, the rise and fall of their breasts and their breath, which, in the crepuscular silence, made the sound of two tiny invisible bees following one another rhythmically. And they were very pale.

It was Sophie who woke up first from that torpor, slowly, with a gradual raising of the eyelid and a hesitation of the hand, on the carpet, toward Emmeline; then, suddenly, for having touched her, she revived ardently, and, shaking all her short thick hair with the pride of a little wild animal that already has a mane, after waking Emmeline, she spoke to the sacred image.

What did she say? Almost a story that would be a religious poem; futile infantile stories in which were mingled transports of devotion; they would go to heaven by the grace of the holy virgin; they would be transported there one day, after having been very good and having prayed a great deal, in a magnificent golden carriage harnessed to twelve great white horses opening vast wings; and up there, it would be very pleasant; even palaces built by enchanters were not as splendid as the good God's paradise. They would hear music such as one never heard on earth, music made with sonorous light; and they would have a house built of diamonds and pearls, the windows of which would overlook the great white road that is the busiest in heaven, and is called the Chemin de Saint-Jacques.[1]

---

1 The phrase "le chemin de Saint-Jacques," initially applied to the Camino

48

Oh, they would receive many visits in their beautiful house, because all the elect would be very glad to make their acquaintance because of their good renown; but even in heaven agreeable to see everyone; without being impolite to anyone they loved, when they returned home after fulfilling their duties as seraphim on the steps of the celestial throne, after having sung canticles and swung censers, they would love to remain alone together. They would sometimes go for a walk, however, with pleasure, in the evening, on the Milky Way, in order to respire the celestial air. There, thousands of stars are the stones of the road, there, one passes between bushes of white roses, which are flowers of flame, but one can pick them without burning one's fingers, because in heaven, very different from the nasty and vile inferno, flame does not burn; and one sits down there on banks of luminous clouds that are like golden cotton wool.

Sometimes, Emmeline said: "It must be very high in the air, the Milky Way; if one fell, it would be frightful!" for she was timid, easily frightened, and, childish as it was with its reminiscences of enchantments, Sophie' paradise still seemed very grandiose and redoubtable to her.

But Sophie said: "Well, no, one can't fall; one is as light as the air and the clouds, and then, falling wouldn't do you any harm, because I'd catch you very quickly, and if you were tired I'd lift you up between my wings, and from time to time, we'd stop at some star in order to rest."

On the morning of the ceremony, sunlight streaming through the stained glass windows sent the church ablaze in places, where the motionless communicants, in two files blossomed, broad and white, in their heavy muslins, like regularly planted flowering thistles. The majority of them, their faces reddened, either by sacred emotion or the effect of the reflection of the stained glass, displayed that stupidity, the ridiculousness of simple conviction, that moves people to tears, and the ugliest were the most touch-

de Santiago de Compostela in Spain, became a general term in France applied to any popular route of pilgrimage.

ing; one sensed that they judged themselves especially august in their solemnity of little idols; it would have seemed a sacrilege, one divined by the precaution of their stiffness, if their veil were a trifle frayed or their robe torn; they already had the responsibility of the god that would be in them shortly.

The first communicant in each file was, to the right, Emmeline, and to the left, Sophie: hazard, or the intention to honor the two mothers, who lived so simply although they were among the richest people in the town.

Heroic fervors burst forth on Sophie's face. She woke up, so pure and so ardent, which a kind of chivalric piety in her eyes, with her robust slenderness sheathed by a narrow dress, an armor of snow-colored silk, giving the idea of a little sacred warrior, and Templar nun. She was haughty, almost archangelic, but delicate in the proud challenge of her faith. She was truly going to the conquest of salvation, and it would have been a bad idea to put up any resistance to her, for she would have broken down the gates of paradise with sword-thrusts.

By contrast, like a fortunate martyr whom torture, by virtue of some pity, did not finish, and who, before dying, wants to render testimony to God one last time, in her inclined languor, in the plaintive ecstasy of an invisible wound, Emmeline appeared, already plump; over her mild forehead, tenderly vanquished, where even the pallor was rosy, the nimbus of her hair trembled, so palely blonde, silver gilded by the sun.

After the processional march, when the communicants were arranged in the choir in front of the altar, when all those whitenesses were kneeling under the veils, Sophie and Emmeline, in the midst of their companions, found themselves neighbors again. At the moment when a priest on one side and a priest on the other, going from girl to girl, gave God to those children, the light, in a hazard of grouped rays, isolated the two friends with a separating clarity that was like another veil, made of light; one might have thought them, in that place, before the altar, two little brides, without grooms.

The priests, the one coming from the right and the one coming from the left, arrived before them; delightfully, lips parted, they awaited the host; they received it almost at the same time. In Sophie's heart it was a devouring fire, and in Emmeline's a warm melting snow; for God is different, in accordance with souls.

Then, suddenly, Sophie stood up; she seemed to be suffering strangely; she put her hands to her ears, as if she had heard some intolerable noise. The priests who were giving the communion approached her anxiously. But already, a smile of passionate serenity spread over her entire face, and, violently, irresistibly, she took Emmeline in her arms and, in the place where couples receive the nuptial benediction, she hugged her friend and kissed her on the lips.

That might have caused some scandal if the faithful had not been accustomed to the nervous disorders that the divine incarnation produces on a few children; the two children were taken away, half-fainted, still holding hands. The next day, among the devotees, everyone was in accord in praising the excess of fervor that the daughters of Madame Luberti and Madame d'Hermelinge had shown in communicating.

✳

The catechism forgotten, Sophie, at fourteen, was smitten with poetry and music. She obliged Emmeline, who had followed her so languidly toward the paradise in which the joy of angelic couples is eternalized, to come with her, to lose herself, albeit guided and sustained, in the sublimities of the epic and the ode.

To tell the truth, Sophie only lingered in the enthusiastic admiration of poetry for a few months. In verses there were so often mistresses conquered by the victorious desire of lovers, the triumphant kiss of the male; women appeared there like submissive hearts or obedient lips, only finding in coquetry or the vain rebellion of refusal a revenge for vile tyranny. Without knowing why, Sophie was irritated by that. Then again, poets, even those most smitten with chimeras, by means of words and images, made the ideal precise, as if visible and tangible; and her innocent predestination, her instinct, perhaps knowing that to be impossible, found itself ill at ease, as if between walls, in those overly real dreams.

Music, with its sonorous mutism, which gives the impression of not being able to proffer some adorable or sinister dream, which is always on the art of speaking but never expresses itself, was more in accordance with Sophie's soul, ignorant of itself, whose continuous exaltation was like a violent but vague symptom of a disease that was still latent. She loved music with a sororal passion, because it seemed to her immediately that it was striving to say, without ever saying, what she sensed and did not know within herself; she was also convinced that, if she did know it, she would keep quiet about it; and music also kept quiet, in melodious reticence.

Arrangements for the piano, operas and dances, even languorous waltzes—all the pieces that a gray-haired piano mistress, a very old graduate of a provincial Conservatoire, made her study—soon ceased to be sufficient for her; she entered resolutely and recklessly into the terrible dream of Bach and Beethoven. For six hours, every day, she deciphered with uncertain eyes the scores harboring so many hopes and so much melancholy, obliging the keyboard, beneath her initially maladroit and then supple fingers, to reveal, almost, the hyperphysical covetousness of melody, to confess, almost, the torment of desperate harmonies.

She laughed, she wept, she died and revived, penetrating ever further forward in the luminous and tenebrous endeavor of the poets of sound, the divine wordless noise. The word is the sovereign and creative virility and, in accordance with an as yet imprecise law of her nature, that female was infatuated with music.

Emmeline, blonde, plump and smiling, not excessive, would have been quite content to remain with quadrilles and polkas; some slow phrase in which the tremolo of cellos dies away toward the points of the organ, would have sufficed for the formulation of her banal reverie. But Sophie, tyrannically, dragged her into the black and fulgurant opium of symphonies; she constrained her to work all day, to spell out, to read, to understand; she precipitated her into music as one pushes someone into the obscurity of a hole full of flame, and the amiable young woman yielded to the almost brutal despotism of her redoubtable companion.

For two years, for three years, it was their common folly to have the wordless voices of passion and anguish sing beneath their fingers, to plunge their souls, as if in a celestial inferno, into the delectable torture of sensing everything and understanding nothing, into the infinity of the unexpressed. It was said in the town that the two demoiselles were excellent musicians, but that, truly, they chose very difficult pieces, which were not to everyone's liking. However, people acquired the habit—provincial idleness—of opening the window in the evening in order to listen to them, or even of gathering, as one does in hours of military music, under the windows of the room in which they were playing.

They did not know that anyone was listening to them. Sitting side by side at the keyboard, tormenting the keys, drawing appeals and moans from the instrument, they mingled their own voices with the flight of sonorities, ever more bewildered to be experiencing without thinking, to be listening to themselves without divining themselves. When the people, weary of the sound, finally, almost fearful before that house from which a seemingly demonic music emerged, had gone home, at the hour when the silence was only rarely disturbed by the staggering of some drunken soldier returning to barracks, alone amid the sleep of the town and the calm of the sky, they continued, furiously, or, sometimes, with weakening softness, to interrogate or cause to clamor in vain the obscure pythoness of the Delphi devoid of oracles.

And they were obstinate, demanding responses to the curiosities of their adolescence, the urgencies of their nobility, believing that they were grasping in every sound the commencement of a revelatory speech, but only obtaining the promise of another sound that might perhaps speak, and did not. So much so that, in the end, breathless and exhausted, unable to do any more, having exceeded the desire without realizing it, in the ever more violent exasperation of the effort, they let their hands slide, flexible in one another's arms, rolling from their chairs on to the carpet, and wept abundantly beneath their mingled hair, while the window, open whether it was winter or summer, allowed a caress of moonlight or the freshness of rain to enter into the darkness that bathed them.

Someone became anxious about that ardent intimacy in which their souls were married: one of the two mothers.

It was not Madame d'Hermelinge, a debonair old woman, very fat and heavy, her face blissfully indifferent between the black crepe flaps of her mourning bonnet; seeing little, hardly thinking at all, uniquely occupied after mass—for she went to all the matins at the church—with the eternal tapestry in which her patience was obstinate. She only had an alertness in her eye at the thought of her son, a brave and strong soldier emerged from Saint-Cyr, now a captain in the cuirassiers, or her husband, whom she had adored with the ecstatic astonishment of being the wife of that bold and brilliant gentleman, her, the daughter of a farmer, almost a farm girl, who had never been able to have white hands, and whom an aristocratic marriage had barely made bourgeois.

No, the one that became anxious about the two young women, or rather who sometimes observed them slyly, with a little mute snigger, was Sophie's mother, Madame Luberti. She gave the impression of understanding, without being astonished or becoming angry. In her manner of studying the children, there was something that resembled, with an imperceptible wink, the "tee hee" of old debauchees listening to some bawdy story. At those moments, she appeared to know many things—many bad things—that dry and meager female, graying in the hair and the skin, always clad in somber woolens, austere and cantankerous, who had come to settle in Fontainebeleau sixteen years before, in a large suburban house, and who was, it was believed, the widow of an Italian diplomat.

She had chosen Fontainebleau because of the proximity of the forest, the air of which is salutary for those who cough. She quickly acquired and maintained, among the good folk of the town, the reputation of a woman about whom, in sum, there was nothing to say, except that she was a little rude, somewhat miserly—the latter fault could pass as a quality—and she was generally esteemed, even though, because of her negligence in fulfilling the duties of religion and the sometimes brutal liberty of her speech, she was suspected of being a protestant.

In reality, she was one of those quinquagenarians deprived of all amour, all desire and all hope, secretly haunted, despite the ennui of life, by the fear of the inevitable tomb, only demanding the peace of a stagnant abode, to sleep from nine o'clock in the evening until the morning awakening, moderate nourishment, the absence of any shock and any emotion, and the prolonged functioning of a vital mechanism that was almost worn out. She had one single passion: that of amassing, as if piling linen upon linen in a cupboard, the income of a fortune that was assumed to be considerable. It was a passion devoid of trouble, because of the facility she found in satisfying it without exciting surprise or reprobation amid the economic mores of the province. A town, especially a large one, near Paris, is even more provincial, by virtue of a natural effect of antithesis. And Madame Luberti was a worthy woman, utterly irreproachable.

Behind that placid appearance, however, seethed a hideous past, like the mud stirred by tadpoles under the weed-filled surface of a pond.

At twelve years of age, the niece of an attendant in the ground-floor boxes of a theater—no one ever knew exactly who her mother and father were—she was almost always nested in the concierge's lodge, tumbling down stairways between the legs of bit-part players, playing roles of little boys in plays where bourgeois couples went for walks with a child among crowds, and also having the occasional glory of representing some Cherub or Amour, thighs bare in overly large leotards, amid the fireworks of apotheoses.

Phédora, more often known as Phédo, had for principal functions that of carrying from the hall and the wings the notes and the bouquets that ingenuous strangers sent to celebrated actresses—the aunt, Madame Sylvanie, pocketed the louis, and gave sous to the child, in order to encourage her—or going to warn a comedienne about to go on stage that the serious Monsieur, the one on whom it was necessary to count, was walking up and down in front of the stage door, and that "Madame" would do well this evening if she left with the young man, who enjoyed noble parentage, through the public entrance.

Having carried out the commissions, out of breath because she had climbed up rapidly, she sat down in a corner, or collapsed—her term—against some piece of scenery, watching beautiful girls undress and dress, with eyes that judged the flesh, or attentive to the gesture of the assistant director who pushed the figurants on stage with his fat hands rummaging under their skirts.

During that apprenticeship, she would have been perverted all the way to the marrow if she had not been perverse by nature to the point of mistrusting the bad examples. She had the incorruptibility of accomplished corruption. It would have been as unnecessary to teach her a vice as it would to pour poison into a calyx of aconite or belladonna. The insalubrity of the wings only served to maintain her evil; there was no difference between the air that she breathed in and the air that she breathed out. She received and returned the same miasmas. There are the mysteries in that of childhoods consecrated to infamy by some obscure law of atavism, or by the inexplicable will of an evil providence. There are cradles that are little beds of prostitution.

She had adventures.

Once, a minor player, rather pretty, plump, her breasts emerging from her corsage, who lit up the room with her underarms, brazenly offered in the flare of black silk, a girl not yet arrived, who did not even have her monthly carriage but already supped every evening in chic establishments—there is a commencement to everything—said to her, with an air of indifference, as if it were of no importance (for it is necessary to be suspicious of little girls, who might talk, and there are parents no better than anyone else, but more malevolent, who speak readily to the police):

"By the way, child, if you didn't know, that lady who gave you a bag of bonbons for me the other evening, asked me, talking about you: 'What about that girl, then? She's amusing.' I replied: 'I don't know; she has an aunt who's very honest.' Anyway, the lady wants you to come with us, this evening. I told her that it isn't possible, that you're too young."

The child only went home the following day; but she gave Madame Sylvanie two gold coins wrapped in torn-up newspaper.

"And where did you sleep, if at all?" her aunt asked her.

"At the home of Madame Ernestine, who is very kind to me."

"That's different."

Other adventures: prolonged sojourns in the dressing-room of the third dancer, who got bored between the ballet and the second act and the ballet in the fourth, and in that of an old comedian, dirty, with tobacco in his nose, fat and saggy, known for the pleasure he took in having his costume put on or taken off by very young girls; everyone knew that, and laughed at it;

he was a worthy fellow, fundamentally, who had a wife and children at home.

Amid all those villainies, however, and encounters with seamstresses on the ladder under the stage, and being flattened against the wall with no matter whom behind a door pushed by the tumultuous exit of the figurants, Phédo was a virgin, in the vain virginity of the body, but soiled in her flesh, in her slender, meager flesh, only retaining of intimate modesties that which can remain after the obstinacy of femininities or senile impotency, and afterwards, in some insufficient dark corridor, the brutality of fingers that do not have the time under her short skirt.

A great good fortune arrived.

Because young Thevenard, then celebrated, died of an influenza aggravated by consumption, the director took it into his head to give Phédo a moderately important role in a drama he was putting on. It was a matter of personifying an enraged gamine, who was like the diabolical providence of a gang of burglars. She was the one who had to say, while lifting the eiderdown under which an old man had just been choked, "How soundly the fellow sleeps!" She pronounced that line, and other analogous ones, in a tone so prettily roguish, with so much mischief in the crapulousness, that she had a success; after her act she got three curtain calls, with the result that she alone made the fortune of the play. The director, who was an honest man, gave her a seven franc bonus. That was enormous.

At the fiftieth performance, a scene was added in which the gamine, woken up by the arrival of the police, descended from a window on a rope, in a chemise, without a leotard. Naturally, if she had been a woman, or even slightly plump, the director, an honest man, would have said: "She needs a leotard," even though he was very devoted to verity in art; but for such a thin child, there was no need of an envelope of silk or cotton; it would have been necessary to be very rascally to have ideas regarding a kid who was nothing but skin and bone. It was even not thought inappropriate—verity before all—that she stopped momentarily in her descent, level with the entresol, in order to grip the rope more firmly, which had nearly escaped her. And the receipts in the orchestra stalls increased because of those little bare knees. The director gave her a ten-franc bonus.

In spite of that stroke of luck, the aunt was not satisfied. A success, yes, which wouldn't last; Phédo succeeded because, being small, she was interesting; but a girl and a young woman are not the same thing; for, in spite of her long, fine hair—that was all she had going for her—she was not pretty, and would not become so in growing, with her nose that was too long and her eyes that were too small, and her thin lips, already deflowered, and her dry skin, almost rough, bulged by large bones. One doesn't quibble about the quality of early fruit, but Phédo would be utterly banal, not appetizing, when she was no longer utterly extraordinary. As for talent, true talent, did anyone know whether she would have any? She, a worker, because of the specialism of her experience, only attributed a mediocre value to that mysterious thing, talent; to make oneself a place in the theater, what was necessary was to be beautiful and not stupid. Not stupid, good. Phédo was that, but beautiful—go and see if they're coming!

With the result that Madame Sylvanie considered as a stroke of unexpected luck the proposition made to her one morning by a well-dressed, fat, imposing individual with no beard or moustache, who talked with a foreign accent and was holding in his hand a brand new silk hat that seemed a badge of quality—the appearance of a great lord who would turn out to be a domestic. He was, in fact, a domestic. His master, the Comte, had greatly appreciated the gentility of little Phédo at the theater the other evening. As he was a passionate lover of the theater, he offered to take the child to Russia, where he would give her masters and even enable her to make her debut in a theater in Saint Petersburg. Naturally, being very rich, and as generous as could be desired, he would not hesitate to make considerable advances to the aunt and the child right away on the salary that Phédo would not fail to earn one day.

Advances, eh! thought the worker.

After a few pleasantries—"Is it built yet, the theater where my niece will play?" and "How old is your master? Sixty? Yes? He wants to adopt the child, then?"—she immediately got down to discussing the conditions of the deal, and demanding precise details.

The name of Comte Tchercelew removed all difficulties. He was known, that Russian, he had spent money with loose women during the six months that he had been in Paris. He was the one who had bought a town house for the scrawny Anatoline Meyer. And with him, there were profits without pain. He did not resemble those old men, more fatiguing than young ones, who were always after a woman. No, he was known, even with the prettiest, not to be demanding. His mania, a tranquil, very honest mania, was to undress the young woman to the waist and to comb her hair with a golden comb, and then with his fingers; that amused him and was sufficient for him.

Thus, the bargain was concluded there and then; a sum immediately agreed—*I didn't ask for enough!*—would be deposited in Paris, at the Banque de France, in the name of Madame Sylvanie, and Phédo could depart when desired. Only her aunt, her second mother, would accompany her; without that, the voyage would not have been appropriate.

A fortnight later, they set forth, in the same compartment, the comte, the worker and the child, who had been dressed as a boy, again for the sake of propriety. With his seemingly melting weight, the obese old man—his face enormous and soft, in which the lifeless eyes, the long eyes of a Tartar, almost closed, put a yellow line between the wan swelling of the eyelids, and a tongue as pale as a bloodless piece of meat hung down toward the glabrous chin—Monsieur de Tchercelew, in one corner, resembled a landslide of flesh. He was holding the girl seated on one of his large thighs; with his fingers, very short and very thin, emerging from an immeasurable broad and fat palm, like the pointed teeth of a rake, he was slowly combing the full length of the child's unrolled hair. Sometimes, the yellow line of his gaze, like the eyes of a greedy animal lapping, was extinguished entirely beneath the wrinkles of fat.

In Saint Petersburg, in the Tchercelew household, for a long time, Phédo was a kind of little domestic animal who performed tricks. She climbed up on a table at the end of suppers to amuse the guests; she danced and sang songs between the bottles, sometimes dressed as a boy and sometimes a girl. It was one of the preoccupations of the old comte to imagine disguises, which rendered the little Parisiennne's songs and dances more piquant. At dessert she appeared by turns as a Tzigane, a Kirghiz, an Egyptian and a bourgeois Russian; sometimes she wore the robe of a prioress or the habit of an archimandrite, and that was amusing, very amusing, because of the unexpected contrast of hearing cheerful popular songs under the veil of a nun in the accent of a faubourgian gamine, making the pendants of the chandelier tinkle with high kicks while lifting the skirt of a monk.

As for complete undress, Comte Tchercelew never demanded that. Decent in his fashion, he had a horror of nudity, except above the waist. In spite of that species of virtue, the presence of Phédo in the house of one of the highest dignitaries of the imperial court, and the anecdotes that ran around the town in that regard, could not fail to produce some scandal. After several years of patience, the authorities finally had to act, because of a more brutal adventure, which remained mysterious, in which the supper tablecloth was not only reddened by wine. A request came from high places, for the comte to retire to his estate in Finland and to remain there until further notice. The impossibility of disobeying counseled smiling submission.

Phédo did not envisage that change of residence with as much resignation; Saint Petersburg, undoubtedly, was not Paris; she got very bored there, even on the days when she danced on the table. It was, however, a great city, with people who were somewhat civilized. Now she was a woman—her aunt, having consequences in mind, already made her wear short skirts—it did not displease her to have the occasional caprice, on evenings when the comte, under doctor's orders was observing his diet, for a student who took her for a drink in a traktir, or an officer who offered her supper in a fashionable restaurant. On those evenings, she undressed entirely, with pleasure.

Even when she has neither a heart nor senses, even when all the vital force of her being has atrophied in the overheating of precocities, a woman cannot help experiencing, momentarily, something that resembles a crush or a desire. "It's nature that determines that," said Madame Sylvanie, indulgently, "but it doesn't last."

It lasted in Phédo; the idea of going to bury herself in a country of savages was insupportable to her. For two pins she would have packed her trunk and returned to Paris. Fortunately, the aunt was there, who had only amassed, as yet, forty or fifty thousand roubles, and was counting on a legacy written into Comte Tchercelew's testament. So they departed for Finland with the domestics; the master was to join them when he had put his affairs in order.

In the middle of one last party, a fit of coughing, which seized him when he was dead drunk, unhooked the life from his belly and he vomited up his soul.

The two women only learned about that accident after arriving in Finland. Was it painful for them? Not excessively, since the former worker was sure of the testament, and Phédo exclaimed: "Good! It's over! En route for the Boulevard du Crime!"[1]

But Madame Sylvanie was not a person disposed to be satisfied with a modest ease. What would they have, according

---

1 The Boulevard du Temple was known as the Boulevard du Crime because it was host to an accumulation of cheap theaters that staged popular melodramas; it was presumably in one of them that Phédo had grown up and made her debut.

to the opened testament, counting the sum deposited in the Banque? Six or seven hundred thousand francs, not more. She was ambitious; she saw herself grand; if she ever returned to Paris, it would be to shine there. She replied to Phédo: "Go away? Are you stupid? Well, what about the heir?"

There was, in fact, an heir, the only son of Comte Tchercelew, thirty years young, who, an invalid since birth, had never left the mansion in Finland, the dwelling of his oldest ancestors.

All day long, clad in black furs from which emerged at the end of the bald neck of a vulture, a smooth and glabrous face, almost devoid of breadth, everything stretched lengthwise like the figures one sees in a convex mirror, he sat, with his palms on the knees of his dead legs, and leprous white patches on the back of his hands, in a rolling armchair, in the middle of a great hall with marble paving stones, alternately black and white, walls of somber walnut, windows that were always closed, and a very high ceiling, from which an iron lamp hung down, incessantly lit. He had the appearance of a dead man sitting in a sepulcher.

Life—an ardent, violent life, often furious with scorn and hatred—only persisted in the eyes of that near-cadaver. The faculty of movement that the legs had never had and was almost abolished in the arms, was concentrated in those terrible eyes; and via them he desired, ordered and detested. But what was most frightful about that less-than-human being, who never budged, could not hear very well and rarely spoke, in a shrill and clear voice, as halting and jerky as breaking crystal—the voice of a stammering dwarf—was that, at times, he laughed.

Without any joy illuminating beneath his eyelids, with nothing but a start of the furs over his belly, he laughed, not with all his face but with his mouth and a part of his cheeks and tremulous chin: laughter that showed, behind the drawn-back lips, the atrocious teeth of a beast, all the way to the gums. That voiceless grimace resembled the vibration of the jaws of a cadaver that an electric discharge might produce. In that strange face, it also evoked the idea of a macabre parody of joy mimed by a spectral Pierrot.

Accustomed as they were to the fashions of the cripple that they had the mission of watching over and caring for, the young comte's four valets, and even Monsieur Luberti, a steward of sorts—an Italian, a former music master fallen from his artiste's dreams all the way to the functions of a nurse—could not help shivering because of that laughter, a persistent symptom of a family disease, or even, if the whispers of the oldest serfs could be believed, the sign of an ancient damnation that the Tchercelews had incurred.

A legend soared over that mansion in Finland, as if with the black wings of a crow: a legend of windows illuminated at an hour when everyone was sleep, of girls abducted and abused under the flamboyance of chandeliers, in the exasperation of wines and spirits, puerile nudities eaten, even as a communal dish, by guests who were almost wolves and almost wild boar, muzzle and snout, while the Devil—yes, the Devil himself, standing in a niche from which the Panagia or Saint Alexandra had been kicked out—burst out laughing, full of satisfaction, with a breath so violent that it extinguished all the candles in the hall.

Certainly, Monsieur Luberti, a practical man who had been a hirer of little girls and little boys in the cafés of Genoa, where he played the guitar, did not attribute any importance to those tales of serfs drunk on vodka or troubled by the ghost stories that were told at nightfall in village taverns. The truth was that the Tchercelews, masters in the manse and throughout the region, had led, as they say, a merry life with the local girls, and that, wearied by the fatigue of his forefathers, their last son could do no more. And nothing was simpler. That explanation did not prevent Monsieur Luberti, serious and solid as he was, denuded of reverie, from having a chill in his spine when Comte Stefan Tcherchelew suddenly laughed, silently, in the great hall.

It was the conquest of that invalid for which the two Parisiennes—Madame Sylvanie, a culpable old woman, and Phédo, a young woman, even more horrible—hoped.

This time, it was not a matter of a small sum deposited in the Banque de France or a mediocre legacy, but of an almost inestimable fortune: platinum mines, a palace in Moscow, a palace in Saint Petersburg, and five estates in Finland, where serfs pullulated like the swarm of an anthill. And it depended on the will of a sick man, paralyzed, almost voiceless, only living through the eyes, the supreme heir of an opulent and abject race, whether that fortune might belong to them!

There was one sole obstacle: the cunning of Luberti, who had arrived first, and to whom the invalid was linked by the habit of being dressed, undressed, washed and wiped by him. But if that competitor could not be evicted, he could be made an accomplice; and with a glance, a long, fixed glance that they exchanged after vague words, the aunt and the niece conceived the possibility of the triumph. In their harmonized covetousness, there was something akin to the amazed joy of two professional thieves who suddenly see, within arm's reach, the key to a strong-box full of gold and wads of banknotes.

Comte Stefan welcomed the foreigners, apparently not opposing any resistance to their design. The two women, moving around him, diverted his immobility. Did he make any differentiation between the old one and the young one? No one could say. With a slow half-turn of the long neck protruding from the furs, he followed their comings and goings with his gaze, and willingly accepted that they tell him things about Paris, in French, with a boulevard accent. After hours in which he had Monsieur Luberti—a polygot by virtue of having been an interpreter in Constantinople—read books in German or English to him, with a preference for works in which science was already observing facts and studying the laws of despairing atavisms, he listened with a species of satisfaction to the chatter of the Parisiennes; and then, if he laughed, his laughter was not as frightful as before, less horrible for having a plausible pretext.

The life of the two women in that solitude, next to that motionless being, was as bleak as a sojourn between the four walls of a sepulcher, with no other distraction than games of bezique with Luberti in the hours when Comte Stefan, closing his eyes without inclining his head, his upper body still upright, appeared to be asleep. Was he asleep? Sometimes, as if in a dream, he laughed. The games of bezique went on for a long time, with the rustle of the cards on the green baize of the card-table, brought close to the rolling armchair, and in the intervals between hands they talked in low voices.

Months, and years, went by—many years—and still the same existence: watching over that corpse of sorts, trying to please him. Such daily monotony, in the hope of a perhaps distant future, still so uncertain—for would the invalid leave his fortune to them?—would have discouraged the most obstinate cupidity. On snowy days, Madame Sylvanie wondered whether, already being rich, it might not be better to renounce her hope and return to Paris, where she could live reasonably well, after all, on the income of her capital. It was now Phédo who was obstinate in pursuing the opulence already in her grasp, it seemed to her. And, desiccating in ennui, aging twice as fast in the long duration of the hours, she did not want to let go.

In that soul, where nothing luminous or proud had ever risen, to which the precocity of instinctive depravity had forbidden even the amusement of the novelty of vices, there was no longer any but one sole thought: to seize everything, to carry away, possess and keep that fabulous wealth. And she acquired, by virtue of the obsession, a more aquiline outline of the nose, with a habit of holding her hand in front of her, hooked. One might have thought that, as among birds of prey, all her vital energy was summarized and concentrated in the long curve of a beak and avid claws.

In truth, Madame Sylvanie admired her. The former worker, finally nostalgic for corridors, wings, and the dressing-rooms of little actresses who caused the foam of champagne to rise up, did not find sufficient compensation for her enunciations in Monsieur Luberti—"You know, we hold him like that!"—and she was astonished, with a species of veneration, by that woman, still young, who forgot everything in the unique covetousness of a fortune that might perhaps escape her.

One day, Madame Sylvanie's amazement was boundless.

"But . . . but . . ." she stammered, looking at Phédo, "one might think that you were . . . pregnant!"

"Yes, pregnant."

"Oh! By whom?"

"The comte, of course!"

"That's not possible. You're bored, you've had someone, a domestic, or perhaps Luberti."

"Don't be stupid! It's by the comte, no one else, that I'm pregnant. That's good, eh? Come on, stop looking at me with wide eyes. It's the comte, since I tell you so."

Then Madame Sylvanie threw her arms around her niece's neck. That result—being pregnant by the comte, by Comte Stefan, still nailed to his armchair, paralyzed in the legs, almost paralyzed in the arms, only alive, it seemed, in his eyes and his spectral laugh—revealed such a prodigy of patient determination, of subtle complaisance, and, during some absence of the valets, of adroit suddenness, implied, in sum, so much impossibility overcome, that she wept, sobbing with joy, like a woman who has suddenly learned of some unexpected heroism on the part of a child in whom she had invested all her hope. Phédo, the mother of a scion of the Tchercelews, perhaps a son to continue the race: what a glorious and useful adventure! The heritage was assured.

But something terrible happened.

On the day when, in the great hall poorly lit by an obscure lamp, in the sole presence of Luberti, who had approved and admired Phédo's conduct, Madame Sylvanie, holding her blushing niece by the hand, advanced toward the invalid in order to make him, not without moderation, a few honest reproaches for having abused—him, the master—the innocence of a person so long irreproachable, that day, at that minute, as soon as he had understood what she was talking about, Comte Tchrcelew, standing up on legs that had been motionless for forty years, and moving his arms, cried in a voice as heart-rending as that of a martyr whose skin is being ripped away:

"No child! I won't have a child! I don't want any child to be born to me. It will die with me, it's already dead, since I'm a cadaver of sorts, the abominable race of which I bear the ancient sins like a burden of filth. The evil from which I suffer is the vice of my family, become leprous in their last heir. The grimace that contracts my mouth is the frightful bitter laughter of their damnation. Have you not been told anything, women who come from so far away? Have you not learned anything during your long isolation in this accursed solitude? They know, however, my old serfs, the story of my family; it is the horrible legend with which the men and women entertain one another in low voices, which one doesn't tell to children.

"My father, the old man who vomited up his soul with meat and wine—my father, not fattened by fat but swollen by the purulence of his intimate crapulousness—was the least hideous of those who bear our name. The past of my family is the joyful astonishment of Hell! If our breed had been a dynasty or a princely lineage, it would—men and women, young and old alike—have left in the consternated memory of people an illustrious trail of abominations, like the Caesars and the Borgias. Between the walls of this manor and in our palaces in Saint Petersburg and Moscow, all of our generations, the heirs and legators of shame, were Caligulas and Lucrezias, Messalinas and Alexanders.

"By virtue of what immemorial malediction, perhaps the punishment of an original sin, or by what fatal transmission from generation to generation, of the execrable flaw of an ancestor, were we constrained to the perpetuity of evil? I sometimes think that they are not lies, the old tales that hover, with their wings of a black bird, over this dwelling, and perhaps the Devil did indeed preside over our nocturnal joys. If my own legs had been able to move, it is toward crime that they would have borne me; for it is in me as it was in them, the abject soul of the ancestors; I have been saved from vile acts by the impossibility of acting; it is to my infirmity that I owe my innocence. But I have had horrible thoughts!

"And my race will not die with me? The ancient infamy will be reincarnated in a son or a daughter, who will be worthy of the ancestors and who, engendering or giving birth in turn, will propagate the hereditary filth until the end of days? No, that shall not be, I do not want that to be. And if you are not lying, if you are indeed pregnant, you, woman, prostitute or ghoul, who came one evening, by means of ignominious and omnipotent caresses that my still-living inertia of a mummy could not, alas, repel, to extort from my loins the semen of monsters, know that you shall not give birth to a living child. With these resuscitated hands, whose fingernails have grown with immobility into claws, I will open your womb in order to snatch out the fetus, not yet born and already guilty!"

He advanced, palms open, toward the two frightened women, who recoiled, their foreheads under their arms, toward a corner of the room, while the prudent Luberti slid toward the door. And the heir of the Tchercelews was so terrifying, with his appearance, truly, of a walking corpse emerged from death in order to accomplish some frightful administration of justice, that the excess of fear rendered some courage to Madame Sylvanie. As Comte Stefan reached out his arms, perhaps with the intention of strangling, she rushed at him and seized him by the throat with the strength of a madwoman. She dug her fingernails into the neck and kept squeezing.

She let go when, because of the weight of the body that had abandoned itself, she thought that the comte was perhaps no longer alive. He fell full length on to the paving stones as a plank falls, and after a few gasps, expired.

A question was frequently raised thereafter between the aunt and the niece as to what had caused that sudden death.

"Surely you strangled him," Phédo said.

But Madame Sylvanie objected: "No, I scarcely touched him. He must have had a heart malady, and the effort and the emotion—bang! no more person."

At first, the accident troubled them; it alarmed the Italian no less, who had entirely linked his interests to those of the Parisiennes. That the men of law would worry about the comte's death seemed improbable—he had been ill for such a long time—and then, in any case, they were innocent. But what was certain was that the abruptness of the death would disrupt their projects. Tchercelew would not get up again to make a testament in their favor, and from the invention of Phédo, who, in the hope of a succession, perhaps a marriage, had dared a species of abominable rape, nothing would result but a fatherless child.

She said: "This way, it's me who has had and will have all the trouble, without any profit."

But they were not people to be discouraged. In default of what they could not have, it was necessary to be content with what they could obtain. Madame Sylvanie, who had been keeping a weather eye open, as they say, knew the coffers and cupboards where the sums brought by the comte's farmers were amassed, and knew where to find the keys to drawers full of bonds and jewels.

After the funeral, which was beautiful—all the serfs followed the master's body, with abundant sobs—the three accomplices left the country in a telega, followed by larger carts loaded with trunks that were not empty. They were allowed to depart without anyone asking them where they were going or what they were taking with them—who would have dared to inter-rogate people who had had the confidence of the comte?—and during the voyage, the aunt and the niece, in conversations in low voices, calculated the figure of their fortune. They added various further sums to what was deposited in the Banque de France, and which had naturally produced interest—that sum had more than doubled—and the considerable bonds that they had appropriated.

"A hundred thousand livres of income," Madame Sylvanie concluded.

"Better than that," said Phédo.

Then they became pensive, their eyes closed, in haste to be on the other side of the frontier.

Only Luberti, who possessed little more than the product of his quotidian thefts, experienced some anxiety. What if his friends let him go? It would then have been without advantage to himself that he had helped them pull their chestnuts out of the fire. But he kept quiet, waiting.

With common accord, they went to Paris. It was only there that they debated the grave question of the equitable distribution of the profits. The two women quickly fell into agreement: "Fifty-fifty," the said, almost at the same time. It was agreed that the total fortune, realized in cash, would be divided into halves, one of which would belong to Phédo, the other to Madame Sylvanie; then the aunt and niece would each go her own way, wherever they wished. They were now in haste to separate: a natural desire in those who have brought off some nasty coup together. It seemed to them that the embarrassment of the crime committed would be diminished by the disappearance of one of the guilty parties; an absent accomplice is a fraction of innocence recovered.

"Very good, but what about me?" asked Luberti.

"You aren't the most unfortunate," said Phédo. "You can marry me."

"What?"

"Yes, if my aunt isn't jealous."

There was no humorous intention in Phédo's words. Now rich, she aspired to be honorable; the child that was going to be born required a father; and for that employment Luberti was more suitable than any other, obliged to discretion by the fear of a quarrel with his accomplices. In any case, she had not thought for a minute of veritably being the wife of that rogue.

"We'll marry, I'll give you sixty thousand francs, and you'll depart for Hamburg, where you can blow your brains out if you don't break the bank."

"No," he said, "I don't play roulette. One can't cheat at roulette."

But he accepted the marriage and the sixty thousand francs.

All accounts settled, Phédo found herself alone, and very glad to be. Initially, pride advised her to install herself in Paris, to throw parties, to humiliate her former comrades in the theater, much older and much less rich than her. But long years of cupidity had developed a frightful avarice in her; with the same ardor that she had stolen the money of others, she wanted to keep her own. Certainly, she did not fear developing a weakness for some foppish ham, who would have beaten her and ruined her; the heart and the senses, if she had ever had any, were quite dead in her. On that side, there was no danger. But receiving people, hosting balls and dinners costs a lot of money, and those who amuse themselves in your home are the first to mock you. Then again, to triumph it is necessary to be pretty; she knew full well that she was scarcely that; she was not old yet, scarcely thirty-two, but was desiccated and atrophied by vice, by the pleasure of others and by the long, tortuous obsession with the money to conquer.

What it was better to do was to become—was she not married, authentically?—an entirely respectable person, about whom there was nothing to say, who could live alone, tranquilly and happily. For several months, less than a year, she stayed in Paris, in a small apartment that was not expensive, summarily furnished. She sometimes went to the theater, not recognizing anyone there, getting bored; and as soon as her child—her daughter, Sophie—was born, she told herself that the best thing to do would be to establish herself in a province, in a healthy climate, because she was coughing slightly, having caught cold in Russia.

She thought of Fountainebleau, bought a spacious house there with a garden, settled down, and was an honest bourgeoise, rich, esteemed, well-nourished, going to bed early, looking after herself and preserving herself, in order to live as long as possible, economizing her life as she economized her income. A good mother? Yes, why not? Devoid of tenderness, but very appropriately alarmed every time Sophie suffered from some childish misfortune. Perhaps, with regard to the child, she had a vague ambition.

And it was a calm and easy existence. No incidents, except, five years apart, two items of news, equally good: that of the death of Madame Sylvanie, from whom she inherited the share of the common profits that she had abandoned to her; and that of the death of Monsieur Luberti, which delivered her from the worry of seeing him appear, poorly dressed, without a sou, looking for a loan.

Today, in that provincial, forty-eight years old, thin, a little hard, almost austere, who had wherewithal, in that widow of an Italian diplomat who had died in service in France, in the respectable friend of Madame d'Hermelinge, there was nothing—except for a few haphazard words, here and there, strange and brutal, which confessed reminiscences of the wings and lucrative suppers—that could have led to the recognition of the little actress who had climbed down a rope, without a leotard, from the second floor, pausing at the entresol, and who, before being the execrable rapist of an infirm near-cadaver, had danced on the table of Comte Tchercelew in the costume of a prioress or an archimandrite.

II

Amusing as it was to embrace in the woods, it was nevertheless necessary to go home when it was time for dinner; it is hamadryads, not well brought up young women, who live eternally under the trees. So, toward the end of the afternoon in which they had had so much pleasure drying their hair in the sun, the two friends, Sophie and Emmeline, went back to the house, the hand of one on the arm of the other—it was Sophie who offered the arm—with very serious expressions, not tousled at all, for they had put their hair up again, and giving the example of correction that befit well-bred demoiselles.

They were very astonished when they went into the main road of the quarter, florid and green in the gardens neighboring their two houses.

Madame Luberti, who usually did not worry about their absences and returns, was leaning out of a window and, with the gestures of a broken down automaton, was making them signs to hurry up, to come immediately.

They ran, and went into the vestibule. Sophie's mother, who had come down to meet them, was dressed to the nines, in a red dress, with sequins in her hair. She had retained from her former life a liking for violent colors and tinsel jewelry. She was hideous—desiccated and jaundiced—under the elegance of her coiffure, giving the impression of a skeletal acrobat.

"Come on, let's go, people are waiting for you," she said. "What the devil were you doing in the forest? You're mad . . . yes, yes, you're mad, but all that's finished. Go home, Emmeline, you'll find someone there that you'll be pleased to see. It's a surprise that's been kept in store for you. Sophie, go up to your room and get dressed, quickly. Your most beautiful dress. Go on, upstairs; I have to talk to you."

A few minutes later, Emmeline having traversed the gardens, Madame Luberti found herself alone with Sophie in a room on the first floor.

"This is it," she said, "it's quite simple. It's a matter of a marriage. The fiancé is dining this evening with Madame d'Hermelinge. I know, seventeen, it's a little young; no matter, we had the idea a long time ago, the neighbor and I, and better sooner than later. Oh, except, you know, I intend this to go as if it were on castors, and there not to be any tears or wailing. You see, gamine, I know you; I'll tell you this, I know you much better than you think. If you take me for someone stupid, who doesn't see anything of anything, you're mistaken. But it's necessary to finish with that silliness, No more of these sighs at the piano and all these attacks of nerves. One is a demoiselle, one marries, that's in the order of things, and it cures syncopes."

With that, Madame Luberti went out, adding: "Get dressed, we're dining at seven."

Of her mother's words, Sophie, standing against the wall, had hardly heard any but two: *marriage* and *husband*. She repeated those words, her gaze fixed, as if she did not understand them. Then, suddenly: "Oh, my God, Emmeline is getting married!" either because in her mind, dinner at Madame d'Hermeline's implied that it was a matter of Emmeline, or because the hypothesis of being married herself appeared to her to be utterly absurd, unimaginable.

She had never thought, no, never that she might be anyone's wife, that she might sleep in a man's bed. Among so many dreams, that one would have been a nightmare, had never occurred to her; it was different from her, a stranger to her. So, no hesitation; she murmured: "Emmeline! A husband!"

An immense desolation, like the solitary night air filled with rubble, penetrated her entire being; it seemed to her that she had no more blood, no more heart, that she was emptied of everything that could live.

She tried to reason. First of all, it was not certain that they were thinking of making Emmeline a wife. Madame Luberti often said things that had no meaning that could be attributed to them; she was very scatterbrained in spite of her grave expression. Then again, in sum, well, a girl is made to become a young woman. People get married every say. What was there that was extraordinary in itself, and so painful for her, in the incident, so natural, of the marriage of her friend? Would it prevent them from being good comrades that one of them had a household, children? And certainly, Emmeline would be very pretty in a white dress with a train, under flowers attached to a long veil . . .

She had a vision of Emmeline in the arms of a man, of that frail mouth, as pink as an unopened rosebud, under the brushwood of a bearded kiss. And, hurling herself against the wall, she struck it with her head, crying: "No! I don't want her to be married! I don't want her to be married! And I say that you won't be married!"

At that moment, after an "Are you ready?" from the other side of the door, Madame Luberti came back into the room.

"Yes, ready, let's go," said Sophie.

"You're not changing your dress?"

"I'm all right like this, let's go."

She spoke in a rude, staccato voice. She went out first, very quickly, she wanted to see the man who was destined for Emmeline right away. What she would do, she did not know; but before even sitting down at the table, she would do something brutal, something terrible, that would break the marriage.

The idea crossed her mind that, having poison, one could put it into the glass of someone drinking beside you. *Poison! If only I had any!* She would find another means, just as frightening. Or she would simply say to the man: "What have you come to do here? You've come to marry Emmeline? I don't want that. Go away."

Yes, *I don't want that*, and she would be obeyed.

The gardens traversed, she went up the staircase of the neighboring house, very rapidly, her head high, with a dry flame in her eyes, her hands trembling.

Emmeline threw her arms around her neck.

"Look! Look! It's Jean, my brother. He has a leave, he's staying with us for three months. Look at him, then! Isn't he handsome in his uniform? Doesn't he have the air of a general? And a general he'll be."

Sophie ran her eyes around the room, looking for some other man next to Baron Jean d'Hermelinge, captain of cuirassiers, who saluted her rather awkwardly, with embarrassment before a demoiselle, with his ornamentation and his saber rattling.

No one, just him.

But in that case, the one they want to marry isn't Emmeline, it's me!

She experienced a great relief, a caress of warm milk running over a burning wound that had been inflicted on her. And, considering her friend's brother, she had a surge of gratitude for that man, who could not marry Emmeline. She was not preoccupied with the idea that he had come for her, with the project that the two mothers had formed. It was not a matter of that. It was a matter of Emmeline remaining a demoiselle; that was what was important; for the rest, there was time before her; she would see. Sophie melted entirely into ease.

The dinner was very cheerful, amid the ecstasies of Madame d'Hermelinge, who could not weary of admiring, touching and embracing that tall, robust and jovial man who had emerged from her, and the gaieties of Emmeline, who, for a moment, put around her waist the centurion from which the saber hung; with the kepi on her head and her fists on her hips, she marched from one wall to the other with a warrior stride, crying: "By the left! Forward march!"

How lovely she was, with the air of a bellicose little girl!

Sophie showed herself entirely joyful; and then, with the aid of the champagne—for they were drinking champagne to celebrate Baron Jean's arrival—the dessert concluded in bursts of laughter.

Monsieur d'Hermelinge laughed more loudly than anyone, red from the edge of his collar to the roots of his short, crew-cut hair, guffawing until he had a fit of coughing into the napkin into which he was plunging his mouth: the laugh of a worthy man who is quickly amused by everything and who is content because he is good.

He was a strong fellow, too tall, stout but not fat, with heavy bones and muscles, with no softness in his flesh; when he walked, he shook the floorboards; when he sat down, he nearly broke the chair. No more than thirty-three, his face congested even when he was not laughing, under his rude salt-and-pepper hair, which gave the impression of a beard on his head, his nostrils flaring and sniffing, beautiful scarlet lips, between which large healthy teeth shone, he gave the impression of a benevolent force; and in his large sky blue eyes, chaste and inviolate, there was a child-like candor; he made one think of a kind of virgin mercenary. He was rude and gentle, brutal and pure. One sensed that life had not spoiled the man.

Well, damn it, to be sure, one is not a demoiselle; the evenings in garrison are long, and after the punch, having a spree with nice girls is not forbidden. In Algeria for instance, one can't amuse oneself every day. If there are days when one amuses oneself too much, that provides a compensation. But in that soldier, everything that, in joy, was not frank humor, and in flirtation, was not prompt pleasure with no tomorrow—"Adieu, adieu, my girl! Pleasure to see you again, you or another!"—had remained unknown; and, deprived of complication, not going to look for midday at four o'clock, as they say, loving war and pleasure, he had the simplicity of being a hero and an excellent fellow.

Thus made, with his familiar roughness and his gross laugh of a giant child, he was not importunate to Sophie; she spoke to him without embarrassment, as cheerful as he was; and as, for his part, the cuirassier looked at and listened to that young woman, who was neither simpering nor coquettish, frank of gaze and prompt in repartee, with a pleasure he did not hide, the two mothers, who had premeditated the marriage of Sophie and Baron Jean a long time ago, during walks in the garden—an entirely suitable marriage, in which all the proprieties of fortune came together—made one another sly signs from one end of the table to the other, which meant: *It's going well, it's going as well as possible!*

But the person who was most content was Emmeline. *If Sophie marries my brother, it will be as if she were becoming my sister.* She was moved by that thought, to the point of having tears in her eyes. She would have liked the marriage to be made already. As long as Jean didn't displease Sophie! As long as she seemed pretty to him!

Emmeline continually got up from the table to go and arrange her friend's hair, always disordered, or to remake the knot in the narrow green cravat that she was wearing around her straight collar.

Only Sophie was giving no consideration to the fact that there was a suitor there. The possibility of having a husband still remained so foreign to her that she had not even thought about it, and no apprehension prevented her from saying to herself that it would be very agreeable and very amusing to have that good companion during the captain's leave.

After dinner, they walked side by side in the garden, followed, not too closely, by the two mothers and Emmeline. They talked about a thousand things: life on campaign, the battles in which he had found himself; she admired him for the four wounds that he had received; she envied him them. He said to her: "I'll teach you to ride a horse, if you like," and she accepted right away; and when they separated they gave one another a firm handshake, like two men.

It was a cordial camaraderie, a life of good fellows, which did not engender melancholy; they went for long excursions in the forest, Jean and Sophie on horseback, the mothers and Emmeline in a carriage; they dined in the arbors of inns; several times, the two comrades followed hunts, furiously, at a great gallop, crossing ditches, leaping over rocks. One day, they threw their beasts in the water along with the pack in order to follow a red deer that was crossing the pond.

In those hard exercises, that virile activity, Sophie felt herself rejoicing and developing her life normally, and as the Baron never talked to her about amour, and looked her in the face without any sighs or languid expressions, had never even kissed her fingertips—a worthy man who, sure of marrying the young woman, did not want to diminish with the vain joys of betrothal the entire happiness of the marriage, not wanting to be the thief of his own treasure—she liked him, frankly, without a hidden agenda, with a more vivid affection every day. With the result that when Madame Luberti suddenly said to her one morning: "By the way, Jean has received ministerial authorization, you'll be married in three weeks" she replied, perhaps while thinking about something else: "Good, good, as you please," and hurried off to put on her riding costume, because Monsieur d'Hermelinge was waiting for her. They were due to go, with Emmeline, to lunch at Franchard's.

For an entire week, getting up early and in the evening, after the healthy fatigue of rides in the wind and the sun, going to sleep rapidly, she did not have the leisure to think about the consent she had given. But finally, in conversations in repose, in travel plans, in the arrival, in large carriages, of the furniture that would furnish the second floor of the Luberti house, unoccupied until then, in the noise of furnishers nailing up hangings, and the chatter of couturiers summoned from Paris for the wedding dress, the idea of the marriage began to haunt her at every moment, evident, precise and inevitable. And since she had said yes, it was too late to say no: such an insult to Baron Jean, to that honest and loyal comrade, was impossible, as impossible as resisting all the pressure around her of desires, exhortations, things prepared and seemingly impatient. She would not break her word, she would be married, certainly—imminently! And she was alarmed, her eyes suddenly fixed, in a frisson that left her motionless and frozen.

Now, she refused to go out, wanting to remain alone, spending the greater part of the day in her room; and by night, next to the extinct lamp, she did not sleep, her elbow on the pillow, her forehead on her fist, looking straight ahead. At what? She did not know; at nothing, the darkness. And, as if between the jaws of a vice, she felt caught between two convictions, between two certainties: that she could not marry Baron Jean and that she could not avoid marrying him.

That was it: marriage inevitable; marriage impossible. Impossible for what reason? She could not find a response. Didn't young women marry? Was Monsieur d'Hermelinge not worthy of amour and esteem? She remained cruelly troubled. If, in order to marry Emmeline's brother, she had been obliged to distance herself from Emmeline, to whom she was linked by such a dear tenderness, she would have understood why the marriage would be intolerable to her, but no; the two friends would not be separated; wherever they went, it was agreed that Madame and Mademoiselle d'Hermelinge would go with the two spouses.

No reason, therefore.

Nevertheless, she sensed, she understood, with a perfect instinctive lucidity, that she ought not to be the Baron's wife, nor that of any other man; it seemed to her that marriage, for her, was uninhabitable, irrespirable, that she would die therein right away.

Before the imminent union she was like a bird bound feet and wings, which someone wants to throw into a river; it does not know what water is; other creatures live in it, but it cannot live in it, and it struggles in a frightful terror.

And anger came to Sophie: against herself above all, not like others, and inexplicable to herself; against the Baron, such a brave heart, however, such a jovial companion—would he not be able to stay in the regiment, would his presence not be needed there?—against Madame Luberti, against Madame d'Hermelinge, the important thing for the one being to have a titled son-in-law, and for the other to give her son a rich heiress; nobility and money were things she scarcely cared about, herself. And she was also angry with Emmeline; should she not have detested marriage for her friend, as Sophie had detested it for hers? Oh, the traitor, the ingrate.

Treacherous? Ingrate? Why? Sophie could not find a motive for the horror that Emmeline ought to have experienced, any more than she could explain the horror that she had felt herself at the idea of Emmeline married.

The day fixed for the wedding drew nearer.

A continual expression of fear was seen on Sophie's face. For, by virtue of the proximity of the event, the probable details, such as her virginal innocence could perceive them, became more precise in her mind. Relentlessly—no smile by day, no sleep by night—she saw the nuptial chamber, the common bed, and the threat of caresses; she imagined the proximity of a body, the contact, perhaps, of skin . . . a frisson shook her entirely; in every one of her pores she felt the sting of an icy needle.

Occupied as he was by his imminent happiness, the Baron could not help noticing the coldness, the pallor, and the frightened eyes of his fiancée, who had changed so completely in a matter of days; he thought that she was ill; perhaps it would be a good idea to postpone the marriage; he would have consented to wait for a week or two. But Madame Luberti insisted with a great vivacity that there should not be any adjournment. Such fears of a young woman on the point of such a great change in her life were very frequent and quite natural. If one listened to these gamines they would never marry!

Perhaps Sophie's mother had some reason, which she did not confess, for hastening the marriage. And it happened in accordance with her will. The marriage took place on the day fixed.

It was before midday, on a bright autumn day; the sun illuminated the church through the stained glass windows, while, her pallor excused by the white transparency of her veil, and driving back in an effort of will of which she would not have believed herself capable the gasp of anguish that rose into her throat, Sophie marched through the guests a little rapidly, in haste to abridge a torture that so many other tortures were, alas, to follow, toward the choir resplendent with gold and candles,

It seemed to her, with a tenderness soon changed into bitterness, that she recognized that sunlight in the nave, that sunlight on the holy sheet, and the gleams of the gilded altar; she rediscovered and saw again something delectable; she felt that she was living in an old joy, renewed; clad in white, as today, she had once advanced in this church, under the light, but was so happy then . . .

The present reality reclaimed her, squeezed her heart; it was as if she were falling that she sat down in the bridal seat.

During the celebration of the rites, however, while the nuptial voice of the organ sang majestically, or the priest, after having bowed before the retable, turned toward the husband, or the little bell rang that ordered kneeling, with her eyes lowered toward the carpet on the steps—unconsciously, perhaps, requesting from the resurrection of an exquisite moment the strength to submit to the frightful moment—she evoked the previous ceremony.

The veil over her forehead, over her arms, over her whole body, was like a consoling caress that enveloped her with the past, isolated her from present sadness; and then, in a realization of memory, she sensed passionate fervors rise from her heart to her lips, reveries of paradise in which angelic couples loved one another spread through her mind, and, at the moment when the officiant gave her the paten to kiss, at the moment when the reminiscence of the divine incarnation put into her a devouring heat that had already burned her, suddenly, in a great jet of clustered radiance, she turned in order to embrace Emmeline.

It was Baron Jean that she had beside her, holding up the ring that the priest had blessed, and which she would wear on her finger.

III

After the good humor of the family meal, the violins having fallen silent and all the guests having departed, mild nocturnal peace was established. Between the sound of a shower of fine and urgent rain that was beating on the windows, the house, in its quietude, was isolated, like an island of silence.

There were footsteps along the wall, in the corridor where an opaque lamp, descending from the ceiling, spread something like a diaphanous muslin. Baron Jean stopped before a door and knocked. With his finger? No, with a sprig of orange blossom that he had detached from the nuptial robe on leaving the church. An unsubtle imagination, an almost stupid superstition; it was thanks to the chaste unopened flowers, sisters of the virgin, that he would enter into the wife's room, where the mysterious enchantment of the marriage would blossom; and that idea, childishly tender, which resembled a memory of sentimental romance, which would have made intelligent people smile, was touching in that tall robust fellow, slightly coarse, not complicated or elegiac, as simple as a hero.

No response. He had only made a slight sound, the impact of the frail buds against the wood of the batten. Doubtless Sophie had not heard it. The husband knocked again, as forcefully as he could, but with precaution, in order not to break the flowers. This time, Madame Sophie d'Hermelinge—he said that name to himself, in a very low voice, to which he listened with delight, because that double name was hers and his, mingled, their two tendernesses in a single indivisible happiness—this time, his wife—he also thought: my wife!—would surely respond: "Is that you, my love?" or even: "Is that you, Jean?" and then would add, after a slightly fearful silence: "Yes, come in."

An infinite contentment entered into him at the thought that he would possess, entirely and forever, that beautiful and young creature. He was not one of those, too subtle, who wear away their emotions in wanting to refine them, or disperse them in minute analyses; he experienced them *en bloc*. Amorous and married, he saw nothing but that; he was happy, his entire being blooming, and his eyes moistened with good tears.

At the same time, there was also some dread. A demoiselle like Sophie, well brought up, timid in spite of her boyish airs, knowing nothing about anything—he had not wanted Madame Luberti to speak to the bride, to explain things to her; he thought

84

that stupid; there was the husband, damn it!—a demoiselle of seventeen has nothing resembling, thank God, the sluts of garrison towns, who had no longer been astonished by anything for a long time. He wondered whether he might not appear coarse to that candor, brutal to that delicacy.

To touch a young woman without doing her any harm would not be easy; naivety is even more fragile than fine porcelain or crystal; and he knew himself that there was no one like him for breaking glasses and plates. But he would use so many precautions! He would have fingers of cotton wool, more sensible than the friction of a snowflake that was not cold; and in his goodness, in his fear of being fearful, he made resolutions to be sparing, to embrace as if cradling, to caress as if lulling to sleep, to attenuate the kiss to the lightness of a breath . . .

Sophie had not responded. The idea that she was alarmed redoubled Baron Jean's timidity. He wondered whether he dared go in before she had said: "Yes, my love, come in."

Get away! He was a soldier, damn it! And, gathering his courage, he grasped the door handle and pushed the batten—oh, not very hard, not hard at all!—and slowly went in. Then, when he had seen, in the penumbra of the room, in front of the blazing logs, the whiteness of the peignoir that enveloped his wife, all the healthy desires of conjugal love, all the pride of honest possession, rose to his throat in a surge of joy; his rude face was radiant.

The bride did not budge.

He approached, on tiptoe, knelt in front of the armchair, and extended his hands as if to pray. Truly, there was piety in his tenderness.

A few minutes passed. He felt almost annoyed. Why did she not turn toward him, why did she not look at him with a smile? Her eyes were closed in her exceedingly pale pace. What, she still retained that melancholy of the days that had preceded the wedding day?

He had understood that she ceased to laugh as the august moment of the marriage had approached; while judging it excessive, he had not disapproved of the often morose reserve she had shown; but at the end of the day, it was necessary not to push the most delicate sentiments to the extreme. They were united, they were alone. Fearful as she might be of the imminent intercourse, no matter how wildly her young modesty recoiled, she ought to have been able, since she loved him, since she was good, to look at him a little, to say something.

Oh, by means of what words, which would not frighten her, could he convince her to raise those eyelids, to part those lips?

Words, he did not find, or rather, those he found seemed too bold; after a long silence, as one wakes up a convalescent, slowly and without shocks, he brushed her hand with his mouth: the dear, slender and pale hand that Sophie extended along the arm of the chair.

As one bounds when burned by a red-hot iron, the young woman started in her peignoir, held tight against her in bewildered arms, and threw herself to the back of the room.

Her back against the wall, her hands crossed over her breast, pale and haggard, she opened her eyes wide; and in the attitude of a cornered beast that would like to bite and flee, there was such an expression of fear in her staring eyes that Baron Jean nearly fell backwards, as if hit on the head with a club, his hands dangling, stammering: "Oh my God! Oh my God! What, the matter, Sophie? Oh my God!" And the despair traversed him that never, at any moment of his life, would he forget the gaze that Sophie was directing at him at that moment.

But come on, she was ill, or mad. Had he not been told that when she was very young, she had had attacks of nerves, convulsions? He pulled himself together, drew nearer, but only by a few steps, and spoke in a very soft voice. He had divined correctly, hadn't he? She was in pain? Yes, it was because she was in pain that she had that sinister face; it was not possible that she had against him, veritably, the kind of rage and terror that she was showing. Alas, he loved her so much that he was worthy of love, not hatred. Had she need of something? Did she want him to call the domestics, to wake Madame Luberti? No, she was right; he would care for her, better than anyone else.

Oh, how cruel it was! A night that ought to have had all the dreamed of joys, and where there was only space, as yet, for such a sadness: Sophie ill. But it would be nothing, it would pass quickly; if she consented to tell him what it was, where the pain was, he would find some way of healing her, of curing her.

What? She didn't want to explain? Why didn't she want to? But perhaps it was precisely her illness that was making her like this, silent, with a surly expression? In a little while, feeling better, she would no longer be nasty.

The most urgent matter was not to leave her there, standing against the wall. She was going to lie down on the bed, fully dressed; she would be much better on the bed; he would sit beside her, would not talk to her if she didn't want to hear him speak, nor touch her, if him touching her would importune her. Oh, she could be tranquil; he would not do anything that might alarm her, and she could sleep peacefully, sleep for a few hours, and have pleasant dreams, while he, like a mother watching over her baby, would watch her sleep, and, after that repose, she would wake up calm, smiling, astonished to have felt ill, and not feeling ill any more, but happy . . .

Softening to the point of maternal soothing the rudeness of his voice and the customary energy of his gesture, he tried to take hold of the sleeve of her peignoir in order to guide her to the bed—but as soon as he reached out his hand, Sophie's teeth clashed frightfully, and her eyes, widening further, darted the cold glint of a more menacing horror.

Then he stood up, and, after a blow of his fist on the marble, which made the candlesticks on the mantelpiece tremble, he cried between oaths: "You hate me! You hate me! Wretched girl, you hate me!"

One might have thought that she was challenging him, with the same terrible gaze; he nearly threw himself upon her.

He controlled himself, he stepped away, biting his knuckles; he started pacing furiously back and forth at the other end of the room. If he had stayed close to Sophie, he might perhaps have killed her. As he came and went he cursed, and stammered:

"That's it. I can see it clearly. You don't love me. You can't stand me. Ill? Oh, well, yes. If I weren't here, me, your husband, beside this bed, on which I have the right to lie you down, you wouldn't be grinding your teeth, you'd be smiling and laughing. I should have suspected that it would happen, anyway! It isn't the expression of a loving fiancée, the expression you've had these last few days. I was stupid, because I love you; and then, I was told that all demoiselles are anxious about the wedding night, of the unknown that there is for them in amour; that they're afraid of marriage while desiring it. Triple idiot that I am! It isn't marriage that you were afraid of, it's the husband. But damn it all, since I horrify you, why did you marry me?"

He stopped, in order to look her in the face, not too closely, and say: "Speak. Answer. I want you to answer. Why have you married me, if you don't love me?"

She still remained speechless, motionless, with the eyes of a madwoman. Exasperated, tapping his foot, almost stamping, he went on: "Do you hear me? Do you understand what I'm asking? You'll give me an answer, I hope? Oh, answer. If you don't answer, beware!"

The same silence, the same furious immobility. He could no longer stand it; he launched himself toward her.

"Say something! Say something!"

Very close to Sophie, however, courage failed him; his legs buckled; he sobbed.

"Oh, forgive me! I'm shouting, I'm getting angry. I was about to do you harm, me, who adores you! But after all, also, you're there, you're not saying anything, and you're looking at me in such a frightful fashion. Oh, I'm not threatening you any longer, no. I'm begging you, I'm pleading with you, I'm imploring you, speak to me, say something, a single word. Tell me that I'm mistaken, that you don't detest me; or, if you detest me, explain why. I want to know how I've displeased you. Oh, God, anything that it will please you for me to be, I'll become, in order for you to be content, in order that you no longer have that expression of cruelty and anger. If you knew all the tenderness I have for you in my heart, my treasure, my darling, my wife! To give you pleasure, I'd die if you wanted; to spare you, to spare you chagrin, it seems to me that I'd have the courage to live without seeing you. Oh, I have too much love for you not to have a little. Come on, be good, don't detest me. After all, think, I love you, we're alone, and it's our wedding night!"

With those words, and yet others, stammering and weeping, he marched toward her, on his knees, and, without anger, with a fearful tenderness, he put his arms around her skirt.

But she repelled him with a kick full in his chest. The blow was so rude that he nearly fell over backwards.

He got up, finally crazed by anger.

But she had had time to run to the window and open it; she would have thrown herself into the street if he had not seized her by the hair with one hand and around the midriff with the other, lifted her up and carried her to the bed, where he fell on top of her.

Then, holding her firmly, with the bewildered fear, for he loved her so much, of having seen her so close to death, and also with rage at seeing her so rebellious to his love, he held her against him and held himself against her. Through the fabrics he sensed the flesh that was his due. Oh, his anger exasperated the desire so long constrained by the respect of betrothal. He had her! He had her! Now he had her!

He closed his eyes for fear of seeing the frightful fixed gaze, but from the body beneath his body, from all the stiffness that opposed intercourse, from the mouth that was grinding teeth, which did not cry out, which contorted, and from that cleavage without a heartbeat, and those thighs clamped as if by catalepsy, he acquired a furious desire to oppress, to twist, to plunge, to open up.

If she had proffered a plaint, of she had said to him: "Please!" oh, how he would have released her, how he would have fallen beside the bed and begged her pardon, and how happy he would have been to hope that one day, later, when she wanted to, she would have opened her lips, smiling.

But no, the resistance of marble, the immobile insensibility of which was made of hatred, that was what he had in his arms, and in a hazard of menace or prayer—he made gestures that might have been of fury or supplication, which were those two frenzies mingled—he parted the muslin of her peignoir; he had the breasts before him! He had touched, he saw, the cold and ferocious flesh of the young woman, the flesh that he wanted, which was his. And he was animalized. All of that worthy man was no longer anything but a male.

Thoughts, however, were mingled with instincts: that she was horrible, that she was obliging that harshness, that she was recalcitrant, having consented, that she was refusing herself, having accorded herself, and that she had preferred to die rather than belong to him, and that he had the right to take her twice over, having married her and having saved her; then, in a softening, that perhaps these refusals, this anger and this scorn were the supreme fears of the virgin, the tenderness, tomorrow, of the wife . . .

No matter. That skin that he had touched, he wanted it. Oh, how he wanted it! He tore off the peignoir, he tore off the chemise, and he tore off his own clothes. He was still holding her, with one hand. He was naked on top of his naked wife, who fell silent, save for the grinding of her teeth. He oppressed her, crushed her under the weight of a charging bull, and with a frantic, irresistible double separation, he obliged the virgin to submit to the triumphant intromission of the husband.

She did not utter a sigh, or a single plaint. Her teeth, beneath her clenched lips, had ceased grinding; that was more frightful. He persisted over that silence, over that immobility, with the vehemence, more hectic for being sacrilegious, of a violator of a tomb who would like to oblige a corpse to the resurrection of pleasure. The soldier put the fury of an assault into that tearing, that breaking down, His victory would only be completed by the admission of defeat!

But he did not obtain that admission, not even in a cry of horror, not even in a sob. And he hurled himself upon the martyr with the effort of a torturer drunk on the blood of torture, who exults in torment. So much so that finally, as a drunkard falls down, he collapsed beside her in a bestial slumber.

✳

In the nuptial—alas!—chamber there was a long silence between the small patter of the rain on the windows.

Finally, Sophie, left there on the sheets like a murder victim, stirred, straightened and sat up. Beneath her eyelids she had the infinite horror of a return from Hell. She closed her eyes, as one does when one wants to think more profoundly.

She remained thus for some time. Then, very rapidly, she turned her gaze toward the man who was asleep beside her; a cold zigzag ran down her back. Closing her eyes again, she resumed thinking, with an effort that creased her entire face. She gave the impression of someone resuscitated, still frightened by having been dead, who would like to recall the panic of the death-throes and the tomb

After a few moments, she slid out of the bed on to the floor, soundlessly, like falling underwear. She picked up her night-dress and her peignoir and got dressed. Now she had the resolute and methodical gestures of a somnambulist. She did not hurry. She took her time.

When she was dressed, she walked to the door. Before opening it she turned her gaze toward the alcove again and considered the man asleep there; a flash of ferocious hatred sprang from her eyes; one might have thought that she was about to pounce on the husband who had vanquished her.

She maintained herself; she opened the door silently, found herself in the corridor, and went down the stairs from the second floor.

She had to go past her mother's bedroom; she continued her route, still silently. Phantoms traverse sleeping houses thus. The other stairway, found by groping, offered itself. She went down again, went along the wall of the vestibule, and unhooked the chains of the entrance door.

She was in the street, where the persistent rain was beating the pavement. Then, when she was outside the dwelling, outside the family, outside the marriage, a cry emerged from her breast, a cry followed by sobs, like coins spilling from a split sack; and abruptly, without knowing where, she began to run, her hair and her sleeves agitated behind her; she did not stop, even when she was out of breath; she fled, pale and wan, in the moonlight that filtered through the rain here and there, and continually, without slowing her pace, she put both hands to the bottom of her abdomen, where she felt, like a dead weight, the dolorous shame of the nuptial wound.

So that was what marriage was! That was what a husband was! A man in a night-shirt, with roughness of skin and hair, falling upon a young woman, lying on her, stifling her, tearing her, and, if he has said between two faints "I adore you!" thinking that he has paid in amour for the virgin's disgust. He is like the purchaser of a field who, having sunk the blade of the plow into the soil, awaits the thanks of the labored earth—and that earth gives birth!

Sophie kept going, past the houses; the rain, she wanted; that water of heaven was washing away the marital embrace, taking away from her breast, her belly and her thighs the heat of the coupling; it seemed to her that she was delivered by the downpour of a skin upon her skin, even of her own dishonored skin; she had the impression of a fresh renewal. She kept going, she ran, like a beast shaking the saddle and the bit, more rapidly when she thought she felt, in the illusion of a weight, the stubborn assault of the marriage; and the pain between her legs spurred her flight.

All her horror detested triumphant masculinity. She had had, which was frightful, the mouth of that man on her mouth, the teeth of that man on her teeth. Oh, how she understood, how she approved now of her instinctive fear of weddings and matrimonial nights.

Oh, my God, Emmeline! Emmeline, if she were married, would also have to endure that execrable outrage. Sophie was almost happy, in her despair, to have been the victim herself; the vision of her friend suffering as she had suffered herself was so frightening that she almost rejoiced in the evil that she alone had supported; it seemed to her, in a strange need for sacrifice, as if realized by being so ardent, that she had been a replacement that night, that she had substituted herself; she had the proud joy of an expiatory host.

But the chimerical pride of devotion could not prevail over real terrors. She still felt the weight of the ignominious wound in her loins. She would have liked to be dead: after that man upon her, the earth upon her, the coffin after the bed. She would have liked, in the mortuary crypt, the lamp of the conjugal chamber. The cloth of the sheets would have pleased her, as a shroud! Dirt for dirt, the creep of putrescence must stink less than the kiss of a man.

While she was still fleeing past the houses, she wondered, in the tumult of a thousand thoughts, how she would die. Kill herself, certainly, but in what fashion? What she would have liked would have been fresh water, very pure, very clear and deep, in which one could clean oneself at the same time as dying there. She felt so soiled that she had a love of the cleanliness, the kind of physical innocence, that there is in water. The rain exasperated her by only satisfying partially her need to be clean. But a river into which one could throw oneself, upon which one could float afterwards with the languor of Ophelia, she would not find. The Seine? A long way away.

To die, however, no longer to be, that was what was necessary. Well, no matter how, she would die. One can break one's head against a wall, strangle oneself with hands that do not let go, stifle oneself with a handkerchief in the mouth; and the peace of the tomb is the same after those various deaths.

At that moment, she found herself in front of the railway track. Even at night, trains pass by. To hoist herself over the hedge and lie down on the rails, and wait for the locomotive, face down, to be crushed, broken, flattened beneath the thunderous passage of the machine and the wagons, and then no longer to think, no longer to move, a kind of rag of bloody flesh: that was possible, that was offered.

And, crazy because of the bed behind her, she was about to climb over the hedge when she remembered Emmeline.

Already, during the hideousness of that night, during that flight toward salutary death, she had thought about the very pure and very tender child who, at that moment, was asleep, without bad dreams, in her inviolate bed of a young woman. Yes, often, into her anguish, the thought of her friend had slid, as the light of dawn enters into a room full of darkness and specters. But she had rejected it, for fear of finding too much charm therein, and losing in that tenderness, in fond reminiscences of their childhood, the strength to seek in death the forgetfulness of that abominable hymen. She no longer wanted to love life; it was therefore necessary that she excise from her mind and her heart the only being that rendered it dear to her.

But now, so close to the accomplishment of the fatal resolution, so close to being a corpse—for perhaps, scarcely having lain down across the track, she would hear the train rushing forward with the thunder of wheels and the spitting of its funnel—she could not snatch herself away from the caress of happy memories; she saw the darling child again, so blonde and so pretty, and their excursions through the woods, and their games in the gardens, and, in the hammock in the shed, their siestas as little husband and little wife.

The word "husband"—for reverie proffers silently words that are nevertheless heard, as if the mind were talking to itself in a whisper—ought to have troubled her, irritated her; on the contrary, a contentment came to her because, in that word, in the idea of marriage, the idea of Emmeline was mingled; and nothing, as soon as Emmeline put her grace into it, could any longer be ugly or cruel, as if, by virtue of the presence of an angel, Hell would become paradise.

Sophie understood that it would be impossible for her to die without having seen Emmeline one last time; she needed to take away a little of that light in the great somber voyage.

Yes, to see her.

At this hour? How?

In a rapid clairvoyance, she thought that everyone was asleep, on both sides of the double garden, in the neighboring houses; that Baron Jean, drunk on his dirty victory, sleeping off his ignoble joy, would not wake up. She would go back home— she remembered that she had not closed the door—and traverse the gardens; as for getting into Madame d'Hermelinge's house, nothing was easier; because of the solid gate and the high walls garnished with iron thistles, they almost always neglected to lock the glazed doors of the perron; and on the other side of that door, Sophie would have no need of light in order to find Emmeline's bedroom.

Very quickly, she retraced her steps, along the walls.

The rain had not stopped falling, fine and dense. Just now, in fleeing, Sophie had already rejoiced in the downpour, but she had not felt wet, as if her fever were drinking the water. Now her peignoir enveloped her with an icy caress that was agreeable to her, calming her and soothing her, putting over her body—

her sad, bruised body—a sensation of cleanliness, of health, and also putting into her mind a pure freshness; with the result that she wondered if that well-being was coming to her from the rain or from the imminence of seeing Emmeline.

As she went into the vestibule of her house—obscure, with opaque darkness—a terror gripped her. What if Baron Jean were no longer asleep! What if he suddenly appeared on the staircase, a lamp in hand: him, the husband, in a night-shirt, perhaps naked, enormous! What if he launched himself upon her, picked her up, carried her off, laid her down again under the execrable conjugal rape, touching her everywhere with his coarse hands on which there were hairs, covering her with his entire mouth in a broad, panting kiss?

She was on the point of fleeing again. But no, there was no one: shadow, silence. She went in, groped, went down into the garden, and rapidly followed the path that led from one house to the other.

As usual, the door to the perron was not locked. Sophie only had to push the glazed batten; she took a few steps, without making a noise, encountered a brass handle with her hand, and, with the furtive slowness of a cat sliding through a gap in a doorway, penetrated into Emmeline's bedroom.

At first she could not distinguish anything because of the closed curtains and the almost extinct night-light. But, a perfume and murmur of breath, there was a floral odor in that young woman's bedroom, and a tiny buzz, like a bee.

Shall I wake her up?

Oh, no, Emmeline would be so surprised, perhaps so frightened; and then, what would she say to her? How could she explain that nocturnal presence, that rain-soaked peignoir?

I'll only look at her. I'll bid her adieu without her hearing me, and I'll go away forever.

In order to see her it was necessary to move a curtain, the one over the window facing the bed; even during the blackest of nights, there is some light in the air. Silently, Sophie moved along the wall, arrived at the casement, and lifted one of the curtains, which she suspended from the peg. But how thick the darkness was! However, the room was suddenly illuminated, not very brightly, but brightly enough. Had moonlight or star-light suddenly entered? No, the night-light, in its little open jar, under the ceiling, had reanimated with a sizzle; and on the bright pillow, amid the tender gold of unrolled hair, smiling in a dream, pale in the forehead and cheeks and pink in the lips, was Emmeline's face. The sheet came up to her chin. How pretty it was, that child's face, pink and pale in that blonde fleece!

Around the narrow iron bed, from which a muslin coverlet lined with blue satinette had slipped, the cretonne of the walls and hangings mingled flowers, butterflies and birds; it seemed that Emmeline was asleep in a florid aviary; if those flowers were not stirring in a gentle breeze, if those birds were not fluttering and chirping, it was in order not to disturb the sleeping child.

On the furniture and the mantelpiece were a hundred small objects: gloves, ribbons, frills, little nacre caskets into which bonbons were put, work-baskets from which red, green and blue wool hung, portraits in crystal frames of the mother or the brother, and Sophie too. And in a corner there was another bed, all lace and beribboned blondes, much smaller: that of the doll that Emmeline had undressed and put to bed before going to sleep. Between the arms of a dainty chair lay the little shirt, the little batiste pantaloons, the silk stockings and the little black varnished shoes; on top of all that, on the chemise folded in four, was a blue satin hat with one edge turned up, with a fantastic plume that was the tail-feather of a pink bird.

In a large armchair near the big bed, Emmeline's garments were arranged exactly like the doll's garment on the little chair; she did the same for her little sister and for herself. And the motionless spring of the walls, the smiling childishness of the small, scattered things, surrounded the sleeping virgin with freshness and innocence.

In that bedroom, where they had spent so many pleasant hours as little girls, and then as young women—for they sometimes came to rest there after playing in the gardens, or after walking in the forest—in that room, where everything was smiles, modesty and tranquil reverie, so different from the other bedroom, on the second floor of the other house, with the horrible bed full of a man, Sophie felt reborn within her the calm and the ignorance of childhood years; she forgot what she had learned, alas. She even seemed better than in the time of the ardent devotions of her adolescence and the transports in poetry and music; she persuaded herself that she was, here, exactly like Emmeline; and because she found her so worthy of being loved, she loved resembling her.

For more than an hour, standing beside the bed, with a paradisal smile on her lips, she watched the pale pink face sleep.

Then, an astonishment came to her, for the first time.

It was singular, in sum, the tenderness that she felt for her friend. Yes, singular. Young women doubtless took pleasure in laughing with other young women, preferred some, could not abide others; Sophie, watching from her window the inmates of convents and boarding-schools filing past, had noticed how ordinary the same faces were that she recognized in the same ranks; and there must be, in those amities of girls, needs that never let up, devotions and jealousies. But it seemed to her that she had a sentiment for her childhood friend that the most tender neighbors in class or the dormitory could not know. Perhaps one sister might cherish another as Sophie cherished Emmeline, and perhaps, by a strange coincidence or because of concordant similarities and differences, even though they did not have the same mother, they were, in fact, like two sisters?

No; in spite of the simplicity of that explanation, which might have satisfied her, she could not believe that she loved Emmeline as one loves a sister. She loved her, not less but much more, differently. And she was astonished.

In the past, in their infantile promiscuities—little husband and little wife in the hammock in the shed—in their soon-faded transports before the holy image or the mute keyboard, she had not felt that disturbance to the extent of not understanding it, saved from anxiety by ignorance, candor and instinct, and she quickly renounced interrogating herself because she would not have been able to respond.

Now she had grown up, however, and a horrible incident had made her a woman, and had revealed to her frightful male desire—so different from what she experienced, but with resemblances—now that she could conceive, by virtue of having suffered the indecency, the passion that precipitates mouths upon mouths, loins against loins, she wondered, sometimes with pride and sometimes with disturbance, whether there was not something in her, adoring Emmeline's sleep, almost similar, or, rather, analogous, to the ardor of the husband who had hurled himself upon her, and whether she had glimpsed the chimerical possibility of being her friend's husband.

Yes, Jean's concupiscence, by a strange transposition, and in spite of natural female decency, awoke in her a kind of clairvoyance of her own covetousness. Since a man embraces the person he loves, why should she not embrace the person she loved? Her very innocence, to which a single experience, in its rapid rudeness, had rendered a poor knowledge of virility, inclined her to confusion; and because she had only learned about male amour in a frightful promptitude of rape, but had nevertheless learned it, she was able to imagine that such an amour, tenderized and purified by the very impossibility of its criminal violence, was not impossible between two women.

But those ideas passed rapidly and were effaced, were no more. Since she was seventeen years old, since no unhealthy reading had ever unveiled her own perhaps-unhealthy soul to her, and one soldier's intercourse had made the child, not a wife, but a bloody virgin, since she was ignorant of everything she knew, her mind could not settle on dreams neighboring crimes that she would not have been able to commit; and she let everything go to chaste delight, so distant from the bed of torture, to contemplate Emmeline, asleep amid her blonde curls on the whiteness of the virgin pillow.

She was anxious, however, because, involuntarily, she was gazing with a precision of pleasure at the lips, so fresh, and the cheek, so pale, and a little of the slender neck of the sleeper. She might have chased away the strange thoughts that had followed her from the conjugal bed, from which the nocturnal rain had not delivered her, but she sensed that she loved her friend tenderly, recklessly and desperately. All the modesty that radiated from the latter toward her entering into her and making her similar to that same modesty, did not prevent her from being delectably and bitterly troubled, and she did not know why.

For an instant, she shuddered, and quickly put her hands to her ears. Was she about to be ill, as in the times of the puerile crises? She had recognized, vaguer and also more ironic, the little laughter that had disquieted the physician and her family.

No, the noise was extinguished. She was not suffering. It was with an infinite tenderness that she considered the repose of the infantile darling in all the scattered hair. But, happy and surprised to be, she continued interrogating herself.

It happened that Emmeline, either partly awakened by a noise or because of the instability of sleep changing a dream, shifted in her bed, and, without opening her eyes, she pushed back the sheet with an unconscious hand as she turned her head toward the wall, with a sigh.

Both Emmeline's breasts were naked.

Because, being so blonde, she was a trifle plump, she had a woman's breasts already, extended curves, firm with an elasticity of swelling, ripe whitenesses tipped, almost rosier on the middle of a circle that was almost not rosy, by two fine summits like those that interrupted the roundness of peaches; and a single blonde hair, very short, so thin, like an imperceptible gold thread, stood up next to one of the scarcely-rosy tips, quickly inclining like a drooping blade of grass. That cleavage of a child-woman, in its rise and fall, was delectably alive; because of the warmth of the bed, a sweat, whose dewy droplets were confounded, had flowed in a smooth warmth, moistening everything, under the night-light, with a gleam.

After the sigh of an incomplete dream, Emmeline moved again, so slightly, entangling herself in slumber again. But, the fabric having followed the slope of the elevation, a smooth pallor running from the cleavage along the pure abdomen, scarcely inflated, slid all the way to the mysterious reflection, over the gloss, thinned here and there and blue-tinting the skin, of a vaguely gilded shadow, which the folds of the sheet, still in place, veiled like a cluster of modesties. And the odor that might emerge from a sandalwood box, closed for a long time, in which white roses and a single tea-rose were enclosed, emanated from that virginity offered in its partial bloom.

Her hands on her temples, in order to compress the throb of her veins, and sensing life rising from all the parts of her body to her lips and eyes, Sophie contemplated that young nudity; within her, there were warmths everywhere, and furies that wanted to conclude in swooning. Did she understand herself? Could she finally explain by what amour she was driven? She did not think so; she was not able to think so. Only the vague and intermittent idea that he, the husband might have experienced something resembling the exquisite and omnipotent intoxication that mastered her. She no longer had any but one consciousness, she no longer had any but one desire, because of that cleavage and those loins. There was not an atom of her flesh that was not demanding contact with all that flesh.

And for that sensual delirium, there was no excuse. She was not admiring that virginal beauty as an artist; she was not allowing herself to be delighted by the auroral innocence that was upon Emmeline like snow on a bunch of roses; she coveted that living thing, that was all; she coveted it with the folly of a hungry beast. The monster that was had always been in her wanted to get out and satisfy itself.

Finally, because Emmeline, while sleeping, had pushed away her sheets, the instinctive passion that had tortured Sophie—who had thrown herself upon her friend on the day of the almost nuptial ceremony of first communion—since childhood, became precise.

That the marital rut had revealed to her, by the desire that it had made her experience, the possibility of experiencing an analogous desire herself, is probable; she did not reflect, she took, and she drew toward herself, all her gazes as absorbent as obstinate tentacles, Emmeline's nude sleep. One sole sentiment differed slightly in her unique desire: the satisfaction, the appeasement—in spite of so many residual troubles—of having found, detestable or not, her path. But she did not dare what she wanted. Precisely because of the excess of her covetousness, she feared—in the troubled lucidity that the deliria of instinct permitted—frightening and bruising the person who was the object of that covetousness.

She was also afraid of the astonished awakening of those childish eyes. What would she reply to her friend saying "You're here? Oh, my God, why are you here? What do you want? Leave me alone; go away!" To impose on Emmeline—for she felt strong, with virility in her arms—a minute resembling the wedding night to which she had been subjected, appeared to Sophie to be impossible. It was men who were violent, who were brutes! For the first time, the idea occurred to her that feminine enlacement might have everything that was tender in male caresses, without anything of what was tearing. To be a husband with the tenderness of a friend; to be the force that does no harm, which wants, no less than its own joy, the joy of the adored: that possibility appeared to her, distant, but so pleasant!

She would not hear, under her mouth, Emmeline grind her teeth as her teeth had ground under the mouth of the man. She consented to forbearance, to waiting, calmed by the prayer for mercy that emanated from that tender, immaculate flesh. But she could not help loving that body, which she refused herself.

She gazed at the two bare breasts and the smooth abdomen, so pure, and the reflection of the shadow. The desire for the embrace was succeeded by a hope of friction, perhaps because, in her prompt senses, the very excess of desire had brought her, in an unconscious swoon, to tenderness; she wanted less for having wanted too much, but she wanted nevertheless, in her languid concupiscence; and, slowly leaning over, with the lightness of a breath over the slumber of a cradle, she brushed one of those sleeping and living breasts with her lips: the one whose scarcely pink summit was traversed by the shadow of a single hair like a perceptible gold thread.

The entire casement, in a shattering of woodwork and glass, fell on to the carpet. Jean d'Hermelinge was standing on the window sill, scarcely dressed, in short-sleeves, and cracking, like a kennel valet, a short whip with a strap hardened by knots. What whip? The one with which the coachman whipped the bulldogs, which was hung up next to the perron at the stable door. Jean had picked up that whip and he threw himself into the room, and with his arm raised, rushed upon the woman who was leaning over a woman's breast.

"Bitch! Bitch! Bitch!"

While Emmeline, woken up with a start, crazed by surprised and fear, uttered little plaintive cries as if in a nightmare, he had grabbed hold of Sophie and, holding her firmly, he lashed her with great strokes of the knotted strap.

She moaned with pain, she tried to flee, but, her wrist caught as if in the jaws of a vice, she could only circle; he circled behind her, still flagellating her.

"Bitch! Bitch!"

Now he was striking less precipitately, with regular blows, with the method of an executioner, and at every stroke, the word "Bitch!" accompanied the torture with insults. Under the whip, the flesh appeared between the tatters of the peignoir and the night-dress.

He whipped the bare flesh, and Sophie finally howled. Lacerated, striped with red and blue, it was bleeding, that flesh.

He whipped it more slowly still, raising the arm higher in order to bring it down more violently and more trenchantly.

The pain caused by the indefatigable stirrup-leather was such that, with an irresistible surge, the martyrized girl escaped the wrist that held her; she fell full length on the floor; in the impotence of her rage, she bit and chewed the wool of the carpet. Then he broke the handle of the whip over his knee and he spat on the near-naked woman who was beating the air with her arms and legs, and with a kick that would have disemboweled an animal, he sent her flying against the wall, where her skull crashed into the wood of the plinth.

IV

He had the impression of suddenly waking up. What was he doing there in the gray darkness of the pre-dawn twilight, before this table, at the door of some sort of tavern where gas jets were still burning? He looked around. To his right, the railway. Liquor-shops near railway stations never close, in the expectation of nocturnal arrivals.

He recalled, vaguely, what he had done, and what had happened afterwards: the appearance of the two mothers and the domestics, summoned by Sophie's howls and Emmeline's plaints. He had not dared to say for what abominable vice, for what crime, he had chastised his wife, only these words, with the feverish, still-broken voice of someone delirious calming down: "Maman, take Emmeline, put her in your bed and lock the door. You, Madame, take your daughter away and do whatever you wish with her. If she dies, so much the better."

After that, through all those frightened women, who did not understand, who were interrogating with arms raised, he had gone out. He had walked for a long time, without thinking, merely with an instinct of no longer being there; then, all his limbs exhausted, and his breast heavy, as if his heart were made of stone, he had fallen into this chair in front of this café. Now, he remembered. He gazed at the pavement with the stupefaction of someone before a great black hole that has suddenly opened.

Yes, that was it, there was no saying the contrary, nor doubting it, such was the woman he had married. He had given his name to that profligate; he had linked himself to that filthy creature. It existed, then, the desire of the female for the female!

During evenings in the garrison, Jean had heard mention of that filthiness; the lieutenants and the young captains, who read Parisian newspapers and books, recounted strange things in low voices when they had found lines in the gossip columns of some rag such as: "Constance Chaput and her inseparable companion, little Jeanne Chien-Fou, were observed in a ground-floor box near the stage; they ordered champagne and, behind the screen of the box . . ."

But damn it, those were things that people wrote and repeated to amuse themselves, for a laugh.

"Come on, come on," said Baron Jean. "It's not possible that women make love to women. For start, in order to make love to one another, how do they do it? Yes, how, I ask you? There's something missing, damn it!" And he laughed out loud, forthrightly, and ordered another beer.

Well, he was mistaken; that passion, that inclination for a woman toward women, it existed, yes. He had seen Sophie's mouth on Emmeline's breast. Damnation! It was in his sister's bed that that woman was going to finish the wedding night. His sister, poor child! Oh, her he didn't accuse. First of all, she was asleep while he was looking through the window. Then, he divined that, if she was guilty, it was only out of weakness, because she had yielded to Sophie's ascendancy. She was so meek, so obedient to everyone, the darling.

But the other! Oh, the wretch! The slut! He understood now why she kept quiet, why she ground her teeth at the moment of the nuptial accomplishment, why she clenched her legs on the bed. It was not a fellow, it was a demoiselle that that bride required! Name of God, what a slut! And at the thought of his sister, soiled, and his wife, a corruptrice, such a rage took hold of Baron Jean again that he regretted not having strangled Sophie, not having choked her with a knee in her stomach.

However, there was no sentiment of jealousy; only anger and disgust. The vice whose reality had just been revealed to him, which had appeared to him previously as chimerical, and had always remained foreign to his thought, appeared to him at that moment so absurd in its filth that he could not even see the resemblance of a treason therein. Cuckolded by a woman! He would have burst out laughing, in spite of his dolorous anger, if that idea had occurred to him.

In his eyes, a woman kissing a woman was indecent, that was all; he could not conceive either of tenderness or amour. Yes, it was just dirty—but to such a point that it made such a creature something less than a beast eating excrement on a street corner, that it nauseated him; and he shouted: "Waiter, a fine champagne!" because his stomach was turning.

But in sum, what was he going to do?

Of course, it was neither complicated nor difficult, what he was going to do. He would leave, by the first train that stopped at the station. It was even for that reason that he had come in the direction of the railway. And no more mention would be heard of him. To return to the house where he had had that frightful wedding night, and the other house to which his wife had gone to marry herself in her own manner, would be impossible for him. He would escape from all that villainy, shaking it off like a dog emerging from a muddy puddle, and he would return to the regiment, where his good comrades were, where one had a mind and heart in repose after healthy fatigue. If some war came along and a bullet struck him full in the chest, in truth, he wouldn't be sorry, and he'd say "Thanks!" because, after all, living with such memories behind one isn't cheerful, and there's nothing finer than a fine death. In the meantime, neither one nor two, let's go—*en route!*

A blast of a whistle alerted him to the arrival of a train. He paid the check and hastened toward the station.

He stopped.

To leave, that was precisely what he did not have the right to do. Because of Sophie? Oh, no, of course not. She could become anything she wished, it was all the same to him, that was not his concern. He had loved her, yes, they would have been happy together, so happy, but now . . . the whore! He repeated, his foot in the empty air, the movement of brutal scorn with which he had slammed her against the wall.

As for Madame Luberti, he could not fathom her, and he was suspicious of her; she must have had a riotous past, once. He had always thought—without daring to say so, because of his mother and his fiancée—that the old miser, who made herself up when she had people for dinner, had something of the retired libertine about her, who was hanging on tightly to ill-gotten gains. An odor emerged from her like an old coffer in which banknotes and unguents were going moldy together. Who could tell? Perhaps she was the cause of everything; she must have brought up her daughter very badly, or had given her, without meaning to, the vices that she had in her blood.

And Luberti, the Italian whom no one had ever seen, whom no one knew, who had died who knows where? Some riff-raff, no doubt. Was he even the father? A knight of industry, encountered while traveling, and whose name is given to a child that is born or going to be born. Sophie's mother sometimes let words escape that admitted that she had lived in Russia for a long time. What she had done in that country no one knew. Not honest things for sure. Perhaps Sophie had emerged from some libertinage out there, some lord who beats his serfs and rapes their daughters.

Baron Jean remembered, as he was reflecting, a tailor in Montpellier who repaired officers' uniforms. He was hunchbacked, that tailor. When people mocked him because of his hump, he said, with a laugh that was painful: "What do you expect? It's in the family. My grandfather also had one shoulder higher than the other." Perhaps moral deformities are transmitted, like physical deformities. Baron d'Hermelinge almost felt pity for Sophie, frightful, but the innocent heir of a race inoculated with infamy. But that pity he chased away quickly. "Bitch! Bitch" Oh, damn it! As long as he hadn't made a child in that marriage bed!

What had retained him at the moment of departure; what constrained him to remain for a few hours more, at least, was Emmeline, poorly protected by her mother. A good woman, Madame d'Hermelinge, but not seeing anything of anything, content if she got a little further with her eternal tapestry between mass and vespers. To leave Emmeline, as if alone, prey to her execrable friend, that was impossible.

So, he wouldn't leave immediately; he would go home, and say to his mother: "Come on, pack the trunks, and quicker than that," and he would take the old woman and the young one with him, to Algiers, where his regiment was. And out there, he would watch over the child. If she had already done something bad, well, she wouldn't keep it up there, closely watched and well defended. At seventeen, to become an honest woman again, nothing was simpler. Vice, among the very young, is a wound that closes quickly because of good blood, and afterwards, one doesn't even see the scar, One day or another, Emmeline would marry a military man, a solid fellow, who would appear much better to her than guttersnipes who kiss or bite with mouths without moustaches. But there wasn't a minute to lose. It was necessary to take the gamine away, with the maman. In advance, he was firmly determined not to take any account of astonishments or weeping.

And he set off toward his home.

But no, he wouldn't go back right away. It was scarcely five o'clock in the morning. The local women, awake since dawn, would be surprised that that bridegroom hadn't spent the night in the nuptial chamber. It was necessary to avoid the old women, to wait for broad daylight; it would even be better to wait until ten or eleven o'clock. That way, people would suppose that he had gone for a walk in the forest while his wife was getting dressed for the family breakfast.

Yes, wait.

He walked through the streets of a quarter where he was unknown, on the other side of town. When he walked rapidly he experienced a sort of tranquility, as if all torment of the mind or the heart were dispersed in physical agitation. But if he halted momentarily, the disgusts of the night returned to him, agitated him, swarmed everywhere within him. He resumed walking again; he only stopped when he was out of breath.

Finally, going past a chapel, he heard a plausible hour of return chiming, and, after having asked for directions—for, troubled by so many ideas, he had got lost—he recognized the two houses separated by the two gardens. What might happen, what Sophie might say, what the mothers might say, did not matter: only taking his sister away.

As he went into the vestibule, a maidservant was running upstairs; she turned round and said: "Oh, Monsieur, you don't know—they've gone."

Gone?

"What are you saying?" he cried.

The maidservant had disappeared into the first-floor corridor, but Madame d'Hermelinge appeared, leaned over the banister, and said: "There you are, finally! We've been looking for them everywhere; nobody knows where they've gone."

And Madame Luberti showed herself in her turn, waving her arms, while the domestics came downstairs in a tumult; the entire house seemed full of the agitation of a madhouse whose padded cells have been opened.

Jean seized his mother's hands.

"You say they've run away!"

"Perhaps they're hiding," said Madame d'Hermelinge. "We'll find them."

"But what happened, in sum?"

"This. As soon as you'd gone . . . by the way, have you lost your head? Beating a woman, you?"

"Yes, what got into you last night?" Madame Luberti interjected.

Madame d'Hermelinge continued: "Anyway, as soon as you'd gone, we did what you wanted. I put Emmeline in my room, and Sophie, dragging herself as best she could, went with her mother. But you're a monster, you know! She was bleeding all over, poor thing!"

"Good, good," he said. "The monster is me. What then?"

"Then, well, you understand, your marriage, the awakening, all those emotions, we were exhausted, we went to bed and we went to sleep."

"But this morning," said Madame Luberti, "when I woke up, I went up to Sophie's room. No one there!"

"And I, when I opened my eyes," said Madame d'Hermelinge, "I saw that Emmeline was no longer there, and since then, we've been searching, and no one knows what's become of them."

Baron Jean swore frightfully.

"They're in some corner, the sluts, eating one another's bodies!"

And he ran into the garden.

Madame d'Hermelinge had not understood what her son had said, but the other mother, slapping her forehead, ran to her room. She seemed to have understood. Meanwhile, behind the bushes, in the labyrinth at the back of the garden, in the little arbor, in the shed where the hammock was still hanging, Baron Jean searched, ran around, but did not find anything. And his mother and the four maidservants were following him, searching like him, in a hubbub of exclamations and appeals, when a cry emerging from a window made them all turn round.

They saw the meager Madame Luberti extending the arms of a dislocated marionette toward them.

"Don't search any longer! It's pointless. They've gone in order not to come back. They've taken thirty thousand francs in gold and bills, which were in my glass-fronted cupboard. It's Sophie who's done it. Go fetch the police."

Because of all the stir and all the noise, the doors of the neighboring houses had opened. Women were coming out in search of information. People were coming into the garden. Baron Jean had collapsed on a bench.

He leaned over the sand, with menacing eyes, with teeth that wanted to bite, while the old lady at the window was gesticulating and shouting: "The police! The police! It's necessary to have them arrested!" and the domestics, gathered around the consternated Madame d'Hermelinge, were standing there stupidly, not understanding.

Now, as happens at the beginning of autumn after nocturnal downpours, the sky was full of radiance and freshness among the still florid gardens; sparrows were fluttering, blackbirds were singing over the tragic disaster of Baron Jean, over the comical dolor of the despoiled miser, still screeching at the window.

The curiosity of the approaching neighbors put a chorus of chatter around those sadnesses and those buffooneries, caressed by the breeze and gilded by the sun.

V

The twilight of an October evening was rose-tinting the river, the meadow and the rusty gold of the trees of the forested isle. That light was softer for being so close to extinction, and had the infinite melancholy of a supreme gaze of amour. There was no sound in the soon-to-be-nocturnal solitude, except for that of the water that was flowing, like a vast glide of silk over silk, or by abrupt awakenings, soon returned to sleep, of the chirping of birds in a bush, and also, sometimes, coming from far away, the music, perhaps merry out there, of some inn piano, so attenuated, so sparse and so vaporous for having traversed the silence and the shade of branches that it faded into a murmur in the reverie of the closing day.

And around the little wooden house posed on the water's edge, there was the languorous somnolence that rises, amid the terrestrial mist, from the last autumn flowers, in which a perfume of adieu sighs, and the mysterious peace that descends from the darkening azure. An hour and a dwelling well made to be preferred by wounded hearts still bleeding from the cruelty of old amours; a moment and an abode that also had the wherewithal to please young loving souls, happy to be in love; for even the impulses of the first tenderness adapt to prolongation in melancholy, and there is no tender happiness without a little sadness.

A last jet of radiance, in a gap in the cloud, splashed the balcony of the little house, and, bathed in ruddy solar light, the delightful couple appeared, their lips close, under the envelopment of tousled hair that only formed a single mane of mingled pale gold and dark gold.

It had already been several days since Sophie had brought Emmeline into that solitude, kept her there, and protected her there.

In the rage that the flagellation in front of her friend had excited within her, she no longer thought of dying. The shame of the punishment counseled her an amour, a pride in the sin that someone had wanted to punish, which she now understood. And since a kind of confrontation, the same night, between the violating nudity of the man and the passive nudity of a sleeping virgin had revealed to her, in an opportunity of choice, her disgust for the one and her desire for the other, well, her choice had been resolved.

To tell the truth, if she knew very clearly why she fled the husband, she could not understand with as much lucidity why she aspired to the friend; the employment that the former had wanted to make of her—had made of her, alas—only informed her very confusedly of the employment she might make of the latter. The certain thing was that, on the one hand, she did not want it, and on the other, she did. And she had taken Emmeline away. The humiliation had incited her to furious courage. But above all, she had taken her away because she was no longer living except in the desire to have her.

Scarcely was her mother asleep before she got up, with pains in her back and pains in her loins—two wounds in the abdomen now, that of a boot after . . . the other—oh, that man! that man! oh, men!—and she went, groping her way, toward Emmeline. That latter, at the same moment, frightened by the horrible adventure, had escaped from her mother's apartment, was searching for Sophie, wanting to know, to understand.

They bumped into one another in the antechamber in Madame d'Hermelinge's house.

"It's you!" exclaimed Emmeline. "Are you suffering a great deal?"

"Lower your voice," said Sophie, "and don't worry about anything. I'll explain it to you. We're leaving. Yes, you and me. Why aren't you responding? Are you hesitating? I want us to leave; we're leaving."

She said those words without raising her voice, but in an imperious tone that did not admit any reply. At that moment, if Emmeline had refused to go with her, she might have strangled her.

Emmeline was afraid; but then, she did not know, she did what she was told; she responded: "Yes, we'll leave, if you want . . ."

"Ah!" said Sophie. "Wait; it's necessary that I go get the money upstairs. Finish dressing in the meantime; then, come over to my house; I'll wait for you outside the door."

"Yes, yes," said Emmeline, her head lost.

A few minutes later, they were in the street. Sophie was carrying a valise.

"What are you taking?" Emmeline asked.

"Underwear, dresses."

"We're not coming back today, then?"

"Neither today nor tomorrow. Come quickly; there isn't a moment to lose; people are going to wake up in the house, in the town. The train goes through at six o'clock."

Emmeline was full of anxiety; at the same time, she admired her friend, who had thought of everything. They drew away very rapidly.

What prevented them from being caught the next day or the day after is that, either by mistake or by virtue of an adroit calculation by Sophie, they left the train before reaching Paris, at one of the last stations. Because of that, the pursuit was fruitless.

The woman at the station replied to Baron Jean and Madam d'Hermelinge: "Yes, I recognized the demoiselles; it astonished me to see them so early in the morning. They bought two first class tickets to Paris." And while people were searching for them in the immense city—"All the police in the air!" as Madame Luberti put it—they were in one of the little localities near Paris, a village that was almost a suburb, where no one took it into their head to look for them.

It happened that the owner of the hotel where they stayed had a house for rent—or, rather, a chalet—on an island between two arms of the Seine, where a painter had put his studio in the previous year. "During the week it isn't very cheerful," the owner said, "but on Sunday, I promise you that people enjoy themselves."

Sophie did not hesitate for a moment. She met the price that was asked. A few hours later they were installed on the water's edge, in a pretty wooden house, defended from tumultuous Sundays by a curtain of trees. And while Emmeline asked: "Oh, my God, oh, my God, what does it mean, all this, and what will Maman think?" Sophie rejoiced in being alone with Emmeline, so far from other people.

As for the owner, he thought that the two little demoiselles, who were genteel, wanted to lodge there in order to receive messieurs from Paris, and that it was a stroke of luck to have let the house, because truly, during the week, the island wasn't cheerful, especially in autumn. He hadn't hired the shack for three years. What completed his delight was that his tenants asked him to send them breakfast and dinner every day from his inn: a fine windfall. Certainly, he asked them their names, which he wrote down in pencil in the margin of a newspaper, with the intention of transcribing them in the hotel register, but when he got home he couldn't find the piece of paper—what the devil had he done with it? Anyway, it didn't matter, since they had paid in advance.

They were alone now.

During the first hours of that isolation, Emmeline retained the fearful alarm of the nocturnal departure, the furtive journey, her mother's anxiety and her brother's anger. If she had dared, she would have cried: "Let's go back! I don't want to stay here." Then too, it tormented her that she did not know why Sophie had hazarded that adventure and dragged her along in it.

Her friend always replied: "Things happened that obliged us to flee. You'll know everything soon. Above all, don't torment yourself. What can you dread, since I'm here? You know that I love you, darling, that I'll defend you. Come on, I love you so much! And it's so good to be separated from all the wicked men."

Sophie's will subjugated and surrounded Emmeline, who lowered her head, a consenting and resigned captive. In sum, she thought, it was an escapade that wasn't very serious, something like a schoolgirl adventure during the vacation; afterwards, the parents would scold and forgive. In any case, she liked the island, less grim than their forest and vaster and as pretty as their gardens; and because it was sunny, she wasn't sad.

A charming life commenced. At first, because of the wounds from which Sophie was still suffering, they were only able to go for short walks around the house, but soon, the pain was attenuated and faded away. They could go out early in the morning.

"Are you coming?" Sophie, the first one dressed, shouted from downstairs.

She had made her dress into an eccentric boyish costume; the bodice fastened over a chemisette looked like a man's waist-coat; the skirt, in two pieces, wrapped around her legs, imitated trousers, and beneath a large straw hat devoid of flowers or ribbons she struck a proud pose, a fist on her hip.

Opening the window slightly, Emmeline showed her pretty tousled head and a little of her shoulder outside the chemise slipping down the plump slope of the arm.

"I'll come down right away."

"What, idler, you aren't ready yet? Hurry, or I'll come up."

"No, don't come up; I'm coming."

A few moments later Emmeline emerged from the house. She had not yet had time to say "Here I am!" when Sophie had already taken her by the waist and lifted her up. Very strong, she held her in the air, putting abrupt, multiple kisses on her eyes, in her hair and on her neck.

"Stop it, stop it, you're hurting me."

Sophie let her go immediately and looked at her anxiously. "Am I really hurting you?"

"Of course. One can kiss without stifling."

"Teach me."

"Here," said Emmeline. "Like this."

Very gently, her arm around her friend's neck, she put her cheek on her shoulder, and brushed with a breath, a breath that might have been a rose, the fine gold down that Sophie had under her chin; and Sophie tottered. Then she did, in her turn, what the other had done.

"Like that, right?"

"Yes—no, your breath is hot."

And Emmeline drew away. Then Sophie shook her head sadly, her eyes moist.

"You don't like it when I kiss you!"

"Yes, yes. Only, are we going or a walk or not. If you pull faces, I'll shut myself in my room and sulk all day."

"Let's go, let's go, quickly."

They set forth, arm in arm, jumping like untethered goats, uttering bursts of laughter at the birds, laughing even more madly when low branches shaken by their passage made them duck their heads, having brushed them lightly, the scattered gold of their October leaves falling, hesitantly, some along their backs and others merely tickling their necks. Usually, they returned to the house for the morning meal, where they found the cold dishes on the table that the waiter from the inn had brought.

At other times, bolder, in a desire to see and challenge the world, they emerged from their insular solitude, and went in a boat hailed from the bank to some guinguette on the other side of the water. But there were always the same charming meals, with hunger that made light of meat that was too tough or fruits that were half-spoiled, and thirst that drank from the same glass a nasty little wine whose acidity tickled the lips and the tongue and made the eyes sparkle; and while one of them, before the full plate, searched or pretended to search the tablecloth for some indispensable utensil, the other—one makes use of these niches—tried to hide the stolen fork between her knees.

For they were two children. Sophie herself, in whom the demonic appetency was incessantly exasperated, being only eighteen, was a little girl, although she was a frightful woman, and still had all her grace along with all the monstrosity; in spring, the most venomous plants flower like eglantines.

After the morning meal, returned from the guinguette or escaped from the house, they went into some corner of the island, under the most distant shade of the large stand of trees. One might have thought that the autumn, because of those children, became spring-like. Around them, there were flowers everywhere, and birds everywhere. The redness of the leaves ready to fall did not know what they were saying, since golden buds were still rattling under the glide of the breeze, since the blackcaps, gamines of the bushes, were chattering from branch to branch.

The two friends sat down in the grass, sparse but still warm and green in places; they played games like those played in the courtyards of convents. "Warm hand" is very amusing. Can it be played when there are only two little girls? Yes, and this is how: it is not a matter of naming the person whose hand has touched you, which would be too easy, but of divining with what—the end of a ribbon, a cluster of leaves, the nail of a little finger, or the tip of a lock of hair—she has touched you. Sophie almost never guessed, either because her thought was elsewhere or because it pleased her to be the one who hid her face in the other's dress. Often, on her knees, her head bowed, she delayed replying for a long time.

"Come on, I've touched you; are you asleep?"

She finally replied, with a slow sigh that died away: "With your hair, I think."

The other burst out laughing. "No, silly, with grass!"

When Sophie raised her head she was very pale, her eyes closed, her mouth open, vacillating on her knees; then she took her friend in her arms, recklessly, and hugged her, putting her head between her breasts.

But Emmeline said: "You lost; let's start again."

"I want to," said Sophie; she buried her head, in accordance with the game, in the skirts, and silently, with her hand behind her back, she started spasmodically, like someone sobbing.

"Are you crying?" asked Emmeline.

"No, no, why do you think I'm crying? Let's play."

Once, on a very warm afternoon: "Look! Look!"

Emmeline pointed at a stream that was running over pebbles between gladioli and irises. The water was so clear, so diaphanous, that they would not have perceived it if it had not tinkled like the shrill sound of a harmonica as it rippled. They were quite astonished by that stream, which they had never seen, even though they knew the island, their island, well. They gazed at it, their eyes refreshed and charmed by its fluid transparency. But Sophie's gaze quit the running water momentarily for the varnished tips of Emmeline's two little ankle-boots, advancing from beneath the skirt like the black beaks of two birds. She shivered because of an idea she had had,

"What's the matter?" Emmeline asked.

"I've just thought of something. You've walked a long way, and you're tired; would you like to dip your feet in the stream?"

"I believe I would! You'll put your feet in the water too, won't you?"

"Me, I don't mind. Sit down here on the bank."

Emmeline sat down swiftly, her legs over the fresh stream. But she became irritated.

"No, I don't want you to take my boots off; I'm quite capable of taking them off myself."

Sophie, kneeling on the bank, had already undone a few buttons.

"Come on," she said, "let me. Why don't you let me serve you, like a chambermaid, since I'd like to? You aren't polite. What I desire, you never want."

She pulled off one of the boots. In the whiteness of the stocking, the foot was so dainty. It resembled a little dove alighted there, which had closed its wings. Sophie unbuttoned the other boot. Her fingers were trembling slightly, like those of someone caressing a little bird or a flower, who scarcely dares touch it for fear of crumpling it.

"Now," said Emmeline, laughing, "since you're my chambermaid, take off my stockings."

If she had looked at her friend she would have shivered, Sophie was so pale, her lips stirring.

"Hurry up then! We haven't got all day!"

Sophie, her hands clenched by desire and fear of the skin that, suddenly encountered, had rendered her foolish, searched under the skirt—her hot eyes were hurting her—for the knot of the garter. One of her fingernails brushed the flesh. She moved away very quickly and stood up.

"No, no, do it yourself—I'm too clumsy."

Emmeline shrugged her shoulders. "Yes, it's true that you're clumsy."

And, very rapidly, she slipped off her stockings, which she threw behind her. Her two little bare feet were in the stream, the heel on the tip of a pebble. The water rippled around them and passed over them, enveloping them in a gliding or broken crystal. They were exquisite, for being so slender and so delicate. The heel was the color of amber, the big toe slightly separate, with a golden nail; the other toes, plumper, were slightly curved; blue veins ran over the smooth skin, intersecting here and there.

Sophie, fallen to her knees again, gazed at those dear bare feet. She leaned further and further forward, as if she would have liked to drink the flow that was wetting them.

It was very cold, that flow.

"The water's icy!" said Emmeline. "I'll surely catch cold. You always have bad ides!"

But Sophie said: "Wait, wait. You'll see; it won't feel so cold."

Entirely inclined, she had taken the two little feet in one hand, and her lips opened; she sucked in the water, which she allowed to fall, a little further away, over the beautiful little bare feet, warmed by her mouth, like a streaming kiss. Then, a mild burn having run all the way from the toe to the throat, Emmeline fell backwards, with a cry that expired in a plaint, her eyes extinct under fluttering lashes, and Sophie, after a sway of the upper body, lay down alongside her, weeping and dying delightfully.

❋

It was their returns, above all, in the evening, that were pleasant, because the laughter counseled by the hazards of walks in the sun never interrupted their languor. The dusk does within souls at that hour what it does in the sky; the whispers of everything about to go to sleep—leaves, nests, blades of grass and appeased breezes—give an example to reveries of mysterious babblings and drowsiness. So weary, Emmeline walked more slowly, sustained in Sophie's arms, to whom the pride of being like an elder brother gave the strength almost to carry that frail fainting sister; and in the darkening mystery of the sky and the earth, the temptress, so voluptuously tempted, spoke, troubled by her own voice, although almost mute.

"Darling, darling, go to sleep on my shoulder. Nothing can happen to you that would be cruel, since I'm here, and I'll defend you, since I love you. Oh, how I love you! If you knew! I can feel you on me; it's like a treasure that I'm carrying. The best thing there is, is to be together, as we are. Do you understand that I adore you and am protecting you, that I'm enlacing you with my tenderness as well as my arms? I love you! I love you!

"Don't be annoyed. You're often bad, when you sulk or when you laugh. Especially when you laugh. Turn round slightly, put yourself against me completely, so that your heart can beat over mine. Wait, you'll feel my heart beating. Can you feel it? They beat one after another, our hearts, and then together, and it's only a single beat, and it's the same heart. Oh, little darling. Lower your head. Would you like me to bite, while we walk, the little hairs that you have near your ear? You have an odor in your hair that doesn't resemble any other odor.

"Don't reply, don't say anything. You hurt me, when you're afraid. Afraid of me! Oh, those whom it's necessary to dread, my darling, are men, wicked men. You know full well that they're cruel. You saw how he beat me and tortured me and killed me, because I was watching you sleep. But the most frightful thing, you don't know. I learned it, since I was married! The amour of men, you see, is more frightful than their anger.

"Me, I'm gentle, am I not? I'm strong too, but so tender. I would never do you harm, my frail and tender darling. Sometimes, it resembles the perfume of a blonde rose that one has burned on a little piece of sandalwood, the odor of your hair behind the neck. I'm saying things that I don't know; I'm searching for something that might smell better than anything else, to compare it with the aroma that you have in your hair, but there's another perfume, more exquisite, and I know it, for having respired it once; it's the one that emerged from all of you, when you push away the sheets, which slide a little and stop . . ."

Their evening meal was silent. Sophie, previously emboldened by the penumbra full of lowered gleams that did not gaze, no longer dared talk under the seemingly observatory fixity of the lamps.

Emmeline, vanquished by the fatigue of walking and troubled by the whispers in her ear during the return in the twilight, turned her eyes away, would have liked to ignore the fact that her friend was there, would have liked not to be observed. What was she experiencing? A very submissive tenderness, which was nevertheless fearful, a tenderness that feels that it is wrong, which dreams of escaping. It often happened that, her elbows on the table—under the captivating eyes of Sophie, to which she was subject without seeing them—she took her head in her hands, and stammered several times, without knowing what she was saying, the word: "No . . . no . . . no . . ."

They did not talk, did not read, had not had the idea of sending for a piano, the music of which would have occupied their evenings. They dreamed, one with fear, the other with desire, and also fear of the hour when they would find themselves in their rooms, the nocturnal hour when nothing would happen to them that did not come from themselves, that did not depend on themselves alone, which might be the moment that determined, which directed, their eternal destination.

On those evenings they had the impression, sensed variously but as strongly by both of them, of being very close to a kind of abyss, from which, if they fell into it, they would never emerge again. In that closed room, far from the noise, far from all the world, far from dangers—and help—something decisive and irremediable might be said, or done, and there was in both of them a vertigo: in the one, with an instinct of flight, and in the other, with an instinct of precipitation.

Hence, long silences and indecisive reveries.

Then Emmeline stood up, took one of the lamps, said "I'm very sleepy," without even trying to smile, and went to her room. Sophie got up in her turn, and followed her to the door, in the corridor. All that in slow motion, as if accomplishing a mysterious ritual, thanks to which a god or a demon might surge forth. Before the door, Emmeline remained motionless, her eyes closed because of her friend's gaze, and their breasts heaved. Sometimes, Sophie, with a surge . . . but she stopped; and, as if having drawn courage—the courage of being entirely fearful—from the threat that she had perhaps desired as much as she feared it, Emmeline went into her room quickly and locked the door.

Sophie, alone in the dark, leaned on the wall, and stayed there, her ear cocked, her eyes wide, listening, thinking that she could see garments falling, one by one, on the other side of the wall, and shivering when a noise told her that the dear pale pink body was lying on the bed . . .

What! Did she want it less? Had the discreet, frantic covetousness that she had experienced next to Emmeline's bed on the wedding night that was also a night of betrothal, relaxed into the mildness of tender camaraderie? No, she desired Emmeline more every day, entirely. Oh, to see that young ripe skin again, so smooth, to put her mouth to the bare breast, at the rosy tip of which a single hair traverses the shadow like a golden thread! During their walks, furious desires came to her to tear off the dress on which she rubbed herself with an insistent feline slowness; in the evenings she would have liked to break down that door behind which the young woman was undressing. And, returning to her own room, going to bed in her turn, she had sweats everywhere, warm, then cold, then warmer, like a fiery dew, heavy breathing that swelled her breast and neck; she searched for, she touched with her hands, on her own body, the resemblances of the dear body that she had not embraced, her rage expiring in a hot yawn that released the bitten pillow.

But her desire was afraid of frightening, and always retreated in order that Emmeline would not be alarmed. She did not know whether the ingenuous child discerned anything, in her tenderness, but the charms of a permitted amity. Was the amorous Sophie loved herself as she loved?

It might be—the dear child was so unastonished by ardent words, accepted caresses so calmly—that she found nothing therein but something very simple and very natural, and if, one day, she had to be astonished by an ardor that even the most perfect innocence could not misinterpret, she might get annoyed and flee!

To remain without Emmeline, that would be the worst of disasters. Sophie had not dared to demand everything for fear of losing what she had. It was already so adorable, that life together, all alone. In gazing at Emmeline, she had a dazzle that put into her eyes, into her heart and into her entire being a kind of luminous warmth; in listening to her, she seemed to be hearing an angel of paradise—a memory of puerile chimeras—descended to murmur in her ear; she would die if Emmeline disappeared.

✳

Sunday arrived.

When they went out, as usual, from the house on the edge of the water, they saw that there were people on the island. People were walking in the pathway that traversed the stand of trees; further away, in the meadow, a few women with a bold air, in bright dresses, with flowers in their large hats, were pursuing one another with laughter and cries hurled into the air.

The two friends went back inside very rapidly, frightened. They remembered that the owner of the house had warned them about a tumult once a week. The waiter who brought them breakfast every morning furnished a more complete explanation. On Sundays the island was a port of call for boaters. They took advantage of the good weather, those young men, with their mistresses. But the funniest thing was the ladies who came from Paris on Sunday evening, in bands, to have a party. Loose women, naturally. They slept in a white house at the other end of the island, facing the village, which had a kind of sign over the door: *Maison Charmeloze*. That was sufficient. Everyone knew Félicie Charmleloze, a former fay in leotards in magical plays, who kept a table d'hôte in Paris where hardly anyone but women ever ate—a specialty—and who had bought the white house with her savings. She received her clients and her friends every week, who came to repose there, and tire themselves out. What a life they led in there!

"If you get bored all alone you can go to Madame Charmeloze's house; they won't throw you out, for sure!" And the waiter had a sly suggestiveness in his laughter.

Sophie interrupted him and dismissed him. She felt nervous and ill tempered. Why? Because they could not go for a walk under the trees with everyone on the island? Yes, because of that. Then, she thought that those women, running and laughing in the meadow, might have seen Emmeline just now. Did she understand, then, the implication contained in what the waiter had said? No, or very vaguely, but with an awakening of a very distant thought, a very vague dread, scarcely a dread. But it would be much better if, that morning, Emmeline did not go outside.

Before sitting down at table in the ground floor room, Sophie closed the shutters of the two windows that faced the direction of the meadow.

"Why are you doing that?" Emmeline asked.

"Because of the sun; it's going to be hot."

In fact, a storm was gathering, on white clouds, a storm of warm autumn days that weigh heavily.

That day, they did not do what they did every other day. Sophie was anxious—about what?—her eyebrows sometimes frowned. Emmeline was more cheerful, more coaxing, like a child who has something to request. The truth was that it did not please her to stay shut away in the house with the shutters closed.

Eventually she said: "Come on, just because other people are walking, that's no reason why we shouldn't go for a walk too."

Sophie shuddered. "What are you saying? No, no, I don't want you to go out."

"But why not?"

"Because . . . someone might recognize us. People from Fontainebleau."

"Oh? All right."

Emmeline went to sit down in a big armchair, crossed her legs, tipped her head back, and did not say another word. She was sulking. She did that sometimes. She had those fits of malice, almost coquetries, with her friend.

She would not sulk for long, because Sophie, on her knees, would say to her: "Whatever you want! Whatever you want!" But today, Sophie did not hasten to humiliate herself, to admit defeat; on the contrary, after a movement of ill temper, she left the dining room and went upstairs.

What was wrong with her, then? Emmeline's desire to go and get a little air had nothing culpable about it; it was mingled with a sort of desire to see, after a week of isolation, the people who were walking; that was only natural. However, Sophie was almost irritated, would have liked to get annoyed with someone.

By chance, while going back and forth in her room, she found herself next to the window. Two or three women—some of those who had been laughing on the lawn a little while ago, the ones about whom the waiter from the in had talked—were approaching the wooden house, seemingly looking inquisitively at the shuttered windows.

Sophie ran downstairs immediately, as one hastens to bring help. Why? What danger was Emmeline running? Do not people in the country, passing by, look curiously at shuttered windows every day? Yes, undoubtedly. She finished going downstairs more slowly. But when she went into the dining room, she saw her friend inclined between two shutters, looking outside.

"Emmeline!"

She ran forward, seized her by the waist, carried her to a corner of the room, sat her down in the large armchair, and while the other stared at her, very surprised, she would have liked to reproach her, to force her to beg for forgiveness. What reproaches? Forgiveness for what? *Am I going mad?*

Well, yes, mad; because Emmeline had wanted to go out, because two women had been inquisitive, because she had looked out between the shutters, perhaps because of the storm. No matter: mad.

And in a fury that she had never experienced before, as if, having lost her, she had found her friend again, she put her hands behind her neck, drew her toward her and kissed her violently on the mouth. It was the first time that she had kissed her on the mouth. Sometimes, previously, her lips had brushed those lips in a touch that left the regret of a perfume; but now, it was a kiss.

And that kiss was so long, so profound and so tenacious that Emmeline, resistant for a moment and tensing her whole body, suddenly abandoned herself like a broken or bent branch, and fainted, her eyes staring. With another kiss, the obstinate Sophie obliged her to revive. And she was no longer thinking about anything except the mouth that she had under her mouth. It put into her entire being warmth, fragrances and an infinite delight. Oh, those lips, and between those lips, those teeth! She was exultant, divining herself. What joy! And what pride in sensing her sudden intoxication by Emmeline, dying and renascent.

Their mouths only parted rarely for the passage of sighs and words that, in admitting the delight, redoubled it. "How good your lips feel, my darling, and what an intoxicating moisture comes from them! One might think that one were drinking the blood of a little living cluster of grapes. I'm not doing them too much harm with my teeth? I'm afraid of being bad without meaning to be. Don't go, if I'm not hurting you, come back."

The two mouths came together again like two beautiful rose-buds that are being plunged one into the other, and the languid gazes were extinguished. Sophie spoke again: "Are you happy, speak? Do you feel very glad?"

The other responded with the acceptance of a more ardent kiss.

"No, I want to hear you."

"Yes, happy."

Then Sophie: "You see, your mouth is everything. If flowers exist in heaven, they resemble your mouth. But no, there's nothing in paradise worth as much as your kiss." Then, in a lower voice: "I don't know if it's the same for you, but when your lips open, when my desire draws in your breath, it's your heart that I'm drawing in, and it comes, and it enters into my body, and our confounded lives beat delightfully in me alone."

Their mouths seized one another more impetuously and did not let go again . . .

Almost at the same time, a lurch in their breasts, oppressed by one another, obliged them to separate, with neither words nor gasps, in the continued caress of their loosened grip. In the silent room with closed shutters, there was a soft shadow over them.

And all day long, the kiss, the paradise finally found, enchanted them. Dinner, as usual, was silent, not because Emmeline dreaded hearing or because Sophie dreaded talking, but because they closed their lips with their lips, drinking in the dew of their mouths the freshness of fruits and the warmth of the wine. Then they leaned on their elbows, in the rosy dusk, on the balcony of the house on the water's edge, and they breathed in, infinitely all the silence of the penumbra, under their unkempt hair, which only made a single mane of mingled pale gold and dark gold.

Then, when night fell, there was not the every-night adieu outside Emmeline's door. They went in together, without dis-uniting their mouths.

Their mouths! Oh, how they wanted one another, to be possessed by one another, how they possessed one another, and wanted to be wanted by one another, those mouths! Their mouths, henceforth, were the unique and double focal point at which all their radiation converged; and for having mingled, mingled, and mingled again the breath in which their vital sap was essentialized, they no longer had any but a single warm soul between the teeth, like two aliments which are made one by chewing them.

More rapidly than the vanishment of the mysterious clouds in which goddesses veil themselves, Emmeline's dress disap-peared, torn to shreds, useless rags; the virgin, her nape on the pillow, offered herself, blushing and quivering, on the mysteri-ous bed, by the pale light of a single lamp with a frosted globe.

Sophie saw her entirely, snow roses, gilded gleams, but all of that, flesh, all of that, woman. She recognized the golden thread as slender as an eyelash that stood up near one of the tips of the breasts, and she was maddened. In the instinct of a closer embrace, or the memory of an almost similar night—oh, no, no, not similar!—she threw off her own clothes; naked, she saw Emmeline more naked; her own nudity was like a mirror that doubled the nudity of the friend; and for having embraced Emmeline thus, she suddenly ceased to embrace her, and fell back on the bed, and did not move again.

When Sophie opened her eyes again, Emmeline, still lying down, her head toward the wall, seemed to be waiting. Shudders were running through her entire body, her eyelids were flutter-ing. What was the matter then? For what was she waiting?

In looking at her at close range, Sophie suffered frightfully, for she divined that she had not given the incomparable and frightful joy that she had known; that neither the embraces nor the caresses, nor the body next to the body, were the realization of the desire to which she had given birth; she had not kept, and perhaps would not keep, the promise that she had made! Neither with her hands nor her lips had she obliged ecstasy in the one in whom she had obliged the hope of ecstasy.

However, it was impossible that there would not be an accordance of satisfactions when there had been an accordance of desires; it was necessary that, in one as in the other, the exasperation would conclude in a divine annihilation. Yes, since Emmeline was there, since Emmeline had not resisted, since Emmeline had abandoned herself, it was necessary that Sophie recompense that presence, that passivity and that sacrifice with an excessive delight.

She had the horrible thought that perhaps men alone are capable of giving young women the definitive intoxication. But no, no, men are torturers whose assault tips over, tears, collapses. It is not to them that virgins can owe smiles of amorous gratitude. And yet, she had her friend beside her, and neither kisses, nor bites, nor breaths over the down of the arms and neck, had succeeded in causing the string of desire to vibrate to the point of delectable rupture, no matter how taut it was; they only increased, and rendered more difficult to satisfy, the demands of nubility.

Emmeline, her teeth clenched—she could hear Emmeline's teeth grinding!—was palpitating hectically, but she did not faint, and still, in spite of slow embraces or furious enlacements, seemed to be waiting. Then Sophie understood that she did not know.

That was it: she did not know. The hope that Emmeline had confessed by the acceptance of lips upon lips, which she had confessed by her nudity on the bed, that hope of some unknown delight, Sophie could have realized for her—but she did not know how, she did not know how!

And the other, still, was still breathless on the bed, still virginal, alas, almost convulsive; in the impatient expectation of the spasmodic body, which could not calm down, there was, along with the challenge, and insulting reproach: "After all, you ought to know, since you have induced me to want to know. I didn't ask you for anything! You constrained me to demand it; are you now going to refuse me what I didn't ask for?"

And before that dolorous unappeased friend, before the virgin formerly so ingenuous and so placid, who, seduced and damned, had become the avid creditor of the inferno, Sophie experienced the remorse of a tender tempter who could not, in exchange for the renounced salvation, give the promised joys.

Her impotence was a disloyalty. That soul, she had stolen, since she had not paid or it. And she multiplied in vain, almost ferocious in the futility of her desire, her kisses and her ignorant bites . . .

But suddenly, she rolled off the bed on to the floor. She held her head between her hands, she closed her mouth desperately in order that a cry whose tearing she foresaw did not emerge. She recognized that evil! She heard, as she had heard it so often before, the little laughter in her ears.

But after all, what was that laughter?

It encouraged her and mocked her. One might have thought that it was inviting her to the effort at whose abortiveness it was laughing. And it was horrible—more horrible, this evening—to have a sniggering evil counsel in her ears.

Alas! Emmeline! That thought did not calm her down. She sensed, irresistibly, the approach of a crisis that would torture her and twist her.

An insupportable idea: in a little while, in a few seconds, perhaps she would be—convulsed, livid, drooling between her teeth and clawing the parquet—an object of repulsion for Emmeline, for that child whom she had not been able to make a happy woman. That was not possible.

With the determination of a drunkard who does not want to vomit in front of guests, she got up, tottering, holding on to the furniture, and walked—her legs, which she could not bend, seemed like crutches on which she was perched—reached the door, found her way along the wall to her room, and fell on to her bed.

The crisis, suppressed momentarily, escaped like a beast breaking its tether. Her eyes vitreous beneath immobile eyelids, her fingers splayed, with gasps resembling muffled barking, Sophie rolled on the sheets; sometimes, her body raised itself up in the curve of an arch, only touching the bed at the heels and the cranium. Finally, she succumbed; motionless, her mouth twisted, her face creased, she was like a corpse still contorted by a frightful agony.

VI

The house was empty. Having awakened—or, rather, having been resuscitated—from that catalepsy, that temporary death, Sophie found the house empty.

"Emmeline! Emmeline!"

No response, and no one anywhere.

Well, so what? She's gone out while I was asleep; she'll come back.

Wait? No. Sophie threw herself outside. She was sure that she would find the dear child in the path, or on the bank of the Seine, or over there, under the trees, perhaps near the stream tinkling over the pebbles. That Emmeline had fled was impossible. *I'm crazy!*

She ran hither and yon. Certainly, she would see her, perhaps suddenly, at the bend in a path, between the branches. That idea—Emmeline disappeared—was so absurd that she expelled it, did not want it. To someone that was within her, and who said to her: "You won't find her," she replied: "Get away!" What a joke! She, Sophie, without Emmeline! She nearly burst out laughing, so imbecilic was it, that idea. As if they were not linked forever, that nothing would ever separate them! And after all, Emmeline was walking on the island.

Sophie came and went, hastened from one edge to the other, returned to the chalet—perhaps the child had come back; no, she had not come back—and set out in quest again, untiringly.

At one moment, she found herself in front of a large white building: *Maison Charmeloze*. Oh, yes; she remembered what the waiter from the inn had told her, and women in extravagant dresses in the meadow, and those among those women who had slid toward the dining room like spies. An imbecile suspicion traversed her: perhaps Emmeline was there. Someone might have called to her, taken her away, imprisoned her.

It was not even supposable. Although it was rather late—ten or eleven o'clock in the morning—the Maison Charmeloze was silent, still asleep, with shutters like closed eyelids. And then, her darling, among those women! She retraced her steps, she searched the island again. Soon, when she found her, how she would laugh at her anxiety. Anxious? No, although she could feel her heartbeats leaping all the way to her neck, she did not want to be anxious, she would not be.

She stopped, she called out: "Emmeline!"

Sometimes, she said: "Come on, it's a joke, you're making me run after you. Where are you? You've tormented me enough Come on, let's go."

After all, it was singular that Emmeline wasn't showing herself.

On returning, for the third time, to the chalet, she saw the waiter from the inn on the perron, making signs to her, holding something white in the air. She ran.

"Oh, there you are," said the man, "I've been waiting for you for a while. It's a letter that your friend gave me a little while ago at the hotel, before taking the train." He added: "Breakfast is on the table," and he left.

She had the letter in her hand, but she did not open it. At the hotel! Before taking the train! She heard the sound of those words again, without perceiving their meaning. What they would have made her understand was so frightful that she did not want to understand it. She remained motionless, the piece of paper between her fingers

"Ah!" there was in that cry, almost like a gasp, all the horrible need to know the truth of which one will die. And she tore open the envelope.

Yes, Emmeline's handwriting, a delicate and long, neutral handwriting, like that of all demoiselles who have had English instructresses.

Emmeline apologized for her departure; with words devoid of tenderness, in correct phrases like those of young women who have carried out many grammatical analyses, she said that she thought that it was necessary to return to Fontainebleau, that her mother and her brother must be anxious; she confessed that she was very afraid of being poorly welcomed, of being scolded; she was also afraid of traveling all alone, but she would go into the ladies' carriage.

And she advised Sophie not to be obstinate in her revolt, which had something too eccentric about it. "Jean hasn't been gentle with you, it's true, but perhaps there were wrongs on your side." She thought that Sophie would return to better sentiments, and that she would return home. When one is married, it is necessary to live with one's husband, just as, when one is a demoiselle, it is necessary to remain with one's mother.

In any case, everything would work out. "Hurry up and come back." And she embraced her with all her heart.

That letter, Sophie raised to her mouth and bit it, and tore it apart with her teeth, ferociously

So, a French species of duty regarding the necessity of being good, obedient to her family, to her husband, that was what Emmeline, in quitting her, had sent her by way of an adieu!

But that letter was nothing; there was the abominable thing that the wretch had gone—and was not coming back! For, out there, she would be closely guarded; and then, even if she were poorly guarded, she would not come back, since she had gone of her own free will

It seemed to Sophie that two hands had opened her heart and that a beast armed with teeth and claws was squirming in the rip, biting and lacerating her.

She started circling around the house, in the garden. Alone! Alone! She was alone! What dominated her, what was stronger in her than all the other sentiments, was a fury against the cowardly child who had left her. So, for fourteen years they had not quit one another, they had grown up together, played together, learned to think and to live together; and for seven days, in this solitude, they had been so happy that their puerile dreams of old had never dared suppose such happiness of angelic hymens; and now—like a madman throwing his treasure out of the window—Emmeline no longer wanted all those memories of childhood, nor their recent joys, so violent and so tender!

Yes, yes, yes, that was true; there was no doubt about it; Emmeline had gone. And, prowling around the house, out of breath, in that circular course, Sophie stammered: "Gone! Gone! But after all, why?"

She stopped.

She understood why Emmeline had fled. And it was against herself that her anger turned, then. To that child whom she had disquieted with strange, unconscious caresses while very small, in the hammock at the bottom of the garden, whose placid devotion she had troubled later with mystical frenzies, whom she had obliged, as one forces a young beast to drink while holding it by the scruff of the neck, to the intoxications of poetry and music, to the young woman destined for the simplicities of some honest marriage with children swarming everywhere, and whom she had carried away into the alarms of an extraordinary adventure, to that virgin, finally frightened yesterday evening by the mouth upon her mouth, and no longer resisting, and offering herself and accepting, what had she, Sophie, given in recompense for so much submission, torment and sudden covetousness and finally mutual appetence?

Nothing.

She had been the imbecile conqueror who does not use her victory. She had been the temptation that lied and tricked, which damned without having divinized: a stupid, unfinished, infirm creature, loving without knowing how to love, coveting without being able to possess! Emmeline had gone with reason, because, in sum, it was not worth the trouble of renouncing all modesties, of exposing oneself to all the reproaches of a conscience that will remember, that will examine, for the exasperation of waiting for an intoxication always refused.

Oh, Sophie would willingly have torn away with her fingernails all the flesh of her useless body, which, wanting and experiencing, could create the desire but not the experience. She did not pause at the idea, already rejected, that man alone can oblige a woman to supreme joys, since she knew that those joys, women could know by means of other women. Only, the mysterious rites of the cult of which she was the instinctive oblate, she did not know.

Absolutely? No; she suspected them, she glimpsed them, she almost divined them, but—so scarcely possible did the means appear to her—they were so strange, those rites, that she was afraid of misunderstanding them, and, in the dread of a sacrilege, she had not dared to resolve herself to try.

And Emmeline had been right to flee, as a god might desert an altar where no one knows how to pray to him.

For an instant, Sophie thought of a strange similarity; she was now abandoned, as Baron Jean had been abandoned. Emmeline was running away, as Sophie had run away. Each of them had fled, in the same way, a different bed; and the excessively violent rut of the husband and the inactive desire of the lover had resulted, in a similar solitude, in the same despair.

But all that was of no importance. What was important was to get Emmeline back. Oh, one thing that she knew was that she wanted her, happy or not, and that she would have her. Gone? She would follow her. Yes, she would go to Fontainebleau. The mother? The brother? They were people about whom she did not care. Emmeline, there was no denying it, was hers, and only hers. No one can prevent someone from taking back what belongs to them. She possessed Emmeline, since the marriage in the hammock, since always. The family? Thieves.

I'll arrive, I'll say: it doesn't matter to me what you think, or what you don't think. And she would take the darling by the arm, and she would take her away. That would be the end of it. They would go away together, further than France, to Italy, or Sicily, or further still, beyond the sea. They would be fine anywhere, provided that they were together.

In sum, that was it. It was necessary to do it

✻

She went back inside quickly, in order to get her hat and cloak. A train? Trains pass through all the time. Dressed in haste, she went across the island, toward the edge where a boat, moored to a tree trunk, transported people to the other side of the river, in front of the inn. She marched ever more rapidly, not looking at anything; she had only one thought: to take Emmeline by the arm and flee with her.

Something cold wet her feet. She looked down. She was crossing—she had not thought of making any detours—a stream that ran between gladioli and lilies. Oh my God! Oh my God! She dissolved in tears; it was like the downpour of a storm cloud that suddenly bursts.

She had recognized that stream, that moist verdure. In that stream, Emmeline had dipped her bare feet, pale, pink and veined in blue, with amber on the heel and gold on the nail of the big toe. "What does it matter to you if I serve as your chambermaid?" And then the darling: "Take off my stockings!" The end of her heel, on the tip of a shiny pebble, amid the water, that was making a little noise. Sophie saw it again. She wept, in the softness of an infinite tenderness.

Her nerves relaxed, a lucidity came to her, like respirable air beneath the sky, after a thunderbolt. She was thinking more clearly, her eyes still moist. She could not get Emmeline back. No. A mother has rights; a brother has rights; they would say to her: "What do you want? You've lost your mind. Emmeline is ill; you shan't see her, leave us alone."

And it would be necessary to be a man to break down the door.

Another thing: the husband! Jean would want her back, to keep her, not to let her go again. That was frightening! She could not return to Fontainebleau without exposing herself, without offering herself, to the sure, inevitable peril of being recaptured. And recaptured, so close and so far away from the imprisoned Emmeline, what could she do? One does not escape twice from the same prison; the first flight alerts the attention of the jailers for a long time. In any case, Emmeline would not consent to escape.

It was finished, then! Separated forever, they would never be united.

A rage counseled her to take her head in her hands and smash her skull against a tree trunk nearby.

But a hope interrupted the commenced impulse. She did not know at what time that morning Emmeline had left the house. There were not many trains in the morning; perhaps the fugitive was still at the station, waiting? It was possible; at least, it was not impossible. She did not know, poor thing, either how to buy a ticket or how to climb into a carriage alone, or anything. She might have lost time. Perhaps, also, in making her escape, she had forgotten to take the money to pay for a ticket. It happens every day, even when one is calm, when one is habituated to traveling, that one forgets to take money.

At any rate, yes, it was possible that Emmeline had not yet departed. That would be too beautiful, too fortunate! To find her again right away! Sophie ran breathlessly. She arrived on the edge. No boat. Yes, a boat, but far away in the middle of the river, a little closer to the other bank. The ferryman responded to cries of appeal with a gesture that said: "You can see very well that I have passengers; wait until I come back."

To wait! But it was true, the boat was full, full of women. Sophie divined them rather than recognized them: the ones who were laughing in the meadow, the ones about whom the waiter had spoken. From a distance, the boat, with their multicolored dresses and their large hats with verdure and roses, resembled a flower-cart gliding over the water; and a noise of chattering, and the refrains of songs, was coming from the group. At moments, because of a burst of sunlight, ten umbrellas opened simultaneously, bumping into one another, covering the boat with gray, blue and red roundels, and there were agitations underneath, arms waving that were trying to push the umbrellas away, and as if through the gaps, loud voices launched forth; one might have thought that it was the flesh of the arms, outside turned-up sleeves, that was singing and laughing.

The ferryman came back.

"Have you seen . . . ?"

She did not have time to finish.

"Yes, yes," said the man—an old man, very shrewd, who had heard it all, was no longer astonished, indifferent and mocking— "your little friend? She hailed me early this morning; I hadn't got up yet. If you're running after her you'll have to hurry, she took the eight o'clock train to Fontainebleau."

And he sniggered into his russet and gray beard.

"Hey! Look out!"

In putting her foot into the boat she had nearly fallen into the water. He caught her, she sat down; there was a sound of oars cutting the water; the old man was hurrying. Oh, it was all the same to her that he was hurrying, since Emmeline had gone such a long time ago, had already returned home.

Sophie was on the point of saying: "No, I've changed my mind, I'll stay, let's turn back."

But staying, she could not do that either! Oh, a new fear, which made her jump! It was evident, it was inevitable. Emmeline, in her mother's house, would reveal to Madame Luberti and Baron Jean the secret of the retreat where they had spent an entire week, and they would come to look for her, and they would oblige her to go with them, being the daughter of one and the wife of the other.

That was the supreme, unacceptable horror. What? Her friend had escaped her, the dear creature that was more precious to her than the daylight and the air; she had lost her, could not get her back; and it was necessary that, to that catastrophe, another would be added, so probable, so certain?

Jean, in a matter of hours, would appear, take her by the hand, take her away, and that evening would be the second conjugal night! He would crush her under his body, with an amour redoubled for having been mocked, with a desire for vengeance. The cuts of the whip, the tearing laceration of the strap, had been terrible, but it was nothing compared to the caresses of that man; she would have endured torture rather than accept a husband.

No, she did not want that mouth on her mouth—her mouth that had, alas, kissed Emmeline's lips, which were still perfumed, still warm, still sugared by them. And it seemed to her that she could feel in her abdomen, as if recent, the execrable tearing of his virility.

"Surely," said the ferryman, "you're upset. Bah! It happens every day. People meet they get together, they let go. People don't die of it. It's true that she was nice, the little one, with her modest air. Those ladies, who saw her through the windows of your house, said that she must be a very nice person. But it's necessary to be reasonable. I've seen them, those adventures, since I ferry Madame Charmeloze's clientele."

What was he saying? She had been divined, then? Her amour for Emmeline was an anecdote among the locals?

But her thoughts went elsewhere. The conjugal bed! That hideousness frightened and chased away all other sentiments. Even—if those two achievements had been able to accord— the joy of embracing Emmeline would not have compensated for the horror of being embraced by Baron Jean. The latter she execrated more than she adored the former. A shiver ran down her back and the memory of that abominable moment.

But let's think what to do, she said to herself.

Oh, no hesitation was possible: flee, hide, disappear, never to be found again.

What? Renounce Emmeline? No. Except that there was the man who was going to be alerted, who was going to arrive; it was necessary, above all, to get away.

"Well, you're brave!"

In fact, after dropping some loose change into the ferryman's hand, she had leapt out of the boat without the aid of the hand that he held out to her, and she ran up the stairway to the bank. She asked the waiter of the inn, which was a few paces away from the station: "What time is the train to Paris?"

"In thirty minutes."

Good, that was settled. It was in Paris that she would hide. There were a great many people, a great many houses; they wouldn't find her. Then, from there, perhaps, having money, she could get a letter to Emmeline. There are adroit and resolute people. Have her abducted? That romantic idea crossed her mind. But the most urgent thing was to flee, to escape her husband. Her husband! A second time, the wedding night—no!

And she sat down outside the hotel, to wait for the train.

✳

A gray and rose tent descended toward four laurels still in bloom; the warmth that was rising from the kitchen through a ventilation shaft, gave the illusion of a hothouse spring, and there were little round tables here and there, painted green.

"Will Madame take something?"

She did not know what one takes. "A vermouth?"

"Yes," she said.

She was afraid of seeing Baron Jean emerge from the glazed door of the station, facing her. She turned her head away. Close by, laughing, around a few tables joined together, eight or ten women were drinking and smoking cigarettes: Madame Charmeloze's friends.

She had a desire to move away, to go and wait in the station. They were so singular. She had never seen creatures like that. How little they resembled Emmeline! Ugly? No, not all of them. There was one—heavily made up, of course—who was pretty, with an abundant fringe of red hair, descending far enough to tickle the eyes. And they were all saying strange things, which Sophie did not understand very well. In speaking French, one might have thought that they were speaking a foreign language. But in the words that Sophie was hearing for the first time, she perceived a reprehensible meaning; the sound, although uncomprehended, was significant.

They were chatting, with their elbows on the table or slumped against the backs of their chairs, with vocal bursts. Badly brought up people, certainly. In the midst of her anguish, Sophie experienced a disgust for them. Then, from the things that the inn waiter had insinuated while setting the table, and what the ferryman had said, a suspicion came to her that those women—bad women, with eccentric costumes—were not so different from her than one might think.

That suspicion inspired a scorn for herself. To recognize that one resembles something base and vile is already a punishment for one's own baseness. At the same time, a certain attraction results therefrom. But the idea of that analogy was so vague within her that she could not pause upon it. And then, there were so many desperate sadnesses!

What decided her, above all, to go into the station was that she sensed that she was being looked at, watched and examined in the conventicle of all those hats grouped a little while be-

142

fore under umbrellas, and she had definitely seen one of those persons, the prettiest one, the one that had the fringe over her eyes, designating her with a gaze and whispering in her neighbor's ear.

She stayed in the waiting room for some time.

"Passengers for Paris!"

She spotted an empty compartment, climbed into it, and sat down in a corner; after a few minutes, the train pulled away, with a noise of whistle-blasts and rapid water.

Sophie was almost no longer thinking, exhausted by the nocturnal crisis and so many tortures. Finally in repose, lulled by the rocking, she allowed her mind to drift into a vague and desolate reverie.

Later, remembering that morning, she would ask herself more than once why she had not killed herself; it was doubtless the excess of her lassitude after so many physical and mental tortures that saved her from active despair; she would not have had the energy to die.

As for what she would do in Paris, she did not think about that. In her head and in her heart there was something like a very profound, very obscure void, with apparitions here and there of vain things and vague beings: a deserted and fuliginous cemetery haunted by phantoms. And she became increasingly weak and flaccid, entangled in the indolence of her melancholy.

A halt of the train did not extract her from that torpor, but she turned her head because of a woman who came in and sat down at the other end of the carriage in the cheerful turbulence of a multicolored dress: a very odd woman, with little red hairs everywhere. Sophie recognized one of the women who had been sitting under the hotel tent a little while before: the prettiest one.

Pretty? No, the least ugly. The one who had whispered in her neighbor's ear while looking at her. All those women were doubtless returning to Paris. Why, then, was this one alone, and why had she changed compartments at that station? Sophie could not help looking at her, covertly, with rapid glances. Even in the most profound depression, a man would not be able to help noticing the presence of a young woman, and taking an interest in her; of a man, Sophie had that.

She was astonished by that thin creature, as stiff as a stick of wood, and knotty, who, under her blaze of hair, gave the impression of a vine-stock crackling and burning. A very dainty face within the thicket of frills and curls; and in that lively face, a trifle wrinkled although very young, the turned-up nose showed nostrils that were too pink; the rings around the eyes, both blue and bistre, descended almost as far as the corners of the scarlet and fleshy lips, advancing like a little snout that might be pretty.

When the traveler moved—she could scarcely sit still—the beige crepe of her dress, sown with florets, and her sleeves, where the excessively white, almost amber skin appeared of arms that were not fat, and from the gap in her corsage, which was not inflated, and all of her costume, emerged, enlivened by the musk of make-up, a perfume of Russian leather and Levantine tobacco, which was the odor of her body. It was better than if it had been good, that odor, which one divined to be created expressly, very well planned; and all of that little woman was as agreeable to smell as it was amusing to see.

What she had that was utterly charming was her hands, of an extraordinary smallness and delicacy, in gloves that were very tight, and her feet, almost no longer, which she did not keep hidden, for, scarcely had she sat down than she put the end of her ankle-boot on the rim of the door; her skirt slipped slightly, allowing the sight of the white layers of underwear, which also slipped; she had pink silk stockings, perforated, in the holes of which flesh put golden dots.

Because the little woman had looked at her, smiling, Sophie turned her head away swiftly. She no longer occupied herself with anything but the trees that fled before the carriage window. But the other burst out laughing.

"Well," she said, "that's a nice face!"

A brutal insult could not have been more painful to Sophie than that remark, uttered in the voice of a gamine, slightly hoarse, but not too much. What did that person want? Why was she talking to her? She pretended not to have heard and stuck her face to the window.

"Can I smoke? It won't inconvenience you?"

Sophie heard the sound of paper rolled rapidly between the fingers, and the scrape of a match.

"In the next compartment, where the comrades are," the gamine voice went on, "there's a fat monsieur who doesn't like people smoking. It appears that he's asthmatic. Then Charmeloze said, 'Let's sit somewhere else,' and she did as she said: she sat on the fat monsieur; she weighs two hundred! Everyone fell about. But me, I couldn't stand it any longer. I would have given all I had—it's not fat, even in nature—to light one. I left them and came here. It's also a little for you that I came."

"For me!"

After a pause, the little traveler resumed, in a less frivolous voice, that was softened:

"I saw outside the inn that you were upset, truly chagrined. The others were making fun of you, because they'd been told your story. Yes, the girl that was with you, and who'd gone. They thought that was funny. Not all women have a kind heart. I said to them: 'If it happened to you, would you like it if people made fun of you?' They laughed louder. Me, I know what it is to suffer in the heart. I've had those dolors, more than once. Then, it was nice, what the hotel owner and the waiter said. All alone, just the two of you, in the little house, no more man than on the hand. I have the air, like that, of being mad, and it's true, I'm not very serious. But when I see a drama performed I weep all the tears in my body. That's annoying, because it makes your make-up run. Your story, a romance with a drama at the end.

"So, truly, she's gone for good? Why? Did you have an argument? Or has she gone to rejoin her lover? Damn, that's forced, one isn't born with income. Lovers are necessary. If she's gone for that, you can't hold it against her; it would be too stupid to be jealous of men. Everyone knows that it's of no consequence, with them. They know it too nowadays, and they've become polite, not demanding, reasonable. Provided that one amuses them, they only ask to be amused. One has no need to exhaust oneself in making a semblance. Me, it disgusts me to lie, I don't like deceiving, but they only want to be deceived. So, to be jealous of a man, there's no need. Of a woman, I don't say so, that's something else. Look, when I was with the grand Amédine, someone said to me one day: 'You know, your friend she tells you that she goes to a Baron's house every morning in the Champs-Élysées to have breakfast. Well, her Baron is a chanteuse at the Gaité-Rochecouart, Léo, the one who dresses as a man to sing and has a monocle in his eye.' I didn't dither. I posted myself outside Léo's house, and when Amédine came out I gave her such a slap. She still bears the marks."

Sophie was huddled in the corner, applying her forehead more forcefully to the window, instinctively trying not to be so close to the voice that was speaking; it seemed to her that the voice was enveloping her in dirtiness. She would have liked to cry out: "But in sum, I don't know you, shut up, leave me alone." She dared not, and she felt full of disgust, because of what she was hearing. Oh, that woman! And the others, in the other compartment, who must be similar! Emmeline was so pure, so tender, and said such honest words in such a clear accent! What, creatures like this one and Emmeline could exist at the same time?

She experienced something resembling the nausea of a very young lover, a child, with a fresh heart and mind, who, on returning from a first confession at the knees of his cousin, hears a traveling salesman telling stories, with filthy details, about the hundred-sou whores and inn girls whose skirts he has tucked up.

A shame also entered into her, that of not being entirely different from these young women. She might say to herself: "They don't love as I love," because she had felt in herself, for her friend, so much delicate tenderness and devour fervor, but she could not hide the fact that, in the mouth that wants the mouth, in the body that wants the body, they must be comparable to her; no matter that they were hideous and sickening, they were sisters of a kind that she had.

Sisters! At that moment, was the odiousness of the strange desires in her revealed to her by the ignominy of their realization in others? Was she afraid of the dream that she had? Perhaps, by virtue of one of those opening to the future, which soon close, she glimpsed—as one sees in an oblique file of increasingly dark mirrors an image becoming more and more obscure, and finally fading away—the degradation of various versions of herself, until their effacement in dirty darkness?

Then, suddenly, anger moved her, the anger of disillusioned pride. Always, the pride that is the resource of the damned, she had thought that the impulsion toward a dear feminine being, the instinctive desire by which she was incessantly tempted— criminal or not, she had never interrogated herself in that regard—only existed in her. Exceptional, that was what she had thought she was; and probably, the infatuation of being different, extraordinary, had contributed more than a little to maintaining her, to pushing her down the slope of evil desires. But now she saw that she was not alone in being subject to the abnormal attraction. These creatures were only different from her in greater baseness and impudence, and they doubtless knew the humiliation of being banal.

In any case, by what right was she scornful of these women? If she was superior to them in generous ardor, from other points of view she was not worth as much as them, for, in the indecency of their passion, they were at least complete.

Oh! That thought renewed her recent torture. They knew! Nothing of that which was the very goal of their covetousness remained unknown to them; they never saw, amid caresses, the fixed astonishment full of reproaches of two expectant eyes.

And now, amid the disgust and the shame and the anger, an ardent curiosity slid into Sophie, and took up residence there, and developed there: an envy of all their knowledge, so close at hand . . .

✳

The little traveler, rolling another cigarette, continued talking:

"Of course, one can't reproach you for being talkative. Do you know that you're no more polite than necessary? For an hour I've been telling you a heap of things and you stay in your corner, as mute as a carp. Because you don't know me? There's a reason! I call myself Magalo. Naturally, it's not my name. The family name, the true one, is sacred; it's necessary not to mingle it with the indecencies of life. I've been well brought up, by the Sisters, I've always respected my parents, to the point that, when my mother, who's a very honest woman, is in the house, not for anything in the world would I receive anyone. I don't want her to know. A mother has no need to know.

"Anyway, she's very discreet. She sees that I'm well-dressed, that I don't lack anything; that's sufficient for her, she's content, she doesn't ask for anything more. Only she said to me once: 'Aren't you obliged to pay contributions?' To pay contributions, regularly, she thinks that's indispensable, that it's a sign that one has an orderly mind. My mother has that mania: order. Manias are natural at her age. She never calls me Magalo. No, Tasie. But for others, Magalo. A funny name, isn't it? It came to me from a little comrade I had at the great Parisian concert. What she made me see, that one! Would you believe that, when I was outside, at night, she came to install herself in my place, with a whole band of musicians from her orchestra. Once, going home at ten o'clock in the morning, I went to bed, and what did I find in the bed? A violin case. As she was always singing: 'O

Magali, my beloved!"[1] people had nicknamed her Magali, and me Magalo."

The chatterbox came to sit opposite Sophie. "Hey," she continued, "I didn't notice it just now. You have something of her about you. Yes, in the forehead and the nose. Not in the mouth. Your mouth is prettier, fresher. You're very young. Nineteen, perhaps less. Me, I began at fifteen, I was almost not formed, with a friend of Papa, an old man who took me for a walk in the woods at Vincennes. My father kept a wine shop, he went bankrupt, and then the old man took me with him. You, for example, to look at you, one would never suspect it. One would think a young demoiselle who's still in her family. Was the girl who's gone—I didn't see her very well on the island—as pretty as you, with such a distinguished air? Damn, a pretty pair of turtle-doves. Only, that air of Saint-Touch-me-not, it's necessary not to abuse it, with men. It pleases them for a moment, but they don't like it to last; they don't have the time, you see.

"In the end, though, you're aggravating, not saying a word! I'm telling you all my affairs, me. Come on, don't be upset any more. You'll find her again, she'll come back, or if not, believe me, one lost, one found. That's how it is, believe me," she finished, laughing, "me who fell out with Hortense yesterday evening!"

Sophie did not understand. Those words were no longer anything but a noise around her. But she was thinking, with an appearance of sleeping. She could not get away from the obsession that this girl, and her friends, knew something that she did not, had descended into the most obscure mysteries of the caress. Infamous, yes, but knowledgeable.

And, in the rocking of the train, in the languidness of her melancholy, amid the loquacity of the voice that was twittering like the noise of an aviary—and because, also, of the singular perfume, Russian leather and Levantine tobacco, that emerged

---

1 The line is from a popular Provençal aubade.

from Magalo—her reverie was increasingly inclined toward the unknown of strange kisses; it seemed to her that a shiver ran through her hair and over her eyes, very hot, her closed eyelids embracing a penumbra in which white contours lit up in the distance pink or blonde things, rapidly extinguished visions, like a flock of phosphorescent butterflies vanishing, and being replaced by other visions, momentarily more precise, but then becoming confounded and vain in the darkness.

She became anxious, Magalo was to longer talking. Weary of not obtaining any reply, was she obliging herself to silence, out of chagrin?

No, Sophie knew that she was being watched. She was certain that the little traveler facing her, leaning forward slightly, was looking at her intently. It seemed to her that that gaze, if she had wanted to move, would have prevented her from doing so. She felt that she was a prisoner of that insurmountable nothing: the will-power of a gaze.

The idea of raising her eyelids was insupportable to her because of the fear of seeing the eyes that were upon her. Then she had the impression of a successive darkening, as if, in a series of shocks, the daylight was escaping around her; each shock was accompanied by a slide, one might have thought, of a ring on a curtain-rail; and while the darkness thickened beneath her eyelids, she ceased to sense the violent gaze upon her, either because Magalo's eyes had turned away, or because their fixity was blunted by the more opaque obscurity.

But again, the gaze seized her, closer, more insistent, more enveloping; she was touched by it all over; she thought that she no longer had any garments, so closely was her skin seized and clutched by that gaze; and it was so unsustainable that she gasped. At the same time, since a night had fallen around her, she was assailed, surrounded and covered by a double and bizarre perfume: was Magalo sitting on the same banquette, close beside her?

150

Sophie had heard her move, perhaps the aroma emanated from her close gaze. It was as if she had been clad in flowers with eyes. But those flowers did not have the simple odor of those that bloom, wild, on bushes or in a meadow; an odor of artificial roses that had been moistened with intoxicating essences, that was what emerged from them; and at moments, in a recrudescence of the gaze, the perfume warmed and exasperated; the exhalation of perfumed artificial flowers was complicated by an effluence of feminine intimacies, also artificial, but alive, which, as if exhaled by the breath of a cleavage in which the flesh beneath the rice powder was tenderized by sweat, became, in gusts, warmer and more irresistible.

As if bound by the burning and maddening caress, which, however, did not touch her, Sophie, her eyes still closed, did not budge, was no longer thinking about anything, only experiencing . . . what, then? The disgust she had had for that woman, entered here and so impudently talkative, the anger, the humiliations of pride, and also the curiosity about the knowledge that she supposed Magalo to have, was no longer there, had dispersed, had dissolved into a languor under the envelopment of that odorous gaze; and she no longer knew where she was; she sensed, that was all, that she was surrounded by a delicious and dangerous menace . . .

Abruptly, a breath that was like the smoke of burned musk desiccated her lips. She opened her eyes wide. Very close to her face, was an ardent little face, made-up and crumpled, with warm creases and eyes from which flames emerged, and lips that wanted her mouth!

Oh, that woman! Emmeline!

But Magalo, with an arm around her waist, had seized her, prevented her from slipping away, held her against her, and she was whispering in her ear, her breath in her hair.

Sophie could not help listening, immobile, with the stupor of birds that, once caught in a trap, no longer move. The things said now did not resemble those said a little while ago; no more laughter, no more impertinent frivolities; vocal caresses rather than speech, but words nevertheless, whispered, begging, which wanted to soften, which promised, sometimes with strange precisions, an infinity of unknown delights; and at each promise of the tempting susurration, a sigh from Sophie was the confession of desiring its realization.

She would have liked to resist, because it was, after all, criminal, because she loved Emmeline so much; and then, she was subject to the embarrassment of a transposition; what she was hearing, she would not have able to say, and yet it seemed to her that it would have been up to her to say it, and to hear someone else saying it was like a humiliation.

But the whispering persisted, more desirous, more promising, recklessly, and she was dying in the enlacement of the voice, the gaze and the odor.

For a moment, she almost pulled herself together; that was when Magalo, drawing away slightly, asked abruptly:

"By the way, what's your name?"

"Sophie."

The other burst out laughing.

"Oh, that name! That's a silly name, damn it! It's good for concierges' daughters. I surely wouldn't call myself that. Look, three years ago, in the house where I was lodging, I knew a girl who had your name. She was very chic and very pretty, very well maintained, decent. And she was astonishing, when we were alone together. But Sophie, you understand, wasn't possible. So, I don't know why, we called her Sophor. Sophor's odd, it isn't common. Say, would you like to be Sophor too? It's agreed, isn't it? Come on, Sophor, a little smile."

Because of that silliness, she drove away, with her hands, the detestable visions of a delectable nightmare; she wanted to throw herself into the other corner, opposite. But Magalo had taken hold of her again, was clasping her tightly; the prayers in her ear, the alluring promises, in warm breath, recommenced more tenderly, more powerfully tempting.

With the perfume that was coming from Magalo, Sophie sensed a perfume mingling that was coming from herself; it was like a marriage, that mixture of aromas. Under the weight, barely, of a hand that was touching the back of her neck, which was caressing her hair with little fingers, it was necessary, finally, that she incline toward the dainty woman . . . it was with the mouth that she received the moist babbling of the excessively rosy lips that advanced.

But Magalo, with a stir of her entire dress, exclaimed: "Sapristi! We're there! We'll be at the station in three minutes!"

Immediately, from window to window, she separated or lifted the blinds. Broad daylight bathed the compartment. As alarmed as a nocturnal bird frightened by sudden torchlight, Sophie had thrown herself back into the corner, hiding her head in her hands. But the other, straightening her hat and restoring a probable disorder in her hair near the temples, said:

"That's not all, let's talk quickly, let's talk well. You understand that because of the others, we can't leave together. No, that Hortense would tear your hair out. But listen carefully: this is my address." After rummaging in her pockets she handed her the envelope of a letter. "You can pick me up this evening, at seven o'clock, and we'll have dinner, the two of us, just us. You want to, don't you? Oh, she's pretty, with her little air of coming back from the other world, and having been beaten. You won't regret her, the other one, the kid who's done a bunk. But come on, speak, seven o'clock? You'll come? For sure?"

Sophie did not reply, tried not to hear, shaken by a tremor. She hated herself, she despised herself. Alas! Emmeline, so pure, with such fresh candor in her lips. Magalo, by contrast, her mouth sweating like the damp heat of a fever, like a kind of nasty melting honey, too sweet, which intoxicates.

And then, they were so singular, those women. Whores. Badly brought up, coarse, infamous. And she saw herself—it was frightful—similar to them, later. She understood that her destiny depended on this minute. No! It was *no* that she wanted to respond. It was not possible that she should yield to such a temptation, that she should desire the villainy of those banal caresses. But the desire, with the blood, was running in her veins, seething and bubbling; it was so maddening, the unnatural odor that emerged from that little creature, all make-up and fire. No matter; she did not want it. She would certainly say no.

The train was slowing down, was about to stop, stopped. The door having swiftly opened, Magalo set her ankle-boot on the footstep; Madame Charmeloze's other friends were leaping, one by one, on to the platform, with laughter and a hundred overlapping voices.

Then Magalo turned round and said, before getting down: "Well then, are you going to come? Decide, or Hortense will scratch your eyes out. It's agreed you'll come?"

"Yes," said Sophor.

BOOK TWO

I

Having arrived near the Opéra, the two strollers stopped. Almost alone at that corner of the boulevard, they could see further on, to the right, between the cafés illuminated with a yellow splendor, beyond the long line of a curious crowd, the open area of the square, black and slick after recent rain, like a frozen lake of ink; and the great stone staircase, white with light, rose toward the façade with the fronton bordered with a thousand little flickering flames, obscure nevertheless, and the details of the sculptures, the nuances of the marble, were extinct in a shadow that made the light of the interior gallery, full of blue-tinted luminous vapor, seem more intense.

Doctor Urbain Glaris asked: "Are you going to the club?"

"Yes," said Monsieur de Maël-Parbaix.

"Good. Gambling is a resource against thought. The modern living have only one goal: to escape consciousness without recourse to suicide; and of all the passions, gambling is perhaps the most jealous, the most absorbing, the one that annuls most completely the faculties that are not indispensable to it; it suppresses everything that is not itself, condenses and simplifies humanity into a single erethism. But know this: gambling is the last resource, and the day when, with the chips on the table, when the cards are falling one after another in front of you, you think about something other than the imminent draw, it's finished; you're doomed."

Monsieur de Maël-Parbaix replied, smiling: "Your ideas are well-known. The forgetfulness of having lived, the non-sentiment of life, that's what the men of today are seeking, and ought to seek."

"Not all. A breaker of stones on the highway, a miner in a narrow tunnel, and a peasant sowing or plowing, can think, without being frightfully unhappy, about what they did yesterday, what they are doing, and what they will do. But the man of the new cities, the man who has finally exceeded the abuse of the desire or the dream, and the lassitude or impossibility of realization, the man who has his complete manifestation in the Parisian, can only find the alleviation of his perpetual anguish in an abolition of himself as perfect as possible. To forget! Not to know! There's no contentment other than in unconsciousness. But it's difficult, forgetfulness. Everyone seeks it, few find it. The drunkard isn't always drunk, the madman has intervals of lucidity. One might think that immemorial human despair has dried up the Lethe."

"Well then, come and forget with me, by gambling."

"No, I have duties that interest me—oh, not very much. I even believe that they don't interest me at all. I fulfill them out of habit. I have to attend to my invalids."

"Your invalids? After midnight?"

"It's my time, and theirs."

After shaking hands, the two men separated. But on turning his head, Monsieur de Maël-Parbaix saw the doctor traversing the open ground of the square, heading toward the Opéra. He caught him up, and said, with a hint of irony: "Your invalids are there, in that fête?"

"Undoubtedly: the most gravely afflicted. I'm going to study the progress of the malady—without any hope, alas, of curing it."

"I scarcely have any desire, tonight, to win or lose. Would you permit me to accompany you?"

"To my clinic? Gladly."

156

"At least the disease isn't contagious?" said Monsieur de Maël-Parbaix, slightly ashamed of his mediocre pleasantry.

"Certainly it is. But what does it matter, since you'll inevitably be afflicted by it, if you aren't already?"

They went up the stairway pale with light, pushed a leather-clad door, and went in.

Monsieur de Maël-Parbaix was a celebrated clubman. The name "clubman" was already given to those amiable idlers who get up late and trail the indolence of their indifference from the fencing school to the gambling club, and from the club to the alcove of some actress who has not yet gone home but is waiting, lying down, with a cigar in her lips, on the chaise-longue in her dressing-room, where the perfumes from twenty bottles mingle with that persistent, ineradicable odor, the odor of washed amour. Yes, washed, since it was dirty. Between the assault in the establishment of the famous master, and the baccarat on some famous green baize, there has been dinner in a fashionable eatery, consumed without appetite.

Hunger! That admirable health is refused to *viveurs*, even those who are well—these days, one says "viveurs" as one once said "Eumenides," by virtue of antiphrasis. Oh, if they dared to eat boiled eggs! They dare not, because of the poor devils on the other side of the glass, on the sidewalk, who envy the woodcock or the grouse. And before the menu, presented with an obsequious familiarity by the waiter who says "Monsieur le Baron" or "Monsieur le Comte," a yawn confesses the ennui of their stomach. Witty? Certainly. Intelligent? Not at all.

Monsieur de Maël-Parbaix was slightly superior to the majority of his peers. He was convinced of having, and had, higher aspirations. No, playing baccarat, betting on horse races, becoming indecent with whores, was not all of life; he permitted himself to have taste, did not lack literature. He had read at least the first few pages of all the books published in the last twenty years. He wrote himself, on coming back from the Bois, before breakfast. He put things on paper that he had thought of in the

Allée des Poteaux. It was extraordinary how the horse, in jolting him, stirred his ideas. He had even put on a very amusing revue at the club, with couplets sung by an inmate of the Comédie-Française. Oh, he had no prententions; but, after all, one needs one's distractions, and the vulgarity in a little vaudeville isn't unbecoming to men of good family.

At any rate, although mediocre, he was not nasty-minded—a rare thing. The man did not hate that which was foreign to him, forgave genius and glory; he admitted heroism. Undoubtedly, what inclined him to those indulgences was that, being very elegant, good-looking, with the good taste not to dye his graying hair—what age? forty-five, the age at which one ceases to grow older—he still had a success in the worldly boudoir appropriate to inspire a contentment in him that blossomed into generosity. And he was a happy man, very happy, because, in truth, having an income of a hundred thousand livres, few debts, good banks and beautiful mistresses, nothing was lacking to make him the sort of happiness that Dr. Urbain Glaris had the impertinence to doubt.

One day, that eccentric physician, to an illustrious banker, reputedly honest and surrounded like a golden idol—in real gold—with universal genuflections, and who was pleased to say: "Look at me, I have no complaints; all possible felicity I have," had replied, "As to that, I'd like to know the opinion of . . ."

"Of whom?"

"Your pillow?"

There was a little charlatanism in the eccentricity, which was also slightly ridiculous, of that savant. Savant? Yes, incontestably: his works, his books, had obliged to a certain esteem even the rare men who, solitary in their laboratories, hide from the curiosity of reporters: hence his extraordinary renown and his almost triumphant authority in Parisian society. To those alarmed by the excess of his paradoxical loquacity, the objection was raised of the solidity of his entitlements to confidence. Women, who were mad about him, were delighted and proud to be able to justify their enthusiasm, and what he had of similarity to Berthelot or Pasteur authorized liking what he had of similarity to Cagliostro. He was not devoid of resemblance to a prophet who reads cards; he told fortunes well.

The specialty of the studies to which he had devoted himself for a long time contained such a narrow vicinity to the rites of magic and sorcery; the reality of his experiments—in search of the unknowns of hysteria and magnetic suggestion—was so close to realized impossibility, to prodigy, that he appeared as an investigator who might be a species of thaumaturge; but he excelled in using that which they certainly had of the scientific, in order not to marvel too much at what they had, perhaps, of the illusory. And the perfect distinction of his person—very slender, with long, fine hands in gloves that molded the fingers—his belated youth of the thirtieth year, a languor in his eyes, the slightly pursed smile of his almost colorless lips, the fatal curve of his nose, his only obedience to the tradition of outdated Mesmers—in a word, the grace of being a man of the world who was the greatest of scientists, perhaps of sorcerers—added to the curiosity of an exoticism that was never entirely clarified; for, although he admitted to being Swiss, Russian or Polish, many people affirmed that he had been born in Serbia, and made him someone charming, who might have been frightening if he wished.

He made science and mystery elegant. Once, in the house of the Marquise de Portalègre—oh, after many supplications, for it is, after all, something slightly blasphemous, that familiarity with the unknown—he had obliged a young demoiselle—Cagliostro would have said "a dove"—by means of a hand on her forehead, to confess the name she was thinking of giving a kitten that someone had promised her.

"What I like about him," said Madame de Lurcy-Sévi, "is that he performs miracles as one is assured that he performs autopsies, without taking off his gloves."

In any case, the modern woman has a dominator: the physician. And it could not be otherwise. In the times when she had a soul—or believed that she had one, which is absolutely the same thing—a woman depended on the priest; now that she is only a body, a body quivering with nerves, or imagines herself to be nothing but that—which comes to exactly the same thing— she is submissive to the physician. It is impossible for her not to confess; confession—the triumph of the Catholic Church emerged from having understood this—is the law of feminine instinct.

It is necessary for a woman to talk about herself, deceptively or not, whether she delivers herself or only pretends to deliver herself. A liar? No. As soon as she speaks she is convinced that she is telling the truth, and her involuntary hypocrisy relieves no less than the frankest abandonment. Now, since the fashion has fallen from sentiment to sensation, from passion to neurosis, it is her flesh, her muscles and her nerves that she confesses, veridically or not.

The confessor was the physician of souls, in the days of souls; the physician is the confessor of bodies. But if he wants to master his patient, his penitent, perfectly, he must put into saving the physical a little of the religion that the confessor put into curing the moral being, in the same way that the priest, under penalty of a deserted altar, once had to charm with a little tender bewitchment the anxiety of scruples or the torment of ardors. Since woman was once a spirit who had nerves, and since she is now nerves that have a spirit, it is necessary—hence Grandier of Loudun—for there to be in the priest a little of the physician (physician and sorcerer are the same thing) and it is necessary—hence young physicians with suggestive eyes and slow, soothing gestures—that there is in the physician a little of the mage (between priest and mage there is no difference).

The story is told of one illustrious practitioner who, seeing a student come to his clinic who was something of a peasant, with the stout knotty fingers of a laborer, he said: "Good, good, you'll practice in the provinces; in Paris one only practices with the hands of an archbishop." He was right. It is indispensable, especially if it is a matter of a woman, to treat a patient with an air of benediction, and, in the benediction, a resemblance to a caress does not harm to the convalescence and even concurs with the analepsy. It is unimaginable that there cannot be—what am I saying? there must be—sacerdotal elegance, the prettiest of all elegances, because of the sacred aura by which it is originalized, in a man who is admitted to take the pulse of a Parisienne; he is a boor if he is not a kind of apostle who, elsewhere, would be liable to kneel down.

To care for the modern woman—I mean one who lives in a quarter where there are only town houses—other than with the soothing and benign hands of a director of conscience, a man of the world inclined to indulgence, would be a perfect incongruity. After venial sins, there are now venial maladies; there are no others under the curtains where the odor of drugs annuls in batiste and lace perfumes with sandalwood or opopanax. But the complaisances of the physician, in their mundanity, ought never to go as far as abandoning his quasi-ecclesiastical prerogatives. He must resemble the priest who, in a little while, will be solemn with the little girl whose chin he has just caressed with an encouraging hand in the courtyard of a convent. A woman is only pleased with grace when she divines a strength therein. Although she loves to be victorious, there are those who can vanquish her; she only wants to be adored by gods, and it befits the physician, amid familiar courtesies, to remain ceremonial, strange, seemingly distant and omnipotent. A prescription is a penance imposed; a pill is now swallowed as an *ave* was once recited; "You are cured" is an absolution; and there is a paradise: morphine.

As soon as he was seated in a box, alongside Monsieur de Maël-Parbaix, Doctor Urbain attracted all gazes; behind fans there were whispers in his regard. They were his clients, all the beautiful persons who had come to that charity ball—his admiring clients, since, to the emphatic gravity of a great deal of science, he added the amusement of a little devilry. But what earned him the ardent sympathy of socialites above all was, more accomplished in him than in anyone else, the almost clerical delicacy of his interrogations, in the mornings by the bedside when the chambermaid, after placing two lace pillows under the shoulders of the patient, said "Monsieur le docteur may come in."

He had a fashion that was only his of almost not asking, but of immediately divining, the cause of the malaise. With anyone else, one would have been embarrassed. Truly, he was the only one by whom, with a wheezy chest, one could allow oneself to be ausculated. It was impossible to describe the reserve with which, in the almost dark room—"Oh, no, no, Rosette, don't open the curtains!"—in the bedroom perfumed by the warmth of a slightly feverish slumber, he inclined his ear toward the bronchi or the lungs. He never requested that the chemise be moved aside; it was through the malines that he listened to the coming and going of the breath; but he excelled at making felt a slightly insistent pressure, with which he observed the firmness of the breasts; and when a more mysterious illness constrained him to more intimate observations, he had such a scrupulous manner of half-turning away while the patient, with a long-hesitant hand, stripped naked, and in circling with clustered batiste the narrow area where something pink, less than a bud, the object of great anxiety, protruded.

Often, on those occasions, he had innocent hypocrisies, which were well designed for him to conciliate the esteem of persons careful of their good renown; and more than once, he contrived to counsel the most complicated medicaments with regard to a trace, slightly red and slightly blue, on the upper arm, which was the persistence of a kiss. There is no better taste. But he became grave next to patients who were not ill but were suffering infinitely. There, he no longer smiled, he ceased to be courteous, he became once again the savant, the thinker, the dreamer that he veritably was.

He believed in imaginary maladies. He believed that one can have, in a healthy body, more frightful sufferings than can be contained in a flesh bitten by wounds, and he was full of pity for the incurable. He judged that the people attained by nephretic colics had, in fact, less of which to complain than those who said, with a fear of being mocked: "Truly, doctor, I don't know what's wrong with me," and who are dead in the soul while having life in the body. He took his head in his hands, full of merciful thoughts, before the beds of young women who held out their hands murmuring: "Oh my God, oh my God, I'd rather die!" and who were going to a ball that evening.

The theory of some practitioners is to treat those maladies with whiplashes, or buckets of water thrown in the face. Perhaps they are right. He did not want to be right like them; he was convinced that a broken leg is trivial by comparison with a slow anxiety between the eyes, which endures, and that the fear of a frisson that might make one shiver in a little while—yes, again, it was certain, the return of that frisson; one was accustomed to it—exceeds in cruelty the most brutal pains; and he listened to the melancholy plaints; and sometimes he did not say no, when the eye of the patient implored one of the benevolent poisons that make one sleep, dream and forget.

✳

That evening, the gratitude of those who were suffering so much in the morning—in Paris one is never ill under artificial light—surrounded him with smiles and thanked him with gracious inclinations of the head; for there was not a single woman at the fête, among those who counted, who would not have confessed to him with the confidence that the nuns of Loudun had in Urbain Grandier. But he was very reserved, never having used his power to the extent of losing it. And, regarded by all the boxes luminous with diamonds and flesh, saluting them appropriately, with reticence in the familiarity, he no longer even knew—albeit with a little affectation in the forgetfulness—that he had seen all, or almost all, of those dazzling and desirable creatures in chemises, or naked.

The fête—concert, ball and tombola for the benefit of the victims of the conflagration in Segovia—laughed, sparkled and agitated noisily under the splendor of the chandeliers; all the beautiful women in Paris were there, since the most illustrious socialites, patronesses of the charity, had solicited their presence and collaboration personally. What would one not risk with a charitable intention? There were not only famous actresses but also bit-part players to whom the undeniable plentitude of their leotards assured a rich clientele.

While Céphise Ador of the Comédie-Française recited a poem on the immense platform where a hundred musicians were gathered, the duchesses and the marquises, in the foyer and the corridors, were introduced by their husbands or lovers to Mademoiselle Anatoline Meyer of the Bouffes or Constance Chaput of the Nouveautés, sellers of flowers and programs. A curiosity devoid of malevolence, a desire to see at close range the pretty creatures about whom the newspapers and gossip columns talked, attracted the escapees from salons to the refugees from the wings; and in the rapprochement of tresses, shoulders and arms there was a resplendent confrontation of family diamonds that had been the pride of ancestors with the recent jewels, ill-acquired and hard-earned, of sellers of pleasure.

It was the night of that fête, you will remember, that for the first time, the two estates of woman, prostitution and aristocracy, the whore and the grand dame, found themselves face to face and considered one another in the totality of their triumphs, resembling one another in their luxury; not neighbors, and perhaps distant, as at première performances and the standard of racecourses, but mingled, rubbing shoulders, only making a single crowd. And they treated one another as equals. There was not, on the one side, pride and suspicion, nor on the other, disdainful courtesy. No, seeing one another at close range, measuring one another and observing one another, they recognized that they were two equally considerable forces; that their disparities of rank and education did not exclude their equivalence, just as two plates of different metals can have the same weight; enemies, no doubt, but enemies between whom the victory would remain doubtful.

That night resembled those truces between civilized warriors in which the officers of the besieged city sup in the trenches or under the tents with the besieging officers, not without felicitations on good conduct in recent battles. After having offered a glass of champagne to Léo Nicot, who emptied it very prettily, her nose in the glass, and retained a little foam on her nostrils— "Oh, how amusing that is, how do you do that?"—the Marquise de Belvélize did not fail to compliment her on the fashion in which the lovely actress had ruined Monsieur de Marciac, who had been reduced to raising sheep in South America; and at the buffet, near the tzigane orchestra, Mademoiselle Rose Mousson, costumed as a Louis XV flower-girl, dared to offer a cigarette to the Comtesse de Lynnès (the Comte was Rose's lover), saying to her: "In truth, in his place, I'd prefer you!" Madame de Lynnès appeared very touched by that flattery.

Since they were there, the whores and the socialites, the majority of the men who counted, by virtue of family, fortune or talent, the old and the young, had not failed to come to the fête: an elegant crowd of frock-coats and uniforms, traversed and illuminated by hair, bare arms and shoulders. And because the most reserved could not help continuing with regard to the grand dames the familiarity permitted with the little actresses, because the moistures of flesh vaporized in the heat of the lights and the music whipped the nerves and the muscles, and a few glasses of champagne, amid all that bare flesh, were sufficient to stimulate brains and set eyes ablaze, a delighted exuberance blossomed. The exuberance of fine Parisian fêtes, especially charity fêtes, in which the sentiment of a good deed accomplished legitimizes, and, so to speak, tranquilizes the pleasure, added, to the gleam of the lights and the beauty of the women, the flame of the satins and the splendor of the diamonds, and to everything, joy—joy!

"Damn!" exclaimed Monsieur de Maël-Parbaix, who was laughing, like everyone else. "Those are invalids whose appearance is as sinister as can be!"

Doctor Urbain pretended not to have heard the laughter.

"Aren't they frightful?" he said. "And isn't a hospital ward, with its beds, from which the odor of wounds and gasps emerge, with the livid faces of the moribund with hollow eyes, whose fingers claw the bedclothes, with all the hideousness of disease and imminent death, less horrible to contemplate than this fête? Oh, the poor things! Oh, the wretches! It would be less lugubrious to see them weeping than to hear them laughing like this. There's no torture as atrocious as their pleasure. How merry they are, how happy they are, how they're amusing themselves, alas! How I pity them. I've seen many despairs, I've penetrated all the human gehennas, the tortures of which I've counted and annotated, but those despairs and those tortures are nothing compared with this desolating joy."

"At least agree, doctor, that they're hiding their suffering well?"

"Yes, they're hiding it from one another, and they're trying to hide it from themselves; it's precisely the refusal to confess it that redoubles their illness and exasperates it to the point of rage. Oh, if they were at home, if they were alone, in front of the fire, under the lamp, their torment might slow down in the peace and the silence; there are in solitude invisible soft hands for the worst wounds. But they dare not stay at home! They're afraid of the void of noise in which they would hear interior voices, afraid of the mirror in which they might see their image, of the desert of insomnia, and of slumber too, populated by nightmares; and all of them, men and women alike, have come here in order to distract themselves, the unfortunates, as they'll go to some other fête tomorrow. But the illness will follow them

166

there obstinately, as it has followed them this evening, more acerbic for having been stirred and shaken. The beast that is biting them doesn't like to be made to dance, and becomes enraged in not having been left tranquil."

"Are you really talking seriously, doctor?"

"As seriously as possible."

"You believe that Parisians and Parisiennes are suffering under their apparent good humor?"

"Frightfully. Some of them are spared—the perfect imbeciles, of whom there are a few in that crowd of black coats, and the perfectly unconscious, of whom there are a few among the young women. But anyone who is capable of reflecting and experiencing, whatever he experiences, has more of which to complain than the most ill-treated of convicts."

Monsieur de Maël-Parbaix finally judged that there was some bad taste in that emphatic and ill-tempered paradox. Then he asked again:

"And their illness is . . . ?"

From the boxes, from the platform, where the allegro of a choir was quivering tickled by the pizzicato of the orchestra, from the entire hall and the corridors, more joyful noise and dancing folly was coming. With the slightly affected solemnity or which he was reputed, and which accorded well with the grace of his melancholy, Urbain Glaris replied:

"Their illness is Remorse."

Then Monsieur de Maël-Parbaix burst out laughing. The doctor observed that hilarity with the appearance of noting a symptom; and the other, still laughing, said: "Remorse! What? Remorse?"

"Yes."

"You'd go so far as to claim that those young women, whose husbands, brothers, friends or lovers we are, and those men, whose hands we are glad to shake, have really committed crimes, have melodramatic rascalities on their conscience?"

"And do you dare to affirm that there are no murderers here, nor poisoners, nor bankrupts, not forgers, nor seducers of virgins, nor traitors to the fatherland? In any case, I haven't talked to you about the remorse produced by brutal crimes, atrocious or infamous actions punished by the law. There's another remorse, that of faults that implicate neither legal chastisement nor even social scorn, and those faults exist, alas—or, rather, that fault exists, for, although innumerable and diverse in circumstances, they are only one in their essence, and if it pleases you that it has a name, you can call it Sin. Not in the sense that it had in the times when simple souls loved and blessed the repentance that earned the delicious absolution, but in the sense that it is necessary to give it at the present time, the time when living beings devoid of faith no longer expect anything from the heavens devoid of paradise.

"Sin used to be the transgression of divine law; now it's the transgression of human law, and the torture by which it is fatally accompanied is all the more frightful because it isn't softened by the hope that it might be pardoned; for the offended isn't a god, terrible but perhaps clement; it isn't a person, or even a thing; it's blind, deaf and non-existent. And the unnamed, the unnamable, holds us, obliges us and imposes rules upon us, marking our limits. While knowing that it is not, we sense that we are its slaves, and if we don't obey it, if we revolt against the will of that nothingness, if we break its law, then the irremediable horror is installed within us: discontent with oneself. Isn't it frightful to be punished for offending—nothing! And since God no longer exists, why does Conscience?"

"Yes, champagne," replied Monsieur de Maël-Parbaix to an adorable young woman clad in a white satin marmiton, who was going from box to box offering sandwiches at twenty francs each and Moët at two louis a glass.

Urbain Glaris went on: "Now these men and women have committed the Sin, have transgressed human law, not that imposed on humans by humans, but that imposed on humans by an inexorable necessity, or perhaps by respect for the ancient divine rule transmitted by the ancestors and surviving faith. They haven't wanted, they haven't been able, to limit themselves to what they ought to be, toward the ideal above or toward the ideal below, they've launched themselves outside humanity.

"They could, simple of mind and simple of body, have rejoiced in the satisfaction of natural instincts: drinking, eating, sleeping, loving like pigeons in the woods or dogs at crossroads—in brief, only asking for, and only hoping for, that which was their wealth, their patrimony; they would not have known anguish! They would have accomplished life with the normality of water flowing where it has to flow, or a stone rolling where it has to roll, of everything that follows its path or its slope. But they believed, the unfortunates, in the ancient promise: 'You shall be like gods!'—for if there is no longer a Tempter, there is still Temptation—and they have fallen into the trap of the more than human; and now they are the damned of an inferno devoid of demons, but no less torturing.

"Perhaps those who bore sublime ambitions, who dreamed, if they were poets, of soothing dolorous humanity with songs, if they were soldiers, of delivering fatherlands or, if they were scientists, of conquering the unknown, ought to have some consolation, in their vanquished and frustrated efforts, in the glory of their martyrdom. Undoubtedly punished, because they have broken the circle in which human life has to be restricted in order to be peaceful—which is to say, happy—they can believe that they have been punished unjustly, and their fine pride is scornful of the victorious rule. But those who are attracted to the inferior gulfs, those who demand of eating the exasperation and continuity of hunger, and obtain gastritis; of drinking, further thirst after satiation, and obtain nausea; of sexual intercourse the excess of pleasure and subtle depravities, and obtain disgust and impotence; those who, violent or refined, furious or methodical, try to constrain their senses to the beyond of sensation, develop the beast that is within them to the point of monstrosity; oh, those, it is not only the overflow of vain desires or the eventual ennui of the excessive—the worst ennui of all, irremediable because it is caused by the very thing that might detract it—and not only the horror of habitude leading to immeasurable insufficiencies, nor the sickening of everything, that chastises them and breaks their hearts. No, because they are Sinners, because they have transgressed strict duty, Remorse is in them, and does not quit them, and never lets them alone. A reproach that squeezes their heart and chills their blood speaks to them in a low voice in solitude, and speaks to them in a louder voice, in order to be heard, in the streets, in the music of fêtes.

"Oh, they do not admit that they can hear it, that reproach. If you say to them: 'Can you hear it?' they will burst out laughing—as you did just now, Monsieur de Maël-Parbaix—and even succeed sometimes, too rarely, in persuading themselves that they do not, in fact, hear it. But it speaks and never ceases to speak. And they cannot run away from that voice, since it is within them, and they cannot escape the remorse, since they carry it wherever they want to flee.

"You say: 'Physical malaise, not moral anguish. A malaise of overworked nerves. A night of repose and one gets up in a good humor.' Yes, there is a night that can cure them: the night from which one does not awake. So, what does it matter if they are suffering in their bodies, not in their souls, from nerves and not from thought. They feel, so be it, I grant it, something analogous to what one feels the day after a night of debauchery; they have 'hair that hurts,' as they say; but for those for whom life is a long abuse of evil joys—sad joys, alas—the day after is always, and they have hair that hurts interminably. Oh, how deplorable they are! So little worthy of esteem that they're worthy of pity. To forget themselves, to ignore themselves, there is nothing they can do; nothing tempts them, but they try everything; they demand accursed drugs, opium, hashish, morphine, the death of memory, the dream that scarcely thinks, vague annihilation. But after the apotheoses of opium, the puerile phantasmagorias of hashish and the excitations or the delectable languor of morphine, their nerves, their senses, and their entire being, like a string that snaps, having been tightened excessively, falls more irremediably into a more profound desolation; and if they are still alive—they call that living!—it is because they dare not die.

"Once, salvation might have been possible for them. Religion was offered to the desperate; it was the place of refuge for souls; they might have experienced resurgence through the exaltations of fanaticism, or numbed themselves with brutalizing faith. But now the times have come predicted by the diabolical prophets, the times of empty or closed churches, and soon the stones of the roads that climb toward calvaries will have forgotten the bare feet of pilgrimages.

"In any case, the overworked are too worn out to dare to believe, the refined are too subtle to be able to believe. With the result that only one frightful issue is offered to them: madness. Yes, madness. They are afraid of death, but they would like madness. The tomb, no, the asylum, yes. Insane! They will consent to be insane. Oh, they don't admit that abominable desire to their peers, they don't admit it to themselves, and when one of them, after so many apparent joys and real tortures, loses his reason, they pretend to feel sorry for him. Deep down, they envy him. No longer to think, no longer to remember, no longer to know the desolating apprehension of an unexpected noise, a hand on the shoulder of someone who suddenly looks at you as if they understand you—what deliverance!

"Undoubtedly, they're odious, and they're dirty, in the great courtyards with regularly spaced trees, those wandering with extinct eyes and mechanical gestures, those sitting with the head between the knees, drooling, or, in padded cells, those fanatics who are biting the bars with bestial teeth. But they have forgotten! They no longer know what they are doing! And even those who are suffering do not know from what they are suffering, the frightful sickness of oneself, slow, continuous, disastrous remorse.

"Truly, I dare not criticize your contemporaries, Monsieur de Maël-Parbaix, for aspiring to that living annihilation. I even wonder sometimes whether someone would be culpable who, having discovered a sure means of abolishing the personality of a human being without killing him, did not refuse him that abominable cure. For they are so unhappy! And in spite of the lies in which they are obstinate, in spite of the hypocrisies of their laughter, their amours, their endeavor, in spite of the feigned resemblance of their despair to pleasure, oh, how they would rush, like country folk marveling at a plumed empiric, if there suddenly emerged in the midst of one of their fêtes a merchant of a drug that drives one mad; how rapidly they would throw away their fortunes, their titles, their renown and the beauty of their mistresses, as those peasants their copper coins, in order to pay the vendor of eternal forgetfulness!"

While Dr. Urbain took pleasure in these declamations—speaking in the box as if in a professorial chair—Monsieur de Maël-Parbaix, who was no longer listening, scarcely hearing, because he had finally become bored, turned toward a forestage box, which two women had just entered.

"Look," he said, "there's a person who gives the lie to your ill-tempered theory, in a singular fashion. More than any other living creature, she has dared to transgress what you call human law. She is Sin and Scandal. And look what a serenity of proud joy illuminates her face! There is something feverish, it's possible, perhaps disquieting, in the gaiety of all those Parisiennes and Parisians; but she displays the imperturbable peace of tranquil consciences."

"Are you talking about Madame d'Hermelinge?" the doctor asked.

II

Baronne Sophor d'Hermelinge was, indeed, there, in that box, with Céphise Ador, and she was magnificently triumphant.

All the other women, very décolleté, were displaying their shoulders and their cleavages; she was not. Her taut black satin dress, rising all the way to the neck, opened over a white pique vest, gripping the solid slenderness of her hips and upper body; and beneath a toque similar in color and fabric to the dress, a few short curls, brown and tawny, protruded. Her eyes, small, and round, were sparkling in the pale face like furbished steel. Her lips, which she bit at times, had the redness of a recent wound. No jewels, either in her ears or on her wrists; only rings, heavy and broad, on the index fingers of the long hands, devoid of gloves, with which she was gripping the edge of the box. And with her gaze, her attitude, she was challenging . . . who?

Everyone. But it was more than a challenge: it was a provocation to outrage, with a superb scorn at the ready. She had a curl of the lip toward the cheek from which a sort of arrogance seemed to emerge, and a riposte. She invited and mocked insult. And she breathed broadly, her face expanded in a proud smile, every time sections of the crowd directed glances toward her that designated her and whispers that recounted. She opposed to curiosities the "thus it is" of revolt that does not lower its eyes and plants its fist on its hip.

She divined, she knew, that those women and those men were talking about her, listing in whispers the details of the extraordinary adventure with which she had astonished Paris for six years; who, then, could have been unaware—since it was brazenly and gloriously admitted—the furious strangeness of her amours without lovers? It pleased her that no one was unaware of it. She took pride in being singular and detestable.

At the commencement of damnation, that pride is the assistance of the Devil. When a few individuals pointed at Céphise Ador, the beautiful actress who was sitting, her arms and breasts offered, so radiantly while beneath the sunlit avalanche of her hair next to Baronne d'Hermelinge, the latter was even more impudently triumphant, and, pretending to forget all the other presences, she possessed, one might have thought, with her fixed gaze, as grasping as hands and kisses on the lips, that beautiful flesh of warm snow, which blossomed.

Sometimes she leaned toward her friend, suddenly quivering; one divined that with an inhalation, through the hair and the fabric, she was savoring that body. She rejoiced in the redoublement of scandal. If Céphise Ador, with a mute prayer, had not retained her, Barone d'Hermelinge would have stood up, would have carried her to the back of the box, after the arrogance toward the entire fête, of a gaze that confirms and proclaims. She seemed a species of strange goddess, who took pleasure in scorn and hated and glorified in the incense of insults.

Looking at her from a distance, one person seemed to be suffering cruelly. That was a little creature sitting in an armchair of the amphitheater, dainty and not very pretty, withered but not old, with the crumpled air of an artificial flower on which someone has stepped. She was not very well-dressed, in a ball gown that had served others, lent by a comrade or hired from some cloths-merchant.

Who was that that small, poorly-clad creature, then?
Magalo.

Through a piece of lace that she had pulled down to the middle of her face, one could have seen shining, at the end of the lashes, a tear that was about to fall, and sometimes, she put a handkerchief to her mouth, very rapidly, which she bit in order not to cry out.

But Sophor paid no heed to that dolorous little creature. She reigned, radiantly. Even when they paused on the nudity of shoulders and breasts, her eyes remained hard, their imperious mastery unsoftened. They took possession, it seemed, of beautiful creatures, not saying: "Would you like . . . ?" but "I want." No plea. They were tyrannical, not admitting that anyone could escape them: the gaze of a conqueror over the multitude of the vanquished, who belong to him; of Don Juan over a feminine crowd, who will belong to him.

And many women were troubled, blushing, a little breathless; they felt unfastened, undressed, by the pointed jets of those eyes, as if by fiery fingernails; unconsciously, they made the gesture of bringing fabrics over them, turning in another direction.

A very beautiful person of the corps de ballet of the Opéra, famous for the audacity of the flesh outside her corset, sleeves that did not cling and the impudent offer of bushy armpit, closed her elbows rapidly as she passed close to Sophor, because she had sensed, under her arm, the sharp burn of a glance.

Now, increasingly, the attention of the crowd was aimed, obstinately, at that forestage box. People were astonished, people were frightened, of Baronne d'Hermelinge, but they saw no one but her, they were occupied with no one but her. Finally, in spite of the scorn, the anger, everything there was, in so many men, at that moment of the fête, desires toward breasts, toward arms, toward mouths, needs for tearing and needs for tucking up, scattered lusts, flowed toward Sophor like flames precipitating toward a more powerful hearth, like currents combining in a whirlpool; all that concupiscence she absorbed, along with the air charged with the odors of women; she lit up her eyes with them; she swelled her breast with them; and the universal heat converging in her only exasperated the passionate effluvia with which, soon turning toward her friend, she enveloped, surrounded and embraced Céphise Ador, so white and so plump, everything offered and everything taken, and who, her eyes lowered, palpitating, would have liked to veil with her hair her beautiful, throbbing and moist breasts.

Meanwhile, Urbain Glaris, leaning on the edge of the box, was no longer talking, observing Baronne Sophor d'Hermelinge with eyes full of an intense reverie.

"How silent you are, doctor, all of a sudden," said Monsieur de Maël-Parbaix. "Can your theory not respond to these living objections: the happiness and the pride of that monstrous creature?"

Then Urbain Glaris said: "Yes, full of joy, in fact, and superb. And her joy is not lying: no rancor, no hidden agenda; that woman seems very well in her ignominy, like certain beasts that are adapted to mephitic air."

After a pause, he added: "But that health, by virtue of its very excess, denounces that, while being sincere, it is not true. In the course of certain maladies, there are exuberances of force and life—grave symptoms; the patient, who does not believe that he is suffering, borrows from the exaltation of the fever that he does not feel, a kind of delirious spirit. But soon, like a fallen rag, the entire being collapses, limp and flaccid; and two empty eyes which are fearful, gaze without seeing anything.

"Look, she's getting up, she's taking her friend away with an arm around her waist, like a husband with a wife; she's beautiful, all in black satin, with that very blonde and very pale woman whom she is enlacing. She is challenging Paris, which, in sum, reproves and is indignant, with a final gaze, and, regal in the arrogance of her vain virility, she magnifies her shame with so much audacity that a kind of glory surrounds her. Well . . ."

"Well?" asked Monsieur de Maël-Parbaix.

Doctor Urbain went on:

"In walks through the nocturnal city, toward unknown haunts, in quarters of poverty and crime—walks otherwise devoid of interest, counseled by ennui and the disappointment of so many other curiosities, have you suddenly seen, at some street corner or on a bench near a stream, or near the glazed door of a tavern painted blood-red, some old lady with her arms dangling, her head tilted forward, her tongue sticking out of her mouth—not very old, but with the air of a centenarian—staggering forward, holding out her hand toward you, stammering as if about to vomit, showing you, beneath a knotted handkerchief from which dirty wisps of her protrude, her face carved with pale wrinkles, with a gray moustache, in which two little crimson and yellow eyes are bleeding, like ulcerous holes?

"That old woman, frequent in the outlying streets along the fortifications, is the supreme point at which feminine decline stops, in the impossibility of going any further; it is the end of the ugly and the vile, the body more hideous than a cadaver, the intelligence more soiled and more annihilated than a rag trampled in the mud, the inutility of life."

"Pooh!" said Monsieur de Maël-Parbaix.

"Well," concluded Urbain Glaris, the prophet of bad taste, "I swear to you that before long, Baronne Sophor d'Hermelinge, who is twenty-five years old, who is beautiful, who bears a name that is almost glorious, who has an income of two hundred thousand livres, who, this evening, happy and furious, is taking her mistress away and launching against Paris entire, with a royal insolence, the challenge of infamous amours, will, in her desolate desire for a little less self-disgust, envy that old drunkard of the back streets, tottering and falling over, ready to render her soul, along with her wine, in the mud of a street corner."

III

The day after the irremediable night, Sophie woke up first. So weary, she moved slowly, her eyes vague beneath eyelids that were scarcely raised and fell back very quickly; and in a languid idleness she could not recover full possession of herself. Half-awake and half-asleep, like a bird caught in a trap, flapping one wing while the other is still captive. She did not know that she had quit the wooden house on the island; she did not recall the disappearance or Emmeline or encountering Magalo, but she felt strangely troubled, by distress and delight, as if after a dream that had been very cruel and had then been very pleasant.

Finally, she opened her eyes wide. Was she still dreaming? She did not recognize the room. Everywhere, appeased by the pale light through the curtains, brightly colored silks and small objects, ivory and porcelain, on the furniture, amid the disorder of scattered lace and ribbons; at the foot of the bed, two dresses laid out, which might have been mistaken in the semi-darkness for two women lying there.

From all those things an insipid and warm perfume emanated, delightfully sickening. And that perfume, it seemed to Sophie, did not only come from the hangings, the trinkets and the lying dresses; it also came from herself. She had it on her hands, on her lips, in her unkempt hair, everywhere about her, as if she had slept in furs that had that odor.

My God, what had happened? Where was she?

And she had scarcely emerged from that lassitude, as enlacing as a caress when she uttered a cry. She had just seen beside her, on the other pillow, an odd and pretty face, which was asleep, with a crease of laughter, the mouth open in a pink roundel. She threw herself toward the wall.

But Magalo, woken up like a bird leaping from a branch, had seized her by the neck, brushed her eyes, temples and nose with little moues, and there were a thousand stammered words, tender and delicate, thanking her and complimenting her.

"No, as genteel as you, there's never been one, ever! Oh, baby, I adore you. Say whether you love me, say it, say it, then. What? Not a word? There, perhaps it's because you were a little drunk yesterday, after the dinner that you wanted; me, I had no need of champagne to be mad. And for whom am I mad? For you, darling, for always. You want that, always? Hortense? No more Hortense. Your little one? No more little one. Both of them, let go. We don't care about the others. Turn your head so I can blow in your hair. Only, it's necessary to cut it, the hair; it's funnier, and it's the habit, and it will flatter me, because everyone, seeing you, with short hair, with me, will guess right away. I'm proud of you. You talk so well! You're so well brought

178

up! And yesterday evening, utterly innocent. True, you didn't know anything about anything, or put on a semblance. No, not a semblance? Then, with your friend on the island, nothing? The first was me? Well, my darling, I adore you!"

During this chatter, of a mouth so close to her mouth, Sophie remembered everything: her marriage—the horrible nuptial rape—the escape, the sojourn in the chalet, the impotent lust, the night next to Emmeline and the flight of the dear child, and Magalo in the railway carriage. Or rather, no, she only thought about Emmeline, and a horror of having betrayed her counseled her to get up and away. How ashamed she was to be in that bed! The awakening of a very chaste male lover who, after supper with comrades, allows himself to be persuaded to go home with a prostitute, has no more rancor than that of Sophie next to Magalo.

But other memories came to her. Since yesterday, so many delicious hours with terrible instants! All the knowledge revealed, and so quickly acquired! And the employment, finally, of all her being in the extraordinary delight for which she had always hoped without conceiving the exquisite and almost frightful accomplishment! Immediately, from the first example—not like someone learning but like someone suddenly recovering her memory—she had understood, dared, realized, and, eyes burning with gazes, nostrils burning with odors, mouth full of inhaled breath, with the recklessness of swoons, with cries and stammers, as crazy as a troop of honey-eating beasts precipitated upon a beehive, she had subjugated, tamed Magalo, had reduced her to the tears that asked for mercy and did not want to be granted.

And now, this morning, from all of Magalo's little person, quivering and shivering so close to her, rose, with the odor of musk and Levantine tobacco, the reek of the night's abandonments; and because Sophie sensed the warm amber skin on her skin, she no longer thought about anything but the ecstasies of the night, which were offered again; and, the tension of her femininity exalted to the point of virile energy, she clutched Magalo, all of her, all over her, proudly maddened by that slender, slippery and supple form, which obeyed the mold of the embrace, those thin little bones, which she sensed cracking in spasms, as if broken in her arms.

It was done; she had fallen into the sin to which the law of mysterious atavisms, if not some diabolical providence, had destined her; and she would not reemerge. Ill or possessed, she was vanquished. She would not have been able to resist; she accepted her destiny, she wanted it.

And amid caresses, they agreed that they would live together henceforth; yes, Sophie and Magalo together—so different, however: one a demoiselle of a good family, who retained, even in the vehemence of desire, the bearing and speech of bourgeois education; the other, a suburban gamine, corrupted in childhood, a dancer in a music hall, who exercised at home in the morning, the tip of her bare foot at eye-level, and who, knowing all the vile words, pronounced them.

Those words—and it is the condemnation, and one of the punishments, of lust that, in order to express itself and name its implements, it has only been able to find the filthiest terms— Sophie dreaded and detested, not consenting to proffer them, and yet unable to hear them, even without fully understanding them in the beginning, without warmth moistening her eyes beneath her fluttering eyelids.

One grave question was of deciding whether they were going to rent a larger apartment or whether they would stay in Magalo's.

"Why change?" said the prostitute. "It's nice here, isn't it? And we don't need two bedrooms, do we? Well, if we had two, there'd be one that would hardly be used, for sure!"

With that, she burst out laughing; and they did not move.

"You'll see that it'll be very nice, all alone. Other women, they're not necessary. If the comrades come to see me, I'll shut the door in their faces. You can't receive them, you're too decent. And you can count on me not setting foot in Madame Charmeloze's again! No, just the two of us. We'll never be apart. We'll go out together, dressed the same. We'll go everywhere, to the restaurant, to the theater—not to the dance hall, because of you. The society's too mixed in those places. Then, the others will make eyes at you, just to annoy me. I know them, the sluts. They'll be enraged when they know we're stuck. Stuck, eh—that's nice? You have no idea of the pleasure it gives me to have you here.

"You're laughing? Good, good, I see what you're thinking. You're telling yourself that I don't have much to complain about, in fact. Well, word of honor, I wasn't thinking about that. Yes, it's agreeable, surely, but there's something else, there's not only the sex, there's the love, there's the heart. I love you so much, you see. You have such good manners. You can't divine the effect that it has on me to be with you. It seems to me that I was a poor girl, a seamstress, a grisette, and that I've just married a prince. It will be jolly good, our life."

And life did, indeed, for days, for weeks, seem very sweet to them. Sophor, in whom some childishness persisted, was amused by everything: boulevards, which she had scarcely glimpsed in brief trips to Paris; dinners with dishes she did not know, with wines whose names she did not know; plays in little theaters, circuses and café-concerts, where the jokes in the songs often made her blush. But Magalo did not like taking her to see fantasy plays because once, as the Châtelet, she had noticed that Sophie was looking at the legs and breasts of the dancers with an indecent expression.

"You know, if you cheated on me . . . !"

But that was said while laughing. Jealous? No, she wasn't jealous. At least, she hadn't had the habit of being. It might be that it would come, one day or another.

What amused Sophor very much was going into clothes shops and jewelers. Not that she was a coquette; a very simple dress was sufficient for her, and she didn't wear any jewelry other than heavy gold rings without stones, men's rings. But it was a charming pleasure for her to buy rich fabrics, in bright colors, with flowers and gold, for Magalo, of which they made dressing gowns, earrings and necklaces, all the gleams that make a noise on the skin when one comes and goes beside the bed.

Those gifts Magalo accepted, even asked for, because of the habitude with men, among the merchants who gave a percentage to the person who prompted the sale; but when she had them, she seemed sad; it embarrassed her to have accepted something from Sophor.

To be maintained by Sophor, oh, no, no way. One day, she said to her: "You have money, good; I can't prevent you having money. But understand that you paying all the expenses isn't funny. You mustn't believe that I'm with you because you're rich. So, if you were good, if you wanted to give me pleasure—what do you expect, I'm proud, one can't remake oneself—you'll let me go out alone in the evening from time to time. Oh, you don't imagine, I think, that I'd go back to Hortense, or Madame Charmeloze's? No more! But, you understand, at the Peters, at the Helder, I have friends . . ."

She fell silent under a violent gaze on Sophie's part, and did not dare mention her project again. But she said to herself: *Well, they won't last forever, your thousand-franc bills, and then I'll be content, because it will be necessary for you to let me do what I want; you'll see that I'm not interested, nor ingrate.*

She had that delicacy—as much as she could have, poor girl. And why? Because she loved Sophor. Yes, she loved her, entirely, veritably. "You're so pretty, with your hair, which is red and black, and your little blazing eyes, and your skin, different from other skin, no make-up, an honest skin."

Then too, along with that tenderness, a sort of respect was mingled, which made her more serious, more profound. If Magalo talked to her friend with familiarity, it was because she had acquired, in the times of the others, the habitude of camaraderie, and because, being shrewd as well, she took account of the fact that it did not displease Sophor, that girlish chatter with indecent words, very funny—on the contrary, it tickled her. There are also men, very young ones, who like that. But truly, she was sometimes embarrassed to be so free and easy with her; at times she had a desire say *vous* to her. Not when they were in bed, of course; oh, then, one is what one is; one certainly doesn't pay attention to what one is saying when one no longer knows what one is doing. But, dressed, she respected her, without letting it show too much, and she experienced a very tender gratitude to that person from high society who had wanted to come with her, who lodged with her, and who went out with her.

At the same time, she admired her. Sophor spoke so correctly, in sentences like those in books. And she was so knowledgeable! One could ask her no matter what question, and she wasn't embarrassed. At the theater, she explained things about which Magalo had never thought. She knew the ancient history that characters talked about in dramas. Once they listened to an operetta, very gay and very amusing, with tunes that made one want to dance. Magalo was very astonished to hear Sophor say that the music was stupid, but she didn't raise any objection; she admitted that the music was, in fact, stupid. Her friend couldn't be mistaken.

Such was her humble amour. And she testified that amour by a thousand tender cares. It was her who washed Sophie, with the enormous sponge, in the tub, combed her hair, laced her corset, not only because of an amorous mischief that wanted to profit from the toilette in order to kiss the top of a shoulder damp with perfumed water, or to see her breasts swell in the overflow of whalebone; no, it pleased her to be her friend's maidservant, her chambermaid.

"Don't call Antoinette, let me button your boots, I beg you."

At that remark, Sophie had reveries that the other could not comprehend. As they went out, Magalo knotted the strings of her capote herself, and said to her: "You haven't forgotten anything? Do you want to take a mantle? I'll carry it, so that it doesn't inconvenience you, and you can put it on this evening, if it gets cold."

Then, at dinner, it was always her who served, and if the waiter was slow in coming, she even got up to take the bread or the plate from a neighboring table. And it delighted her that Sophor seemed content with that kindness. Merely by a "Thank you, darling," Magalo was so moved that she felt her eyes moistening, and in order not to weep she tried to laugh.

Did Sophie love Magalo? No, or doubtless very little, even though she showed herself jealous to the point of wanting to hit her and to insult her, if, in the street or the theater, the little slut looked at someone too attentively; the jealousy of a miser rather than a lover. Certainly, there was no resemblance between the sentiment that she felt now and that she had known with Emmeline. But she was cheered by that frivolity, incessantly awake, moved by that tenderness, always ready for caresses, infatuated with that submission, which, for being so feminine, made her, Sophor, more masculine. Then there were the frenzied enchantments of the nocturnal hours, the acceptance, weeping with delight, of her insatiable kisses, her pleasure exalted by a radiant pride in the certainty of being able, her, a woman, to constrain a woman to perfect hymens; she palpated in the glory of conquest in hearing Magalo scorn the virile embrace, in preferring hers, and then she loved her, in giving her so much joy.

However, sadnesses came to her, and came to her more frequently after the first weeks. She remembered the friend of childhood, lost. Was her regret augmented by the chagrin of not having revealed to her the unsuspected intoxications, now known? No, the knowledge that she had acquired, she did not dream of sharing with Emmeline. It was not that, in the docilities of Magalo, her desire for the pure child relented—many a time, Magalo heard her stammer a name that was not her own—but it seemed to Sophor, in reveries that were not very precise, that the things in which she had been instructed were not those that

184

Emmeline ought to know, that those obscure mysteries were different, distant from her, and did not concern her.

She did not repent of her delightful conquests, nor judge herself culpable; on the contrary, she experienced the ease of developing in accordance with her nature; and she wished that all women might be similar to her—all except one; Emmeline was not like the others, ought not to become like the others. Sophor was almost happy to have spared the virgin abandoned by virtue of ignorance. If it had been given to her to go back, to see her again as she had had her, on the bed in the wooden house, she would have striven, in spite of the pressure of covetousness, to forget all that she had learned, in order not to teach it.

But her love for the absentee was no less great for having been purified in the very experience of sin, and very often, in the amusements of walks, dinners and the theater, and even nocturnal delights, she thought about the preserved child. Only, she did not want to see her again on the island, in the perilous hours of solitude; she distanced the memory of the bare feet in the stream, of the dear sacred body on the bed, which would have been sacrilege. Of their amity, she only evoked the puerile candors, the games in the gardens; she was even afraid of thinking about their excessively passionate devotions, and the excessively ardent musical evenings.

Since she had had Magalo, she constrained herself not to desire of Emmeline that which she now knew that she had once desired of her, unconsciously. She accepted the realized joys for herself, but not for the innocent creature. If she had believed herself to be diabolical, she would have been able to compare herself to a demon having pity for an angel. But her memories were no less cruel for being chaste, and many a time, her dreams were melancholy. She was like a young man, very smitten with a beautiful and amorous girl, who thinks with a bitter tenderness about a fiancée returned to the country, whom he left pure, and whom he will not marry.

Those fits of sadness, Magalo perceived, and because Sophie had told her the whole story, she knew that her friend was thinking about Emmeline, unable to help it. That caused her great chagrin. When, on her knees before Sophor, motionless and her eyes half-closed in a dream, she took her hands and tried, with her chatter, to make her smile, and could not even make herself heard, a desolation constricted her heart, and she could hardly hold back her tears—but there was almost no jealousy, and no anger at all.

She recognized that she was such a little thing, compared to Emmeline, who must, like Sophor, be a very well brought up demoiselle. She did not feel that she had the right to be jealous: her, a slut, nothing at all. It is necessary to see oneself as one is. Well, yes, she had a heavy heart; nothing is sadder than not being loved by someone that one loves so much, but it was natural that Sophor had tenderness for the other, who was prettier, and honest.

It's already very kind of her to stay with me, not to scorn me.

Such was that little creature, very humble in spite of her bold airs, very simple in spite of her shrewdness, corrupt and ingenuous, a depraved child whose soul had remained tender. But a right that she had was to suffer from Sophor's dolor; and the latter, after hours when she had not embraced Magalo, or even said a word to her, often found her sitting in an armchair in the living room, her head in her hands, sobbing, the poor tormented child.

"You're crying? What's the matter? Have I done something to hurt you?"

"No, no, nothing, it's nothing. It's my nerves. It's over."

And Magalo laughed, with moist eyes.

✳

Once, having gone out to book a box at the Varietés, Magalo did not come back in the evening, and Sophie was gripped by a rage. She remembered! Magalo had talked, one day, about resuming her old life, because of money, of going to Peters' or the Helder, where she had friends. Perhaps she had gone back to Hortense, or to Madame Charmeloze? At that moment she might be letting some man who had offered her supper take her by the waist, or be sitting on the knee of some woman who was kissing her on the neck.

The idea of Magalo, who was hers, being touched and caressed by others exasperated her, made her march from one wall to the other, her fists clenched. Twenty times she was on the point of going out to look for her in those restaurants or at the whores' homes. She would have taken her by the arm with the brutality of a man of the people dragging his mistress away. "What are you doing? Come on, go home." And on the way, she would have beaten her, as one beats a dog that has run away. But those restaurants, she was not sure on what street or boulevard they were located; and she did not know the address of either Hortense or Madame Charmeloze. Then, the hope that Magalo might still return counseled her not to go out, to wait. She listened for the sound of fiacres, for the bell at the coaching entrance, for footsteps on the stairs.

Magalo did not come back.

Until daylight, not undressed, Sophie waited on the bed with her elbow on the pillow, her eyes fixed on the vision of her friend lying in another bed.

She fell asleep as the morning light filtered into the room through the curtains—a sleep shaken by nightmares, with teeth sometimes grinding behind drawn-back lips.

The sound of a door closing woke her with a start.

"Where have you been, wretch?"

But Magalo had already thrown herself into her arms and was weeping hot tears on Sophor's shoulder.

"Oh, don't scold me, don't scold me, I beg you. I swear to you that I haven't done anything bad. I couldn't tell you where I was going because you would have stopped me going. Perhaps you thought I was with a man, or a woman? Oh, how foolish you are—I love you so much. I haven't done anything wrong, I tell you. Don't scold me, my baby."

Then the other, pushing her way: "Where have you been?"

"I have nothing to hide from you; I'll tell you everything. I've seen, for a long time, that you were thinking about the little one, the little one from the island. You still love her. I don't hold it against you. You must have noticed that I don't hold it against you. I understand things, and I don't have any illusions. If you have me, it's for pleasure. She's something else. Anyway, you were sad because you didn't have news of her, because you couldn't go in search of her because of your mother and your husband, who would have kept you. So, what you couldn't do, I've done."

"You! You've been to Fontainebleau!"

And a fury took possession of Sophie. That girl had dared to think about Emmeline! Had seen her, had perhaps talked to her! She almost hurled herself upon Magalo. But the latter was looking at her with such great tenderness, with such a pleading, humble expression, of a dog that does not want to be beaten and yet would consent to be.

Sophor told herself that she was very hard, very bad, to the poor child who had not thought that she was doing anything wrong. And then—dominating all the other sentiments—there was the desire to have news of Emmeline; and, very quickly:

"All right, I don't hold it against you. Speak, speak quickly: what have you learned?"

Magalo threw her arm around her neck.

"Truly? For sure? You don't hold it against me? You're not annoyed? Oh, my God, how kind you are!"

But she did not stop weeping, because it was not good news that she had brought. This was it. She had left for Fontainebleau on the seven-thirty train. When she arrived there was no one in the streets; it was too late to seek information. She had slept in the hotel near the station. In the morning, she had asked questions, of anyone, of passers-by. As, in provincial towns, everyone knows everything, it wasn't difficult for her to find Mademoiselle Emmeline's house; she said Mademoiselle expressly.

"Oh, I hadn't, as you can imagine, any intention of going into that house. Me, I can't be received in bourgeois houses, noble houses. But chatting with the neighbors, with servants going out to go to market, I can do that without any impropriety."

That was what she had done. Well, the tobacco merchant three doors away asked for nothing better than to say what she knew, and hadn't taken long to tell her everything.

"Well, what did she say? What did she tell you?"

"Oh, my poor Sophor, my poor Sophor! A few days after Mademoiselle Emmeline's return, your husband left with his sister and his maman, and they didn't say where they were going, and no one knows what has become of them. Even Madame Luberti's domestics don't think that they'll ever come back, because Baron Jean, as they call him, summoned a notary on the eve of his departure and he signed documents to enable you, his wife, to be able to direct your affairs and dispose of your fortune, as if he were dead."

Sophor, her eyes moist, murmured: "She's gone, gone . . ."

It seemed to her, knowing that she was further away from her, that she had lost Emmeline for a second time.

"Is that all you were told?" she asked. "You don't know anything more?"

Magalo turned her head away, stammering, hesitantly: "No, no . . . I assure you . . . nothing more . . ."

"You're lying!"

The little prostitute burst into tears. "I beg you, don't be chagrined, don't do yourself harm. It appears—you know that domestics listen at doors—that if Baron Jean took Mademoiselle Emmeline away, it's to marry her immediately, far from Fontainebleau, far from Paris. He had the intention of leaving France, after his sister's wedding, asking for service in the regiments that are in the Colonies, because he had a great deal of chagrin and anger because of you. And now, Mademoiselle Emmeline's marriage must be made, at present."

Emmeline married! Emmeline in the arms of a man!

In Sophor's head, and in her heart, it was as if claws were scratching. Married! Which is to say, possessed, tortured, that dear pretty delicate body—as she had been herself—by the brutality of the male!

Faint with pity, Sophor fell into an armchair. Then, suddenly, she went horribly pale. She thought—and it was more frightful than the idea of Emmeline tortured—she thought that her darling, in the conjugal bed, might be happy. Perhaps she liked the tearing caresses and the oppressive embrace. The joys that Sophie had been unable to give her, that she would not have dared to give her now, Emmeline might accept, and desire, from a man. She might be delighted and charmed and dying of ecstasy in the arms of a husband, like Magalo in Sophor's arms! Oh, that idea was intolerable, lacerated her and devoured her.

She turned toward Magalo. She cried, in an enraged hatred: "What are you doing here? What do you want? Get out. The cause of everything is you. You'd do well to get out and never come back, I have a desire to kill you. If you hadn't talked to me, in the carriage, if you hadn't intoxicated me with your nasty-smelling perfume, I'd have returned to Fontainebleau. I might have been able to live with Emmeline if I hadn't had you. I detest you, because you consoled me. Yes, I'd have gone home, in order to see her again. My mother? My husband? I wouldn't have cared about them. One can't lock a woman in her bedroom as in a prison; and then, locked up, it wouldn't have mattered, I'd have been living near my darling, and they couldn't have prevented me from hearing her voice through the walls. By leaning out of the window, I'd have been able to see her going through the garden, I'd have made signs to her, and she'd have smiled at me. And my husband wouldn't have been able to take her away without taking me away too. That way, no more marriage for her. I'd have given him a fine reception, the suitor who came! Then, one day—yes, it would have finished like this—I would have found a means of taking Emmeline away, so far, so far way that they'd never have found us, and she wouldn't have quit me this time, because I'd have kept good guard. Oh, I wouldn't have loved her as you've taught me to love. She's not one of those with whom one takes pleasure, as one eats when one's hungry, as one drinks when one's thirsty. I would adore her with prayers and hands that rise up without touching! We'd have been more content than the married angels are in heaven. But you, you took me away from her; because of you, I almost forgot; and she's married, a man has her, is keeping her, and won't let her go! She loves that man. Everything that I didn't have of her, she's giving it to him, she's content to be a wife! And without you, she wouldn't be one. It's you who've put her in her husband's bed. Get out! I hate you! Yes, I hate you, because of my desire for you, because of the pleasures I owe to you, above all because of the pleasures I've given you, since I know, thanks to you, what Emmeline is also experiencing, with someone else!"

Sophie marched toward Magalo, menacingly.

But the latter did not turn away, was not frightened by that fit of temper, not irritated by those insults. She wept, in little sobs, that was all, having nothing but sadness because of her friend's pain.

"Oh, my God! Oh, my God!" she said. "My baby, my darling, how you're suffering!"

She would even have liked Sophor to beat her, to dig her fingernails into her neck, to tear all her body, because maltreating someone relieves a person who is angry; it is even better than breaking furniture or smashing porcelain.

Besides which, there was perhaps a little cunning mingled with her abnegation—but such a tender cunning. In order to do someone harm, it's necessary to touch them, isn't it? And she knew full well that Sophor, touching her, wouldn't remain in a bad mood for long. Well, one knows oneself. One knows what one is worth. A skin like the one she had, and an odor like the perfume that was only hers, changes people's ideas quickly.

Clutching her friend like a child clinging to the skirts of an angry mother, extending her lips, she would have liked nothing better than to be grabbed and bitten, since that rude handling would quickly have turned into enlacement and kisses, and after the brutalities, she would have consented without rancor to caresses, not because of the pleasure—oh, she had far too much chagrin to think about that—but because it would be good for Sophor to be nasty, it would console her more than being gentle.

She therefore offered herself, seductively, to blows, to wounds, in order that Sophor, finally, exasperated by the tender challenge of that sacrifice, would pick her up, with I know not what crazy need to throw her out of the window, to crush her against the wall, or to use her body to batter down the doors by which she would flee toward Emmeline.

But because she felt her friend's heart beating, because of the eyelids palpitating over those tearful eyes consenting to everything, because in the efforts of that almost fight, a warmth, from one as from the other, would emerge and mingle them in their confounded emanations, Sophor threw on the bed, her shirt and voice torn, the dainty creature sighing without complaint, fell upon her to strangle her—and kissed her. She bit her everywhere, furiously, delectably. It was the extraordinary joy of the kiss that would like to lacerate, the embrace that would like to stifle.

Never had Sophor wanted so intensely that creature whom she hated for the first time. For the desire ignited by anger, as by despair, stimulates lust! And hatred and amour exasperate one another until both succumb in a common annihilation.

❋

Sophor and Magalo resumed their life as before. There was never any question between them of that bad moment. With a common accord, they wanted to forget it. Was Sophie no longer anxious about Emmeline, then? Did the horror of knowing that she was married, or near to being, not haunt her days with bitter reveries or her nights with nightmares?

She seemed tranquil, laughed with Magalo, went out at the customary hours—one of Magalo's joys was that they had a coupé to go to the Bois, where people saw them! And, in truth, a peace had descended on Sophie. She was no longer angry with anyone. Weary of the initial horrors, or resigned, she told herself that destiny had arranged things well. Emmeline, by virtue of the separation—by marriage, alas—would find herself out of range of Sophie's desire, which was better for the poor child, destined for calm joys. She would not pursue her, would leave her tranquil in the distance. Certainly, she would suffer, she would suffer for a long time, always, from not seeing her; but she wanted to sacrifice herself to Emmeline's happiness, and she did, indeed, sacrifice herself.

At least she had the conviction of her sacrifice, so natural and pleasant is it to give as a motive for what one is doing or what one is experiencing a sentiment of which one can be proud. Sophor did not even ask herself whether it might be to her contentment with Magalo that she owed her resignation in Emmeline's regard. And the two of them, Sophor and Magalo, were content, with occasional sadnesses that they did not admit to one another, and which vanished quickly—in sum, content.

But one morning, sitting beside the bed, Magalo cried: "Ah! Do you know that you're pregnant?"

Sophor did not understand, and, pulling away her arms—less thin, because she had become a little plumper in the idleness of satisfied desire—she murmured, yawning: "Are you up already? Did you say something? What did you say?"

And she would have gone back to sleep if Magalo had not said: "Well, I said that you're pregnant."

Sophie d'Hermelinge leapt out of bed. Her, pregnant! How? Pregnant? She put her hands on her friend's shoulders, looked her in the eyes and said: "You're joking, aren't you? Come on, say again. I'm mistaken, you didn't say . . . ?"

"Yes, yes, I said it, and it's sure, unless I'm ill, or you're not made like others. That's possible, but it isn't probable. Well, think, for three months . . . I know, though. At first, I didn't want to talk to you about it. I thought that it would annoy you. Then, the first time, that doesn't prove anything, but now . . ."

Sophor repeated the frightful word as if she had not understood what it signified. She pulled herself together, pushing away the wisps of her short hair from her forehead and her eyes.

"Come on, pregnant by whom?"

"Oh, not me, for sure—by your husband, stupid. Do you think it isn't sufficient to have a baby, what you've told me?"

Sophor fell full length on the carpet.

When Magalo had picked her up and carried her to the chaise-longue, they spoke together in low voices.

Sophor stammered: "Yes, yes, you're right, that's true." Then she fell silent.

But Magalo chattered: "What do you expect? It's necessary to expect these things. Me, I haven't had a baby because I started very young, with an old man, and because the men who go with us after a dance or supper aren't demanding. People think they're buying a woman? Not at all; they're hiring a bed. I've heard plenty of men snoring! Anyway, there are precautions. But you, you were married; your husband, who wanted you, didn't go to sleep, and what's happened is quite natural.

"That it's annoying, I don't say no, because one suffers a great deal, it appears. For that alone. Don't go imagining that afterwards, one has a belly with creases, or breasts that fall. Bourgeois wives, perhaps. They don't look after themselves. It's all the same to them to be pretty or not to be. What do they want their body for? They're honest women. It even pleases them that their husbands can always see that they've been mothers. They're like soldiers who don't hide their wounds; they'd like to be decorated for having had children. But us, giving birth doesn't change us.

"Look, Hortense—you know, I've told you about her—she's had four kids, three dead, one living; well, if you saw her you'd

194

say: that isn't possible! It's because she had a good midwife, a friend of Charmeloze, Mademoiselle Lavenelle, who knows what she's doing. With her, it's as if one hadn't had a kid. That woman could make a girl out of Mère Gigogne. So, don't worry. And if you suffer, you'll see how I look after you. I don't say that it will amuse me to go out with you when you look as if you've got a pillow under your skirt; that won't go with your short hair at all; too bad, we'll stay in the house. We won't get bored, will we, all alone? And I'll coddle you when you're ill, I'll give you things to drink that will do you good; when you scream, I'll scream louder, to make you laugh.

"Then, when it's all over, think how amusing it will be to have a baby, the two of us. We'll choose a nurse in the country, near Paris; we'll be able to go and see the kid every week, twice a week. It'll be pretty, of course, since it'll resemble you. I'd rather have a boy; boys are less affectionate, but they're more cheerful than little girls. And I promise that, boy or girl, it won't have anything to complain about. I'll pamper it, you'll see. I love it already, your little boy or girl. If it's a boy, we'll call him Rodolphe. That's my father's name, who was very honest.

"When the little fellow can walk, we'll take him out with us. We'll look like two mamans, and to have made him ourselves. That will be funny. Two mothers for one baby, with no papa! We'll say to people, laughing: 'We had him in the first year of our marriage.' No, really, it will be funny. And you know, it's not for laughing, I sense that I'll adore him, your child. I was wrong to talk about a nurse in the country. Never in this life! She'd let him die of hunger. We'll keep him at home, we'll have a cradle in our bedroom, and at night, I'll get up to give him something to drink."

But she stopped talking, because of Sophor's eyes. She was sitting with her fists between her knees, her eyes cold and ferocious, like murderous steel. Magalo had never seen such a gaze, so full of inexorable hatred. She understood everything that she might say, everything that she might do, would not prevent Sophor from having that desperate and atrocious gaze. Without adding a word, without waiting for a "Leave me alone, go away!" she stood up, crossed the room, lifted a door-curtain and disappeared. She felt useless, divining that if she stayed she would become odious. Evidently, something was happening in her friend's soul of which she could not take account; she had been wrong to try and console her.

Alone, Sophor looked at the carpet with those frightful eyes.

So, veritably, pregnant. She had in her body a being—perhaps a man—that a man had put there, and since that was so, it could not henceforth be different. She would give birth; she would be like other women who gave birth, who nurse, who rock a cradle; what there was in her different from other women would be thwarted, annulled. The husband had not limited himself to stifling her and lacerating her; he had pushed his brutal and detested triumph as far as engendering in the violated womb. The extraordinary desires beyond human normality had not saved her from the common fate; a virgin in love with a virgin, she had been made into a wife; a wife who had escaped in vain; she would be the mother of a family; desirous of ardent sterility, she would be fecund; and a living thing would emerge from her entrails, which would proclaim the nuptial kiss. To bear the virility within herself for long months, after having been torn, and to emit it in the most frightful tearing!

That excess of the defeat was intolerable. She started to march between the furniture, full of furious projects. No, she would not give birth. She would not accept that resemblance with female animals. Die? So be it. Give birth? No.

For a moment, her fury calmed down in the hope that Magalo might be wrong, might have spoken stupidly. Alas, instructed now regarding sexual laws, she could not deny the evidence; she was heavy with an impending humanity. But she would not allow the fruit of the execrable semen to develop; she would not admit her maternalized femininity, would not hear the cry of a newborn.

It was not the horrors of the parturition she feared; in order not to bring a child into the world she would have consented to dolors a hundred times worse. She did not want to be a mother, that was all, because she was not a woman. It was to females smitten with males that fecundity was appropriate. A crime, then? Yes. And nothing was more just. A crime for a crime. Had she not been the victim of the most abominable violence on the night when Baron Jean had carried her away and crushed her on the conjugal bed? For evil she would return evil. She had been tortured; she would kill.

And then, criminal or not, it did not matter, the action she was premeditating was necessary, inevitable. Have a child, her? No, no, no, it was absurd. Her entire being revolted against a function that was not hers; that nothing, not yet alive, which wanted to live, she would prevent from being born, even if she had to open up and rip apart her entrails with thrusts of a knife, even if she had to flatten her belly against a wall every day for months; and after all, it was not her fault if she was as she was!

But that wretch was not completely monstrous. A little light always persists in the most obscure sciences. After the folly of the first fears, she recovered her reason. She saw the abject horror of the crime that she had conceived. She sensed that she would be incapable of committing it. Anything, even a fecund womb, rather than the suppression of a life, even scarcely alive. She set aside the execrable temptation, with an indefectible determination, once and for all. She accepted the destiny, the catastrophe; since she was pregnant, she would be a mother, so be it.

But there were horrible days, weeks, months. She no longer went out, wandered silently from room to room, sat down, stood up, resumed marching with neither gestures nor words, all her faculties immobilized by the obsession of the fixed idea. She was going to give birth! She did not think about anything but that, only lived in the bleak despair of that expectation. In her, the hatred of maternity—more frequent, alas, than modern hypocrisy admits—increased and was consolidated, to conform logically with her other instincts; it was normal, because of their abnormality; an aberration legitimated by an aberration.

Magalo tried in vain to distract her friend; Sophor drew away with a movement of the arm, an unsmiling gaze, which did not permit persistence. And there was the incessant walking from one wall to the other. At meals—now they had their morning and evening meals at home—there was silence; with her elbow on the table and her head in her hand, Sophor gazed at the plate without seeing the meat that she did not touch; and in the evening, when it was raining or frosty, she opened a window and remained standing there, her hands on the sill, considering the passers-by, the carriages and the comings and goings of the Parisian crowd with an atonal gaze, and then the deserted street, or the reflection of the street-lights. She resembled someone no longer alive, a corpse, the lowering of whose eyelids had been forgotten, which had been propped up in the embrasure of a window.

She was thinking that she was going to put into the world the resemblance of a man, and anyone who had touched her during those moments would have recoiled in astonishment, so taut was her skin, as if frozen in a motionless shiver. From the bedroom, Magalo, in bed for a long time, called to her, saying: "Come on, baby, you're not being reasonable; come to bed, you'll catch cold." Sophor did not reply, pretending not to have heard. She sank ever more deeply into her bleak reverie.

And to think that other women awaited with enchantments the hour when they would be mothers, when a tiny creature would be born from them, adored already, who would be a little image of the husband; the more they loved the one who had given it to her, the more they loved it, and they rejoiced in advance at the first cry, the first smile, the hiccup between the lips and the blank slumber in the swaddling clothes.

One night, a voice ripped the air, a shrill yelp, the clamor of someone who sees a murderer emerging from underneath a table or from behind a curtain. Magalo leapt out of bed and ran into the next room, saw Sophor standing, her fingernails digging into the wood of the sill, her face as gray and cold as a disinterred corpse. She was no longer crying out, she was grinding her teeth.

"Do you want to kill yourself? Staying in the air, in that state! It's so cold. Come to bed, I beg you. Come on, what's the matter?"

Between the grating of her teeth, Sophor replied: "Nothing's the matter. I was frightened by a shadow on the house opposite. Leave me alone, I'm all right here."

What had wrung the cry from her was that, for the first time, she had felt something moving in her belly.

✳

An event deflected her from her anguish for a few days. She had to go to Fontainebleau because a note in the newspapers announced the sudden death of Madame Luberti; the old woman's notary had had the notice published in order that it might come to the attention of Madame d'Hermelinge, the daughter and unique heir of the deceased.

When Sophor descended from a carriage in the street on which the two houses stood, the funeral procession was setting forth for the nearby church, but what she saw first, with a rapid glance that seemed to her to carry her soul, through the gate, was the window on whose sill she had so often leaned with Emmeline—the window of a room now empty, alas. Emmeline had departed, she was married, but the house was still the same; nothing had changed in that door from which the darling had emerged, never to return.

Sophie was irritated by that indifference of things. But she loved the garden, desolated by the winter, as sad as she was. It was necessary to warn her that the procession was already turning the street corner. She hastened, in spite of the heaviness of her loins, which tugged at her. She caught up with the people behind the hearse and placed herself in the first rank, amid the whispers of the neighbors, who recognized her with her face inclined beneath a veil, and followed her.

She did not feel any grief at her mother's death. Perhaps, if she had seen her during her illness, if she had cared for her, kept vigil, held her in her arms at the moment of her last breath, she might have experienced some disturbance or chagrin now; she would at least have had a nervous lassitude that might have been mistaken for melancholy. But that coffin, which she had not seen filled, did not move her. It was as if she were accompanying, out of politeness, the body of someone from the neighborhood she scarcely knew. Only a hypocrisy counseled her to raise a handkerchief to her eyes.

Then, for the first time, she was traversed by a fear of herself. What was she, then, since the greatest disaster that one can suffer—the death of a mother—left her impassive; since the greatest happiness permitted to a woman—a husband's kiss—had been odious to her; since the most magnificent employment of life—the creation of a living being—was a cause of horror and hatred? Neither daughter, nor wife, nor mother, what was she, then?

But she knew very well what she was; she was the passionate lover of virgins and women, the triumphant rival of males, the searcher and giver of intoxications forbidden by the imbecile law of the sexes; everything that was not those delights or was not attached to them seemed to her to be superfluous, was even insupportable; she was an exclusive lover of love stolen from man, and in being so extraordinary, a pride inflated her breast and made her nostrils quiver. While between the black drapes of the church, over the meditation of the crowd kneeling before the catafalque surrounded by candles, the increasing tempest of the organ rumbled, the insolent memory and desire for beds full of whiteness under long hair caused her to raise herself up against the divine threat, and to the thunder of the *Dies irae*, the glory of her eyes launched the challenge of beautiful nights of joy.

After the funeral, in the office of the notary, things could not be concluded without too many delays; Sophie d'Hermelinge had to remain in Fontainebleau for a few days. Although Madame Luberti, surprised by death, had not made any testament and the authorizations left by Baron Jean, absent for several months—departed for the Senegal, it was supposed—were entirely in order, it was necessary to fulfill a certain number of formalities.

After a week, the orphan returned to Paris. She had an income of more than two hundred thousand livres.

The cares of those days and the initial dazzlement of the fortune had diverted her from the obsession, but, having returned to Magalo's apartment, she returned entirely to the dismal thought and was more profoundly wrapped around by it. In the rooms, there was the sinister impassive muteness, the gaze aimed at nothing, the relentless march.

Since she could not remedy that species of madness, Magalo had made the decision not to worry about it. Her friend, after giving birth, would return to what she had been before. And to pass the time, the little prostitute occupied herself with the layette. On all the furniture there was a disorder of white fabric and lace, with a great many blue or pink ribbons. He would arrive naked—it would definitely be a boy—but would soon be dressed; of embroidered baby-clothes ornamented with frills there were enough for five or six newborns; every day she cut, sowed and adjusted; she had bought a large doll, on which she tried out the small garments. When the little mannequin was clad in batiste and malines, coiffed in a ruche bonnet, she lifted it up in two hands toward the ceiling, moved around the room in a waltz rhythm, and, her lips laughing at the wax face: "Come on, Rodolphe, give us a smile!"

Of all that, Sophor did not see anything, or pretended not to see anything. With her continuing terrors, a new fear was mingled, aggravating them. She had heard it said, and had read, that of all human sentiments, maternal love is the most intense, the most ineluctable. A woman can detest the birth, and curse her fecund womb, but her child, as soon as it is born, she cherishes with passion, no longer wanting to quit it, snatching it back from everyone as if recovering a fragment of herself.

Sophor wondered, shivering, whether she might experience that instinctive amour. To her horror of physical maternity was added the apprehension of moral maternity. She belonged, she wanted to belong, so entirely and so absolutely to tyrannical and electable Desire, that she envisaged with terror the possibility of a sentiment that might deliver her from it. She feared the diversion of loving her child. At every lurch of her belly she was afraid, in an attentive observation of herself, of hearing a heartbeat of her own respond.

And time went by. Now a serious anxiety gripped Magalo, who had finally divined, albeit obscurely, that hatred against the child who was about to arrive. What would Sophor do, at the moment when the urgency of giving birth twisted her? It would be frightful, between two howls of pain, the malevolent fury of that mother who did not want to be a mother, and perhaps it would be necessary to hold her hands in order that she did not make a little cadaver of that newborn.

Vain anxiety. On the evening when Sophor felt herself gripped by pains, she went to bed without being aided, said in a placid voice: "Send for Mademoislle Lavenelle," and did not add another word, not even a glance of gratitude for the encouragements of Magalo, who hastened with the tenderness of a sister and the activity of a neighbor. Sophor showed the calm of a condemned individual resigned to suffering a torture, who submits to it without revolt, since it is necessary.

For many long hours, the torment did not wring a cry from her; the pride of her patience triumphed over the pain; one might have thought that she believed herself observed by someone who would render testimony of her stoical acceptance of the evil.

"No," said the midwife, "people like that I've never seen; one would swear that it isn't her who's giving birth."

There was no symptom of suffering except, at times, a frightfully rigid tension of the entire body and, from the temples to the chin, creases of the skin that confessed an effort not to howl.

But when the little being—a girl—was born, and when, entirely enveloped in frilly sheets, she was presented, limbs stirring, to the young woman buried in the torpor of relief, Sophor, whatever was done to retain her, raised herself up on her hands and gazed at her daughter avidly. One might have thought that her entire being was converging in that intense fixity, but it also seemed that she was listening for a word that was about to be spoken in a very low voice.

Yes, she was listening.

To whom? Herself.

She was interrogating herself: "That child, my child, will I love her?" And she awaited a response from herself. After a long silence in which no response came, she lay down again, tranquil, abominably reassured.

In the following days she remained immobile, her head on the pillow, very pale, her eyes closed. Magalo knew, undoubtedly, that women who have given birth are recommended not to move and not to speak, but that did not prevent them, as soon as the midwife or the nurse had turned her back, from chattering with their friends, and she was annoyed to see that Sophie was obeying the recommendation so sagely. She would have liked to chat and laugh, since the most annoying thing now was that there was no longer any reason to worry.

In truth, she had a somewhat heavy heart because, on the express order of the young mother, a woman who had been summoned from the nursing bureau had taken the little girl far away, to Touraine. All the lovely plans deranged! They would not be going for walks with the little one, both mamans. At least

Sophor would have talked to her; one can't live without talking to one another.

But Madame d'Hermeilnge retained her inert attitude, did not emerge from her silence, almost always seemed to be asleep. What was she thinking, in the inert solitude in which she had interned herself? Perhaps she had made a resolution that she would accomplish when the time came, from which she did not want to be distracted.

She accepted cares without paying any heed to them, not even responding with a gesture to the words: "Are you feeling all right? You're not in pain? Do you have everything you need?" If, rarely, she raised her eyelids, she revealed fixed pupils that saw nothing of what was there, which gazed at a distant goal. Then, very quickly, she closed her eyes again, as if with a determination to veil her thought.

On the twentieth day, when Magalo came back into the room, with a cup of broth in her hands, she saw Sophor on her feet, fully dressed, coiffed with a capote and gloved, ready to go out.

"Oh my God, what's this? You're up? You're going out?"

Sophor replied: "Yes, I'm going out."

Magalo dropped the cup.

"You're going out! What about me?"

"You can do what you want. You can go or stay, as you wish." Then, very closely: "Listen to me carefully. I'm leaving. I don't want to be followed. I don't want anyone to worry about me. Adieu."

And, in the tone of those words, there was such a chill, such a clear resolution, that Magalo fell into an armchair, numb with astonishment, and did not even make a gesture to retain her friend.

Yes, she was going. Since she had not died in the dolors of the hideousness of childbirth, since she had recovered her health and strength, she was escaping from the dwelling where she had suffered the shame of maternity, and she was fleeing at the same time the person who had been the witness to it, almost the accomplice, by virtue of her seeming approval of it. A scorn had come to her for Magalo since she had seen her cutting out bibs, sewing nappies, being a woman like those who accommodate men, a little maman; then too, everything that had been in proximity to the defeat of her pride, things or people, was insupportable to her. Her horror of being a mother had rendered horrible everything that was around her when she became one.

Young, rich and free, she wanted a life without a past. What life? The one for which she had always been destined; beyond the bonds of yesterday, she would blossom in the full development of herself.

✳

In the first days, Magalo was as unhappy as possible. So many broken dreams! So many joys that she would no longer have! She looked at the items of layette scattered on the furniture, for the nurse had not been able to take it all away with her; she considered the bed in which Sophor would no longer sleep; and she wept, with great sobs, abandoned. It did not suffice to console her that her friend had left banknotes in the casket where they put the money; a fine affair to have hundreds and thousands! She wept again.

Oh, would she never correct herself? Would she always be a dupe, always attach herself to people who have no heart? It was not the first time she had been left. Léo had left her too, and others, before and after. This time, it was even sadder. Sophor was so beautiful, so loving! And then, such a good education! Oh, my God, she would never see her again. What would become of her now, all alone?

On the evening of the third day, she finally revolted against her own stupidity. Sophor? A snob, that was all, and surely she wouldn't mope around regretting her. There wasn't only her in the world. "Zut!" And she went to dine at Madame Charmeloze's table d'hôte. They drank champagne to celebrate her return. Yes, they made fun of her a little, because she had been stuck on no one knew whom. But as she showed them the money, they ended up admitting that the person in question must have been a very well-to-do woman.

And for more than a month there was, with Hortense and with others, a spree such as had never been seen. Everyone at Madame Charmeloze's was always drunk; then, for hours, there was baccarat and rams. Magalo lost all she wanted; it's true that Madame Charmeloze would have fallen ill if she hadn't cheated. Between two games, Magalo, her nose in Hortense's neck, said: "The other? I don't give a damn."

She was lying. She had death in her heart. She couldn't think about anything but Sophor. She had mad desires to look for her, to find her again; but she was afraid of being poorly received. In her home, Sophor had been her comrade; elsewhere, Madame d'Hermelinge was a grand dame, who might have her thrown out.

And Magalo amused herself all day and all night, so racked was she; she might have died of the pain of being so gay and so sad at the same time, if her money had lasted longer. But when she no longer had a sou, it was necessary to think about serious things. The old life resumed: going out in the evening, supper, coming back late, or not at all. The cares of necessity absorbed her more than pleasure had; already, she had almost forgotten; soon she would forget entirely.

No, she still remembered! When she came back, accompanied, to the bedroom that had been their bedroom, rages gripped her, because of the lost friend, against the man who was there. One evening, she threw out a very adequate monsieur because, on approaching the mantelpiece, where there was still a photograph of Sophie in a crystal frame, he had said: "Who's this filly?"

In any case, it would have been difficult not to think of the absentee very often; at suppers, chic fellows named Baronne

Sophor d'Hermelinge, who had become, in a very short time, famous.

Yes, famous. She had triumphed very quickly. A few visits, under the pretext of charity, had taken the place of an introduction into society, and as soon as she was known, her name and her fortune opened Parisian salons, including the ones into which it was very difficult to be admitted. Who would have taken it into their heads to recognize, in that very distinguished person, with perfect manners, the irregularity sometimes glimpsed in a hired coupé, around the Lac?

Since the departure of Baron Jean, discreet, as if furtive, had not caused any scandal, she was—so far as anyone could know and say—married to a gentleman officer whose military duties obliged him to expatriate himself, and who had not wanted to expose his young wife to the perils of distant voyages and bad climates. In fact, a keener sympathy accumulated because of her solitude, almost a widowhood, and also because of the misfortune she had recently suffered in losing her mother.

Three months after the day when she quit Magalo, she was living in the Avenue de Villiers, in a sumptuously furnished town house, from which emerged, at the hour of the Bois, in a coupé or a huit-ressorts, harnessed to Russian horses. She received the noblest families, the most illustrious artists. What rendered her worldly renown incomparable was a fête in the vast winter garden that surrounded her dwelling, with music, dancing and enchantments of light and flowers; having quit mourning-dress for the first time, she appeared in a pompous antique costume in crimson and gold, carrying a lyre instead of a scepter, and, her forehead crowned with laurel leaves made of diamonds, she resembled, imperious and as if inspired, some royal Sappho.

Her singular, almost brutal beauty, with red and brown hair like clusters of somber flame, the eyes of a hawk in a fading ring of bistre, with the audacity of excessively red lips, would not have failed to earn her a few sly intimations among pretty women anxious about being surpassed if an irreproachable virtue had not served as the excuse for that beauty. Many men among the most noble or the most famous wanted her; a few loved her—one above all, Monsieur de Ligneris, who, for her, refused to marry the richest heiress of a member of the Chambre des Communes—and when it became undeniable that she rejected the adroit and passionate suitors with a gracious and firm austerity, that she intended to remain faithful to Monsieur d'Hermelinge, the most subtle denigrators among her friends proclaimed her perfect in every respect; and "the beautiful Baronne Sophor" was a phrase that was heard everywhere.

In any case, she excelled at winning support from women by means of a frankness and a passion in amity that, on the part of someone like her, could not displease. She was prone to abrupt eulogies, sometimes, with regard to a shoulder at a ball, or a little ankle-boot perceived on the footstep of a carriage, and also sudden caresses, entirely unexpected; people were slightly astonished, without being offended; it was quite natural, such childishness, in a young woman, almost not married, who brought into society the candor and zeal of convent camaraderies; although she resembled an almost wild adolescent, people were tempted to say to her: "Stop it, little girl," and were very flattered by it. Madame de Lurcy-Sévi, famous for the delicate slenderness of her fingers, of which she was very proud, said to anyone who cared to listen: "When Baronne d'Hermelinge holds my hands, she no longer lets go of them."

In sum, all the socialites were delighted with her, and if she was thought to be eccentric, she was judged above all to be charming.

The Comtesse de Grignols, delectably thin, plaintive, elegiac and slightly consumptive, who died of a brutal noise and swooned over music—she played Chopin nocturnes with fingers as gliding and fluttering as the wings of nocturnal moths—conceived a veritable passion for her. At the Bois, at the Opéra, they were seen together, gazing at one another, talking in low voices; two sisters could not have been more tenderly united.

They were opposed, as a decisive example, to chagrined spirits who claimed that amity cannot exist between women.

Furthermore, in the general opinion, Baronne Sophor was much more sincere in that touching intimacy than Madame de Grignols; the latter, whose affairs were somewhat disordered since the death of her husband, perhaps did not give proof of all the desirable disinterest; once covered in debts, she no longer owed a sou since she had made the acquaintance of Madame d'Hermelinge. Then, suddenly, they ceased to be seen together; they scarcely spoke to one another in the salons in which they found themselves in one another's presence. Had the Baronne perceived that she had been duped? The other—perhaps because of new debts—played Chopin's nocturnes with a more desolate melancholy, her eyes expiring toward her former friend.

✳

For an entire year, Madame d'Hermelinge did not appear to have a preferred companion, only acquaintances, to whom, in the mornings, she rendered visits in order to agree what they would do in the evening, the theater or the salon to which they would go. She loved those casual conversations in the boudoir or the dressing-room in which people talk about whatever comes to mind.

Sometimes, on arriving, she said to the chambermaid: "What? Still in bed? It doesn't matter, announce me, I'll wake her up, the idler." And from the drawing room, the chambermaid heard: "Oh, my God, you! What time is it?"

"Yes, dear beauty." Then laughter.

After a few moments, Baronne Sophor, who was often in riding costume on those mornings, cried: "Well, what if we were to take a turn around Auteuil, or Suresnes?" And it was not rare that the whim took them to have breakfast in some country tavern.

But no serious amity: the smiling banality of worldly relations, into which Madame d'Hermelinge put a little boldness and extravagance.

She experienced a more violent sentiment, and very complex, for Princesse Leilef, who was the most extraordinary young person that one could imagine.

Scarcely any taller than a little girl of twelve, svelte and vibrant, all sinew but not thin, Marfa Petrowna, with her little golden eyes, blinking very rapidly, and her turned-up nose, and her impertinent laugh under the russet down of her lip—almost a moustache—gave the impression of a young boy always in search of a quarrel. In Saint Petersburg, where she had resided until the end of her third marriage—for at thirty, she was a widow for the third time, her husbands not lasting long—she had astonished and also alarmed the court and the city with her diabolical mischief, which was never in repose.

On the ground floor of her palace she had a fencing room where, clad in leather and with a cigarette in her mouth, she matched foils with officers from a neighboring barracks, whom she buttoned very nicely, and then invited them to dinner to console them for their defeats and get them drunk. She was delighted by people who became extravagant after champagne, and when she was drunk herself she adored people to lack respect for her—but only up to a point! If an arm went around her waist or breath put a warmth in her ear, she did not like it; that had no consequence, and there was a great risk in hazarding anything further; she would have recommenced fencing with the insolent who had offended her, with unbuttoned weapons.

Did she have lovers? It was believed so; it was probable, but no one knew. To one of her husbands—the first—who had had the indecency to seek information, she had replied with the refrain of a song taught to her by a Parisian chambermaid, and, the husband having persisted, she slapped him on both cheeks with her pretty hand, as swift and sharp as a monkey's paw. The other two husbands were more discreet, either because they were confident of their natural right or had recognized the futility of not being.

In any case, being of high nobility, almost related by distant bastardies to the imperial family and rich to the point that, in spite of all prodigalities, she had never succeeded in diminishing her fortune, Marfa Petrowna was a person of whom to be careful; having married her, one made every effort not to quarrel with her, and she used the consideration that was due to her in order to act, in every regard, in accordance with her whim, repaying complaisance with generosity, seeming not to see it, saying to her husband: "You're scolding me? How much do you owe at the club?"

What had initially rendered her famous was her intrepidity as a horsewoman. She rode an enormous black stallion, scarcely trained, which reared up, waving its hooves in the air, and in order not to slip off she had to let go of the reins and grab hold of the mane; then, her spurs bloody, there was a frantic gallop along the streets, the highway and the plain, punctuated by "hups" and strokes of the crop; and, very tiny on the huge animal, she raised it over hedges. Once, a kick threw her against a garden wall where she struck her head; she got up immediately, her temple bleeding, launched forward, caught the animal, clung on, regained the saddle and, enraged, obliged the horse to jump the wall on which she had nearly cracked her skull. In the evening, at the Théâtre Michel, still in riding costume, with her arm in a sling and a pink wound near her eye, she had applauded an actress from Paris with little raps of the riding crop on the edge of the box, or laughed like a child at a comedian's joke, tipped back in her armchair with her legs crossed.

One adventure completed her celebrity. For some time, a student arrived from Courlands—he was the brother of Marfa Petrowna, whom he resembled singularly—had been spreading terror among policemen and tavern-keepers. Almost always drunk, like other hooligans of his species, he sometimes belabored local watchmen with punches, in broad daylight, and in order to get something to drink he was wont to break through the shutters of wine shops at night. Encountering a girl even in a street that was not deserted without grabbing her arm or wanting her to lift up her skirt had never happened to him. In addition, very much gentleman in his deportment and brave to the point of folly, he fought duels twice or three times a week, for a misheard remark, a glance that had displeased him or for no reason at all, to pass the time. One morning, he laid out in a meadow, with a wound in the chest, the fiancé of a demoiselle of a good family because the fellow did not like the fact that she opened the little garden door to the student when everyone was asleep. When it was discovered that Princesse Leilef had no brother, it was divined with astonishment in the drawing rooms of Saint Petersburg that the rogue, drunkard, fighter and gallant was herself!

The scandal was considerable, and the petulant person, who had just lost her third husband, judged that it would be stupid to remain in a city where people were astonished by so little. She departed for foreign lands, almost amused herself in Vienna, nearly died of boredom in Berlin, and only felt entirely at ease when she lived in Paris.

The first time she encountered Baronne d'Hermelinge—it was at a five o'clock tea at Madame de Ligneris' house—she cried: "Damn!" and looked at her for a long time. Sophor observed her with an equal insistence. There was no mildness in that exchange of glances, but a mutual challenge that resembled a clash of swords. It was a commencement of hatred, but a strange hatred, in which there was no more quarrel than veritable intimacy, which implied above all the impossibility, whatever might happen, of indifference between the two women. After that obstinacy of their intersecting gazes, they both lowered their eyes at the same time, and they were out of breath, as in a battle. Then, when they had been introduced to one another, they pretended no longer to see one another among the comings and goings of visits, only chatting together over tea; evidently, they had no desire to link acquaintance.

It is true that they left at the same time and went down-stairs together, but without saying a word, without alerting one another with a glance to their presence; and, with the air of two women who had never met, they headed for their carriages, Madame d'Hermelinge stopping beside her coupé and Princesse Leilef beside her Victoria. Then, abruptly, Sophor said: "Well, come on!" Marfa Petrowna had not waited for that word; she was already in the coupé, and when the other had joined her, when the horses had pulled away they grabbed one another's hands recklessly, and that first embrace left scratches in the flesh.

Then they remained mute for some time, not looking at one another; but they felt the sharp pressure in their palms, ever more penetrating.

The coupé stopped.

"Listen," said the little princesse, abruptly, "I have my yacht at Le Havre. I'm leaving tomorrow to go who knows where. Will you come with me?"

"Yes," Sophor replied, "but we're making a mistake. You can see that it will be terrible. You don't resemble anyone else. You attract me and you irritate me. I have a desire to embrace you, and a desire to hit you."

"Hit me; I'd like that. I'll hit you too. Until tomorrow,"

And she slipped away.

Their life aboard was extraordinary; in the beginning, one long quarrel, sometimes with sudden furious tenderness. The sailors were astonished by the two women, who got carried away in outrageous arguments and then suddenly embraced frenziedly, until they were rolling on the deck. There was not an order given by Marfa that was not revoked by Sophor; a continual irritation put them at odds. Why? Because each of them was, almost, what neither of them ought to have been; at every moment there was the collision of two virilities, more excitable for not being real, and they detested one another, not being sufficiently male, for similarly resembling two men.

A calm would have resulted from a consent, on the part of Baronne d'Hermelinge or Princesse Leilef, to inferiority, but both of them, Sophor more imperious and Marfa more teasing, had the pride of domination. And by night, in the cabin, after bottles of liquor drunk together, their rages were exalted to the point of madness, because one revolted at accepting from the other the pleasure that she had tried in vain to impose on her, so that in the end, frantic with the same desire that, in an equal desire for masculine mastery, the realization of which Marfa refused to Sophor and Sophor to Marfa, they separated after brutalities and insults, resigned, hatefully, with exchanges of obstinate gazes, to the illusion of triumph.

But for not possessing one another, they coveted one another all the more, and became even more exasperated. The mildness of solitude at sea, under slow clouds upon slow waters, enveloped them and rocked them in vain; their tempest did not yield to the calming of the wind and the waves. The peace of the infinite did not enter into them; they were angry beneath the tranquil middays or the beautiful stars.

Once, however, leaning on the rail, the night was so mild, so pacifying, that Marfa felt languid, and a reverie counseled her to weakness between Sophor's stronger arms, which enlaced her. An idea occurred to them almost at the same time: to bathe together in the silently moving water, so clear and so blue. Why not? The crewmen, confident in the calm, were lying down in the crew cabins or asleep under the benches. They were alone, and it was so easy to descend by the rope-ladder into the sea, where they were enveloped in a smooth warmth, almost lulled to sleep by the scarcely sensible sway of the waves.

Having taken off their dresses, they let themselves slide down, one after the other, and the water received them. Madame d'Hermelinge was a rather poor swimmer, having only had a few lessons in Parisian pools, to which Magalo had taken her because it was then the fashion to go there, but the sea was undulating so calmly that there seemed to be no peril in confiding herself to it. Sophor, hanging on to the ladder with one hand,

and Marfa further away in the deep water, bathed nonchalantly. Their paleness, in the azure of the water sown with starlight, was delectable, and blossomed, as if swooning under the caress of the night.

Sophor gazed at Marfa, who was gliding boldly through the waves with the suppleness of a little siren. And on seeing her clad in transparency, her desire was ignited more ardently, solicited by the embrace of the water, which enlaced and penetrated her everywhere; and as the little princesse, drawing closer, swimming on her back, shouted to her, while laughing, in her challenging manner: "Well, what are you doing? Come on, coward!" Sophor leaned forward, seized her by the leg, pulled her, took hold of her, all wet, and, carrying her with the strength of a man, climbed back up the rope ladder, laid her down on the deck, in spite of her twisting and turning like a cat trying to escape, and maintained her there victoriously.

From then on, Princesse Leilef was, for a long time, with Sophor, like a pretty animal formerly wild and suddenly tamed. She had renounced resistance. She was a very obedient little person, who did not refuse anything, who wanted everything that was wanted of her. She still had her gamine enragements with regard to other people; she abused the crewmen and scolded the captain, but with Madame d'Hermelinge her mildness was like the humility of an affectionate servant. One defeat had convinced her if the inutility of victory; she took pleasure in a defeat that had been so pleasant, and gazed at her friend—her triumphant friend—with eyes charged with a gratitude that desired further motives for gratitude; always rubbing against Sophor, like a little amorous kitten, purring and mewling with retracted caws.

And by night, in the cabin, they no longer quarreled and no longer rejected one another; the victor, by means of the omnipotence of pleasure, held the other in her hand like a little bird that one would stifle if one squeezed a little harder.

For having been mastered, however, Marfa's puerile pride had not abdicated, fundamentally, and, on the contrary, wilder and more acerbic in being obliged to so much submission, it burst forth in furious jealousies. Absurd as the suspicion was, she imagined that Sophor had looked too tenderly at the pilot of the yacht, a young Norman whose arms and legs were always bare. She flew into a delirious rage and swore that she would throw the man in the sea. Hence, in nervous fevers, a prompt return to Le Havre.

In Paris, however, Marfa's jealousies did not dissipate. Once, after a ball, in the antechamber of a town house, Sophor, perhaps with some slowness of the hands over the bare breast, fastened the mantle of Mademoiselle de Selves, a plump, tall, brunette with profound blue eyes. Marfa launched herself toward the young woman and slapped her with a stiff hand. There was a great scandal. And because, for several months already, since their departure, and above all since their return, the intimacy of the two friends had given rise to singular suspicions, because the whispers had only been waiting for an opportunity to become jeers, a tumult of reproving and pursuing voices followed Marfa and Sophor down the stairs, into the courtyard, and all the way to their coupé.

For a week there was no talk of anything but that adventure at five o'clock teas and over dessert at dinners, behind fans that masked blushes, and it was also an anecdote that amused the smoking-rooms. Now people recalled things to which they had paid no attention previously, or, ingenuously, had not judged reprehensible: the strange fashion in which, at balls, Baronne Sophor d'Hermelinge gazed at shoulders and breasts; her tenderness for Madame de Grignols, the couturiers' bills paid; her boyish extravagances, the morning visits, the offers of escapades in the country.

Madame de Lurcy-Sévi, her eyes lowered toward her hands, which were so small and slender, said with an air of embarrassment that did not conceal a little contented vanity: "Do you remember? When she held my hands, she no longer let go of them." Many other socialites had abundant memories of that sort. Those above all, to whom a little more familiarity with Sophie might have attracted awkward suspicions, hastened to speak in order that no one would believe that they had any reason to remain silent, citing circumstances in which that extraordinary person had behaved entirely inappropriately.

They had not divined then, what had it signified, oh, no, not divined at all—they even insisted a little too ardently on their perfectly natural incomprehension—but now, everything was explained, and they were indignant against Baronne d'Hermelinge. The abominable creature! It was truly frightful that such things were possible in good society; one has no idea of such horrors.

Sophor and Marfa might perhaps have been able to stand up to the reprobation, and triumph over it to a certain extent. Irreproachable houses, certainly, were closed to them, but there are less austere salons, more accommodating, which only renounce in the last extremity the advantage of receiving rich and highly titled people, not pardoning a scandal but feigning to be unaware of it, only demanding a little hypocrisy in order to believe in innocence. Many doors would have remained open to them, if they had only consented to some reserve; if, for example, they had renounced their impertinent habit of arriving at dinners and balls together, leaving together, climbing into the same carriage at three o'clock in the morning and only giving the coachman one address.

But Sophor was not a soul inclined to concessions. She refused to swallow with the villainy of lies the pride of her sin. She was what she was, and wanted to show everyone, without reticence or veil. She did not deign to usurp esteem. And, in truth, she had felt ill at ease for a long time in the narrowness of the prejudices to which, if one lives in society, it is always necessary to submit to some degree. She had sometimes had to dissimulate, to constrain herself. She had not dared to proclaim her unique joy!

Then again, those women, the ones who, surprised or curious and sure of mystery, only half-rejected her, had such timid hearts and senses. Never a reckless abandonment, but, with frights and recoils, hands over closed eyelids, a gradual consent that did not confess to intention, the furtive hazard of a kiss almost refused in the semi-darkness of a bedroom or a boudoir, insufficient for the satiation of entire desires into which all her vital forces were precipitated. The majority of those futile and prudent ladies, if Baronne d'Hermelinge, in some exasperation, had thrown a memory in their face, would have been able to reply, almost sincerely: "In truth, Madame, I don't know what you mean!"

The Comtesse de Grignols, so tenderly, so languidly acquiescent? A blasé girl, that idealist, a debauchee, who paid her with a confession of pleasure that perhaps she had not had. As for Marfa Petrowna, she was a kind of little incomplete monster, not woman enough to accept amour, not man enough to impose it; and her rages—vanquished for a time but ever ready for rebellion—came from a double impotence in being satisfied or satisfying. Who could have said, anyway, whether that creature, desirous before all of appearing extraordinary, of astonishing, mannered even in her savagery, whose very wrath was perhaps manufactured expressly, might not affect virile concupiscence, as she dressed in male attire, for the sake of the boastful vainglory of an eccentricity?

The result was that Baronne Sophor submitted without chagrin to the reprobation that separated her from worldly society; expelled, she had the impression of being free, and the honest audacity of her desire demanded frank amours.

On the opening day of the Salon, there was something like a riot of astonishments before the painting exhibited by Mademoiselle Silvie Elven. Under the scattered gold of sunlight, green-tinted by virtue of having traversed foliage, a young faun was recklessly enlacing a very delicate and frail hamadryad: a melee of lustful flesh in the long grass in which the long hair of the nymph was caught; it seemed that the stifling lover would not let go of his prey, even dead. It was a banal subject, in sum, to which mythological painters devoid of imagination willingly resigned themselves; but a magnificent ardor of lust singularized that embrace under the trees; the almost naked bodies, on which the heat of the day dried and burned the sweat, were alive with an intense, excessive life, less and more than human; it was a bestial and divine intercourse.

However, attention would not have paused for long on that painting if there had not been something strange and disquieting about the young faun. Faun? Fauness, rather. The sex veiled beneath the modesty of a scrap of crimson fabric, the figure was, indeed, male in the violence of the enlacement, the vigor of the muscles, the short hair as thick as moss; but the whiteness and the harmonious curve of the hips, and, resisting the obstinacy of the pressure, a double swelling of firm flesh in the breast permitted the suspicion that it was female: an almost virile female, of brutal beauty, with little blazing eyes ringed with bistre and devouring red lips.

Groups tightened before the canvas, with whispers and nudges that recommended looking closer; Parisiennes turned their heads away, attracted nevertheless, blushing under the gazes of men who were smiling. Suddenly, there were exclamations of surprise in the crowd; people stood aside to let two women pass, who only darted a brief glance at the canvas and drew away, talking in low voices. One of them, very thin, her skin barely pink under wayward blonde hair, was Mademoiselle Elven, already celebrated; a rapid comparison between the work and the author revealed in the delicate and frail hamadryad the resemblance of Silvie. The other, with a mat pallor and a seemingly bloody mouth, was Baronne Sophor d'Hermelinge; one might have been seeing the young faun or virile fauness walking, in a spring dress.

✻

In the bright daylight, Silvie Elven's studio, not too vast, was lovely, colored by japonaiseries and sparkling with glassware in which the light glinted. On the walls hung up like suspended sultanas, Oriental satins, gold and multicolored, sometimes stirred in the draught from an open windows; and, sliding from the chaise longue, from armchairs and from the ebony piano encrusted with tin, muslins spangled with silver brushed the skins of white bears, the fur of which was gentle on bare feet.

It was there that Silvie Elven, scarcely more fully dressed than at the moment of awakening, her shoulders and arms outside a cream silk chemise tightened by a metal belt, painted all day long, sitting in front of the easel, the smoke of the cigarette in the corner of her mouth rising toward the almost ungilded curls of her hair, also reminiscent of light smoke; while Baronne Sophor d'Hermelinge, in a long dress of dark cloth, more like a frock-coat than a dress, red, was lying on a mass of cushions. But the book did not interest her for long; she continually turned her head toward the little painter, and, her neck extended, considered her with an ardent passion; it was hers, that charm, that youth and that entire body, more precious for being weaker, and all that thought too, infatuated with light and form, which made colors with the tips of frail fingers.

Several weeks had gone by since she had entered that studio for the first time, a grand dame coming to commission her portrait from a renowned artist. The true reason, or a pretext? There was a legend around Silvie that must have interested Baronne Sophor d'Hermelinge. Born into a very bourgeois family, Mademoiselle Elven had never wanted to marry; it was not, people claimed, in order to dedicate herself entirely to art that she refused marriage. Female friends loved more than is appropriate were attributed to her; each of the pastels that she exhibited—spring in a pathway where a Parisienne costumed as a shepherdess was laughing; summer traversed by a beautiful young woman coiffed with poppies; yellow autumn with a redder grape-picker; winter whose snowflakes flourished over the chilly nudity of a girl—passed for the evocation of a tenderness symbolized in seasons; and the painted lips of her figures would, if alive, have rendered kisses.

But people did not believe that she hazarded herself in her intimacies as far as the brutal villainy of entire sin. She fled husbands or lovers because men are rude, and it was her love of flowers, birds, perfumes and things that are gracious and light that inclined her toward women; it pleased her to love what it pleased her to paint, but she refrained from asking more from any of her friends than one asks of a beautiful rose; she desired nothing more than the delight of a breath or a touch that was barely a caress; the nudity of the lovely actresses who consented to serve as her models—lilies are also naked—only troubled her with a reverie devoid of any evil thought, and left her the charm of a memory devoid of remorse.

In any case, so frail, like everything that is going to wilt, languish and etiolate, evoking the idea, with the diaphanous quality of her sin and the bright frisson of her hair, of those downy flowers, the angelic flowers, that one can blow away with a breath, she would have been crushed even by the ardor of feminine embraces. One day, a very redoubtable woman, an illustrious poet and famous debauchee, accustomed to the excess of joys, who had premeditated tormenting her to the point of extreme pleasure, quickly renounced her design, softened by seeing her place her head, with the eyes half-closed, on the shoulder of a friend and remain there, her lips parted in a smile, content with the teasing of a breath toward her lips, under the hair mingled with hers. And, close to the crime, Silvie Elven had not been afraid, knowing that she would never throw herself into it, sure that no one would ever have the cruelty to push her into it, so happy on the edge.

On seeing Baronne Sophor d'Hermelinge, however, she was troubled, hearing within herself a kind of counsel to flee. That woman, as soon as the banal words of her first visit, enveloped her with a gaze that threatened as it caressed, which ordered and wanted to be obeyed. Alas, that one would not be gentle with her, like the others, would not remain similar to a tender, affectionate sister; there was no hope of being spared; and she sensed, beneath that fixed gaze, violent, sharp and penetrating, that she could not resist it, that she would submit with the vague plaints of a little bird charmed by a snake. One resource: to send her away this time, and not to receive her again.

In spite of her efforts, however, Silvie could not resolve herself to that which she judged indispensable. That slightly grim beauty, with the velvet redness of the lips and the tyrannical persistence of the gaze beneath the tawny blackness of the hair, attracted her and frightened her. How beautiful she would be to paint: Penthesilea in the horrible helmet, clad in gold and steel, or an ardent satyress of the woods who, lying in the grass of a shore, was extending her arm toward mists in the form of women drifting over the lake.

Previously infatuated with everything rosy, bright and sweetly tender, the pallors of water color and the languors of pastel, it seemed to Mademoiselle Elven that with such a model she might dare to attempt more ambitious works, in which her talent and feminine grace might be reinforced as far as the conception of virility. But she was not without some fear, in her thought given to amiable futilities, of that development in herself of a more vigorous labor, in the same way that, a poor little heart accustomed to discreet amities, she feared the passion divined in Sophor d'Hermelinge. And truly, she would have liked that visitor to have departed already; she was about to say to her that, busy with other works, by virtue of too many commissions . . .

Sophor was still looking at her, more ardently. Silvie Elven replied: "I'll be very happy to paint your portrait, Madame." And, while blushing, she lowered her eyes.

Now, they were united. Sophor was infatuated with that thin and frail body, that pliant slenderness, which abandoned itself with the paints of a turtle-dove that is being hurt, and always had, during intercourse, a bewilderment beneath the eyelids at the imminent joy, and a kind of fear of death. She was also infatuated with that futile and curious, almost infantile, mind, the primal naivety of which the subtleties of Parisienne life, the camaraderie of the workshop and the wings had not spoiled, and which, in being so tender, had remained so ingenuous.

Silvie, for her part, adored Madame d'Hermelinge, while fearing her, like an infernal goddess that one has in one's home, and her terrors augmented her delights. They were exquisite: the gazes that entered her via the eyes, like drills of flame, all the way to the heart; the caresses that subjected her, impetuously, to violence. Or, more efficacious for being less vivid, they exhausted her with a long insistence, and finally left her inanimate.

Did she sometimes think, with a regretful softness, about the almost pure charms of her previous amities, the incomplete pleasures that were scarcely pleasures and did not alarm her conscience? No, she belonged entirely to the despotic lover. If she was frightened by her joys, she was glad to be frightened. And as well as being threatened and tormented, she felt protected; she had confidence in the person martyrizing her. When the excess of a strange joy, still unexperienced, maddened her as far as the throes of agony, she had thrown herself, in order to be rescued, into the arms of the person who was killing her, and under Sophor's tenderly dominating gaze, which interrogated her and obliged her to the confession of mortal ecstasies, she had, tipping back her head, the smile of a happy dying woman who would have liked to suffer even more, to die entirely.

Did the former comrades still come to the studio, in spite of the almost perpetual presence of Baronne d'Hermelinge? Of course they did. After the initial astonishments, after a few jealousies, they had come to terms with an intimacy that Valentine Bertier of the Odéon called a *fait accompli*; and in the afternoon, while Silvie painted and Sophor played some sonata at the piano, there was a rustle of dresses between the easels and the frames; cigarette smoke rose toward the beribboned and plumed hats with which the busts were coiffed.

Yvonne Lérys, knowing and agile, as thin as a pretty stick, with a shock of black hair under the rust of the dye, who played ingénues at the Comédie-Française and also played them in the city, but with a less probable sincerity, never failed to come and have a glass of Madeira with Silvie after rehearsal, in order to relate the theater gossip and to see where the darling was with her new painting; and before she had even made her entrance people exclaimed: "Here she comes!" because of an excessive odor of sandalwood exasperated with ginger, with which she had a mania for perfuming herself all over; with the result that, when she took off her mantle, one had a desire to open the window, and Valentine Bertier, unembarrassed, said: "She's funny, Yvonne; one might think that she had armpits everywhere."

When Mademoiselle Lérys arrived, there were already many visitors: the stout Constance Chaput—who had been there all morning, having come for breakfast—a former fay in fantasy plays once famous for the plenitude of her leotards, a beautiful girl collapsed into an obese quadragenarian, giving the impression of a fairground somnambulist or the clothing-merchant that she would soon be; Rose Mousson, an escapee from the Operetta who was about to make her debut at the Palais-Royal, too white and too pink, dainty and affected, like a gilded flower; Adeline Nordrecht, enormous and firm, resembling the statues placed in city squares, Dutch, she claimed, while recounting with a strong Hanoverian accent that success she had had in The Hague in the role of Phèdre played in French; Rosalia Fingerly, utterly pretty and very svelte in a clinging dress, like an amazon, a stable-girl made illustrious by the amity of an empress, decorated one evening of dressage with a medal sought after by a queen—out of modesty, she did not wear the ribbon in her corsage, but where it had been placed, next to her skin; Séraphine Thevenet of the Vaudeville, too plump; and Jeanne Vincent of the Gymnase, too thin, with Madame Leverrier, a once-celebrated courtesan who had ended up as a moustached couturier, who dressed and undressed both of them.

There was also Honorine Lamblin, certainly as white as a swan and probably as stupid as a goose, who, on the evening of the premiere of a revue at the Folies-Dramatiques, quitting the stage in order, so the role said, to take a bath, stripped naked in front of the scene-shifters and figurants in an imaginary bath-tub, either because she was stupid or because she was white-skinned; Vivette Chanlieu, a diabolical soubrette, so mischievous, with gestures so lively and so boyish that one might have thought that she was dressed as a man under her dress—when she sat down her skirt billowing, one saw her gilded skin, that of a gypsy, beyond her black silk socks; and that madwoman with hair everywhere in the eyes, Luce-Lucy, stupid to the point that one evening she sat down in a ground floor box at a performance in which she had forgotten to go and play her role, and suddenly, having heard her cue, launched her tirade into the hall; and Germaine Triezin, who had come back from the Théâtre Michel with all the diamonds one can have, not virtuous, saying: "If I'd given a hair to each of my lovers I'd surely be bald!"; and with them, another ten of the prettiest and most elegant stars of the stage, who had, one after another and sometimes several at a time, served as models for Silvie Elven.

Very often, too, more beautiful than all the others in the young splendor of her flesh and her heavy blonde hair spilling in closets from her capote, Céphise Ador came, the admirable actress, the only truly passionate amorous woman of the theater of the time.

And those Parisiennes, dresses trailing over animal skins, or lying on chaise-longues, their mantles fallen and their fans fluttering, mingled in the studio their colors, laughter and perfumes; the air was full of the invisible mist that emerges from fabrics impregnated with flesh. Baronne Sophor—not without some dread of a glance from Silvie—contemplated, listened and inhaled; she absorbed into herself alone all that scattered femininity.

Beautiful, rich and splendid, she conquered all, or almost all, those women; this one with some princely present, that one with an abrupt kiss on the lips when they were going down the staircase, already dark, on their own. One did not refuse to join her in a booth in a nocturnal restaurant, another agreed to go with her, in the evening, to a village on the water's edge, where, after dinner in the arbor of an inn, not much was happening, either because they were accustomed to such caprices or, on the contrary, because the novelty attracted them, or because it amused them to put one over on Silvie Elven, who had made fun of them, truly, with her Saint-Touch-Me-Not airs and her fashion of begging for mercy when someone breathed too close to the little mouth that offered itself only to refuse itself. And some—those in whom all flames were not extinct and all nerves exhausted—remained thoughtful the following day.

They had been disconcerted, even the most perverse, by something terribly unusual, to which they were not accustomed, of which they had never thought. Amuse oneself, fine, why not? Where's the harm? On the contrary; it's very innocent, as at boarding school. But Sophor was redoubtable. In spite of so much experience, Valentine Bertier said: "That one isn't playing a game."

And those pretty girls, scarcely knowing anything of amour except the vice of men, only obtaining brief moments of pleasure from their lovers, the egotistical salary of complaisance, were troubled by having submitted, recklessly, to strange and cruel joys. Several, frightened, went away with a: "No one will have me like that again," in which some regret nevertheless lingered. Others, vanquished, glad of their defeat, resolved to perfect slavery, attached themselves to Sophor, no longer wanting to let go of her, and went pale if they saw a cold gleam in her eyes that did not desire and did not promise anything.

And Madame d'Hermelinge was as infatuated with their anxiety as she was proud of their delights. Undoubtedly, she experienced some remorse, because of Silvie Elven, genteel and seductive, who, so often betrayed, did not complain, allowing her to go away without quarrels and welcoming her, when she returned, with a smile devoid of reproach; often, the infidel knelt down, and swore that she was finished with all those follies, that she would always remain with her darling, and begged her not to be chagrined.

"But I'm not," Sophie said, "since you love me." And she had a contented expression, a smile sometimes interrupted by a little cough. For she had been coughing for some time. Rarely—a little fatigue—in sum, nothing. Sophor was anxious about it, nevertheless. Perhaps it was the voracious obstinacy of her desire that was anemiating the delicate creature. She sometimes feared not seeing her recover from the torpor into which she had plunged her. But concern for Silvie, weary and slightly ill, could not retain her for long; she yielded to the pressure of her destiny toward so many other women; she became furiously smitten with Céphise Ador, the most beautiful of them all, who refused herself.

Céphine was a very healthy creature, with a simple intelligence and senses; she admired an ardent, robust young man with a frank heart and solid nerves; they were superb to see, that beautiful girl and that handsome fellow, content with one another in their healthy happiness. As soon as the first breath with which Madame d'Hermelinge, leaning into a forestage box, caressed her neck, the honest amorous woman burst out laughing and, turning to her lover, who was in the back of the box, said: "That's my mistress!"

But Sophor wanted her, and would have her.

She did not beg, did not humiliate herself, did not try to soften her; she also refrained from audacities that might have earned her a definitive rebuff. Without humility or temerity, she was in the presence of Céphise as often as possible, rendered her a visit every morning, went to see her in the evenings in the foyer of the Comédie; she surrounded her and invested her with gazes, invisible distant caresses that nevertheless seemed close; and what radiated from her put around Céphise a warmth in which the latter experienced a singular embarrassment, in which she was sometimes stifled to the point of being unable to drawn breath; she felt surrounded, penetrated by a desire pressing every more tightly around her; when Sophor was present she made an unconscious gesture of pushing away bonds.

Madame d'Hermelinge's covetousness, exasperated by waiting, became more imperious, more irresistible, and once, as Céphise Ador, after a performance, enervated by a drama in which she had wept real tears, and a quarrel that she had had a little while before with her lover, and the imminent storm that was putting a fiery heaviness through the open window of the dressing-room, began to unhook her bodice with a feverish hand, she felt herself embraced by two convulsive arms, and, turning round, she received Sophor's victorious kiss full on her mouth.

After that, she no longer belonged to herself, nor to her lover. Scarcely possessed, she was enslaved. For Sophor was the violent and savant frenzied giver of incomparable joys, the one who wants everything and can obtain everything, the dear torturer whose matryrized victims always demanded new tortures, and who always invented the most frightfully delicious ones.

The man she loved, Céphise no longer loved, had him thrown out, did not want to see him again. "You alone exist," she said to Sophor, "you alone make life worth living." And the Baronne d'Hermelinge, holding under her despotic and tearing amour, as if under a claw, the most beautiful of beautiful creatures, long resistant, exulted in an enchantment and a limitless pride.

So, it was true. She was accomplishing her destiny. That which she had to be, she was; she had realized herself, absolutely. She had broken the ancient defenses, mocked marriage, had informed and imposed in amities the delights of an amour more enviable than all amours.

Humiliated once by a man in the horrible nuptial night, how she was avenging herself now! How she was triumphing over husbands and lovers! Seduced or tamed, women preferred her to scorned males; for her elect there was no longer any paradise than the one whose largesse she provided for them. Those promised to virile embraces accepted and demanded the feminine wedding! And at times, the excess of her victory inflated her heart, and made her face—her pale, mat face—crimson.

All those charms, the pink and odorous lips as well as the flowers of flesh, the long hair that veiled nipples and loins as if they were jealous, and the throbbing breasts where bloody rednesses already had a presentiment of a bite, and the pretty fleece of napes, and all the whiteness of the body, all the way to the nacreous yellow toenail that separates and turns up, she had them under the so delicate and so masterful friction of her caress, under her kiss, captor of all breath, all blood and all life; she had made of ecstasized woman a delectable regal bed.

And, more than the joy of possession, the pride of that enchanted her. An unpunished violatrix of natural laws or the designs of the divinity, she had, in delirious fevers, the supreme arrogance of a Lucifer who, for an instant, has vanquished God.

But suddenly, she shivered as at the wound of a knife, tightened her elbows against her body and, ordinarily so pale, became white, with a palpitation of lips that were less red. She shrugged her shoulders and shook her hair, with the air of rejecting an obsession . . . in vain.

Oh, it was insupportable, that!

What, then, was *that*? Well, that little sound in the ears, which rang like laughter, which she had hard when she was very small, in times of crises, and near Emmeline's bed, and many other times as well.

Truly, it was laughter, as if something within her were mocking her. For some years it had been less discreet, less distant, seemingly resolved to be entirely perceptible. However, one might have thought that it did not mean to be frightening. No, it was complimentary: "Ha ha! Really? Yes, yes, very good!" Except, when it persisted, it became irritating in the end.

Oh, Sophor was not unduly anxious about it. A tinnitus, that was all, which resembled a snigger. A nervous phenomenon. For sure, if she had consulted a physician, she would have been liberated forever from that importunate little noise, which must have a name in the books of science. But she heard it so rarely, and it was such a little thing! In sum, an illness too slight to be worth treating.

And every day, she rolled more furiously down the slope of her vice, having, although she was descending, the impression of rising. It was no longer sufficient for her, now, to experience her joys; she wanted to display them, in defiance of hypocrisy or social honesty. She went through Parisian life, dragging enamored beautiful women after her, like the impudent Pietro Aretino in Venice, followed by forty Aretines.[1]

After the Bois, where she was like the queen of a troop of amazons, who escorted her and caught up with her, with appeals and laughter, a tumult of joy was heard coming from the windows of her town house or the casements of a fashionable restaurant; Baronne Sophie d'Herleminge was dining with her friends; when the lamps were lit, behind the translucency of the curtains, there were passages of rosy whiteness that were not the color of a fabric. Was Silvie Elven there? No, she would not have taken pleasure in those fêtes, where people made too much noise, preferring to smile than to laugh, and also to weep, almost willingly. Then again, suffering slightly, she did not go out in the evening. Always that little cough.

As for Sophor, she did not linger long over follies after the champagne. Well before the time when the performance finished, she went to the Comédie to join Céphise Ador; she had a continual need to see her, and to be seen seeing her. There was no need of a dresser for the actress's costume changes; it was her friend who put other boots on her feet, who unlaced and laced

---

1 Pietro Aretino (1492-1556) was famous as a poet, satirist, self-declared homosexual and pioneer of literary pornography. Legend asserts that he died of laughing too much.

her dresses, and the corsage not yet flossed, mad with beautiful offered flesh, she laced up in a delicious paroxysm.

Afterwards, if there was some fête at which Paris assembled, she took Céphise there; in the full light, she showed that admirable creature to the finally scornful and angry crowd, her arms bare, her neckline too low, whom none of the men had, who was hers alone.

IV

Imperiously insolent, admitting her infamous amours as a Faustina or a Theodora boasted of her crimes. Baronne Sophor d'Hermelinge emerged from the Opéra with Céphise Ador between a double hedge of indignant whispers; and, scarcely having sat down in the coupé, they embraced one another. Breath mingled with breath, in a great rustle of fabrics. But the carriage did not budge. Outside, a little hand, small, well-gloved in an old glove, had made a sign to the coachman and then posed on the edge of the window.

The two friends drew apart, alarmed. They saw the head of a woman, surrounded by lace, leaning forward. That woman, whose features, doubly veiled by the darkness and guipure, could not be made out, was trembling like a beggar who wants to ask for alms but dare not. In a very low, hoarse, stammering voice, which one might have thought fearful of being heard, she finally said: "Madame . . ."

"Come on, what is it?" asked Sophor.

The other, in a tone that was even more hesitant: "It's that I'd like to speak to you. Yes, to you, Madame, only for a moment. I'd be very content if you'd allow me to speak to you."

At the same time, that person unfolded the lace.

It was Magalo—but so different from what she had been! Her little face, illuminated by one of the coupé's lanterns, had the yellow color and the wrinkles of a dried medlar on straw.

The lips, which had once had a red freshness, seemed dead. Between eyelids devoid of lashes, her eyes, in which there was nothing alive but tears, were bloodshot; and the gaiety of the colorless curls was lamentable.

Sophor divined rather than recognized her. Oh my God, in so few years, such a change! Either Magalo, before, had been much less young than she said, or poverty, and perhaps chagrin, had withered her to this point!

There was a great pity in Sophor's heart. It was so far behind her, Emmeline lost and the shame of childbirth, that she no longer had any anger against the poor little creature. She remembered, above all, that Magalo had been, with so many pretty perversities at first and obedience thereafter, the commencement of her joys. Sophor owed her present happiness to her; and, young, beautiful and fortunate, it was truly a very bitter pain to see her again so old and ugly, and so sad.

Magalo continued: "I assure you that I won't keep you long. You're in a hurry to go home, with Madame, who is very beautiful. I understand that."

She dissolved in tears.

Certainly, Sophor was about to reply: "Well, climb in." But with an abrupt movement, Céphise Ador put her beautiful arms round her neck, and, almost brutally, with a confused suspicion of the truth, said:

"Send that woman away; I don't want you to talk to her. She looks like a streetwalker. She's some whore. Go away."

Then, while Magalo, suppliant, extended her hands inside the vehicle, the actress let go of Sophor for a moment, and, lowering the glass with a feverish hand, shouted to the coachman urgently: "Are you mad? Go!"

The coupé set off so rapidly that Magalo hardly had time to throw herself backwards in order not to be knocked over.

One of the wheels passed over her foot. She uttered the plaint of a small dog that has been trampled.

The carriage was far away. And she was all alone, and the pain in her foot was very acute; perhaps her toes were broken. The agony rose all the way to her heart, but she was so accustomed to suffering in another fashion that she could not really tell whether she was suffering from the wound or from her everyday chagrin, more cruel that night. She sensed that she was about to faint.

She had the idea of sitting down on a footstep; but no, the coachmen, the door-openers and the people coming out of the fête would be astonished to see her there.

She traversed the square, with difficulty, like someone who is dragging something heavy with one leg, reached the boulevard, fell on to a bench beside a kiosk, not very far from a restaurant whose windows were still ablaze, even though the shutter on the ground floor was closed. From the cabinets, through the windows, came the sounds of people having supper, amusing themselves. She was in so much pain that she would rather have been dead.

Thus, it was for nothing that, with ten francs borrowed from the flower-girl at the Rat Mort, she had hired a ball gown, that she had come to this fête—she didn't have the heart to laugh, for sure—with a ticket sold on credit by the hairdresser, that she had had the courage, after so many hesitations, to speak to Sophor?

Baronne d'Hermelinge had not replied with a single word, perhaps had not even recognized her, and the other lady, out of jealousy, had made the carriage depart very quickly, in order to crush her, Magalo.

Oh well, that completed her ill fortune. One could say that misfortune like that was the ultimate in misfortune. And her foot was hurting badly; stronger stabbing sensations, and crawling sensations. She did not want to pay any heed to it; she gazed at the people coming out of the restaurant through a little door, she heard the porter calling out the number of a carriage; she remembered that it had happened many a time, when she was chic, not to finish supper until four o'clock in the morning; but the porter had changed; the other had been stout, with English side-whiskers.

The casement of a cabinet opened abruptly; a woman in a black silk chemise appeared, with white flesh that stuck out, a glass of champagne in her hand; she threw the glass on to the sidewalk, to amuse herself or in the irritation of some quarrel.

Magalo thought that to drink champagne at present she only had this means: to open her mouth under the windows of restaurants, like a beast, muzzle in the air, to lap up the rain. Oh my God ! Oh my God! But fundamentally, it did not matter to her no longer to be fashionable, to be a kind of guttersnipe, to sup in brasseries in Montmartre when she was offered supper. Her true, her only despair was that Sophor had not responded to her.

She had never forgotten her. Can one no longer think about someone who has been so good, and so wicked? Oh, certainly, life is life; it's necessary to look after one's affairs; to pay one's rent, not to die of hunger, it's necessary to let oneself be touched, embraced, for hours; that occupies one, men. No matter, the idea of Sophor always returned to her, and very often, especially when she had difficulties, a kind of rage gripped her to see her again, to see her right away. She threw herself into a carriage, gave the Baronne d'Hermelinge's address—everyone knew it, that address—and she said to herself:

I'll have myself announced, like a visit. She won't have the wickedness to have me thrown out. I'll talk to her, in a proper fashion, entirely polite, as long as the domestic is there, but as soon as we're alone . . .

Oh, how she would have thrown her arms around her neck! How she would have said tender things in her ear! And—one can never tell, can one?—perhaps Sophor might have taken her with her, lodged her in her house, introduced her as a relative, or as a lady companion.

I can certainly believe that I'd keep her company, if she wanted, day and night too!

But when the fiacre went into the avenue where Madame d'Hermelinge's house was, Magalo no longer had any courage at all. She imagined a great marble vestibule with valets in red livery who offered you an ivory plate on which one wrote one's name, They would give her a funny look, the domestics, on reading that name: Magalo. Then they would come back down with a mocking expression. "Madame la Baronne is absent," or even "Madame la Baronne does not know you."

That would truly be too painful. Her heart constricted, she had a desire to weep; and then she remembered a rendezvous at the Café Americain with big Rosa, who was to introduce her to some very nice foreigners, or a dress to try on, or a step to take with the bailiff in order to obtain a postponement of a seizure. She turned back.

Every time she went to see Sophor, it was like that. So many times that, in the end, sure that she would never dare to go there, she stopped forming the design.

She had the idea of writing to her. But she did not know how to spell. Now that her friend, who was no longer her friend, had gone back into high society, perhaps she would laugh at badly written words. Anyway, Sophor would doubtless not reply.

Of course, one pleasure that Magalo could give herself was that of seeing her sometimes, without speaking to her, at a distance. Her comrades did not understand why she did not want to take anyone with her on certain days when she went to the Bois in a hired Victoria. It would have been annoying to have a woman beside her at the moment when Sophor went past in her caleche or her coupé. And if she perceived her disappearing rapidly into the elegant tumult of carriages, she felt her heart full of ease and desolation.

How beautiful she is! How well she's dressed! She resembles a queen now.

And to think that she had had that queen in her little apartment in the Rue Saint-Georges, that she had said *tu* to her.

And the woman who's with her, who's she?

She experienced sadness rather than jealousy. She came back into Paris. She promised herself no longer to find herself in Sophor's passage.

That promise, she did not keep. A month, or two months later, her folly gripped her again; for weeks she ran around the theaters—the grand theaters—where she hoped that she might encounter Madame d'Hermelinghe, where she sometimes brushed her in a corridor without being recognized.

But it was especially when life became cruel, when she lacked money completely, that the thought of Sophor haunted her most assiduously. Bohemia, for those poor women, is immediate misery as soon as they are no longer pretty. Magalo, who had never been very pretty—an amusing little face—who was entirely used up, took on the appearance of a little old woman almost from one day to the next; not at all fatigued previously, she woke up one morning unable to do any more. Her little nerves, too taut, had snapped. She felt like a rag. All right, it was because she was ill. Strength would return to her, and the drollery of her face. She was only thirty-three, after all, and only admitted to twenty-seven. That age, in Paris, is youth.

No, she stayed what she had become. She tried to buck herself up with alcohol, at Madame Charmeloze's or the café, but she only felt wearier. She made herself up excessively, uselessly; when she looked at herself in the street, in some shop window, she found herself horrible. The make-up no longer held together over her little wrinkles.

It wasn't cheerful then, her life! Men no longer paid attention to her, either in the dance-halls or at the open air concerts, not even the very young one who are pressed for time and take the first thing they find. Often, she would not have eaten if Madame Charmeloze, very faithful to the comrades, had not said to her once and for all: "You know, supper is served every evening at half past seven; if you don't have the sou, too bad." But the excellent and ignoble old woman, who devoted herself to gaming and love—a gambling den with alcoves—was arrested one evening and sent to Saint-Lazare. Magalo, who no longer had any furniture, only had one dress, and slept in a friend's apartment in a hotel in the Avenue de Clichy, became utterly miserable.

It was that horrible existence—her last clothes at the Mont-de-Pieté, debts engaged, the two sous' worth of milk that one goes to fetch every morning from the dairy, bareheaded, and in the evening, in some brasserie where one hasn't dined, glasses of green chartreuse or kummel, swallowed one after another, in order to numb the appetite, for which one can't pay; one arranges things with the waiter at closing time. Surely, she would have died of hunger if good girls, when they had won at rams, hadn't lent her forty sous or offered her sauerkraut.

Her lucky breaks were when a monsieur came to the Rat Mort or the Brasserie Fontaine to look for women, two or three; she approached and said: "Well, won't you take me?"

"Yes, yes," said one of the women, and they took her, because they knew that she had liked that once. She no longer liked anything, or anyone. The only tenderness she retained, of the entire past, was the memory of Sophor. The further she descended into poverty, into infamy, the more she thought with affection of the one who was so happy, so glorious, up there, so far away!

But at present, she no longer loved Madame d'Herelimge as in the days when they had lived together in the Rue Saint-Georges, or even in recent times when she was not so miserable, not yet so ugly, and she went to lie in wait in the Bois or in some theater, saddened, almost jealous if Sophor wasn't alone. Well, yes, she no longer thought about stupidities. Now that Magalo had the look of the little old fay Carabosse—for, very weak, she was stooped, and resembled a hunchback—a horror even came to her of the vice that had been her pleasure, now that it was her métier, that she made it a kind of ignoble and supreme resource.

It's extraordinary how one changes! It disgusted her, it made her want to vomit, women, because people paid her to amuse herself with them; and also because she could no longer obtain the end, from being so ruined in the time. And she no longer recalled Sophor's caresses, nor her kisses. If she had thought about them she would have chased away the memory. What she saw, when she closed her eyes, with the dear name on her lips, was something bright, soft and consoling. In the darkness where she was, she turned toward her old friend as toward the light.

That tenderness resembled devotion. It sometimes happened to her, in her worst troubles, to repeat Sophor's name, with laudatory and fervent words, as one recites litanies to a saint. To that obscure little soul, who had never clearly discerned good from evil, led to believe that everything that is pretty or shiny is honest, that those who are fortunate are worthy of esteem and admiration, Sophor, so beautiful and so magnificent, appeared as a divinity, all the more radiant because Magalo adored her from the depths of the deepest darkness and shame. The hope of seeing her again made her eyes blink, like the idea of a sun that is about to rise.

When, in the hazards of conversation, someone pronounced the name of Madame d'Hermelinge, or she read it in a newspaper with regard to a premiere performance, she suddenly became motionless, with her eyes fixed and a smile of ecstasy on her pale, withered lips, as if before an apparition. It seemed to her that if she could find herself in Sophor's presence, if only for a minute, all her misfortunes would be over; one glance from her friend would render her young and pretty again, as joyful as before, completely consoled. She had that obsession, as a little girl has confidence in a fay.

Did she think that Sophor would come to her aid, extract her from difficulty? Yes, perhaps she glimpsed something resembling amicable alms. Sophor was so rich, and she, Magalo, was so poor! But that hope was imprecise. Madame d'Hermelinge was, for her, in a general fashion, peace, salvation and life. In hearing her, she would be content to the point of dancing like a madwoman. Alas, at present, it was even more impossible than before to go to Sophor's house. Old, ugly, dressed in rags, looking like a seller of songs, she would never have had the courage to go into the sumptuous house. Oh, no, she was too ashamed of herself.

Once, however, when she had been even hungrier than usual all day, when she had been refused credit everywhere, at the fruiterers, the creamery, at the baker's, she clung more ardently than ever to the desire to see Sophor gain, to hear her speak; that day, she had read in a newspaper that Baronne d'Hermelinge had paid twenty-five louis for a box at the charity fête that evening at the Opéra.

Then—the intensity of desire can produce such miracles—she succeeded in borrowing ten francs from the floor-seller at the Rat Mort, of getting a ticket from the hairdresser in the Place Pigalle; as soon as the doors opened she went into the hall; she had put on so much rouge and rice powder—and the dress wasn't too crumpled, or the gloves too dirty—that she almost looked good under the double envelope of lace.

But that had done her a lot of good, going to the Opéra! Here she was, at three o'clock in the morning, sitting on a bench in the boulevard, all alone, with her foot in a fine state and a heart so heavy that it was choking her.

※

It began to rain. A very cold rain. And Magalo had a low neckline, with bare arms, with no other mantle than the lace that she maintained over her shoulders; the needles of the rain pricked her flesh. Well, what was she going to do? Feeling sorry for yourself is all very well, but it doesn't get you a bed. She could have gone to her friend's place in the Avenue de Clichy, but she never came home alone, that woman; perhaps there was a man there, or men, in the only room; it would be necessary to laugh, to appear to be enjoying herself. Tonight, after what had happened, it would not be possible for her to be funny. She had so much desire to weep.

Well then, what was she going to do? Was she going to sleep on this bench, in the rain? That wouldn't cure the cough that she's had for three months. It's a terrible thing, to have chagrin and to be ill, when one hasn't a sou and hasn't a domicile.

"Hey, you, haven't you finished resting there? Get up, turn your heels, or I'll take you to the station."

It was a sergent de ville who was speaking to her. She trembled with fear. She had never yet had any dealings with the police; that was all that was lacking! She apologized, said that she had felt very tired.

"I'm rested now. I'll go home."

She drew away toward the Madeleine, along the walls, limping. The rain was heavier, and seemed icy to her. Her dress stuck to her. So, not even a bench, in order to be sad for a little longer at ease!

She stopped occasionally under the arch of a coaching entrance, her back against the stone and the wood. Motionless, she felt even colder; she had a shiver from her nape to her lower back, as if a snowflake had melted on her back. She started to run, her teeth chattering. She ran out of breath very quickly, because of the foot that she was dragging, and her dress, soaked with water, and very heavy. She foresaw the moment when, exhausted, she would fall on the sidewalk.

The fear of being picked up by the police, taken to the station, and then to the depot, rendered her some strength; she would go to the house in the Avenue de Clichy, since she had no other refuge.

She turned right into a street. She walked, and she walked. Everything was effaced from her mind, even Sophor. She was no longer thinking about anything but a bed, where she could lie down, undressed, where she would be warm. *Yes, but how am I going to get up the Rue de Clichy? Can I?* She could scarcely stand up, but was still walking.

As she went along the balustrade that encloses the square in front of the Église de la Trinité, she heard a noise behind her, turned her head instinctively, and saw a man coiffed in a top hat with the collar of his overcoat turned up to his ears. He made a sign to the coachman of a fiacre that was going along the Rue de la Pépinière. Doubtless someone emerging from a soirée had not found his carriage at the door.

The fiacre had not stopped. The passer-by perceived Magalo; he approached, looked at her, could not see her very well in the darkness, through the lace, and he went away rapidly; but, changing his mind, he came back toward her and asked her if she lived very far away.

Immediately, the poor wanderer had the vision of a place where it was not raining, where there might be light and a fire!

In a hoarse voice, even hoarser than usual, she murmured: "Very far. But that's no reason. There are hotels in the Rue de Clichy, at the very beginning of the street. I know one, where one is very comfortable, which isn't dear."

Then, drawing closer she said other words, which she knew how to say.

The man hesitated.

She added: "Me, it will be whatever you want."

He did not reply, but started to walk, very quickly, because of the bad weather; beside him, she hastened her steps, with so much difficulty.

She dared not say: "Give me your arm," because there are men who do not like to give their arms to women in the street, even by night. He might be annoyed and go away. And they did not pronounce a word.

They arrived at the hotel. She asked for a room. The clerk winked, on recognizing Magalo. "Number 5 is free; here's the key. The fire's prepared; you only have to light the faggots with the candle."

They went up a narrow, unwaxed stairway with an abrupt turn, and stopped on the first floor. She was so cold that the candlestick trembled in her left hand, the key being in her right. She had difficulty finding the lock. Finally, they went in. The room, longer than it was broad, was reminiscent of a corridor with a single window at the end; red tiles with a frayed bedside rug; gray wallpaper with pink flowers discolored by damp; and on the mantelpiece of black wood, painted with marble veins, between two fake bronze candelabras each missing an arm, a clock deprived of gilt and devoid of a globe, on a mahogany pedestal. But the fire, quickly lit, gave the place a gaiety of crackling flames.

Magalo looked at the bed. In a bed one can lie down, turn over, stretch oneself. It would have been better all alone, but in the end, it was necessary to resign herself, and earn her money. Perhaps the monsieur wouldn't stay there until morning.

She undressed very quickly, put her dress, her skirt, her stockings and her chemise to dry in front of the fireplace, while, fallen into an armchair with his boots toward the fire, the man who had brought her examined her. All that in silence. What did they have to say to one another?

Naked, she slid between the sheets, the chill of which gripped her as if she had lain down in snow. With a strong will, however, she stopped her teeth from chattering, and although, involuntarily, her body was shivering with fever, making the covers jump, she had the courage to say: "Come on then, darling!"

He had stood up; he was very close to the bed, considering her. She had not yet looked at him closely; she saw that he was someone very young. Naturally. Men of a serious age don't pick up a girl in the street at such an hour. And, his face a trifle plump between bright side-whiskers, he seemed timid and mild, even feeble. A funny expression, too, not the expression of a man who desires to sleep *à deux*, an expression of being annoyed to be there. Oh my God, what if he went without paying for the room!

She pulled her thin arms, which no longer smelled of Russian leather and Levantine tobacco, but had an odor of wet animal, out of the bed, and tried to put them round his neck.

But he said: "No, not now; another time; give me your address. I'll come to see you."

He thought she was ugly. The boy was going to look for a carriage; he would rather go home. And he turned to the mantelpiece, where he put a gold coin, a twenty-franc piece.

This time she had a desire to kiss him, truly, with genuine amity. He was going away and leaving the money! A louis, enough to pay for the hotel and eat for several days. It wasn't an old man who'd behave like that.

Magalo didn't have time to thank him; he had gone, and had closed the door again quickly.

No, she wouldn't let him go without telling him how content she was, how kind he was. She leapt out of bed. She had scarcely touched the tiles with her bare feet than a brutal frigidity rose from her soles to her heart.

She fell back on the bed. Her body and her head too buried under the covers, she extended everything, curled up, and stretched again striking the wood of the bed. She was, by turns, so cold, so hot and so cold that she thought she was surrounded by ice, fire and ice again.

Suddenly, a gust of flame rose from her breast to her cranium, filling her head entirely, and nearly caused her temples to burst. Then, in the terror of a child seized by delirium, she threw off the bedclothes, took hold of the bell-cord between the curtains, pulled it, and pulled it, ripping it away, shouting:

"Help! Help! I'm dying!"

When the hotel clerk came in he saw Magalo sitting on the bed, naked, holding her head between her hands, agitating it from the left to the right and the right to the left, still crying: "I'm dying!"

She also said: "Sophor! I want to see Sophor! Go fetch her. Tell her that I'm dying, that I want to see her. It's Madame d'Hermelinge, she lives in the Avenue de Villiers, number 54, the finest house in the avenue. Go fetch her; she'll prevent me from dying."

Then, while the clerk shrugged his shoulders, making gestures of annoyance, thinking: *Good, here's an invalid now! I have to run to the doctor, to the pharmacist; a fine way to carry on!* She lay down again abruptly, like a falling plank, and, her head still clutched between her hands, rebounded, and collapsed, her arms twisted, her torso and belly throbbing, her breast filled with gurgles and gasps.

V

When, after nine days and nine nights of fever and delirium, Magalo returned to the sentiment of life, it seemed to her that she was emerging from a very profound and very long slumber. She saw around her a rosy shadow traversed by daylight; it was cast by the curtains of a bed, which had been drawn in order to protect her from the light. She had a heavy lassitude in her limbs, with pains everywhere, as if she had been beaten while she slept. Full of molten lead, her head had never been heavier or hotter; her eyes, like embers, were burning her eyelids. She could not remember anything of what had happened to her, and did not know where she was. She did not even have the strength to want to remember; did not think, her soul and body inert.

But a sound reached her through the curtains, close at hand, like people talking in low voices. She could not make out any of the words, either because of the weakness of her hearing or because the voices were covered by another, louder sound. What sound? The one that was coming from her throat, panting and hoarse. But without knowing why, she was worried by those whispers, and, with an instinct that someone was talking about her, she extended an arm to part the curtains, in order to see who was there.

Her hand fell back upon the quilt, like the hand of a corpse that has been dropped.

After a long fatigue of her effort, she tried to sit up; she did not even succeed in raising her head from the pillow, her burning and heavy head. However, a little light dawned in her mind; she understood that she had been ill, that she still was. What was being said, she wanted to hear.

With a tension continually interrupted by weaknesses—and always that rattle in her throat—she gradually turned over, pushed her head with her shoulders, and succeeded in parting the fabric with her forehead. She saw, in a room that she did not recognize, men clad in black, three or four, whose backs were turned.

One spoke, another replied, the others approved with little nods of the head. Words reached her.

"It's serious. It's necessary not to dissimulate the disquieting condition of the patient. A more robust constitution might have been able to resist the illness. This person, doubtless, has abused her strength and her nerves for a long time; she didn't eat, committed imprudences. We've been able to observe that, even before this crisis, doubtless due to cold, she had a disposition to tuberculosis. The pneumonia has therefore found a terrain very favorable to its development. We regret to be obliged to tell you that all hope seems lost. The patient might succumb tomorrow or tonight, perhaps in a few hours."

Although Magalo could hear better, she didn't understand very clearly. What was certain, of course, was that they were talking about her, and it wasn't agreeable for her, what they were saying. For sure, she would have been wrong to be content.

Suddenly, she opened her mouth very wide, and, her fists in her teeth, bit them. She knew that she was going to die.

But now another voice spoke, which was not a man's voice. "Poor Magalo!" it said.

Then the dying woman sat up, in a bewildered joy, parted the curtains, and lurched forward, crying: "Sophor!" And she would have fallen on to the tiles if Madame d'Hermelinge had not received her in her arms and laid her down again, kissing her hair.

"Sophor! Sophor!"

Magalo repeated the name and repeated it again. She was so content, her eyes illuminated, that her gasping gave the impression of laughter. At the same time, memories returned to her in a host. She remembered the fête, the rain, the young man who had come with her to that room, who had left twenty francs on the mantelpiece. Doubtless she had been ill for a long time. But all that was nothing, since Sophor was there, touching her, caressing her, with her eyes red from having wept.

Sophor weeping for her! That consoled her for everything. She would have liked to be even more miserable, in order to be lamented more. And her misfortune was good fortune.

When the physicians had gone, she said: "Then you're really here, with me, it's really you who are here?"

With her thin, spare hands, where the skin was wrinkling over meager bones, she touched the cheeks, the neck, the ears; she would have liked to hug her, she tried several times, but had insufficient strength in her arms.

"Yes," said Sophor, "it's me. Don't talk so much. Don't tire yourself out."

"I know, I'm going to die. The men who were here—doctors, no?—I heard them. It's finished. But no, since I've seen you, I don't care about the malady. You've worked a miracle. I'm cured."

"Certainly you'll be cured, if you're sage and reasonable."

"Let me look at you. You're my health, my salvation. Then, like that, you've come?"

"As you can see."

"How did you know I was taken ill, since I was in this house?"

"In your delirium you spoke my name and my address. The hotel proprietor wrote to me."

"I should think that I said your name! Is there any other name than yours? And you've been coming to see me for a long time?"

"A week . . . yes, a week."

"You've come every day?"

"Of course."

"It's you who called the doctors?"

"Yes."

"And you've cared for me yourself?"

"Yes, darling."

"You covered me up, so I wouldn't be too cold, when I threw the sheets and blankets in the air?"

"There's a nurse who helped me."

"You gave me tisanes and potions to drink? Oh my God, perhaps you sat up with me at night?"

"I spent last night with you, because you had a bad fever."

"Oh, my God! Oh, my God!"

And in a paroxysm of joy, Magalo found the strength to clutch her friend to her poor little breast, shaken with sobs. If she had to die, she would have liked to die at that moment, while she was so happy.

The fatigue of her joy finally broke her; she fell back on the pillow, as if inanimate. But between her two hands, where tenderness retained life, she squeezed Sophor's hand, almost, and a sweetness dreamed in her half-closed eyes; the scarcely pink butterfly of her smile alighted on her pale lips. But the gasps, at intervals, swelled her throat and her cheeks, soiling the smile with a little foam the color of rust.

Baronne d'Hermelinge could see clearly that the doctors had told the truth; it was all over for the poor young woman. The thinness of her arms was horrible to see; folded at the elbows, one might have taken them for two little white sticks broken in the middle. The face, in which the cheekbones stuck out, already had the color of the earth that would be thrown over her tomorrow, and the moist odor of long fevers, of rancid sweats, greasy potions that had flowed over the skin, emerged from the whole of that paltry body, once so exquisitely perfumed: an odor scarcely less sickening than the one she would have when she was a cadaver.

Sophor, in considering Magalo, pitied her, the dying darling, with a great sympathy. But she could not escape from a more egotistical dolor. She was witnessing the agony, almost the putrescence, of a being with whom she had once been so mingled that something of herself was dying with her, hideously. It was the most ancient realizations of all her desire, her first complete sensual pleasures, that were lying there. Her cries of amour were expiring in that rattle. Her pleasure was stinking in that bed, and, after the funeral, it would be eaten by the worms, under the ground, with that flesh where it had been born.

Furtively, a disgust seized her for the joys of old, also those since that resembled them, because of the ugliness and the vileness that they would become, before long, between the planks of the coffin, staved in by the expansion of putridity.

Meanwhile, Magalo, very slowly, opened her eyes again. Gazing at Sophor, she dreamed for a long time. No more smile on her lips, nor dolor in her eyes. At the same time, she was no longer groaning, no longer seemed to be suffering. It was as if all the vital force that remained to her was employed in one solemn thought. Yes, at that moment, under the shadow of the invisible wing that death opens over us, that poor little creature was entirely clad in a mysterious gravity, a strange pomp.

Sophor could not help lowering her eyes, with religion.

In a muffled, almost extinct, seemingly distant voice, the dying woman said:

"Listen to me carefully. It's finished, I'm going away forever. You're getting up? You want to send for a priest? No, stay. I wouldn't dare confess. It's too vile, what I'd have to recount. The good God would be offended to hear it. Do you believe there's a God? I went to church when I was little. I ought to have died after my first communion, to be buried in my white dress. But it's not a matter of me. If there's a Hell, I'll go to Hell, that's all; I've deserved it, and what does it matter? A girl like me is no more important when she's dead than when she's alive. You, that's something else; you have intelligence, education, you're a great lady. I want to talk about you, you alone. Perhaps it'll be good for you, what I'm going to say."

She had raised herself up slightly; she had put her hands on Sophor's shoulders. She went on:

"You're very knowledgeable, but I've learned, in an instant, many things that you don't know. You thought I was asleep, didn't you? No, I think I've been dead and that I've come back to life for a few minutes, to tell you what I learned while I was no longer alive. I've never been as I am. I think that I've never thought. Hear me, it's the last thing I'll say.

"Sophor, there's one true thing: it isn't good not to be honest. When you're young, when you're content, you mock people who talk to you about goodness, virtue, you laugh in their faces. That's wrong. It's the bourgeois who are right. They live tranquil, they die tranquil. Me, I've been unhappy for a long time; that's all right, I've had what I deserved. But even before my troubles, when I was happy, I wasn't very. I can see now that it isn't amusing to laugh. And I've expiated, and perhaps am going to expiate again, frightfully, the pleasure that I haven't even had.

"Oh, I'm afraid of what will happen to me when everyone believes that nothing more can happen to me. But you, you, it's necessary only to be occupied with you. I love you so much that I wouldn't want to cause you pain even for your own good, but it's necessary that I speak. You've done things that aren't right. Don't do them any more, in order not to be punished, as I've been, as I will be. It's already bad to have lovers, for money or for pleasure. But the two of us, we've done worse, you know, than giving ourselves to men. We've been friends, as it's necessary not to be, and each on our side, with other women, we've committed the same sin.

"We've been wrong. It's dirty. For some years, I've seen that there's nothing dirtier. In the beginning, because it's different from the habitude, because it's droll, because one's proud of passing up men and enraging them, one only finds amusement in it; then, there's the pleasure that attracts, when one's young. But soon, old or fatigued, you become irritated by what seemed agreeable to you. It sickens you, I tell you. You begin to wonder whether you've ever loved, really, that dirtiness, and you respond: no.

"I've responded that. And when I thought of you, I was ashamed of what we did together; it soiled me, the memory of our amity, that it had had the semblance of love. Yes, semblance. Make-believe. For, in the end, when you think about it, it isn't true that women can love one another amorously. It's a comedy one plays. Here's the proof: of two friends, there's always one who is the man, the master. An ignoble comedy. And now that I've been dead, I see things in yet another fashion. It isn't only vile, that pleasure that isn't a pleasure, it's forbidden.

"By whom? I don't know; perhaps the good God or by what we call the good God. But I swear to you that it's forbidden, more than all the other vices, more than all the crimes. There's someone who doesn't want it to exist, and who punishes in this world, and in the other too, those who have disobeyed him. I know full well that he punishes, because I've suffered. You, if you don't get out of that filth, you'll suffer even more because you're more culpable. In soiling a little good-for-nothing like me, I haven't done much harm, but for being debased, you, so great, so good, who have so much intelligence, you'll merit frightful tortures and you'll suffer them.

"You see, what's true, what's good, because it's permitted, is to have a husband and children like brave women. If I'd married a worker, or an employee, I'd have been spared them, the chagrins! Yes, it's possible that he'd have quarreled with me, even beaten me; never silk dresses or hats with flowers, but frying food and cleaning up the kids; I know full well that family life isn't rosy! But my man would have said to me, sometimes, 'Come here so I can kiss you.' And I would have had a mind at rest; I wouldn't have wanted to vomit after a party with Hortense or big Rosa, I wouldn't have needed, in order to eat sometimes, to lie in Madame Charmeloze's bed.

"You, with your husband, what a happy life! You're so beautiful, he would have loved you with so much tenderness and respect, and think of the god joy of going to sleep beside him, next door to the room in which the little children are lying in their cradles. Let me speak. I believe that the Devil exists. Yes, I believe that. It must be him who has imagined, in order to doom us and aggravate the good God, making women caress women. I've had a demon in me, you've had a demon in you too, a greater demon, because you're worthy of being tempted by a very chic devil. There were many possessed people in times past, why shouldn't there still be?

"I beg you, don't listen to that evil spirit any longer. You're all pale, your features are contracted, you have fire in your eyes. Perhaps the devil is stirring in your body; he's making you angry because of what I'm saying; he's giving you bad advice; listen to mine. I'm like your good angel, who's talking to you. A funny angel, no? Who doesn't have very white wings.

"That doesn't matter, she knows what he's saying, that angel, who isn't very much; she knows what it's necessary to do to be happy, precisely because she did the opposite, and as she's going to Hell, she knows the road not to follow. No, for what I've had of it I've wept the tears that one drinks with cognac, and which give it a bad taste! And it's perhaps true that the Evil cooks you in cauldrons or grills you on griddles. I'd like it to serve for your happiness on earth and your salvation that I've had so much chagrin in life, and that I'm damned."

After a sigh, Magalo's head fell back on her pillow, the eyes wide open and staring.

For a moment, Baronne d'Hermelinge had not been looking at her any longer. For the first time, she was troubled. Her eyelids closed, she could hear Magalo's words within her, prolonged from echo to echo into the depths of her consciousness. Proffered at the moment when Sophor was calculating what there was of herself in that dying woman, the fraction of her that was about to perish and rot with that body, they were like counsel that one part of her being was giving to the other, and what there was of stupid loquacity and memories of puerile catechism in Magalo's words was solemnized by the mortuary hour, the imminent tomb. And now the Laughter was ringing in her ear! Not soft and insinuating, as before, but violent and victorious, with the pride of a mocking master.

Then she was afraid. She leaned over Magalo desperately, in order to ask her to speak again, to retract what she had said—with an instinct, also, of her, living and strong, to be protected and saved by that expiring weakness. But she stood up with a cry.

Magalo was no longer moving, no longer breathing, was dead.

Sophor moved away with a bound, fell into the chair facing the bed, and, because she did not know at what moment the poor creature had rendered her soul, because Magalo had stammered that she had emerged from death in order to say useful things, Sophor wondered, fearfully, whether it was not from beyond the tomb that that warning had come.

VI

Outside the funereal chamber, outside the sort of respectful acquiescence that the vicinity of the dead imposes, when she had found life again in the agitation of the streets, and even when, having returned home to the familiar apartment, far from the unexpected and the extraordinary, she was reclaimed by the envelopment of dear habitude, Sophor did not feel liberated from Magalo's words: "It's dirty, it's forbidden."

Sitting in a low armchair, her head bowed, her fists joined between her legs, she saw once again the alarm-sounder who, dying, perhaps resuscitated, had said to her, in a voice that she had never had, things that one would never have believed her to be capable of thinking.

Oh, that the reprobation of an entire city was heaped upon her, Madame d'Hermelinge knew very well; for everyone, men and women alike—she was not unaware of the fear of her own accomplices—she was a kind of monster; good, that was all the same to her, she mocked the scorn and the hatred, she took pride in the insults. But the reproach of the dying woman had been so unexpected that it astonished her, and obliged her to reveries.

Because it was strange, impossible, that Magalo, a puerile little soul, had proffered that advice and those threats herself, it seemed that they had been dictated by someone mysterious and terrible. Sophor felt as troubled as if she had seen an infant, who had been playing a moment before, writing frightful prophecies on the wall.

Then another thought tormented her. It was bizarre, in truth, that the malediction on the unique pleasure had been pronounced by the very person to whom she owed the knowledge of it; and, unconscious as she had once been in Sophor's eyes, Magalo, for having initiated her into delightful mysteries, retained a competence to blaspheme them.

But, suddenly standing up, she uttered a loud burst of laughter. And, her hair unfastened—her red and black hair, like tenebrous gold—she looked into the mirror at the triumphant pride of her youth and her beauty.

She went pale; it seemed to her that her own laughter resembled another laughter, which she had heard more than once.

Come on, she was crazy. Over what stupidities was she lingering? This was what came of keeping vigil over the sick, of seeing people die. Death, in passing, leaves a shadow that does not disperse immediately. It is necessary to break through that darkness, to the resurgent light. Yes, it was very sad that Magalo, once so lovely, had become a vile little cadaver, but so what? The memory of the dead ought not to encumber existence. The living have the right, in the forgetfulness of tombs, to light, amour and life.

And Sophor, delivered of vain apprehensions, went back and forth in the room, happy and warm, her eyes full of defiance.

She sat down at an ebony and plush table, on which there was an inkwell, pens and scattered sheets of paper. She started writing, with a prompt hand, smiling, her eyes proud and her lips drawn back in an arrogant smile.

Having finished eight or ten notes, she struck a bell and said to the chambermaid: "Have these letters delivered right away. I'm having several people to dinner. Have the table set in the hall."

Then, alone, she resumed marching; at intervals, she stopped in front of the mirror, and her face expanded in a beautiful arrogance.

Dirty! The dying woman had pronounced that absurd word! It was dirty, the flourishing lips of women and the freshness of their bare breasts? Dirty, the embrace of arms washed with odorous water, containing, in living cassolettes, perfumes as fervent as the incense of altars and the myrrh of tabernacles?

What is, in fact, filthy, is male lust, brutal and bestial intercourse, with its sweaty obstinacy, its achievements in which desire is sickened; and, since the virile embrace has for its end the filth of fecundity, conjugal nights are the execrable fear of the pure dream of loving. But all chastities and all tendernesses open in the double flower formed by the joined mouths of two smitten virgins; then, without rancor and without remorse, without the distress of fatigue, inexpressible delights, perpetuated by never-sated desire, haunt the beds of lovers who devote themselves to the divine sterile kiss. And in those unions, similar to snow with snow, an aroma with an aroma, the caressant wave with the wave that follows and surmounts it, the presentiment awakes of

254

a paradise still unrealized, in which the Eternal Feminine consecrates the weddings of ecstatic angels. But what need is there of that paradise, since, on this earth, with all modesties and all ardors the beautiful flesh and souls of female lovers can enchant one another outside the virile mire.

And Magalo had also said "forbidden." A thought more stupid still, well worthy of a mediocre and banal creature, falsely extraordinary, bourgeois in reality in spite of her appearances of mad Bohemia, in whom the insufficiency of pride implied the fear of revolt, the admiration of the ordinary, and the need for consideration in life, in pardon beyond, which torment souls without true boldness sooner or later.

Forbidden by whom? The one who dreams, in the solitude of his divinity, of the eternal evolution of worlds, is scarcely concerned with the sex of ephemeral united mouths, and the heavens light stars indifferent to all evenings of amour. Forbidden, why? Has not the desire, whatever it might be, that impels the person who experiences it, the right to be obeyed? Is it not the case that whatever is desirable is made to be possessed?

Wanting has for a prerogative the ability to attain. To whomsoever is hungry, it is permissible to eat, to whomsoever is thirsty, to drink; the living are the dupes of life if it opposes to their instincts the prohibition or the impossibility of accomplishment. The creator has contracted a debt with regard to the creature. Since I am, I demand. The appetency that was put into me, with the breath that I have not desired, obliges the one who put it there to satisfy it. To yield to its law is more than a right, it is a duty.

Being destined, it is necessary for us to live in accordance with our destination; that which is forbidden is not criminal, if the necessity of the crime is within us.

In any case, what crime? Oh yes, the sterility of enlacements seems contradictory to the natural rule; love in order to give birth, that is what the immemorial succession of races appears to order. Man engenders, woman gives birth, and little beings grow up to engender or give birth in their turn. But there are women in revolt against sexual fatality, and their innate vocation in no less legitimate for being exceptional. Perhaps, since they are infrequent, they are even the preferred of the creative power; the most beautiful flowers do not grow on every bush, and it is in rare couples that magnificent and noble animals wander. That which pullulates, which is abundant, is that which is petty and vile. There are millions of insects for one wild beast; termites are innumerable, a lion is superb.

Those ideas had already been stirring in her for hours when, as dusk was falling, the chambermaid returned.

"Mademoiselle Roselia Fingely has arrived," she said.

"Good. Ask her to wait for me. Have the candelabra and the chandeliers in the hall lit."

Sophor returned to her reveries.

And if there was anything forbidden, if desire did not always imply the legitimacy of realization, would there not be a grandeur in rebelling against the prohibition? To transgress being human, humanity: what a glorious audacity! To infringe the law and brave the punishment is to triumph over the judge. To say no to God is to become a kind of God. The being who makes itself different from what it ought to be recreates itself, equaling the creator, with the additional pride of an obstacle overcome. Woman smitten by man is the primitive rule that nothing opposes; woman smitten with woman is a new rule, more superb for having vanquished the other. The proudest conquests are not taking possession of a deserted country but violent occupations after the first occupants have been expelled and dispersed. It is nobler to build on ruins.

The chambermaid reappeared.

"Madame Nordrecht is here, with Mademoiselle Luce Lucy."

"Have them take their places at table; I'm coming."

In any case, licit or forbidden, glorious or vile, it was not her who had put into her the furious and triumphant desire by which consciences were alarmed. With the arrogance of a

Spanish heroine, she thought: *I am what I am!* but she had not been made what she was. A conflagration has for its excuse the spark that lit it; it has it's fatal development, like a blossoming flower. It is the sower, not the field, who is responsible for the grain. Some women consent to placid hymens, accept the humility of being wives and the bestiality of being mothers. She was not one of those! But, monstrous, at least in social judgment, she had not invented her monstrosity; at the most, she was the accomplice of her sins—sins, so be it!—since she had received the irresistible order to commit them. She took pride in obeying a strange law, but in sum, she was obeying, she was the servant, recklessly zealous, of an omnipotence; happy in her sin, she was not the one who had chosen it. And if, instead of having been obliged to the most extreme delights, she had been obliged to tortures, she would not have been the culpable but the victim; she would have had the right to complain of being criminal. But she did not complain, since her covetousness accorded with the impossibility of not succumbing to them, and since the breasts and loins of women are the divine altars of dream.

The chambermaid came in again.

"All Madame la Baronne's guests have arrived," she said.

"Have dinner served. I'll join them. The time to change my dress."

Had not Magalo talked about the Devil? Well, yes, why not? It was possible that she, Sophor, had some rebel angel within her. She admitted that she was possessed, but by what a glorious, what a delightful demon! A Lucifer as heroic as a Penthesilea and as subtle as a Parisienne counseled all audacities and taught all stratagems. It was formidable and elevated, a sort of God which, for being female, was a Devil. And it had real substance, it must be made of a thousand mouths everywhere ever open and extended toward the odor and honey of lips. It had the fury of the kiss, the need for the embrace and for panting submissions. It knew the words that trouble, disconcert and infuriate. It was the counselor of gestures that envelop and overturn. It put into the eyes, toward the eyes of beautiful women, into the hands, toward their flesh, and into the breast, toward their breasts, the frantic ambition to seize and possess. It was from it that she had the arrogance to look indignant crowds in the face, not to lower her gaze before gazes charged with scorn or hatred, and to bear opprobrium like a radiant diadem.

Between the battens of the door, abruptly pushed, through which entered laughter and the sound of clinking glasses:

"Well, is it for today? Are you coming or not? It's about to finish, dinner, and there's no more crayfish left, or sugared dishes, or Vivette!" said Honorine Lamblin, very pale and too plump, under a candelabrum that a sleeveless arm was holding up.

Sophor said: "Here I am."

With a violent gesture, she tore off her bodice, shook her hair, raised her warrior arms, from which the perfumes of warm sweat took flight, and, all unkempt, her face ablaze, she went into the hall sparkling with gilt and brocatelle, illuminated by twenty candles, prolonged by luminous mirrors.

Around the table abundantly strewn with poppies and red roses, the beautiful amorous women, amid the irradiation, under the chandeliers, crystals and mirrors, were eating, drinking, laughing and saying the foolish things that memory and the hopes of kisses cause to rise to the lips. Almost all of them rose to their feet on seeing her come in. Voices appealed to her, hands grasped her, pulled her into the midst of an upheaval of silky fabrics that made a noise of rubbed flesh.

Yvonne Lérys, always drunk before everyone else, had unhooked her corset, and was pointing the tips of her little boyish breasts like tiny spearheads; and, more forceful than usual, an odor emerged from her of sandalwood exasperated by ginger. Valentine Bertier had taken Vivette Chanlieu on her knees, tipped backwards and showing, beyond her black socks, the gold of her gypsy skin. And those who were not drunk would not be long delayed in being so.

Then Sophor, standing, toward whom all the laughter, all the odors and all the splendors of tresses and flesh converged, considered passionately the subjects of her sovereign desire. Without sitting down she took from Valentine Bertier's hand a Bohemian glass as large as a hanap, from which foam was overflowing. She emptied it, refilled it with champagne and emptied it again; the enthusiasm of the wine, spread throughout her, blazed in her eyes and lit up her mouth. She wanted to drink again, and ordered everyone to follow her example.

What need had she to deviate from her intelligence, to preoccupy herself further with Magalo's sinister chatter? Was she not entirely convinced of the beauty of her joys and her right to possess them? She drained the large glass, with an effort, for the fourth time.

And now, in the midst of the odors of meat and flesh, amid the furious glare of lamps and candles that spangled faces, shoulders and breasts with gold and flames, within the ardent tumult of the troop of young women, whose kisses rang out impudently, Baronne Sophor d'Hermelinge saw the chimera edified of a delectable and formidable Sabbat, in which a multitude of beautiful witches and possessed women said the blasphemous mass of virile amour.

The great hall, with its columns of black marble, extended like a temple illuminated for some glorious ceremony; at the back, the elevation of a dresser charged with gold and silver candlesticks imitated a radiant altar. And from walls opened by some omnipotent spell, young women advanced two by two. Although they resembled Germaine Triézin, Rose Mousson, Séraphine Thevenet or Vivette Chanlieu, they were not all wearing the costumes of Parisiennes.

Some, as if issued from the distant past, were showing faces and breasts panted with a yellow daub that reeked of saffron, and, their legs bare beneath a transparency of spangled muslin, they had little bells on their ankles like the gandharvis of the paradise of Indra, and they were leading domesticated panthers on leashes. Others, who were brandishing thyrsi or shaking rattles, were clad, like the maenads in paintings, in crimsons rent by drunkenness; others, offering lilies and doves in baskets, were imitating the naiads of humid lairs, clad in a fabric woven of verdure and air or the mist of water vapor that rises from springs; and behind them came Aragonese women in red satin and black lace, arched to breaking point, Roman women with mat skin in which two fiery holes opened, helmeted with ebony hair, advancing with a slow stride, as if still asleep in the idleness of sunlit siestas.

Madcap marquises, with faces as white as snowballs, lips the color of peppers, and a beauty spot at the corner of the mouth, frightened a procession of nuns, all blue and pale, holding hands under lowered veils; the mystery of nocturnal caresses in the shadow of cells or under the colonnades of cloisters around moonlit cemeteries enveloped them with a pensive silence. And yet others, between the walls not yet closed, processed toward the sanctuary.

When the host of beautiful tresses was like a dense field of red and black wheat, all the women uttered a loud cry simultaneously. In the passion of a joy so violent that it resembled anger, they began to circle before the altar, running and leaping; their footfalls resonated throughout the temple, and, spinning endlessly in accordance with a furious rhythm, they uttered appeals and howled evocations, or, sometimes, more softly, sang strange litanies in a monotonous voice:

"You who rejoice in nocturnal solitudes populated with dreams and invisible caresses! You who hate the hymen and mock it!

"You who teach young women the enchantment of exchanging their beauty for its living resemblance, who spurn husbands and compliment Sisters!

"You who lean your elbows on the bed-heads of virgins ignorant of the perfect joy and guide toward awakening the uncertain caress of a somnolent hand!

"You who are temptation and salvation! You who invent an inferno sweeter than paradise, and who, for our delight, give a woman's odor to all the flowers of the garden and a woman's gaze to all the stars in the sky!

"You who counsel the Oceanides the fluid bed of a single wave, and beautiful courtesan empresses to drink the drop of blood that a golden needle causes to pearl on the breast of an African slave, and Parisennes to take their baths two by two in narrow bathtubs of cracked faience!

"Enemy of marriage, curser of fecund beds, who takes pleasure in smooth bellies and unwrinkled breasts, exquisite and formidable Demoness, our recourse and our terror, appear on the altar, Demoness,

"In order that we might all adore recklessly your goat's feet perfumed with the hair of queens, and in order that our lips, joined two by two, and our arms enlaced with arms, and our breasts offered, and all our bodies shaken in a frenzied round,

"Will make around you an enormous garland of living flowers, from which all brunette, blonde and red-haired odors, delights of your nostrils, will rise in a single incense toward your starry head!"

And then, out of a smoke that was rent like a veil, a colossal form appeared on the altar. Had it surged forth from the infernal depths? Had it descended from the clear nocturnal empyrean? It was black, red and gilded. It loomed up, diabolical and celestial, prodigious; it was terrible in the enormity of its grace as well as seductive in the infinity of its horror; one divined the torturing charmeress; and, dominating the voices of the kneeling Sisters, her laughter—Sophor recognized it!—sounded like a clarion of victory.

Woman in her long and heavy hair, the mystery of her gaze and the redness of her lips, as fresh as a bloody kiss, beast in the golden hair that covered her arms and legs, and in her caprine feet, she was the female Satan of a Sabbat devoid of men, and while, on a forehead horned like those of satryesses, a diadem of somber diamonds was strangely flamboyant, which evoked the idea of a constellation of damned stars, the Demoness with the divine eyes, tucking her scarlet and gold robe up to her navel, impudently showed and offered to adoration her tawny pubis, like a monstrance.

Then the lovers, extending their arms, waved their tresses towards it like vases of perfume.

"Be propitious, ineffable Mistress, to those who scorn conjugal couches and curse cradles!

"The young men, when we go through the cities, make us signs to follow them and try to take us by the hand; but we, laughing at the thick beards that dishonor their chins, return to our friends with tremulous lips with barely a down of fine gold.

"Be propitious, ineffable mistress, to those who scorn conjugal couches and detest cradles!

"Male lovers throw themselves at our feet, embrace our knees and then, in despair at our refusal, they strike themselves with a blade that enters entirely into their hearts; and we smile, thinking of the pretty ruby bracelets that one might make for the friend with the droplets that spill from the wounds.

"Be propitious, ineffable mistress, to those who scorn conjugal couches and detest cradles!

"We have attempted all the roads toward the excess of delights; by means of frank ardor or sly caresses, we have obliged the most resistant to the confession of perfect ecstasy; for we are the frenzied and the subtle.

"Be propitious, ineffable mistress, to those who scorn conjugal couches and detest cradles!

"However, if labors and joys exist that are still unknown to us, reveal them to the fervent who have merited being instructed in them, O instigatrix of dear sins! Admit one among us to the torturing delight of the communion, in order that, full of you and having become you, she might teach us your science and your will.

"Be propitious, ineffable mistress, to those who scorn conjugal couches and detest cradles!"

But the Demoness did not lower her head toward the supplicants; and there was in her violent eyes, like golden red holes, and the irritated splendor of her diadem, the impatience of a deity to whom the offerings that please her are belated.

Through the parted crowd women advanced, clad not in linen or silk but in fresh red blood, who had knives in their hands; they resembled sacrificers still bloodied by a hecatomb. Behind them, uttering loud screams, mothers were heard fleeing who held their babies in their arms. The bloody women raised baskets toward the altar in which the virilities of male newborns were palpitating; they poured those offerings like strange flowers at the feet of the Demoness; the latter made a sign, and suddenly, wild pigs surged forth, grunting and grunting, which rushed, invaded the altar, and while the living idol laughed mightily, they ate the bleeding future of races.

Then the Mistress, satisfied, designated with her gaze the woman to whom the communion would be given, to whom the new secrets would be revealed, in order that she could teach them in her turn; and it was Sophor who, amid the agitation of odorous tresses, climbed the steps of the altar gloriously toward the radiant and tawny monstrance. All the lovers, their heads toward the floor-tiles, had prostrated themselves like faithful followers unworthy as yet to contemplate the celebration of the supreme mysteries, plunged in a religious terror. But a canticle rose up mutedly from their half-closed lips.

"O triumphant Elect! O royal elder sister! Since you have been chosen among all to receive the ineffable host and to spread the Gospel of new caresses,

"We adore you, and when you descend from the altar our bodies will make steps for your bare feet!

"Since the one in whom the ultimate science and the ultimate joy reside accepts you as a spouse and wants to espouse you, since she is giving to you what you are giving to her, since she and you are simultaneously, in the sacramental office, the communicant and the host,

"We adore you, and when you descend from the altar our bodies will make steps for your bare feet!

"Since you are mingled to the point that if our eyes dared to raise themselves toward you, they would only see one augustly nuptial form; since her divinity and your humanity are joined and confounded in a double feminine unity,

"We adore you, and when you descend from the altar our bodies will make steps for your bare feet!"

And the Elect, in fact, was no longer herself; full of the possessed Demoness she sensed herself becoming. Black, red and gilded, it was her who loomed up, diabolical band celestial, prodigious; woman in her long and heavy hair, the mystery of her gaze and the redness of her lips, as fresh as a bloody kiss, beast in the golden hair that covered her arms and legs, and in her caprine feet; and, while, on her forehead, a diadem of black diamonds was flamboyant, like a constellation of damned stars, she offered triumphantly beneath her scarlet and gold robe up to her navel the tawny splendor of the monstrance!

And the walls vanished; the entire city and the whole country, and the rivers, and the mountains, and the continents appeared such as Lucifer saw them from the height of his star; the universal multitude of virgins, wives and widows headed toward the altar; they were singing, they were dancing, they were joyful, they were kissing one another on the mouth; if men tried to retain them, they threw themselves upon them, tearing them apart and laughing, leaving them beside the roads, bleeding and dying.

They were still advancing; it was like an expanding circle of waves driven by other waves, which was tightening; and when they were closer, they uttered great clamors of joy and, raising their arms toward the somber and luminous altar, launched themselves forward.

The Elect, in the meantime, now felt herself magnified, and further magnified, enormous, immeasurable, as if infinite; under the scarlet and gold garment, now similar to a fulgurant storm cloud, the diabolical monstrance was prodigiously deployed, deepening full of fiery eddies and darkness, and to the passion of the herds of charging women, it offered itself like the vertiginous entrance to a gulf.

BOOK THREE

I

The bedroom blanched by a ceiling lamp was full of silence and torpor. The gold of furniture and picture frames, the light of spangled fabrics, faded away languidly, as if in lassitude. It seemed that things were reposing while the living slept. The armchairs on which no one was sitting any longer stretched themselves vaguely, in the idleness of being unused; it was as if eyelids were lowered over the somnolent mirrors, which forgot to reflect. The inanimate was immobilized and extinguished in more annihilation.

The night went by.

Céphise Ador parted the hair that covered all of her face with two hands, opened her eyes and yawned. Why had she woken up? Ordinarily, she slept for longer, without shocks, without even dreams, in the heaviness of her blonde hair, a little too thick. Perhaps a noise in the street, or a movement in the bed, had extracted her from her repose, or some anxiety. What, then? She turned toward Sophor, who had closed her eyes on the neighboring pillow, after the kisses.

Sitting on the bed, an elbow on her knee and her chin in her hand, Sophor was motionless, turned toward the dark window, as if she were waiting for a commencement of light through the curtain.

Slowly, Céphise put her arms around her neck and drew her toward her, wanting her to come back to bed. But Sophor did not appear to feel that caress, and remained motionless.

"Darling! What's the matter? What are you thinking about? You're not in pain? Come and sleep."

Sophor did not reply. With slightly clenched fingers, which a sort of irritation seemed to retain, in order not to do any harm, she undid the amicable embrace, whose arms fell back, astonished. And she did not turn away from the dark window.

Then Céphise Ador leaned forward, as much as she could, in order to see her friend's eyes, to read her thoughts therein. She straightened up again, almost frightened, so much dolorous reverie was there in those weary eyes.

It did not appear that Sophor was aware of being observed.

She was beautiful, in spite of the years and years. If her pallor, still mat, was less white, yellowed here and there, especially toward the temples, by shades of old ivory, her mouth retained a beautiful violent redness; the reddish black of her hair coiffed her in an ebony and gold helmet. But at the present moment of the present night, the tension of thought wrinkled the skin at the corners of the eyes, and deformed the arc of the lips to the extent of making her appear older than she really was; and the steel of her eyes was extinguished.

"Come on, Sophor, what's the matter with you? You're scaring me. Answer."

This time, Sophor deigned to hear. Without budging, with the ennui of fatigue, she said: "Nothing, nothing's the matter. Leave me alone. I can't sleep, I'm thinking about something. Go to sleep."

But Céphise, raising her voice, said: "It's not something you're thinking about, it's someone, it's a woman!"

She threw back the covers, leapt out of bed, wrapped herself in a peignoir and started pacing around the room, pushing away the chairs and armchairs. With all her undone hair shifting along her back, she said:

"You're thinking about a woman, I tell you. Do you think I don't see anything, that I'm an idiot, and that I don't know that you've had someone in your head who isn't me for a long time?

268

It leaps to the eyes that you're no longer the same. When I speak to you, you don't reply, and if, after making a semblance of not looking at you, I turn round quickly, your eyes are elsewhere, far away from me. You'd like me never to look at you, in order not to be obliged to look at me sometimes, out of politeness. And then, by other signs, I can see clearly that you no longer love me as you once did. For three weeks you haven't come to my dressing room, or to the foyer. I'm obliged to come in search of you now, to come here without you bringing me; and you can't suppose that I didn't see your expression just now, after dinner, when my coachman came up to take orders and I said; 'No, not this evening, tomorrow at midday.' Admit it, you'd rather I'd gone! Admit that you no longer love me. Come on, speak. I want you to admit it!"

She was stamping her feet in front of Sophor, looking her in the face, with rage in her eyes.

With an expression of great weariness, Madame d'Hermelinge said: "You're mad; you know very well that I love you; don't torment me, I beg you, I have worries."

"What worries? You've had enough of me and you want someone else, those are your worries. If you imagine that it's sufficient for you to say: 'Go to sleep, I'll be more cheerful another time,' for me to leave you in peace, you're mistaken. Was it me who came to you? Was it me who offered myself, five years ago? Well, yes. I had a lover, whom I adored, and who loved me. I was happy with him, with him alone; and because, in addition, I was famous, because people applauded me, I didn't desire anything more. You know full well that I'd never thought about women, that I didn't want to think about it, that I was a very simple creature.

"But you enveloped me, you carried me away, you kept me. Five years ago you didn't have these fashions of not looking at me, not replying to me. And now I'm as you wanted me to be, now that I've loved you, and I love you, you no longer want me. Am I less beautiful than before? No, more beautiful.

Everyone says that I'm more beautiful. Blondes, it's at thirty that they're faded, like large summer flowers. But don't imagine that I'm going to accept, like that, tranquilly, being scorned, being rejected.

"What you've made of me you know full well: a woman at whom people point fingers, about whom they talk in low voices. It's nothing to you that people say that you're frightful; on the contrary, it gives you pleasure. You like being hated. Me, I'm ashamed. At rehearsals, respectable people deliberately don't talk to me, move away; even the public—look, I've never talked to you about this, in order not to give you pain, because I thought that you loved me!—the public is no longer for me, as in the past. If I had talent, I have even more; there are evenings when I'm content with myself, when I truly sense that I'm a great artiste. It makes no difference; the audience remains cold, especially on the evening of premieres. Because the people who are there know our whole story. Thanks to you, I horrify them.

"And you imagine that after having sacrificed my lover for you, and my success, and esteem—no, not an honest woman, but after all, a woman like all the rest—that after having become, in order to give you pleasure, a monster like you, that after having been reduced to having you in exchange for everything, I'll lose you without getting annoyed, without complaining, and that I'll say to you: 'You no longer want me? All right, I wish you lots of happiness with the others, adieu.' You can be sure that it won't finish like that, and if you love someone else, you can count on me killing her and you—her first. Yes, I'll kill you, with this dagger, look, with this dagger!"

She had taken from the mantelpiece an ancient silver stiletto, with a sculpted hilt with a little death's-head with ruby eyes; and, plunging it into the breast of some imaginary rival, she seemed, her hair disheveled and her cleavage heaving in the gap in the gold satin peignoir, she was reminiscent of a tragic heroine quivering with vengeance and amour.

Brutally, Sophor said: "Fifth act," and she seized Céphise by the wrists, held her very tightly and forced her to let go of the toy with the pointed blade, which, tip forward, traversed the carpet, plunged into the parquet and remained vertical, quivering.

Then the jealous woman fell to her knees.

"Hurt me, hurt me, I want that. Twist my arms, break my bones, I beg you. I understand that I was wrong. Yes, I was wrong. You have worries that you don't want to tell me, and I, with my ideas, I'm tormenting you. I'm preventing you from being sad at your ease. That's bad. You're right to be angry. I know that it's not true that you love someone else. You're too good, my darling, to love any other woman but me. You can't want me to die of despair, all alone, in some corner. I'm culpable for having imagined that, for having spoken in anger.

"But remember, I have an excuse. I have so much need of your tenderness, in order to take refuge in it, in order not to think about the bad things that are being said about me, the insults that they're heaping on me. It's terrible, I assure you, when everyone draws away from you, or looks at you with a nasty expression, to feel less loved by the only person who loved you. And you've been so cold, so indifferent, for some time. It's understood, you're not deceiving me, you wouldn't dream of deceiving me, but after all, you must agree that you're not the same as the Sophor of old.

"Do you remember the three weeks we spent at the seaside last winter, in the empty hotel? The house was so enveloped by waves and squalls that it trembled and resounded like a ship; but we loved one another in the tempest, as at sea! I don't believe you'd have pleasure, now, in being all alone with me, even in a place that wasn't somber. That's what irritates me, aggravates my nerves, and makes me morose or angry.

"Look. I'm not angry any longer, I no longer have ridiculous suspicions, I'm reasonable. You can talk to me without scolding, generously. Why are you like this with me? Have I done something? If you have some complaint against your Céphise, say so, so that she can apologize. No, she has nothing for which to reproach herself. What you want, I want. Always, I wait for you to speak, I watch out for your gaze, in order to obey you immediately.

"When I'm not with you, do you know what I think about? What I'm going to say when we're together again, of how I'm going to behave to make you content, so you'll smile at me, so you'll touch my hair with your hand, you know, behind the neck, as you did in the early days, and you no longer do today. And you know full well that for five years, I've only loved you, and you alone. Well, you can guess that, pretty as I am—for, after all, I'm not ugly, am I? I'm not ugly—men have prowled around me, rich and celebrated, and women too, who hoped, because they knew . . . but men and women, I don't care about, because there's only you in the world.

"Listen, and promise me not to laugh. Do you remember your big portrait, in riding costume, that you gave me? To begin with, I put it close to my bed, with a lamp, in order to see it right away by night if I woke up. But it was a painting, it wasn't life. Then I thought of putting it in a corner of the room, in such a fashion that it could be reflected at a distance by the mirror above the fireplace; and between the mirror and the portrait there are two gauze curtains that hang down and move slightly. That way, because of the kind of mist that the curtains make in the room, when it isn't very bright, your resemblance is almost you: indecisive, troubled, but real, alive, and as soon as I open my eyes, I blow kisses at the reflection of your image. Then I think: 'Tomorrow, she'll return those kisses to me.'

"You no longer return them to me. I deserve them, though. Order me to open that window and throw myself out on to the pavement and you'll see whether I obey you. How it's happened that I'm like that, I can't explain. You hold me entirely. All that I am, I gave you the first time, and I've never taken it back. So, you have no reason to be sullen with me, to go for hours without talking to me. Oh, you can't understand the desolation

I have when you're no longer paying attention to me, when you seem not to know that I'm there and I'm waiting. What I'm waiting for is for you to love me. That's what I'm waiting for, always. The love that you had for me is like someone who's gone away for a voyage. If it comes back too late, it will find that the friend who stayed on the doorstep all the time to see it return has died of sadness."

She spoke with so much tenderness, her irritation and despair having dissolved into humble melancholy, that Sophor, finally moved, smiled. She looked kindly at that beautiful young woman, so submissive, so seductively plaintive. With a slow hand she caressed her forehead and her hair, as one cajoles a child who has been angry, who has wept, and who is repentant.

Like light into a dark place, a joy entered into Céphise; her eyes were like windows illuminated by an interior fire. Was she about to rediscover her Sophor? Because she remembered the ardors of old, the mad embraces that followed brief sulks, and all the quarrels forgotten in swoons, by lowering her shoulders, while her friend leaned toward her to place a kiss on her forehead, she made the satin of her peignoir slide down her arms, and, under Sophor's inclination, displayed her beautiful plump nudity, the odorous warmth of desire.

But Madame d'Hermelinge stood up then, and, as if seized by alarm, ran toward a corner of the room; there, her head in her hands, she struck the wall with it, with the rhythmic strokes of a pendulum. Then, returning abruptly to Céphise, still on her knees, who held out her arms, stupefied and suppliant, in a jerky voice broken by anger, she said:

"No, don't say another word, don't come any closer. Go to bed, try to sleep. Imagine that I'm ill. You know that when I'm ill, I don't want anyone to occupy themselves with me; I want to be left alone. Well, I'm suffering. What's making me suffer, you can't understand; I don't understand it myself. It's a chagrin, which will pass. At this moment, everything that you could do to cure me makes it worse. You're beautiful, you're good, you're ardently devoted to me; it's true that I'm an ingrate, but I implore you, since you love me, not to touch me, and to shut up. It's necessary."

Céphise took no account of those words; she launched herself toward her friend.

"I won't let you suffer, I'll console you, come!"

But the other said: "I told you to shut up and go back to bed." At the same time she grabbed hold of her, lifted her up, and threw her on to the bed.

"Are you going to shut up now?"

"Yes, yes, if you wish," stammered Céphise.

She abandoned herself on the bed, her head on the pillow, her haggard eyes turned to the wall.

Sophor considered her for a long time, as if to make sure of that immobility, as if to fix it under the threat of her gaze. Finally, she turned away, walked slowly to an armchair, turned it toward the window, and sat down, with her arms on the arms of the chair. She remained still, thinking, her eyes bleak, directed at the curtains. At times, a little sob, retained in a spasm, came from the bed. She paid no attention to it. She never took her eyes off the window.

She seemed to be waiting for daylight, anxiously . . .

※

From then on, Céphise had only one thought: to discover the woman whom Baronne d'Hermelinge preferred to her. For she was not contented by her friend's vain excuses. Does one have worries? Is one ill? The truth was that Sophor was experiencing a violent amour; and, perhaps disdained, she belonged entirely to her desire. But the new beloved, who was it? Céphise searched in vain.

Not for a moment did the thought cross her mind that Sophor might be smitten with one of those mediocre creatures, Yvonne Lérys, or Valentine Bertier or Roselia Fingely. She was

274

not unaware of her friend's meetings, on certain evenings, with those women; Sophor had even confessed to her the strange evening when, upset by Magalo's death-throes and the words she had heard, furious for having buckled momentarily in her pride, and revolted and full of demonic drunkenness, and also bewildered by four large glasses emptied one after another, she had seen a banal sluttish debauchery develop to the point of a seemingly living and tangible, perhaps real, magnificent and prodigious Sabbat.

Certainly Céphise, who wanted everything, having given everything, had suffered from those follies of Sophor, but she was sure that in those perverse adventures, the infidel did not deliver herself entirely, reserving for the best beloved her heart, her mind and her true desires. In any case, those women, and others similar, Sophor had gradually ceased to receive. It was, therefore, in another direction that it was necessary to search for the rival, beautiful enough, smitten enough or reserved enough—for there is an omnipotence in the refusal of kisses—to captivate Sophor.

There had been talk recently in the foyer of the Comédie, in front of Céphise—in order to give her pain—of a great Polish lady, once a singer but now the widow of an emperor's bastard, who had come to Paris and had received Baronne d'Hermelinge; but no, not pretty in any case, almost old, she had departed again for Vienna, taking an Opéra-Comique tenor with her.

Who, then? Oh, wherever she was, whatever she was, the detestable creature who had stolen Sophor, she would find her, and would get to her. A fifth act? So be it. After the dramas on the stage, the drama in life. It was precisely because she had enough strength in her for hatred, and for vengeances, that she had been able to express them in plays so passionately. Well, of that strength, she would make use on her own account. She would be what she had had the ability to appear. And it would not embarrass her to deliver a knife thrust, or to pour poison into a cup, since she had the habit of it. They would see! The certain thing was that she would cease to laugh, the woman preferred by Sophor, and all that would finish tragically.

But her jealousy did not know to whom to attach itself; there was always that question: "Who does she love?"

Once in her bedroom, she considered Madame d'Hermelinge's portrait, and uttered a cry of rage and joy: rage, because of the near certainty of being betrayed stabbed her in the heart, joy because she would be able to avenge herself.

Silvie Elven.

Yes, Silvie Elven.

Why had she not thought of that right away? Once, Sophor had gone very often to the little artist's studio. Their intimacy, then, had not been a mystery to anyone. Baronne d'Hermelinge had even had tender cares and gentleness in her passion for that frail creature; she lowered her voice in talking to her, in order not to shake her with too rude a noise, and made signs to people to walk on tiptoe when Silvie was working. Of course, they had separated, and gave the impression, if they encountered one another, of not knowing one another, but that quarrel might only be a ruse, that coldness a hypocrisy.

Céphise imagined, with a redoublement of anger, that she had been their dupe for a long time, that they had never ceased to love one another; and the more she applied her mind to that idea, the more she judged it probable. Precisely because Silvie, cunning or ingenuous—for one could never tell—gave the impression of a little girl who would fall over if one pushed her a little to hard, and had the languors of a pretty invalid, and had resemblances to the flowers she painted in pastels and which flew away if one blew on them; precisely because she was so different from the ardent and violent Sophor, she must please her, attract her, keep her, perhaps inspire in her some very delicate and very tenacious sentiment, a desire ever renewed because one scarcely dared to satisfy it; the fear of doing her harm by touching her added a delight to the audacity of having scarcely touched her.

Céphise, in the subtleties of her jealousy, understood everything now! She was, for Sophor, something like those beautiful plump and white girls of whom men who are engaged to honest, slightly paltry demoiselles, whom they were not marrying until next year, make use in order to slow down the brutality of their temperament. With the former, they render themselves capable of respect toward the latter. What Sophor's kiss wanted from her was attenuation, the blunting of a desire by which Silvie's mouth, a little sensitive rose, would be frightened; she had enabled them to love one another chastely!

Chastely, no; Céphise knew very well that Baronne d'Hermelinge did not limit herself to the stupid infatuations of little schoolgirls who gaze at one another at a distance, blushing, glancing between the eyelashes, or squeezing one another's fingers furtively under the table in the refectory. She had possessed, did possess, Silvie, but to Céphise's bed she brought back the ardors wearied by not breaking the other; Céphise was employed to spare—but not enough, alas—her rival!

Such a fury impassioned her that if Mademoiselle Elven had suddenly appeared, she would have thrown herself upon her, without a word, thrown her down on the carpet and stifled her with a knee on her breast.

Immediately, her resolution was made. She would go to see Silvie, would hurl insults in her face, would oblige her to confessions, and if the culpable did not ask for pardon and swear never to see Madame d'Hermelinge again . . .

Céphise Ador dressed very quickly, went downstairs, and climbed into a fiacre. She had brought the little dagger with the death's head with ruby eyes on the hilt, stolen from Sophor's.

In the carriage she thought a little more calmly. Her jealousy was not pacified; as before, she was convinced that she had been betrayed and mocked, but after all, she had no proof. Certainty, yes; proof, no. It was necessary for her, however, to confound the little hypocrite. With the result, now, that she hesitated, wondering what she was going to do at Silvie's studio.

She ought to have gone to Madame d'Hermelinge's house first, to search the drawers, to discover letters. Letters? They had no need to write to one another, since they saw one another so frequently, every day, whenever they wished. Then too, Mademoiselle Elven was not one of those who write! A woman careful enough of her repose, her health, to accept fatigued kisses, sufficiently uninfatuated to accommodate herself to an agreeable sharing, to the idleness of amour, would be able to refrain from imprudences that might compromise her.

The evidence, if it was possible to find any, it was in Silvie's studio that Céphise would find it. On some item of furniture she would see a handkerchief or a glove belonging to Sophor. Perhaps the artist had commenced some painting—a warrior nymph, a fauness in the woods—of Madame d'Hermelinge.

Oh, on going in, Céphise would have the indifferent air of a lady who has come to render a visit, but how she would search the corners with her eyes; how adroitly she would dart a glance through a door standing ajar into the next room. Then, she would get up, wander back and forth, admiring the canvases, as one does in studios, suddenly returning to an easel where the resemblance of Sophor appeared.

Thus, it was necessary that she go to Mademoiselle Elven's apartment. And it was with a tranquil step, without visible emotion, resolved to all patient investigations, that she went up the staircase and into the antechamber.

The visitor was introduced immediately.

"Truly, it's you?" said Silvie, astonished. "It's been a long time since anyone has seen you!"

And she held out her hand to Céphise Ador, after having put the tip of her mule on a cigarette, which a little cough had expelled from her mouth. Then she resumed painting. It was a bunch of violets that was beginning to flower on the canvas. It had been months since Silvie had renounced large paintings with characters. Even portraits in pastel no longer tempted her. What there had always been in that delicate and mediocre artist, of the schoolgirl who has dispositions, had regained the upper hand. She also did a few water colors: windmills beating the air near running water, the openings of grottoes veiled with climbing roses under flowering acacias. She took pleasure in those meager works, the natural imaginations of a little soul full of romantic reverie.

The two women chatted, with occasional silences, about the things about which one talks when one does not know what to say. Céphise, smiling and worldly, giving the impression of not having any care, had picked up a Japanese fan, with she was agitating in a hand devoid of fever.

But how she hated her, that creature, still very small, very dainty, who, at twenty-eight, did not look more than twenty, so much had she retained slenderness and fragility in her seemingly unfinished prettiness. And beneath the admirable coolness of her appearance, the jealous woman thought about Sophor's kisses among those light tresses, like a silvery gold down, on those diaphanous cheeks with a rosy pallor, on the delicate flesh of those lips, between which the fine nacre of the teeth shone. That body, not of a woman but barely a little girl, enveloped, loosely here and narrowly there, by the cream silk of the peignoir, had quivered in frail shocks under a savant mouth with lustful tortures; and everything that Sophor had touched, Céphise would have liked to bite and tear.

For a moment, she had the folly of hoping that blood was about to redden the fabric at the place where the peignoir was scarcely inflated by a young breast, and did not understand how she had sufficient empire over herself to chat with ease, not to leap on Silvie and make, in fact, with the dagger that she had in the pocket of her skirt, the hoped-for wound. At the same time, she looked in all directions, covertly, searching for some clue.

Nothing. Animal skins on the parquet, Oriental muslins hung on the walls, and trinkets on the furniture. The door by which one entered Silvie's apartment from the studio was closed. In the next room, on the other side of those planks, they must have enlaced so often! But it was closed, that door; there was no pretext for opening it, to go and make sure that Sophor was not there. Perhaps she had hidden when Céphise was announced.

Another thing occupied her: that large green curtain, which was closed. What was that curtain veiling? After hesitations, she stood up, and made it crease on the rail.

"What are you looking for?" asked Mademoiselle Elven.

"Pardon me, I'm so curious. I thought that you might have an unfinished painting there."

Behind the green lustrine, there was only the modeling table, with a wooden banquette covered with silks and flowers. There, doubtless, in the times when Mademoiselle Elven had not yet renounced considerable compositions, some young woman had lain, figuring a dead Ophelia or a sleeping odalisque.

Céphise came to sit down again with the rage of disappointed jealousy, and she talked about the play that was in rehearsal at the Comédie-Française, about her role, which did not please her much. So, she had come for nothing! She would leave, not only without being avenged, but without having gleaned the slightest indication. Five o'clock chimed on a Boule clock. It was impossible for her to prolong her visit any further.

Then, suddenly, she stood up, went toward Silvie and seized her wrists rudely.

"Admit, then," she said, "that Sophor comes here every day!"

"My God, what's got into you? Why are you hurting me?"

Céphise let go of the wrists.

"Don't make a semblance of being half-dead as soon as some-one touches you. Sophor's hands are more violent than mine, and you don't complain when it's them that hold you. Go on, talk, when does she come? Yes, Sophor, Madame d'Hermelinge. You're not going to tell me, perhaps, that you don't know what I'm talking about?"

Silvie was trembling, like a child caught at fault.

"Ah! You're afraid! You have good reason to be afraid. However, I don't know yet what will happen. First of all, it's necessary that I know everything. So it's true, she comes here often? When? In the morning, when I'm still asleep, or in the afternoon, when I'm rehearsing, or even in the evening, when I'm performing? That's why she's no longer seen at the theater. It's in the evening that she comes, I'm sure of it; she finds you prettier under artificial light!"

Silvie smiled, sadly.

"I understand," she said. "You're jealous."

"Well, yes, jealous. Why not? Isn't it my right to want everything, since I only have her? Speak, quickly. You can see that I've divined things; it's not worth the trouble of hiding anything from me now."

Silvie took her hand gently, led her to a large armchair, sat her down and sat down next to her, on a stool. Then, her eyes tender, she said, in her murmurous voice:

"You're mistaken; I assure you that you're mistaken. It's more than three years since Sophor has come here. You can ask the domestics, the people in the house. It's more than three years."

Then Céphise: "You're lying . . ."

"I'm not lying. I always tell the truth. You've had some quarrel, suspicions have come to you, and you've said to yourself: 'It's to Silvie's that she goes.' No. You can imagine that people have told me things. Yvonne, who is at the same theater as you, doesn't leave me ignorant. In any case, everyone talks about it. And it appears that it's natural to be jealous when one's in love. But you're mistaken. I never see your friend, and I'm quite content, because I'm more tranquil. I'd be dead now if she hadn't left me.

"It's true, Céphise, I assure you, that I scarcely have as much strength as a bird. I'm not ill—it's nothing, this cough—but I'm weak, throughout my body; it always seems to me that my life is only hanging by a thread, that it's about to fall. I must have hardly any blood; sometimes, when I get up from my chair, I'm not sure of being able to go as far as the other room. I need to be treated with a great deal of care, like a convalescent. In the evening, when I go to sleep, I'd like someone to rock me in my bed, as in a cradle, someone to sing me nursery songs in a soft voice, to send me to sleep. When my mother was still alive I sat on her knees after dinner, already grown up, and I closed my eyes, almost dreaming; it was very pleasant.

"Sophor frightened me. She was good, and strove to be gentle, but in spite of herself she had passions that rendered me half mad. It seemed to me that her eyes, via my eyes, were entering into my body and wanted to take the heart from my breast. I loved her very much, with terrors. She had the effect on me of a good giant, who sometimes, perhaps annoyed, would be terrible. Little dogs in a lion's cage must be as I was. Then there were strange hours, when I was afraid of remaining dead.

"With that, she had a very great intelligence, she thought of powerful, elevated things. Me, no. She wanted me to do great paintings, with heroic figures. That's not my affair. What amuses me is to paint flowers and birds. There's nothing prettier than a butterfly on a rose; it scarcely alights, doesn't do it any harm; and if it flies, it isn't very high. Sophor, in that as in other things, embarrassed me, frightened me. She was too superb, too great for me. So since she's been gone, I've had, after a great deal of sadness, a great deal of contentment.

"Oh, if she came back, I don't know what would happen. She's so extraordinary that she does with me whatever she wants. Perhaps the life of old, when I was like a swallow in an eagle's claw, a wisp of straw in the fire, would recommence. I don't think I'd have the courage to escape the alarms, the apprehensions, that were so frightful and so charming. She would kill me; so be it, I'd die. But there's no danger that she'll come back! And everything is for the best. I don't hope for that, because I don't regret her.

"I've become again, entirely, what I was before knowing her. I have my friends, who are very amiable, who don't jostle me, who come to talk to me while I work, as one chatted once in the schoolyard. They're very funny, they tell stories, we laugh; it's amusing. They bring me flowers, I give them water colors or pastels, which they find pretty, and which are pretty, in fact. Sometimes, with Roselia or with Luce Lucy—you see, I'm not hiding anything from you—we stay on, talking in the studio long after it's no longer daylight. It isn't terrible. Merely thinking about Sophor, I have a frisson.

"Are you tranquil now? You're sure now that our friend doesn't come here, that I'm afraid of her. Come on, smile. Don't be angry any more. If you wish, I'll give you this bunch of violets when it's finished; you can keep it in memory of that poor Silvie, who never did any harm to anyone."

Her attitude, while she spoke so softly, asked for tender responses, affectionate acquiescences; she wanted to be thanked for her sincerity, to be pampered in response. In the mingled pleats of her peignoir and her dress she pressed herself against Céphise, tipped back, almost lying in the large armchair. She might have made one think of a dainty little girl emerged from her couchette in a nightgown, barefoot, coming to her mother's bed and stroking her, wanting to be taken into it.

But Céphise could no longer hear Mademoiselle Elven, was no longer looking at her. *If this child is innocent, who, then does Sophor love?* Her mind wandered among so many women, pausing over a suspicion, then another, and then others. At each presumption there as a new bitterness, a stir of bile; Céphise resembled someone making a bouquet in a garden of poisonous flowers.

She stood up and said: "It's possible that I'm mistaken, and it's very lucky for you that you haven't seen Sophor, because, look, I brought this."

And she showed her the stiletto, the little death's-head with the ruby eyes. While Silvie recoiled, frightened, Céphise's eyes lit up with a steely glimmer.

"But in sum, I believe you. Adieu."

And she left, without another word.

Did she, in fact, believe her? Yes. No. Silvie's voice had appeared sincere to her. But, involuntarily, she felt attached to her former suspicion, and could not set it aside entirely, as one only recovers with a kind of regret from an illness from which one has suffered a great deal. It seems that one is clinging to something that one has put into oneself so dolorously. In any case, there was no recovery; on the contrary, the anguish subsisted, more torturing for having no precise object: the same jealousy, exacerbated by the uncertainty of the vengeance.

Well, what it was necessary to do was quite simple. It was necessary, without allowing anything of her interior torment to show, to spy on Sophor, to follow her, and have her followed, to discover, finally, the execrable rival. And on the day when she held her, how delightful and frightful it would be, all the more exquisite for being more terrible. She lived the moment of murder and joy in advance. In a strange décor that was edified in her mind by memories of drama modernized by present habits of elegance, which resembled simultaneously a Parisienne's bedroom and the apartment of a courtesan of Ferrara or Padua, she saw herself entering—her, Céphise, but also Thisbe, clad in shadow and silence. She approached, feeling the walls, with a dagger in her raised hand; she moved aside furniture, parted curtains, parted drapes, and, with a great cry of rage, she awoke the two lovers asleep on the same pillow.

Oh, the sensual pleasure of the hand that plunges the steel into the rival flesh, which draws it out and plunges it again, and thinks that it will never enter deeply enough. Then one withdraws it, in order to see the blood spurt, the beautiful blood, the dear blood, the adorable, avenging blood!

Céphise would drink it, that warm redness; and with her teeth, she would enlarge the hole, because a large glass is necessary for a great thirst; and with her lips, soaked with red, like the wound from which they had sated themselves, she would stifle the scream of horror on Sophor's lips, would spit into her mouth the dead woman's wound, would oblige her to swallow it too. They would both be drunk on it!

Then, if people came, the neighbors, with the police—she saw sbiri mingled with sergents de ville—she would cry out, pointing at Sophor next to the murdered woman: "We are the guilty!"

They would be taken away, they would be judged, they would be condemned.

In her romantic reverie, she imagined a prison, where, from her cell, by night, thanks to the complicity of a warder, is not some open wall, she would reach another cell, Sophor's; there, no one would see, or be able to come and take her friend away from her, and they would no longer emerge from that dear paradisal tomb, and she alone would possess her entirely, as she would be possessed, perpetually.

II

Céphise Ador was mistaken. Sophor did not belong to any violent passion, renewed or new; she did not love Silvie Elven, or any other woman.

What was the matter with her, then?

Ennui.

With her mouth to Céphise's mouth, she suddenly had the sensation—on no matter what evening, one of the evenings of life—that she was kissing those lips without pleasure, that she was kissing them because she had kissed them before, out of habit; that she no longer coveted what she possessed.

A momentary melancholy, the fatigue of the excessive delights of the evening? That was the first idea that came to her; certainly, she would rediscover, in the continuation of the effort toward joy, the accustomed joy; there would be delirious hours: all the violence of ancient desires, with all the science acquired in long perversity, she put from dusk to dawn, in her caresses. Never had she obliged her friend to the confession of the happy death with so much subtle obstinacy, recompensed by sighs; she knew once again—voluntarily, alas—the ecstatic victory that she had so often owed to the precipitation of her entire being into gaping femininity; and, straightening up, gloriously unkempt, she displayed the arrogance with which she had divinized herself on the altar amid the universal multitude of virgins and widows.

For weeks and months, she was obstinate in pleasure, frenetically.

But she sensed clearly that it had ceased to be real, that pleasure, that she was lying to herself, that she now only wanted that which she had once desired, that her instinct would only reignite the old pride of being satisfied. The fear traversed her at times that she had finished being herself.

She quickly chased away that importunate dread. It was absurd to imagine that she loved less, that she coveted with a less sincere passion the flowery and perfumed beauty of lovers. Why not also think that, like poor Magalo, led by her natural stupidity and the disillusionment of poverty to the denial of former happiness, she would soon envy the fate of the honest bourgeois woman who lay down in the bed of a man and gave her breast to her children?

She burst out laughing.

The truth was that the monotony of a unique amour eventually implied some lassitude. But, young and strong, not sated and destined never to be, she still aspired and always would aspire, to the charm of dear pink lips, to the odor of undone tresses. Did the mouths of young women resemble less than before beautiful flowers of flesh? Did maddening warmth no longer emerge, as before, from open corsages and shifting dresses? It was only necessary to shake off this idleness of the senses in which the soothing tenderness of an enlacement that was always the same had gone to sleep. She was like a husband or a lover who, in too many happy nights, has wearied of his wife or mistress, but would love other women with the rediscovered fervor of first kisses.

She threw herself outside the placid life that the tenderness of Céphise had made for her. Taking advantage of the hours when her friend was retained by rehearsals and performances, she returned to the comrades of old, unknown to the actress, and also attempted new adventures on impulse.

Because she was famous, because her strangeness attracted all extravagances, all the unhinged, she saw in theaters and restaurants, as soon as a voice had named her, the eyes of women who were offering and soliciting; she received letters that did not hesitate to propose meetings during the absence of parents or a husband; and young girls—schoolgirls to whom a newspaper read in secret had revealed her—sent her flowers in letters from which an odor of irises and fresh corsage rose.

She did not waste time choosing. In taking all those creatures, who liberated her from the ardent dementia whose hearth was within her, it seemed to her that she was reentering into possession of her property, that she was exercising a right; she also had the impression of fulfilling a kind of duty. It appeared to her that she was accomplishing a mission to which the fatality of her being commanded her. And the laughter that sometimes rang in her ear, the laughter in which she now took pleasure, the return of which she solicited, complimented her for that fidelity to her task.

There were months of fantasy and amusement, of satisfied vanity. She had foolish gaieties, in having been obliged to hide in a cupboard like a lover in a vaudeville at the sound of the footsteps of a jealous individual, in having taken some beautiful woman to supper at the very hour when she was awaited by a serious lover; in having made some divette at the Bouffes or the Nouveautés miss her entrance in a new operetta; and she took provincial ladies into the debauchery of concert-spectacles and nocturnal restaurants. For two days, having said to Céphise: "I'm going on a voyage, don't worry,"—for it was amusing to lie like a husband giving the pretext of the opening of the hunting season—she was the chambermaid of a very beautiful demoiselle who, on the point of being married, had sent her photograph to her.

Mediocre caprices! Almost vulgar lusts! Anecdotes resembling the banality of libertine novels. But in all those frivolous abominations she mingled the solemnity that was within her; she rendered terrible that which, without her, would only have been bizarre, imposing destiny at random. To make every adventure into a magnificent or sinister event merely by virtue of the fact that they are participating in it is the prerogative of heroes or monsters. And her criminal amusements left her accomplices with reveries, ensuring that, suddenly waking up, they would consider the darkness with wide eyes.

She did not worry about the remorse that she was sowing in souls. For almost an entire year she diverted herself with so many passionate pretty women; she had the conceit of a hundred petty victories on her lips, by which her diabolical triumph was augmented. And it was charming, all those mouths full of kisses, which she emptied laughing, as one drinks over dessert a liqueur from the isles or Tokay in little Bohemian glasses. For a long time she thought she had never been as cheerful or as happy.

And the ennui got worse and worse.

There was no way of hiding that lugubrious verity from herself: she was haunted by ennui. And it was not only during the natural languor of aftermaths that it slid into her and took up residence; at those moments, it might have been nothing more than a melancholy of fully sated senses, exhausted nerves, a residue of joy fatigued by having been excessive; even in the most maddening obstinacies of intercourse, the moments when, at one time, universal life was summarized for her in the long-hoped-for spasm of lips under her lips, yes, with the supremacy of a god constraining souls to enter into his paradise, she obliged her elect to joy, there suddenly came to her, next to the most beautiful, next to the most desirable and the most desirous, a sadness in being there, a need to be elsewhere.

Elsewhere? Where, then?

She did not know. Elsewhere.

She wondered why she was in this bedroom, on this bed, alongside a table on which half-empty glasses enabled the idea of an incomplete intoxication, under lamps whose very light awakened the idea of an imminent extinction. And she drew away abruptly, her head between her hands. One sole need: to flee.

She thought, sometimes, that she might run through a country where there was no one, through damp grass, swim naked across a river, wash herself in its freshness, wash not only the body but the soul, and, on the other side of the cold and healthy water, in a meadow, put on white clothes and, far away, travel in the company of village folk who go on Sunday to some friary under the trees. While she was occupied by that stupid chimera of an escapade in the fields, her eyes, it was strange— her dry eyes, as if burning—became humid; and a regret filled her entirely.

Regret of what?

But the person she had left on the pillow turned toward her, looking at her with an expression of astonishment and reproach. The puerile dream of a white dress in florid meadows was not permitted to Sophor. Nor any other dream. She did not have the right to abstract herself from the completion of what she had demanded and undertaken. It was necessary that she keep the promise of her troubling and violent eyes, or her whispers in a low voice, necessary that she justified her renown. One does not throw a woman on to a bed, after having tempted her with frictions whose power one knows to be irresistible, only to quit her thereafter, nervous, her entire being in alarm and blushing in her futile nudity; it is indispensable to accomplish that which one has constrained her to desire, one cannot deny her mouth the kisses that it implores.

To go away, to be alone, would be so good! Joy. No, since joy was no more; but at least it would not be the simulation of joy, which is the most desolating of labors.

Alas, she resigned herself. She owed, she would pay. She gripped the flesh again that she had released momentarily. With a violence exasperated by the lie, she reduced it to the cries of a murder victim, almost hateful for being devoid of amour. She rarely succeeded in being her own dupe, she rarely thought that she experienced, in reality, what she ought to have felt. When she fell back on the bed, as if dying, beside the almost dead woman, her feigned faint was only a pretext for the bleak reveries of ennui; she prolonged that inertia for a long time, for a very long time, so much did she fear the awakening that would oblige her to caresses.

She had thought she owed that kind of spleen to the monotony of her liaison with Céphise; the impossibility of liberating herself from it in the illusion of temporary intoxications led her to believe that it would be better to return entirely to her friend. The only thing that she could not suppose, that she did not want to suppose, was that her ancient desire for feminine beauty was finally weary; she had an indomitable pride in having remained similar to herself. She would never submit to the humiliation of admitting that she was less capable of the exultations of yore.

And, with passionate hopes, she took possession again of the amazed and delighted Céphise. She strove to find her infinitely desirable. She swore that even in the early days of her amour she had not known such an absolute delight in holding her in her arms.

Ennui? There was no question of that now. She had been ill, nothing more. Now health had returned to her, and she was the assiduous friend of the most seductive and the most loving of women. If, sometimes, in the evening, when Céphise went back and forth in the bedroom, all white and pink under the diaphanous mist of her chemise, Sophor felt herself involuntarily invaded by a need for solitude, was tempted to yawn, she went into the next room, took out of a sideboard some bottle of liqueur or heady wine, emptied it almost entirely in a single draught, and reappeared, her eyes lit up; and drunkenness, while she seized Céphise too recklessly, rendered her the illusion of desire.

But soon, neither the determination to love, nor the exasperating alcohol, succeeded in persuading her of the sincerity of her concupiscence. When she rejoined her friend, who extended her arms, naked in lace, toward her, she calculated the length, the morose length, of the time that would go by before dawn, before the hour when sleep would not be an insult.

Of all the embarrassments with which an unknown power chastises humankind, there is none more execrable than pleasure when it has become servitude. To kiss lips, no matter how young, fresh and exquisite they might be, when one has ceased to desire them, is the worst of tortures; and no one can have any idea of the joy reserved for an escaped convict who has not turned her mouth away, finally, after so many breathed hypocrisies, from a mouth she no longer desires. No Hell is comparable to the caress when it ceases to be a paradise.

Baronne Sophor d'Hermelinge knew that chore of loving. Only extreme fatigue delivered her, momentarily, from repugnance; at night, after the labor, she collapsed beside Céphise, finally asleep, in a bleak stupidity; she sank, as if into pitch, into opaque nothingness, wanting to sink even further. But an instinct survived: that of seeing the morning light, of opening the windows, of enabling to escape that odor of mouths with which the bedroom was full, toward the distant freshness of the heavens.

Then, gradually, these projects formed, with the glimmer of an issue: as soon as the daylight had dawned fully, she would awaken Céphise, and tell her that it was time to go. "Aren't you going to take a ride in the Bois? I'll join you, before midday, at the Pavilion d'Armenonville. By the way, you know, you have an early rehearsal today." And often, she put the clock forward, in order that her friend, whom she shook with a seemingly involuntary movement, astonished to have slept so late, would exclaim: "Oh, my God, I need to go!" And, when Céphise was dressed, Sophor found interminable the kisses that they exchanged at the door, under her lifted veil whose friction, on her forehead, aggravated her.

Alone, she returned to the bedroom swiftly, opened the shutters by a crack, went back to bed, threw away one of the pillows—Céphise's—breathed in the bright air, deeply; and there was throughout her being what a woman experiences when she has just taken of a corset that was choking her.

But she did not go to sleep.

She reflected, more lucidly; she strove to understand. That covetousness was dead in her she did not want to admit. No, no, a hundred times no! She affirmed violently to some invisible contradictor that she would always be the woman victorious over humiliated males, the insatiable conqueror of young women. Only—yes, that was quite probable—her desire had been refined by the experience of pleasure, what resembled lassitude was merely a noble disdain for excessively banal joys. She took pride in not being content with mediocre rewards, astonished by once having been so easily satisfied.

She became scornful of the women she had had, whom she had. How had she been able to obtain pleasure with Magalo, a falsely adventurous little creature, fundamentally stupid and not very pretty besides, impudently made up: a whore to whom men made signs in the street or dance-halls, and who went on in order to be followed! Sophor had accepted the leftovers of Provincial advocates who came to Paris during vacations.

Others, after Magalo, had been worth no more than her. Those socialites! She could not help shrugging her shoulders with a pitying expression when she thought about the prudery of their consents, the imbecile reticence of their most reckless abandonments; and some were whores of a sort, more stupid. She had been exploited—yes, exploited—by Madame de Grignols; that consumptive had herself paid with a ring or a settled debt, for the risk of a cough. Marfa Petrowna? A fanatic enraged by the certainty of never knowing the intoxications of which she boasted of wanting, and in whom perhaps even that enragement was insincere.

One alone had been delicate and worthy of affection: Silvie Elven, a poor little woman ever ready to render her soul, who had, when one clasped her too forcefully, suppliant sensitivities, exquisite fashions of dying, a virgin every time and always astonished no longer to be, and becoming one again as soon as there was a threat of a new caress, so desired nevertheless.

As for the others—Roselia Fingely, Valentine Bertier, Luce Lucy and their peers—she only thought of them with a mocking laugh. Amorous women? No, accepters of pleasure, or feigning to accept it, from wherever it came. They took off chemises in the bedrooms of their mistresses crumpled by the caresses of a lover. The least despicable were those who truly abandoned themselves under the kiss to some enchantment, did not make any difference between the feminine mouth and the virile mouth, like vulgar drinkers who cannot discern one vintage from another, nor one glass from another, and are content as long as they get drunk. Yvone Lérys, deceiving herself in the extreme spasm, gasped the name of a man languidly in Sophor's embrace, as she doubtless moaned "Sophor" between her lover's arms. In no longer wanting all those women, in being tired of their deceptive or banal ecstasies, Madame d'Hermelinge found a just pride.

As for what Céphise was, she had no illusions about that beautiful creature. Beautiful, certainly, and emitting perfumed warmth whenever she stirred her hair, but what was she? A kind of magnificent animal, nothing more, refined by life, rarefied by art, but nevertheless still instinctive, loving as one eats and drinks, faithful not to her friend but to her joy, jealous not of her mistress but of the delights she expects for her; bleak after a night without kisses, like a hungry bitch. Simple and direct, Céphise was incapable of conceiving that there was a triumph in the scorning of virile amour. Resplendent, all warm snow and gold, and good, yes, for displaying on an evening of victory, like a fluttering flag of flesh, but possessed of neither grandeur nor revolt. A bed-servant.

Thus, it was legitimate and natural, the ennui that was haunting Sophor; the only extraordinary things was that she had not experienced it sooner. Oh, all her hope, once disappointed, went toward one goal alone, so distant. For some time, already, she had been evoking the years of old, and, in the trouble and distant clarity, like an apparition of an angel amid paradisal mists, Emmeline trembled diaphanously.

✳

Emmeline! That name, she did not pronounce; she heard it like a very ancient echo of a matinal bell. And now she revived the games in the double garden, the walks in the forest, the passionate transports at the keyboard whence their dreams flew away in music. She saw again the flight through the obscure rain, the little wooden house on the bank of the river.

Alas! They had been happy on the island. She would have exchanged the memory of all the sensual pleasures with which she had been infatuated since for the freshness of a single drop of the water that she had dripped on to the child's little feet. Those dear little white and pink feet, veined here and there with blue! The chill of the skin, so delicate and so smooth, shining under the gliding transparency!

And she recalled the tenacious, the infinite kiss in which they had absorbed themselves in one another.

Precisely because she had never been possessed, Emmeline remained exquisitely desirable. The vision, in the distance, of that virginal body on the narrow bed—the body before which Sophor's ignorant desire exasperated—was like a glimmer of very pure snow and dawn. How destiny had frustrated her of the sole being that she had veritably loved! So many women, all women—except that young girl.

And now, henceforth, her entire life turned toward Emmeline. She was like a voyager who would like to retrace his steps, toward the country glimpsed at the awakening. If she had not lost

Emmeline, what divine days they would have lived! Instead of vague avidities toward too many mediocre creatures, one sole, constant, serene, sacred amour would have filled everything; she would have been, eternally, the amorous sister of an angel, the angelic wife of a virgin.

Doubtless, now that the knowledge, alas, was within her, she dared to say to herself that she would not have respected Emmeline's innocence for long; she would have possessed her, since amour is made of desire, since the soul is realized in the flesh; there would have been, there might still be, delirious joys. Oh, God, her mouth! To rediscover the ecstasy of a kiss on that mouth, she would have accepted to drink therefrom, the freshness of the breath, a poison causing instant death. But her ardors would be purified because of Emmeline's purity.

Sophor ended up conceiving the bed that she had shared with her unique friend as an august nuptial couch in which sensual ecstasy was idealized, divinized. Her pleasures with other women seemed to her now to be debauchery; her love for Emmeline would have had the chastity of marriage. And in the penumbra of her ennui she adored that light, Emmeline, whiteness and candor. All that is bright, serene and sacred was summarized in that vague apparition, out there.

There was a resemblance between the devotion that, among the dirty sadness of life, Magalo had had for Sophor and the fervor in which Sophor was now exalted toward Emmeline. On emerging from some monstrous sin, she became innocent in that religion, as one might cleanse oneself in a baptismal dew; at other times, it seemed to her that the vision of Emmeline by which she was brushed settled on her shoulder like a dove—with the result that, long unavowed, the thought of seeing her childhood friend again, and finally possessing her entirely, no longer quit her.

Seeing her again?

Alas, would Emmeline still resemble the young woman of old? So many days, months, years had passed. Married, the so dear must be very different from what she had been. In any case, for what was Sophor hoping? Did the possibility of a renewed and henceforth continuous tenderness appear to her in the distance? Did she conceive the design of a future made of all the tenderness of the past and other tenderness too? She did not interrogate herself. Whatever Emmeline had become—she must still be adorably pretty—and whatever might result from their meeting, Madame d'Hermelinge needed to see her again, that was all, as a mouth rendered tasteless by a sugary liquid might desire a splash of snow that would melt between the teeth and run down the throat. In the presence of the only friend, she would be suddenly liberated from languor and rancor, happy.

And finally, she made the resolution. She would see her again.

The difficulty of carrying out her project made her desire its realization even more; immediately, ardently, she occupied herself with the means of succeeding. In order to recover the traces of the vanished person, what should she do first? What rendered the enterprise far from easy was that Emmeline, married who knew where, perhaps in some foreign country far from France, now had a name unknown to Sophor, and as long as that name remained unknown, how could she orientate her research?

But not at all, she did not know what she was saying; it was not indispensable to know the name of Emmeline's husband; it was sufficient to discover what had become of Baron Jean. He could not have remained in the Senegal for very long; he must have returned to his homeland. He ought, at present, be in some large provincial city, the chief of a battalion, or a colonel, perhaps a general; and after being informed, Madame d'Hermelinge would send someone intelligent and reliable, who would be able to make the Baron's domestics talk; surely they would not be unaware where their master's sister and brother-in-law lived.

Thus, it was possible, it was certain; she would find Emmeline again. Oh my God! An anguish gripped her heart. What if Emmeline were dead? Even very young, people die; the most exquisite are often the first. That idea—Emmeline dead, put in the earth, having become the horrible thing that cadavers end up—filled her with terror and despair. And yet it might be that her darling had ceased to live, during all this time.

But no, it wasn't true. Sophor refused to believe in the impossibility of seeing her again. If her friend had been attained by a mortal malady, she would have received some mysterious advertisement deep inside herself. No, no, not dead, very much alive! And all would work out for the best, since they were surely going to find one another again.

She had a disappointment. Monsieur d'Hermelinge did not figure in the Army List. That was singular. Had he been killed in some skirmish in Africa? Very anxious—for, with the Baron dead, how could she discover Emmeline?—she went to the Ministry of War and had her name sent to a bureau chief, who received her immediately. She was one of the strange celebrities of Parisian life; people were curious to see her at close range.

The bureau chief had, in fact, once known Baron Jean. "A fine soldier," he said, "who didn't steal the rosette of an officer of the Légion d'honneur." But after a few years passed in the Senegal, where he had fought like a demon, and others in Algeria, he had handed in his resignation, on the pretext of eight or ten wounds; no more mention had been heard of him. Sophor listened in consternation.

"In fact, though," the bureau chief continued, "if you want to know what has become of your husband, nothing is easier. Decorated, he has a right to a pension. At the Légion d'honneur, they can't be unaware of his domicile."

She had a great joy. An hour later, she wrote in her notebook: *Colonel Baron Jean d'Hermelinge, at Gemmilly, via Balleville, Eure-et-Loir.*

It was now only a matter of finding an adroit emissary . . .

An emissary, why? She could go to Gemmilly herself, interrogate people herself. That was, she would avoid the anguish of idle waiting; anxiety is eroded in activity, and she would be informed more rapidly.

Did the idea of being in close proximity to her husband not cause her some apprehension?

She was only thinking about Emmeline. In any case, she had no need to risk an unpleasant encounter. In one of the town's hotels—or, rather, at the village inn, for Gemmily only had four or five hundred inhabitants—it was probable that everything that she wanted to know would be known. Emmeline and her husband must have visited Monsieur d'Hermelinge more than once. Then too, in sum, if, in prowling around the vicinity of the Baron's home, she found herself in the presence of her husband, where was the peril in being recognized? Perhaps, in fact, she would not have been sorry to find herself face to face again with the man who had tortured and beaten her, and, now strong, liberated from the marriage and no longer able to be trapped by it, to throw in her husband's face her still-vivacious scorn and her furious rancor.

In sum, that was the thing to do.

Without even having warned Céphise of an absence that might perhaps be prolonged for several days—talking to Céphise at a moment when she had given herself again to Emmeline would have been insupportable—she set forth early in the morning. From the corner of her carriage she saw through her window the green freshness of meadows, woods, and the gaiety of the sunlight traversed by birds. The spring was also in her now. She felt full of living and fresh things; like the landscape, she was reborn. In the same way that those hawthorns flowering alongside the track had forgotten the thorny black skeletons that they had been for so long, she no longer knew that she had been morose and acerbic. And it was not true that so many days had gone by, that she was thirty years old; Emmeline and she were as young as before; they had not ceased to be tender and happy.

Suddenly, she leaned forward, delighted, toward the window, because the grand avenue of a château, in the distance, resembled the path in the forest where, one day, after the rain, they had played like madcaps, and spun and spun, for a long time, holding hands, under the parasol of their mingled flying hair. Well, those little girls' games, they would recommence them; they would go together along roads toward the woods. Sophor did not doubt Emmeline's obedience. At a word, at a sign, Emmeline would come to her, without caring about her husband or anyone else. And they would leave immediately.

Where would they go? To the island. The house must still exist. They would lodge there, without domestics, as before, have morning and evening meals sent from the hotel; they would be alone under the great trees, running after one another, throwing flowers at one another on the lawn. And it would be the adorable idyll of old, more delectably amorous. For now, Sophor was no longer ignorant of all that Emmeline, so chastely and so unconsciously, had desired. They would not separate in the evenings at the door of the finally-nuptial chamber; the hope of the bride would not be disappointed by the inexperience of the kisses; delighted, she would no longer flee, as she had done, as she had been right to do; and no human happiness would equal the pure and perfect joy of the two beautiful spouses.

As soon as had she entered the only inn in Gemmilly, which was next to the railway station, she began to interrogate the innkeeper, a stout red-faced woman with an enormous belly, trailing resounding sandals over the tiles of the dining room, she had difficulty in retaining a cry of joy, so promptly did the success of her project surpass her hopes.

Baron Jean d'Hermelinge did not live alone in the village where he has established himself the previous year; he had his brother-in-law and sister with him, Monsieur and Madame de Brillac; they were well-known, and everyone loved Madame Emmeline, because every time she came into the village she never failed to stop in the square to distribute sous and cakes to the barefoot little boys playing leap-frog around the fountain. The whole family lodged at the top of the road that climbed through the acacia wood.

"Here, from this window you can see the house. It's the finest in the area."

Emmeline's house! One could see it!

Sophor ran forward, and, leaning between the two battens she contemplated avidly the brick building splashed by daylight, with its slate roof sparkling with a seed-bed of golden dust, with its windows enlivened by the sun. She had never seen anything more luminous than that dwelling.

Further away, beyond three large clumps of trees that were swaying harmoniously, the hill was flourishing under the diaphanous azure, and the road rising toward the pink façade, clouded here and there by the vacillating shadow of wayward vines stirred by the wind, was so bright, so gilded between the acacias that were dotted with reddish whitenesses like settled butterflies, that it made her think of the radiance that descended obliquely toward the earth from the glories of paradise, like a ladder thrown down for the return of divine travelers and by which exiled angels climbed back to the heavens. Oh, there had never been an exile crueler than Sophor's! But she would reenter into amour by that road of sunlight and flowers.

Well, what was she doing there, at the window?

Why was she not launching forth toward Emmeline, so close?

She left the room very rapidly, traversed the square almost at a run and began to climb the pretty florid route.

There's someone, thought the innkeeper on the threshold of the inn, *who's in a hurry to see her friends again; it's surely good news that she's bringing them.*

❋

Sophor increased her pace. In all the smiling charm that enveloped spring nature there was, for her, the presence of Emmeline; those colors, that freshness, and the pure daylight, and the odor of the acacias and the twittering of the birds were Emmeline, or the presentiment of Emmeline. As she walked she plucked a branch of eglantine, in full bloom, which she kissed with her full mouth, a little cluster of perfumed lips.

She stopped.

To begin with, in the excess of her joy, she had not been able to reflect, to take account of things carefully. It was necessary to map out a reasonable line of conduct. Nothing would be more absurd than to have herself announced, to go in, to say to Baron d'Hermelinge: "It's me; I've come to fetch your sister; have her informed that I've arrived and that I'm taking her away." He would throw her out, insult her. Then too, with the brother, there was the husband.

The husband! In recent times, since the memory of and desire for Emmeline had haunted her, she had often thought about that man, but, in being unknown to her, in not having a name, he had not appeared veritably existent. Now that he had been named for her, and she could see the house where he lived, he had been realized; and Sophor was jealous of him. "Monsieur and Madame de Brillac." She had heard the innkeeper say it. Those words signified kisses, caresses, intimate forms of address, a bed in which two people slept. Oh, she detested him, the husband!

But she contained herself. Rage would have counseled her to some imprudence. Later, she would imagine a means of slaking her hatred against the man who possessed Emmeline. At the moment, she ought only to see him as an obstacle, an obstacle not easy to overcome. As much as, or even more than, Baron Jean, Monsieur de Brillac had the right to conceal Emmeline, to repel the intruder. It was therefore necessary not to think about a direct conflict, which she would have preferred, but to proceed slyly, to succeed by means of some stratagem.

Alert her friend by means of a letter carried by a village girl? A dangerous attempt; the letter might fall into the hands of the brother or the husband, and everything would be compromised; Emmeline would be imprisoned or taken away.

An idea occurred to her, which appeared to be excellent, but with the unfortunate aspect that could not be put into execution right away, and that the choice of the day and hour would have to be left to chance. However, as no other means was offered, she would use that one. Madame de Brillac sometimes went down to the village, alone, to give cakes and sous to little children who were playing. Well, Sophor would keep watch, from morning to evening, at one of the windows of the inn, on the ground floor; she would wait for Emmeline to come to the fountain; then she would call out to her, have herself recognized, take her into the hotel, convince her to leave, and by the first train, they would flee no matter where.

She therefore resigned herself to waiting. She turned back toward the village.

But no, it was too frightful to sense Emmeline so close by and to go away without even having perceived her. She consented to wait before fleeing with her, not to embrace her yet, and not to speak to her yet; she did not have the strength to renounce seeing her this very day. It was necessary that she see her. And that was not impossible. What could prevent her from going all the way up to the house, from prowling around the gate or along the hedge, watching the windows? What a delight if she divined her, even at a distance, leaning on a window-sill?

There was a danger of being surprised by Baron d'Hermelinge, but a scarcely probable danger. She had changed over so many years, and her veil was thick; she would be patient until nightfall, and then, veiled by lace and darkness, no one would see her features. Yes, she would stay in the acacia wood until dusk, but as soon as the first stars appeared she would slip between the trees toward the brick house and go around it, until, though a door or a window, she saw—oh, only for a moment!—the adored one. Perhaps she would be lucky enough to see her walking in some pathway of the garden, in a white peignoir, all alone and pensive.

An infinite tenderness filled Sophor because of the idea that Emmeline sometimes thought about her while walking under the branches in the evening. She penetrated further into the flowery wood; no longer able to see the road, she supposed that no one could any longer discover her from out there, so she sat down in the ferns and remained immobile, her elbow on her knee and her chin in her hand. Her eyes were brightened by hope; her lips opened with the aspiration of kisses.

Oh, it was quite true that the sole possible salvation resided in Emmeline, since, for being less far away, she felt happy and appeased, in spite of all her impatience. The truly extraordinary thing was that she had remained so long without the need to reconquer her at any price. How many years lost, which might have been so sweet! But it was necessary only to think about the future, so beautiful; Sophor made a paradise of the dream of imminent delights, and wondered whether she might not go mad with pleasure, at the moment when the unique beloved rendered her the unforgotten perfume of her lips.

While the shadows rose, crawling through the undergrowth and climbing the trees to go and dislodge from the branches the rosy gleams of the setting sun, like birds of flame, Sophor went slowly back to the road, followed it as far as the façade, walking on the darker side, clad in an impalpable mantle of twilight. When she saw the gate, and the lawn beyond, with its basket of roses, she avoided passing in front of the house, going along the hedge toward the hill. She slowly made a tour of the little park. She stopped from time to time and hoisted herself up on tiptoe in order to look over the verdure, or bent down in order to look through some gap in the thorns.

No one. She continued walking. It was almost dark, but not one window lit up. Had she been misinformed? Was the house empty? Had Baron d'Hermelinge departed for some voyage with his sister and brother-in-law? Oh, my God, what if her hope was mistaken, if her friend were not in that house?

She was soon reassured. The sound of a piano reached her. It must be Emmeline who was playing; surely, it was Emmeline. Sophor recognized a dance tune. She would have preferred to hear a different music, more subtle or more violent, mysterious, one of the pieces in which they had once mingled their souls in their impulsion toward the unknown. Emmeline has always liked light music. She was wrong. No, she could not have been wrong. It accorded with her ingenuous and futile nature, uncomplicated and not sublime, that taste for simple and lively tunes, which amused and did not trouble. Then again, what did the tune matter, since it flew from Emmeline's fingers! Every note entered into Sophor's heart like a drop of honey that opens and dilates into flame; and the banal rhythm rocked her in angelic arms, toward the heavens.

A bell rang; the piano fell silent; from the perron, the loud voice of a man called up to a first-floor window: "Well, are you coming down? Your husband is already at table; you know we're dining in the arbor. Hurry up; I'm as hungry as a wolf." Baron Jean's voice. Sophor had recognized it.

Instinctively, she moved away, nearly took flight. But she was scornful of herself because of that fear; she found herself near the hedge again just in time to see a white dress disappearing toward a distant light, under an arch of slender branches. It was there, on the far side of the park, that the table must have been set. She walked rapidly along the hedge, turned, turned again, and stopped. She could hear the sounds of cutlery and crockery. Parting the branches, she distinguished five or six guests around a tablecloth, under the globes of two lamps into which moths were bumping; fumes were rising from a large faience tureen.

She saw Emmeline.

She pulled her head backwards very rapidly, because in precipitating herself forward she had scratched her face on the thorns. But she drew nearer and she peered, and continued gazing, breathlessly.

The diners were very hungry. At first they did not speak. They leaned over the table, a full spoon going from the plate to the mouth and descending again from the mouth to the plate; the liquid sounds of soup between inflated cheeks could be heard. Country air gives one an appetite.

With a coarse laugh, Baron Jean said: "I'll have a second helping of soup."

He had grown fat in growing older, His beard and his white hair, short, thick and brutal, bristled on his head like ill-tempered snow, and he breathed from the belly, broadly. Blooming in his jovial rudeness, he had the air of a contented giant. Monsieur de Brillac, robust in his hunting costume, showed a very pink face, which was laughing with ease, for no precise reason, because life is good; and Madame Emmeline, very pale, more beautiful than pretty, plump, without a corset in her white bazin peignoir, tightened by a belt of the same fabric, stopped eating continually in order to make a little girl perched on a high chair swallow a piece of bread dipped in the broth, and she used her napkin to wipe the mouth of the child, who said: "More!"

Two other children, a boy of ten or twelve and a girl a little younger, were sitting between Monsieur d'Hermelinge and Monsieur de Brillac, facing Emmeline; they were kicking one another under the table, without taking their eyes off their plates. The other, who was watching them without appearing to, said to them at times: "Well, Gaston? Well, Constance?"

But Baron Jean, with his mouth full, said, "Bah! Let them amuse themselves. When I was little I was always kicking the table leg. It wore away the wood in the end. One day, when a big dish was being served with a leg of lamb inside, the table collapsed under the weight like a cripple without a crutch."

Everyone burst out laughing. It must have been the hundredth time that the good folk had heard that story. It had never seemed so droll to them.

Emmeline replied, however: "That's how you help me to raise your niece and nephew well! You ought, on the contrary . . ."

She did not finish, because she was obliged to put her napkin very rapidly beneath the chin of the smallest one, who had stuffed too large a piece of soaked bread into her mouth and could not swallow it.

"Something very curious happened to me the other day," said Monsieur de Brillac, while a servant with bare arms changed his plate. "Can you imagine that I was walking along the railway track, and I heard the whistle of a locomotive, and I said to myself: 'Good, there are imbeciles going to the devil, when they could stay tranquilly at home.' But it's all the same to me what others do, and as it was pretty warm—pretty warm for the time of year—I wiped my forehead with my handkerchief . . . you know, my red handkerchief, here, this one . . ." He deployed an enormous handkerchief and went on: "Suddenly, someone threw himself upon me, snatched the handkerchief and disappeared. You'll never guess who it was! The roadman. Probably, he didn't know where he'd left his flag, and I saw him make the signal with my handkerchief!"

Baron Jean, puffing with laughter, did not want to believe a word of that story. "Brissac's telling us tall tales. Just because he was born in the Gironde, it's no reason to pull people's legs."

But Gaston, his fork in a chicken thigh, said: "So, Papa, if you'd had a white handkerchief, the train would have been derailed?"

That remark seemed so comical that everybody writhed with laughter; Emmeline's corsage shook, and after that hilarity, the woman and the two men, silent for a moment, looked at one another with a satisfied expression. It meant, that expression, that it was good to be as they were, together, in that mild evening, between the trees that freshen the air, before dishes that smell good.

A tenderness gripped them. Monsieur de Brillac stood up and, after having wiped his mouth with his napkin, took his wife's neck between his hands and kissed her on both cheeks.

"Come on, René, stop it, will you stop it!"

"Bah!" said Monsieur d'Hermelinge. "Carry on as if I weren't here." He laughed quietly; he had a project—that of taking on his knees the child perched beside Emmeline. While Madame de Brillac defended herself against her husband's caresses, he stretched out his arms, seized the little girl, lifted her up and held her against him.

"There! I didn't have a wife, but I have one now, and I want to kiss her." And he rocked the child, and smiled at her, while the two older children got up from their chairs and grabbed hold of his sleeves. "Me too, Uncle! Me too! Kiss me!"

That tussle only came to an end when Emmeline, in a tone that was almost severe, pushing her husband away with a hand over his mouth, cried: "Come on, you're all mad, the big and the small, and we'll never finish dinner this evening."

Just then, the maidservant put on the table a stuffed shoulder of mutton from which a stimulating odor of spices rose; the reawakening of appetite produced a truce. They resumed eating. Worthy people, happy people, they were taking pleasure in their familial solitude, in their honest idleness; they had peaceful hearts and untroubled minds. For many days, certainly, they had not read a book or a newspaper; the noise of the great cities did not reach them. It did not matter to them that they were only mediocre; they did not think about that; they lived simply, instinctively; they no longer knew that there were, elsewhere, desires, ambitions and troubles.

When dessert was served, Baron Jean said, in his coarse gaiety: "From what I can see, there'll only be the Emperor who won't be dining today?"

"Yes, yes, here he is!" replied Emmeline.

The Emperor was a little man aged six months, whose real name was Félicien. Monsieur d'Hermelinge had nicknamed him the Emperor because the brat resembled, like two drops of water, Napoléon I, and also because the baby was the master of the house, which for him was the world. A stout girl brought the child who, his head round and face plump and wide-eyed, was waving his fingers out of his swaddling-clothes.

"Give," said the mother. But before taking the child she unfastened the corsage of her peignoir and brought out her left breast, very large, as if bloated, with a broad and violet-tinted tip. Then she took her son from the maid's arms, and the Emperor, his eyes almost not open, his hands pressing, sought with his avid mouth, and found, the tip of the breast and stuck his moist lips to it, sucking with occasional inflations of his plump little cheeks; it seemed that the noise of the flux with which he was filling himself was audible. Emmeline's breast bulged under the suction, the blue veins swelling, and the infant's lips were pinker than the rim of the teat.

"The Emperor is drinking!" cried Jean d'Hermelinge, raising his glass.

"The Emperor is drinking!" repeated Gaston.

His younger sister, already in the anxiety of future maternity, did not look in the direction of her mother, only occupied with the cherries on her plate.

But Monsieur de Brillac's eyes were proudly radiant. To see his wife—the person that one has made one's wife—nursing the being that one has enabled to live! To see the body that one has fecundated corroborating the engenderment, what an august joy! He no longer resembled at all the banal country gentleman, or the Gascon who, a little while ago, had recounted the adventure of the handkerchief used as a flag. He was the father, attentive to the maternal spouse.

Invaded himself by a solemnity, Baron Jean, in an instinctive adoration of the august mystery that was being accomplished, and no longer talking, raised his eyes to the sky full of stars, which were radiating complaisantly toward that mother nursing her child.

In the great silence, it seemed that nature—the pacified branches, the flowers that were almost no longer moving, and the luminous azure through the trellis of the arbor, colored with approving mildness the woman who was giving life to the child who owed life to her.

Sophor fled. She went back to the road, and went down at a run, with the rapidity of a rolling stone.

✳

Emmeline's breast! That was what it had become, that pale virginal breast, where a redness had flourished that was almost not pink, traversed by the shadow of a golden thread, that breast on which a slightly too insistent caress had left a wound, that breast which seemed to be made of a flesh of soul! It was swollen like the cleavage of nurses that one saw on the benches of promenades, it widened its violet-tinted and clotted summit like an old flower opened too extensively. And it was lactating! A male was sucking virility from that breast. She had seen white droplets flowing over the round softness. That breast, once so exquisite in its sterile virginity, was vilely and execrably maternal; the suction there dishonored the memory of the kiss!

Sophor did not care, at that moment, about Baron Jean or Monsieur de Brillac, so contented and so joyful, nor about the children, living testimony to marital caresses; she was not even thinking about Emmeline's heavy face, too plump and too white, resembling a fatigued mass. She saw that horrible breast full of milk! And she fled, recklessly.

It was the impossibility of salvation that she had found at the end of her pilgrimage. Full of the ennui of so many revelations, she had launched herself toward Emmeline as toward the sole delight still unknown; her supreme hope had ended in this disappointment.

What, then? What remained to her? One cannot live without desiring something; but what she had desired so ardently a little while ago was an object of disgust and horror to her. She was like a shipwreck victim who had tried to clutch a rotten branch and had sunk again.

To think that it was true! To think that it was so: that Emmeline was now that fecund wife, that nurse. Oh, the gesture with which Madame de Brillac had pulled from her peignoir the breast like an udder! Oh, the gaze full of bestial tenderness with which she had covered the nursling feeding on her!

And the most frightful thing for Sophor was not that it was her final dream mocked and humiliated; it was the thought that henceforth, the Emmeline of the present would spoil for her the Emmeline of the past; in the dreams in which her ennui sought alleviations, Sophor would no longer be able to see her friend candid, fresh and intact, such as she had been. The mother would substitute herself for the virgin. The exquisite form lying in the bed in the house on the island would be that hideous breast, and if, in some chimera, she leaned toward the cleavage in which the shadow of a golden thread trembled, her lover's lips would encounter there the competition of a little, plump, thirsty mouth. With the result that an abominable mockery of destiny had dirtied the unique distant whiteness that had still authorized yesterday her illusion of not being irremediably dark; and her night, which could not hope for a dawn, would no longer even have that little star.

Another idea stabbed her, of which she could not rid herself, to which she was subject as to a nightmare on her breast: Emmeline was happy.

Was she jealous? Certainly not. In spite of the disgust of the recent vision, she retained a very tender affection for her childhood friend; what sickened her was not Emmeline's happiness, but the species of that happiness. She was happy because of family life, because of a husband, a brother, three children already grown and a little one on the teat! Happy for having done what all women did! Happy for having been, for being, an honest and simple creature!

It seemed that an unknown will was imposing on Sophor, at the same time as the dishonor of her first and last desire, the example of the felicity that she had repudiated. She could have been what Emmeline was, sitting down with her husband and her children around a table in a covered arbor, giving her breast to a feeding newborn, and rejoicing in it, and yawning, while playing whist on the ground floor drawing room, toward the good sleep beside a husband, who, as soon as he has embraced you, kisses you on the forehead and goes to sleep.

It is true, however, that they are tranquil and have no sadness, and that they do not have bad dreams, those who are like everyone else. Perhaps the pride of being different is not worth as much as the peace of being banal. One has glories and hallucinations that resemble divine sabbats; one is extraordinary; one looks at the people passing by in couples with their children: "They don't know how astonishing I am!" And one smiles with pity, because they look so stupid in their Sunday-best happiness. Yes, but they go home, where the table is laid, where the lamp under the shade illuminates the mild monotony of being honest every day, where girls ask for a checkerboard after dessert, to pass the time, while the men, the husband, the brother-in-law and the grandparents talk politics, somnolently, their hands on their bellies.

Oh, the imbeciles! Oh, the elect! You know full well that you will die, you who live! And in order to be in repose in the sepulcher it is necessary to have acquired, down here, the habitude of peace. It would be terrible, at the moment of eternal slumber, not to be able to sleep. My God!—for Sophor thought that name, by virtue of a memory of custom—how frightful it would be to be in one's bier, without finding anything there but the continuation of having been awake for so long! A corpse who, beneath closed eyelids, is alive! And perhaps the shroud is not only made of linen but of all the things that one accomplished or thought. Thinking differs little from accomplishing; sooner or later the person who dreams acts out the dream.

Then too, how do we know that our dreams are not incarnate in some sidereal world in which the beings are our chimeras, finally substantial? Sophor while on this earth, had realized herself; she knew full well that she was complete, that joys different from those caused her ennui would never be possible for her. She had made the tour of her destiny. Like a traveler following accustomed roads she was no longer unaware of what she would find around the bends in the route: the inns were devoid of surprises.

No longer to have any hope! No longer even to have anything to dread! To expect all pleasures, as to expect all distresses, to be someone who is no longer astonished, to be the desire that will love all the more for not being sated, and will nevertheless be as it was before. The chastisement of the culpable Ideal is that it can become real, whereas the other, so distant, always slips away.

To live, perpetually, a day informed and sure of its tomorrow, oh, that is installation in Hell—and a Hell in which the uniformity of the tortures does not even permit you the distraction of dolor.

Alas, good people also know the desolating monotony or the bitterness of living. It is necessary not to believe that happiness is so facile; that it suffices not to be criminal never to suffer. If honesty fatally implied happiness, everyone would be honest in order to be happy. There are, in the contentment of duty accomplished, many regrets of faults in which one would not have found veritable joy. And even without those regrets, simple hearts have troubles; there is, for mothers, the cough of little pale children; husbands finally know the ennui of always having the same face on the neighboring pillow. They are satisfied, nevertheless, the bourgeois, as they are called, very satisfied; they have acquired, in seeming to be, the habit of believing that they are.

Illusion, perhaps, but sincere illusion; and as they are excluded from troubles, searches and anxieties, their felicity is like a house of cards that remaining standing because there is no wind. In any case, the resource remains to them that if they wanted to be otherwise, they could be; it is one of the advantages of virtue that, when it becomes bored, it thinks that it would be possible to sin—sin, for worthy people is like a reserve, one does not touch it—while evil, in spite of divine repentance, can never become innocence; and, all returns being insipid, it no longer knows what to do when it collides with the all that limits it.

Sophor could not help having the idea that it would be very good to be similar to simple folk. The calm of that dinner in the arbor caused her, as she went down the road, to seize handfuls of hair. Her anger against those imbeciles exasperated desire.

Oh, come on! Was she mad? It was not sufficient for her, then, that Emmeline, so long desired, had appeared to her unworthy of desire; that from Emmeline's breast maternal milk had flowed before her eyes? She wanted another despair? She needed, after the torture of the disappointment, a humiliation even crueler than that torture? She was not far from thinking that she had been wrong, that her life was mistaken, that it had been necessary to be like the idiots in order to be happy like them? That it would have pleased her to have four children, like Emmeline? That she share the opinion of the dying Magalo, who regretted marriage, the babies one washes and the dinner one cooks?

No, she revolted, scorned and repudiated those cowardly thoughts. She would never consent to cease to be herself! She was what she was! There was nothing more abominable, doubtless, nothing more outrageous, for her ancient dream, than Emmeline's breast nursing; but no matter, she would not admit that she was vanquished; she mocked her friend's happiness.

And she went, and she fled, and at moments, she burst out laughing. Then she heard two laughs in her ears, her own and another, which did not come from her.

III

Having returned to Paris, she plunged desperately back into the infamous adventure. She would find in her sin itself the cure for the ennui that she had. What it was necessary to avoid was the truce between two pleasures, the moment when one judges the previous joy and that to come. Continuity leaves no room for lassitude; intelligent drunkards are those who, when scarcely awake, grasp their glass again and intoxicate the hangover; she would do as they did. Even if she had to die in the effort, she would never accord herself any respite; she would be like a cowardly beast that bites while running.

Then she told herself that her sensations of yesterday were not the only ones that one could owe to the concupiscence by which she was devoured; that there were certainly lusts still unknown to her. She had only had friends who had not experimented very much—even Magalo had shown limited ingenuity—and Sophor thought she still had a great deal to learn. It was impossible that vice should be limited to such scant sensual pleasure. She no longer had any fear of self-abasement; she would not hesitate before any sin, no matter how abominably subtle or singularly atrocious it might be; it was important, above all, not to suffer ennui, not to see in the mirror vague eyes in which hope is dead. She wanted to desire.

To break with what her life had been yesterday was the most urgent thing. She quit her house in the Avenue de Villiers, where the same sights gave her the same thoughts. She no longer received any of the women that her fantasy had accepted; with an insult, almost a shove, she rid herself, after a quarrel, of Céphise Ador—always tender with sudden furies, a good dog with the rages of a she-wolf—and, free, she rushed on.

There are cafés and brasseries in Montmartre signaled by a particularity. By day, there is nothing singular behind the large windows of the shop-front; people eat breakfast tranquilly, play dominoes, play a game of billiards. The waiters doze on the leather banquettes, suddenly shaken by the voice of the proprietor or a customer. In the evening, however, in the flamboyance of gas, the hall is populated by women who come and go, a cigarette in their lips, only sitting down rarely. Some are very young, some very old; Parisian prostitution begins and ends here. One leaves, one comes back. The old are obese, with corsages that overhang all the marble of a table; the new are as thin as errand-girls who breakfast on a croissant dipped in milk. They talk to one another in a species of argot mingled with the jargon of painters—the enormous ones were models, the smaller ones are—and pimps. They are ugly, even those who have been beautiful, and those who will be pretty; the not-yets of the latter are scarcely any better than the already-no-mores of the former.

Their attire gives the impression that they have dressed in haste in a clothier's shop that was being robbed, while the police were breaking down the door, so much does the hazard of their garments assemble various colors, mingling frippery with elegance. Ordinarily, however, the hats are new and bright, with furious flowers and frantic ribbons, hats bought in the morning on the way back from the creamery, from the milliner in the Rue Clauzel or the Rue Labruyère, with the money of a lucrative night. And almost all of them have bare hands, either because they have no gloves, or have forgotten to put them back on before coming down the stairs of a nearby hotel.

In sum, for the man who goes in and comes out, there is nothing extraordinary in the places: something akin, with more baseness and less possible illusion, to the halls of the large nocturnal restaurants, the difference between champagne and beer, and the musk here reeks. But for those who know things, these women—there are sometimes more than two hundred around almost as many men—are distinguished from the rest of Parisian prostitution by a specialty. They are those for whom one comes in search for abnormal and laborious debauchery. They are the adroit and the indefatigable; they know their métier, they are still studying it, they are perfecting themselves in it by exercising it; the place where they assemble would be the drawing room of some brothel if they were naked and if they provoked men. But, although they consent to follow anyone who makes them a sign, it is not to virile lust that they offer themselves, functionally.

They live two by two on the third floor of some furnished house, are jealous, quarrel, sometimes arrive at the creamery or the table d'hôte with cheeks scratched by fingernails; and, although "stuck," having the habit of beds without males, they sell to other women—who know where to find them—what they give to one another. They make a commerce of the vice that is habitual to them and, with some, agreeable. Into the café or the brasserie that they haunt—a sort of ignoble marketplace— the procurers charged with cheering up the conclusions of suppers of unhinged foreigners or mad Parisians come to obtain provisions.

After certain weekly dinners to which men are not admitted, actresses drunk on champagne and laughter, who no longer know how to kill time, climb into fiacres and come to Montmartre; and they mingle with these prostitutes, not in the common room but on the first floor, or in some cabinet behind the billiard table. Because if the waiters passing by, in a dignified manner, lifting on enormous trays taken from sideboard for the occasion, bushes of crayfish or cold chicken, the regular immediately divine that there are "chic people" in the process of "having a party." The waiters close the door rapidly.

And the next day, the actresses, who spend the night in some dubious hotel or some furnished apartment, return through the streets full of sweepers, hailing fiacres; back in the padded luxury of their apartments, they fall like things that have been dropped on to the bed or the chaise-longue, and go to sleep without undressing. For the prostitutes that they have followed practice the filthy mysteries methodically, coldly and terribly, knowing all the embraces that exhaust, all the obstinacies that anemiate, all the violence and all the slowness; but they do not tire themselves out—reserving themselves for their friends—

and, the following day, not enervated, in good health, their eyes tranquil, ready for new labors, they return to the café or the brasserie with the placid ennui, devoid or desire or rancor, of an employee returning to the office or an artisan to the workshop.

Sophor, under thick veils that she sometimes raised brazenly, as if in defiance—who, then, was she challenging?—frequented those sinister places. She was quickly noticed. In those dives she was celebrated, and popular. No one knew her name; they called her "the grand dame." As soon as she arrived there were whispers among the women grouped around the tables. Some threw away their cigarettes, in case she did not like the odor of tobacco. And there was a legend around her: that she was very polite, very proper; that she had lace and silk underwear such as had never been seen; that she forgot banknotes in purses of gold on mantelpieces.

Thus, as soon as she sat down in the least luminous corner, people prowled around her, only waiting for a wink or a vague gesture to run to her, to sit down at her table; those whom she had taken away on previous evenings, had ill-humored expressions if she did not summon them. Did she even recognize those who had gone with her? For that, it would have been necessary for her to pay attention. She did not choose. The first to come along, that was the one she preferred. All of them were equally good, so far as she was concerned, because all of them were equally horrible.

Yes, horrible. She detested them and despised them, but she returned to them as a dog returns to vomit. She had known the ennui of her vice; now she knew the disgust. She felt a frisson run through her loins and a nausea inflate her throat at the thought that, soon, she would be touched and embraced by those hands, those arms, by those mouths, which would put their breath into her mouth. But, docile to some fatality, it was necessary for her to come in search of these prostitutes, that she possess them one after another, all of them, and that after these, she would take others, and after them, yet others. Not only had she to do it, but she wanted to do it. By virtue of an inconceivable aberration, she desired that which was frightful to her, demanded that which filled her with agony. She was addicted to the pleasure by virtue of the horror that she had of it.

To the pleasure! For a long time, she had no longer known maddening joys; she never had sincere gasps of ecstasy in her throat. Even hideous, her sin left her calm. She was not moved by the worst excitations. Oh, what she would not have given for a second of intoxication or forgetfulness! But forgetfulness was exactly what was forbidden to her.

She did not even feel any victorious delight when, in the accomplishment of her task, she constrained one of the whores, astonished by the inaction that Sophor demanded of her and the spasm that she condemned them to suffer, to cry out. She was obstinate nevertheless in her dirty labor. She would not concede the argument to imbeciles, to worthy people! She would continue her destiny, accomplish unrelentingly her office of mocking, by the example of her corruption, the sanctity of mothers, the honesty of wives and the candor of virgins.

There remained to her the pride of being scandalous! A joyless pride, but a pride nevertheless. And she was sustained by the laughter in her ear, the laughter that was now so frequent, which irritated her, spurred her and engaged her. And then, did she know whether, some night or other, she might find in excess some beyond that would render pleasure to her? She was not entirely dead, she might live again. It was necessary to seek, to keep searching.

She descended further into ignominy. She dressed as a man in order to visit the abject places where the perfect brutalization of whores is a species of crapulous innocence. A prostitute is as stupid as an angel. Sophor almost became interested in those wretches in whom unconsciousness is almost equivalent to a purity. But they were still mouths and breasts and arms and loins.

Oh, veritably, the evil spirits, tempters of humankind, lack imagination. How small a universe vice is, and how little time it requires to make a tour of it! How quickly one finds again the places where one sojourned yesterday! How limited the horizon of evil is! The Possessed are dupes, since the One who promises them infinity opens a space scarcely larger than the ditch in which they will soon lie down, with their evil desires having become earthworms. It is scarcely worth the trouble of not being healthy, good, chaste and enouncing a placid conscience down here and paradise on high, that conscience become heaven, if one is only to receive in exchange, firstly dubious pleasures that are always the same, and later, the nausea of having obtained them with the impossibility of conquering others. One gives one's soul, and one receives—so little. Not even a little. Nothing.

Nevertheless, still darkly dazzled by the vision of the One who had displayed herself on the Sabbat throne with a diadem of black diamonds, Sophor dared not blaspheme the Demoness who had chosen and espoused her; she refused to confess that there are no mysteries in which being lives again, is exasperated, only weakening to be exasperated again, and is divinized terribly. In some, she had only known the pleasures, soon faded, of kisses; even in the most orgiastic excesses, she had only coveted agreeable intoxications. She had not tempted dolor, had not tried to demand joy from tortures.

Perhaps it was by means of suffering that she would cease to suffer. To see eyes weeping, to sense hearts bleeding: that was a supreme resource. And what inclined her to think so was that, several times, in the midst of her desolations, she had found a kind of amusement in sensing, not far from her, the despair of Céphise Ador, who, still infatuated, still jealous, lay in wait for her and followed her: Céphise Ador, who, in the morning, on emerging from some dive, she recognized in the back of a fiacre, sobbing and biting her fists. Thus, something in her was still moved by the woman's torture; she conceived the hope of taking an interest in dolorous flesh.

She installed in her new house the strange workshop of martyrdom and debauchery in which the coldness of marble bristles with tearing angles, where creatures, some suspended from trapezes, others spinning vertiginously in steel panniers, suddenly fall, all the cords broken, on to carpets of thorns, from which they only get up, feet bloody, to fall back again and bloody their hands, their breasts, their faces. She saw nudities writhe in baths of broken ice.

A seeker starved of being devoid of hunger, she took her seat, hideous, at the feast of living bodies bitten and chewed, she intoxicated herself in the redness of wounds. She was frightful. She was the diabolical realizer of chimeras invented by the satiety of old kings and weary empresses. Still beautiful, and rich, and illustrious in her ignominy, she was the inexorable tormenter of all the women who gave themselves or sold themselves, and because she seemed to obtain pleasure from their tortures, they were grateful to her for them.

And she was intolerably bored. Even crime did not reawaken her from her flaccid lack of appetite; it was necessary for her to make an effort to smile at drops of blood. Alas, how pleasant it would have been for her not to be frightful, not to seek in ferocities the forgetfulness of her bleak distress. How she would have liked not to do harm, since doing harm did her no good, since, after the frightful attempts to flee ennui, she always found herself facing the limit, the enclosure, the wall, which she dreamed of breaking down, and which would never open.

Oh, a little repose, that is what she would have desired. Repose was not permitted to her. It was necessary for her to follow her path—so fatigued, however—that she go on to the end of the duty that an execrable providence had made for her. To escape her destiny was impossible. An impulsion constrained her to keep going, still; a hand on her nape obliged her to keep drinking, still, the water of the poisoned spring, and even with a drop of blood, that liquor no longer intoxicated her.

Truly, she felt sorry for herself, sometimes. The more detestable she was, the more she merited sympathy; the very excess of her crime, it seemed to her, absolved her from it. But she did not have the right to linger in feeling sorry for herself. She had other things to do. Inevitably, she had to devote herself to the search for the undiscoverable, the recommencement of the ever-illusory effort.

For it would also be too comfortable, after having precipitated herself into the miry abyss, to be able to climb back up, and, not having broken her skull or her back, to shake off the mud and to go on, singing. Are you there? Stay there. All your somersaults will have no other success than to make you penetrate further into the opaque and dirty depths. You are the prisoner of your sin, and the worst despair of your descent, eyes closed, becoming heavier and heavier, will be the thought that there are, so far away from you, up there, meadows with flowers and the sky with its stars.

✳

Once, for one of the abominable games in which her double impotence of not attempting them and taking pleasure therein persisted, a pretty and frail child was necessary, as gentle as lambs that are bled. The experiments of certain mages require those paltry and tender creatures, which Cagliostro called Doves.

Sophor thought, searched in the past, and her mind alighted on Silvie Elven—initially, with pity. But soon, she almost rejoiced. Perhaps she would find a reawakening of sensation in the fear and the torments of that poor darling, so delicate, so slight, immediately plaintive; she would be pretty, that wounded swallow. In addition, although she did not love Silvie Elven, since she no longer loved anyone, she retained a tender memory of her; surely, it would cost her to do harm to that child, so fragile; and that which would be cruel for her in the execution of her design was precisely what resolved her to accomplish it.

On an evening of rain and mud, she climbed into a fiacre and threw Mademoiselle Elven's address at the coachman.

She had an astonishment that made her lean out of the window; it seemed to her that she had heard the rustle of a dress close by, as if someone had been lying in wait, as if someone had drawn nearer in order to listen to the address launched in a loud voice. In fact, she saw a woman, hidden in a long pelisse with a hood, who was now running along the sidewalk, alongside the wall; and that woman leapt into a coupé that drew away very rapidly. Who was it? Céphise Ador? Yes, perhaps; in sum, it did not matter.

"Well, get going!" she said to the coachman.

On the way, amid the jolts of the vehicle, which rolled slowly—very slowly—she thought about Silvie's surprise, about the alarms she would have as soon as she spoke, with so much modesty in her cheeks and fear in her eyes. She would be like a living doll whom one has come to demand that she allow herself to be cut into pieces. She would say yes, however. Sophor knew that with a gesture, with a gaze, she would be able to do whatever she wanted with the docile creature. Or rather, Silvie would not say anything, would allow herself to be taken away.

The fiacre advanced so slowly that Sophor took nearly an hour to arrive at Silvie's house. She went up very rapidly and rang violently at the door on the third floor. She had these abrupt movements; her gestures often seemed to be more the effect of a spring than a human will.

But, when the door opened, she found herself face to face, not with a chambermaid or Mademoiselle Elven, but with Céphise Ador, grim, rude and disheveled, who cried:

"There you are! Come in. Does it astonish you that I'm opening the door? What does it matter? You've come to see Silvie, so come in. What are you waiting for?"

To begin with, Sophor smiled. An almost amusing thought had just crossed her mind. Céphise? At Silvie's? Might it be, by chance . . . well, why not?

But the actress had a singularly pale face, and her staccato voice, her entire attitude, frightened and haggard, did not permit Sophor to believe that she was interrupting a tender melee on the chaise longue or the white bearskins. On the contrary, she had the impression that something violent and formidable had happened, or was about to happen. A curiosity came to her. It had been a long time since she had been curious.

She followed Céphise.

Scarcely were they in the studio, where nothing had changed, where the pretty disorder still laughed, which the comings and goings of so many beautiful young women had once amused, than Céphise set the lamp down brutally on a little table, in front of the green lustrine curtain that veiled the modeling table, and turned toward Sophor.

"Yes, I'm here, me!" she said. "And, you know, we need to talk."

Madame d'Hermelinge sat down.

The other, going back and forth, talked, sometimes grinding her teeth.

"It's true, then, I'm not mistaken. You were lying and she was lying. You still love Silvie, since you've come to her home, since she was waiting for you. Oh, you understand very well that I'm not unaware of what you've been doing for so many months, since you beat me and kicked me out. You're frightful, there's no monster comparable with you. But that was all the same to me, all the women that you took away and who came back the next morning with the faces of corpses. I saw them leave. I thought, on looking at them: *She doesn't love them, she can't love them. As long as it isn't Silvie, I won't say anything, I'll remain tranquil.*

"And I continued to gather information, to watch. It wasn't always easy for me, because of the theater. I'm not rich, and as I don't have a lover, it's necessary, in order for me to live, to act. No! The rage that I had when, suddenly, in the middle of a scene, the idea came to me that perhaps, at that very moment, you were with Silvie, and that you were making jokes about that poor Céphise, busy on stage, who couldn't surprise you.

"But this evening, I don't know why, I had a presentiment. To go to the theater would have been impossible for me. I posted myself outside your door. They're waiting for me, out there. Well, they can wait for me. The audience can smash the benches if they like; it's all the same to me. So, you thought that I didn't know the truth? That I'd never have the proof? I heard you say the address to the coachman. And I set off, and I got here before you. You understand? Before you.

"It's very fortunate that I arrived before you. You don't understand, yet? I tell you that I've been here for a long time—a very long time—and that Silvie was alone and that I talked to her. Look at me! Do you hear me? It doesn't make you afraid that I found Silvie all alone and that I talked to her?"

Sophor could have calmed Céphise's rage by affirming that she had not seen Silvie for several years, and that a circumstance with no connection with those of old had bought her here; the jealous woman, over whom a tender word triumphed so rapidly, would have allowed herself to be persuaded. But Madame d'Hermelinge obtained an interest from the fury of her former friend grinding her teeth and stammering under her shaken hair, prowling around the studio with crazed eyes, like a beautiful and terrible beast; it seemed to her increasingly that a strange adventure had occurred, or was about to occur; it was necessary not to calm Céphise down.

Coldly, Sophor said: "What right do you have to spy on me? I'm free. I can come to Silvie's because it pleases me to come here, and I can love whomever I want to love."

"Wretch! You see that I was right!"

Céphise leapt upon Madame d'Hermelinge, seized her by the neck and tried to strangle her; and she approached her red mouth with hateful teeth, in order to bite. But with a single movement, Sophor freed herself and sent the actress rolling on the floor. Then, standing up, she said: "Enough cries and madness. It's necessary that I see Mademoiselle Elven. Where is she?"

She marched toward the door that opened from the studio into the bedroom. Céphise Ador had crawled toward her, and retained her with her arms around her legs.

"Stay, stay. She isn't in her bedroom. She's gone out. She'll come back. You'll see her in a moment. I swear to you that you'll see her if you absolutely insist. First, listen to me. I have to talk to you. I still have these fits of anger. It's stronger than me. I can't help myself. But I assure you that it's serious, what's happening, that I have to talk to you seriously. And I beg you to listen to me. Afterwards, if you want, you'll see Silvie. Oh, my God, yes, if you want, you'll see her."

And, with sobs shaking her entire body, under the long hair, with which she wiped away her tears, she stifled her cries.

Sophor sat down again. "Well, whatever you have to say, say it, and speak quickly."

Amid gasps and tears, Céphise Ador went on: "I have to say that terrible things have happened. You see, the best thing for us to do is not to stay here; it's to go away immediately. We'll be better elsewhere, far away. Oh, if you wanted to go with me, far away! Not in France. Abroad, where there are people who don't know us. To hide, to put ourselves in shelter, that's still possible. But it's necessary not to lose any time. If you like, we'll take the train this evening. No need for trunks. We'll buy what we need on the way, after having sold our jewels. We'll go to America, if you like. And you won't have to worry about anything. With my talent, I'll always earn the necessary money, won't I?

"But it's necessary to leave right away. Tomorrow, it will be too late. Oh, my love, my eternal love, come away, I beg you to come away. If you only knew how much I love you, and how much I will love you. You can be sure that I'll never do anything bad again. You can do what you want, I won't complain about anything. As long as you're gentle from time to time, after having shouted at me and beaten me, I'll judge myself satisfied; I won't have anything to desire, since I'll have you, my beloved darling! Let's go, shall we, it's agreed? We'll leave this house, where we have nothing to do.

"Sophor, I beg you, take me away, take me away—I'm frightened! We'll go on a great voyage. Give me your feet, so that I can kiss them. I adore your feet. You can see that I'm weeping, Have pity on me. If you could understand how frightened I am, how necessary it is that we go away! Come, my adored. One day, later, I'll explain everything to you. Let's go."

Sophor was finally irritated by that rambling chatter; and with that woman, the refuse of ancient desires! She stood up and said, rudely: "You're mad. Go if you want to. I'm staying. Where's Silvie?"

Céphise Ador stood up, with a loud cry of rage. Then, fanatically, her head forward, her elbows by her sides and her fists clenched: "You're determined, you want to see her?"

"Yes."

"It's for her that you've come?"

"Yes."

"And you come here often?"

"Yes."

"While I'm rehearsing or on stage?"

"Yes."

"And you'd have embraced?"

"Yes."

"On her bed?"

"Yes."

"She would have slept with you?"

"Yes, yes, yes. Where is she?"

Céphie uttered a burst of laughter.

"She's here, imbecile. Where do you think she is? She doesn't go out in the evening, that little girl. She'd be too afraid in the streets. She's here, that's certain."

Astonished, Sophor demanded: "Why doesn't she come, if she can hear us?"

"Oh, I didn't say that she can hear us. No, truly, I don't believe she can hear us." Céphise's laughter redoubled, more

326

brutally sonorous. She added: "If she doesn't come, it's because she's asleep."

"In her bedroom?"

"No, no, not in her bedroom. We have a surprise in store for you, Silvie and I."

"Silvie and you?"

"Yes, we're very good friends. I said to her: 'Sophor, as you know very well, isn't like everybody else. Since she's going to come, since you're waiting for her, since you're going to sleep together, it's necessary to amuse her with the unexpected. A woman in a bed, between batiste and lace, is banal. It's necessary to find something more singular, more novel.' And as she couldn't think of anything, I thought of it for her."

"You?"

"Me. At first, she didn't want to, she hesitated, I made her understand that you'd be very content, and she ended up obeying me. And to amuse you, this is what I imagined. You know that she once began a large painting: an Ophelia, amid flowers. Was it an Ophelia? At any rate, a young woman lying down, with lilies and roses on a tunic, on her arms, on her breast. Well, I laid Silvie down on the modeling table; she's waiting for you there, you'll see how pretty she is. Oh, I hope you'll thank me for having dressed her and laid her down for you!"

Then, lifting the lamp with one hand, Céphise, with the other, slid aside the green lustrine that veiled the modeling table. On the sloping banquete, Silvia Elven, very dainty and pale in her long peignoir strewn with flowers, her hair lightly posed on her forehead like golden butterflies, appeared, delightfully slim, frail and smiling. She resembled a doll of which a statue on a tomb had been made.

And in one of the breasts of the murder victim, so delicate and so slender that even a kiss would have rendered it unnecessary, was the stiletto whose hilt represented a death's-head with ruby eyes.

IV

Now her accomplices were frightened of her. Even those who confronted the bloody works in the studio of martyrdom and debauchery drew away from Sophor, no longer daring to look her in the face, for she had become terrifying. She demanded from alcohol, opium and the pale poison that slides under the dermis like a delectable death the forgetfulness of sad hours, but even in the most furious or the torpid intoxications she could not forget; she saw again little Elven on her bed of flowers, murdered by Céphise, and Céphise arrested, judged, condemned and thrown into prison; other visions were sketched and formed behind those: she discerned in a vague shadowy distance, in addition to a spring evening where a newborn was suckling at Emmeline's breast, another corpse on another bed, Magalo in the hotel room.

And all the horrible memories that the passion or laxity of her delirium had avowed in confused speech added so much fear to the false joys of libertinage made of her—so pale now, the make-up adhering poorly to her convulsed skin—such a spectral companion that everyone was afraid of her. As they drew away they took with them the frisson of having prostituted themselves in a cemetery, of having been embraced in a shroud by a specter to which the flesh remained.

And for Sophor, the mornings and nights were terrible. When she parted her hair, partly woken from such brief slumbers, as if her nocturnal eyes were insulted and scorned by the pure light; when the sentiment returned to her that it was necessary to live again, to be today what she had been yesterday—to recommence, in sum—such a horror of herself and everything filed her, such gurgles of bile rose to her throat, that she sometimes wished that she was about to vomit her life.

O definitive accomplishment, to be there! No longer to be able to hope for anything that has not already disappointed you, and at the same time to know that, by virtue of an inexplicably domineering necessity, you will be forced to do again what you have done, to owe to new disappointed efforts an even more irremediable lassitude, which will not preserve you from further ever-futile efforts. And then, those corpses, and that murderer behind them . . .

Magalo would not have agonized in a bed in a dirty furnished room, Silvie Elven would not have been so pale amid the flowers, and Céphise Ador would not be in prison at this moment, laboring in silence and gazing through the high, unreachable window at the birth and death of the distant daylight, if the three unfortunates had not bitten into the fruit forbidden to woman, the flesh of woman. The law of chastisement even in this world appeared to her.

And how much more was she chastised since, alive and free, she was reserved for other crimes, since she could not prevent herself meriting even more disgust and anguish. She would have liked to be buried like Silvie and Magalo, imprisoned like Céphise. But no, to her it was permitted—which is to say, ordered—to become more infamous still.

In an hour, out of bed and dressed, she would plan some debauchery for the evening, would think about it all day, as one chews over something fetid, and, her senses maddened or numbed by alcohol or narcotics, she would attempt again pleasures more odious than the Hell to which they would damn her. It is by way of Hell that one merits Hell.

In the meantime, Emmeline, with her husband and her brother, on the florid hill, were living in the tranquil house where only the laughter of children troubles the good silence. It was another laughter that Sophor heard.

And something even more terrible than the laughter was all over her.

What? An odor.

Yes, now, almost perpetually, even in the rare moments of repose that morphine gave her in vain consolation, she sensed that she was enveloped by a warm, insipid but intense perfume, which she recognized—which she had loved, alas. It did not come from the furniture and fabrics around her; it was exhaled from herself, from her hand, which had touched breasts, from her hair, which had mingled with tresses, from her mouth, which had inhaled mouths, from her entire body, which had oppressed so many bodies.

She had hoarded the sexual odor of all those she had possessed, and now it was reemerging, like a vapor of sweat, ever more abundant, ever more warmly insipid, ever more sickening.

Sophor could not avoid respiring the aroma, which had become a stink, of her ancient pleasures and her recent repulsions. Cold water, which streams and chaps the skin delectably, did not deliver her from it, nor creams, nor powders, nor the sachets that one puts between silks and batistes. It emanated from her inexhaustibly, it had become inherent in her, like the perfume of a flower. And she communicated it to everything she touched. She rediscovered it in her dresses, in her underwear, in the armchair where she had been sitting; expired by her, it made a mist on the mirror in which she looked at herself. She ate it in food, she drank it in wine. It was a horrible distaste.

Reality, or aberration? Whatever it was, the obsession of that miasma was abominable. And even in the gardens, amid the freshness of the trees stirred by healthy breezes, before the vast sky, she sensed the insupportable odor. Often, if someone offered her a bouquet, she pushed away the flowers, and, her hand at her throat, she retained a nausea. She would have consented to any torture rather than that one. To be lacerated, to be raked with iron claws; to have a needle in the heart that turned, turned and turned again; to be broken on a wheel, and quartered, she would have agreed, on condition of no longer sensing the frightful reek emerging from all her pores and reentering her body through the mouth and nostrils.

So many dolors, finally, fatigued her, exhausted her and wore her out, and the last spring that was sustaining her snapped. Yes, pride was extenuated in her; the pride to which she had ceased to owe joy for a long time, but to which she at least owed the ability to fake it. If she still tried, in a residue of diabolical arrogance, not to confess her defeat to others, she no longer had the strength to deny it to herself. She was vanquished; she could do no more, she begged for mercy, she ceased to mock good simple folk who lived in families, who did not hope for strange pleasures. She had been wrong to be extraordinary, different from other women.

Definitively cowardly, she had even lost the vigor to revolt, to tell herself that, after all, she had not made herself the way she was, that the responsibility for her faults went back to some mysterious power. She did not argue. She admitted that she was culpable. The chastisement had convinced her of the crime. Only, she would have liked not to be suffering any longer, because she had suffered too much, and she was worn out. Oh, that odor, above all! If she could only be liberated from that!

But she dared not even complain. She merely remarked, with timidity—to whom? she did not know; to someone to whom, it seemed to her, her confidences were audible—that she had expiated her sin sufficiently, by the sin itself; that she could, at present, no longer hear that laughter, no longer smell that odor, no longer be obliged to go in search, in the lie of dirty pleasures, of further remorse. She said to herself: "Yes, it's remorse that I have."

At those times—it was, above all, after the excitations of morphine, in the laxity of flaccid enervation, that she abandoned herself to that degree—she would not have refused to be a person like those, of which there are so many, with relatives and a husband. With her face to the window she envied the Sunday strollers who were going to dinner in the country.

At certain times, the thought even occurred to her of begging forgiveness from Baron d'Hermelinge. If he did not want her for a repentant spouse, well, she would be a servant in his house, who did her work well and did not know these frightful languors. But she told herself quickly that her dreams of repentance, pardon and honesty were chimerical; that she was riveted to her evil, that she would never escape its desolation.

There was, however, one way out. To die.

To die? Yes.

The first time that idea came to her, it was as if she had suddenly relaxed entirely into an enlacing mildness, as in a bath of calm sensual pleasure. She conceived, delectably, the wellbeing of no longer existing. Oh, how lovable that hope was! To be dead, which is to say, to longer to think, no longer no act, no longer to have the infamous rancor of yesterday, the more horrible disgust of tomorrow, no longer to be the laborious seamstress of sin and remorse, no longer to hear the Laugh, no longer to smell the Odor! How much better in the nostrils the stink of the sepulcher would be, if cadavers can even be inconvenienced by it, than the perfume of her vice; how she would have preferred the putridity of dead flesh to that of living flesh!

What is exquisite about a coffin is that it is too narrow for a woman to lie within it beside you. At least, when one has no more lips, one is no longer in peril of the kiss; skeletal arms cannot be obliged to embrace bodies that the shocks of pleasure moisten with a sweat stickier and more fetid than the humor of water-snakes; after all, when dead, one sleeps alone! For it would truly be necessary for a prostitute to be very passionate about her trade, very desirous of earning a salary demanded in advance, to go, after having scratched the earth with her fingernails, to bring a corpse the hire of caresses.

Sophor could hope, after her last sigh, no longer to hear the panting of her breast. Then she could leave others tranquil, and would be left tranquil herself once buried. And she would not be stopped by the apprehension of tortures that punish the guilty after death. What torture could be comparable to the one she was enduring? At any rate, it would be a change.

Besides which, even though she had sometimes dreamed of expiatory gehennas, she believed in the peace beyond the tomb. She denied revelations and eternal tortures. To have a demon in oneself is no reason to be convinced of Hell; in those who conclude a pact with some satan, an obscure accomplisher of celestial designs, there is often the absurdity of not believing in the god they have renounced. Many of the possessed are atheists.

Thus, death, in Sophor's eyes, really was repose, a dreamless sleep, delectable inanimation. And nothing prevented her from going to sleep forever. It is easy to die. One can let oneself fall from a window, or throw oneself from a bridge into the river. It is also very easy to have recourse to some prompt and reliable poison; Madame d'Hermelinge, who demanded exasperation or torpor from forbidden drugs, always had within reach—just a few drops more—the possibility of dying.

Why, then, did she not escape odious life? Eternal unconsciousness would be so good, after a few minutes of agony—oh, so good!

She did not dare.

No more than the strength to vanquish the Enemy—the execrable Enemy who sniggered in her ear—did she have the strength to escape him by flight into the funerary shadow. She was so absolutely languid, weak and enervated that she dared not die. Oh, what retained her in existence was not the love of things down here. Nothing was more abominable, alas, than living. But she was not capable of the particle of energy that is necessary to jump, or to swallow water that has changed color in a glass; and above all, above all, she was afraid of being dead. Fear of Hell, of punishments, of tortures? No: fear of no longer experiencing of no longer suffering, of being non-existent. What she judged to be so pleasant, so desirable, was precisely what she feared with a glacial chill.

Such was her cowardice—all her sinews and muscles finally overloaded, exhausted, reduced to rags—that she could not confront, even in the second of a gesture, the idea of immobility in darkness, the idea of going to sleep in a slumber that is not slumber, of being in the cold, in the soft, in the grease—or, rather, the idea of not being at all, of not sensing that one is. If she had hoped for Hell, she would have killed herself, because incessant torment is not death, it is not the obscure, infinite unnamable Nothing. But she was utterly repelled by the thought of no longer having the sentiment of oneself. To die is not only to cease to live, it is to become as if one has never lived. It is the abolition, not merely of being, but of having been. And to that, she could not resolve herself.

Twenty times she raised the mortal phial to her lips; twenty times, having gone up to the top floor of her house, she leaned out into the void looking down at the paving stones. She dared not. And in the collapse of her vitality, she was haunted by the absurd chimera of a death that would undoubtedly be death, but which, at the same time, would be a little . . . oh , almost not at all . . . like life . . .

Then the necessities of her function gripped her again, threw her back into the ignominy of atrocious or nauseating pleasures; and she saw clearly that she would never emerge from anguish, fear and enveloping, adhesive ennui, since all the exits were closed before her—even the beautiful, august ebony door encrusted with black diamonds that, turning on mute hinges, offers to all the living the magnificent silent path descending between royal cypresses toward the pacific and eternal sepulcher.

V

The valet de chambre announced: "Madame la Baronne d'Hermelinge."

Urbain Glaris stood up, not too rapidly, from the sofa where, idly extended, he was leafing through a pamphlet. He saluted his visitor, silently indicated an armchair, and waited, standing up.

The years had scarcely modified the appearance of the elegant physician. With a little gray blanching at the temples and fatigue in the smile, he still had the simultaneously emphatic and discreet air that befits a worldly mage. But at the moment he was hiding poorly, under lowered eyelids, the keen gleam that was sparkling in his eyes—the gleam of satisfied vanity. This woman, whom he had been observing for many years, whose decline he had prophesied, this sick woman, all the more interesting because she had retarded longer than any other the advent of the final crisis, was having recourse to him!

She was, therefore, giving in; she was proving him right; she was vanquished, as he had predicted. He swelled with pride.

But when, having fallen into an armchair like someone fainting, she had raised her veil, he no longer experienced anything but a great pity, so pale was Baronne Sophor d'Hermelinge, in spite of her make up—the decoration of a mummy rather than the adornment of a Parisienne—so much did she have in her fixed eyes, beneath the sparse lashes, an irremediable disillusion with everything.

After a long silence: "Doctor . . ."

With what objective had she come? She could not have said, precisely. Without desire or hope, like everyone that is infirm, everyone atonal, too feeble to endure life or to confront death, incapable of any will—a wreck adrift in a dirty current—she had come, instinctively, to ask for help. Like all the women in Paris, she knew who Doctor Urbain Glaris was; knew him, for having heard him more than once, in earlier days, profess his paradoxical theories in boudoirs. Very often, in fact, in the time of her pride, she had even smiled at that savant of sorts, who had something of the sorcerer about him, who spoiled with an empiric's boasting his very legitimate authority as an experimenter, who had the impertinent bad taste to deny joy and laughter, and not to believe in the happiness of the happy; more than once she had sensed anger against that man whose eyes sought her out, in the Bois, at the theater, not letting go, with the air of observing symptoms. And by virtue of irritation, she had hated him.

But now she shared Urbain Glaris' opinion; she knew what mourning desolated, beneath the exterior in fête, the conscience of those who transgressed human law. Like the sad, envied individuals that he called his clients, she was a lamentable seeker of forgetfulness. And because she no longer had the strength for rancor, because she would have begged pardon even of someone who had offended her, she had come, in a vague intuition of some possible relief. This adept, who refined science with a little magic, might have secrets, ways of putting to sleep, if not suppressing them entirely, dolors similar to those by which she was sickened; she was addressing herself to this specialist, who was something of a charlatan, like a condemned invalid.

After the word "doctor" she did not pronounce another. She had encountered Urbain Glaris' gaze, and quickly closed her eyes. She understood that she had nothing to tell him; that she had for him a soul and a heart open like the flanks of a cadaver on the table of the amphitheater; and, deprived of old arrogances, she did not revolt against the sympathy of that gaze, accepted the perspicacity that would once have seemed outrageous to her. On the contrary, she experienced a sort of satisfaction, like someone who, attained by an ignominious disease, will have no need, thanks to the physician's clairvoyance, to describe its symptoms.

They were silent.

What did he think of the anguish of the vanquished? He divined the ennui in which she had finally succumbed, and the collapse of her pride, and her final gamble of demanding forgetfulness from mortal drugs, and her cowardice before death, and all the emptiness that was within her.

Finally, in a very soft voice, he said: "So, nothing remaining, then?"

She turned away, ashamed. "Nothing . . ."

"You've tried . . . ?"

"Everything," she said, her head in her hands.

"Even prayer?"

"Alas."

"Even being loved by a man?"

She turned her gaze toward him with a perfect astonishment. The misfortune of the woman was even more irremediable than he had thought; she could not conceive the possibility of renovation by some natural amour. Doomed, more definitively doomed than shipwreck victims who have sunk into the profound sea. And Urbain Glaris' pity became dolorous; he thought, he sought, not taking his eyes off the poor woman. Words emerged from his lips, slowly.

"There might, perhaps, be a salvation, or at least a relief from the torturing anxiety . . ."

She held out her hands, and stammered, almost suppliant: "Speak, speak! A means of salvation, or suffering less, do you know one?"

"Perhaps, but that means is precisely one to which you cannot have recourse."

"How do you know? Only indicate it to me. Oh, I implore you!"

He went on: "There is a sentiment, or an instinct, stronger than all human sentiments, precisely because of what it has of the instinctive, of the bestial, even. In those who experience it, it absorbs all desires, all thoughts. As soon as a woman knows it, she no longer feels anything else. It is not subject to differences, to augmentation, to weakening; as long as one lives, it does not die, because it is a bodily need as much as a passion of the soul. By virtue of it, for its sake, one forgets . . . everything. Yes, I think that in the living women that it occupies, it does not even leave room for bad memories. It is so jealous that it does not let anything subsist that is not itself; it is not a virtue, it is a physical necessity, and thanks to it, one lives outside oneself."

"Please, what is this sentiment?"

"The love of a woman for a creature to which she has given birth. It is not true that after the birth, the infant is no longer connected to the mother. Nothing breaks the genetic attachment; the child is always linked to the mother's entrails. But you, Madame, since you have lived without a husband, without a lover . . ."

She lowered her head, frowning, as if, in an effort, she was gazing into the distance of her life, out there, out there in the shadows. She was thinking. She raised her head.

"I have a child," she said,

The doctor was astonished.

"A daughter, the daughter of Baron d'Hermelinge. I saw her for a moment and have never seen her again. She was born, she was taken away. On my order, when she had grown a little, she was put into a convent, not far from Paris. Every three months, I send money in order for her to be cared for and well educated. Her name is Carola. It was Mag . . . one of my friends, who gave her that name. She must be fifteen years old now, or a little more, sixteen. Yes, it's true, I have a daughter.

She spoke in a low voice, without inflection. She repeated: "It's true. I have a daughter. Carola. She's sixteen."

And she reflected, her pupils fixed. After a long time, she asked: "Then you believe that a woman who has a child, who loves her . . . ?"

"Try," he said.

She stood up, went to the door, and went out without a glance at Urbain Glaris, without a salutation. He watched her draw away, traverse the antechamber. She disappeared.

"Who knows?" he said. But he shook his head, sadly, and shrugged his shoulders, like a practitioner who does not believe himself in the effect of his prescription.

VI

To be a mother! To love a child that one has carried, that one has put into the world! Only to live for her, to pamper her, to coddle her, to hold her against one's heart, to find her more beautiful than all the other children, and, at night, to get up and go and listen, through the gap in the door, to see whether she is asleep on the pillow that the whiteness of curtains protects like the wings of seraphim! Sophor knew full well that she was not one of those to whom such joys are permitted; she remembered the moment, a long time ago, when she had looked at her child, and swelled with pride at not feeling her heart beat faster. Yes, she had been proud of not being a mother.

How one changes! How she would have liked, at present, to be capable of the emotion once dreaded and scorned! Alas, she had not changed enough. Still the same incomprehension of the tenderness that inclines a woman toward cradles; the sole difference was that, because of a surplus of desolation, she no longer gloried in being what she was. To her remorse—because it was not repentance, because it was only the ennui of satiety— she owed a horror of the evil, not the possibility of the good. A frightful thing, not to be able, hating and despising oneself, to become quite different from oneself! She did not hope that she would ever love the child born of her, and, for not being able to love her, she detested herself even more: the sole result of the advice that Urbain Glaris had given her.

However, it would have been so pleasant not to be always a monster, that, in a reawakening of illusion, she clung on to the idea of her being a mother, like so many happy women. From groups of children perceived during walks, plays that she had seen performed, and her reading, she evoked maternal scenes, strove to incarnate within her the young women who were laughing at little boys or little girls; asking herself sometimes— what a cruel response in the depths of her being!—whether she was really sure that she would not have any pleasure in caressing the blonde curls of a little head. But the hand that she extended toward an imaginary forehead fell back, discouraged.

Then she imagined that the dream alone had insufficient power to give birth in her to a sentiment that was so strange to her; that the blossoming in question doubtless required the active force of reality. Oh my God, what if, suddenly, on seeing

Carola—she said Carola expressly, repeating the name frequently in order to accustom herself to it—she might experience an ardent and pure tenderness, become mad with happiness, cry: "My daughter!" as in melodramas. What a joy to love a child to whom one would be dear, no longer to think of anything but her, to devote oneself to her, entirely.

Those ideas, still without hope, filled her with a mildness that she had never known. She resolved to depart, to go to Carola's convent. After all, it was not impossible—frightening and horrible as it might be—that something human remained in her.

And thus, in the railway carriage—she had left at one o'clock in the afternoon, in order to arrive before nightfall—Sophor experienced a mansuetude that resembled a presentiment of salvation. Maternity had appeared odious to her, above all, because of the brutalities of the male, the hideousness of childbirth, because of newborns obstinate at the breasts of nurses—of, Emmeline giving suck!—because of all the dirtiness of the marriage and the first infancy. But now she no longer remembered the husband, the pregnancy, the birth, and Carola was grown up. She no longer had the vileness, the puerile animality of early age; she had only retained the healthy innocence and the new freshness. Why could Sophor not be glad to be the mother of a beautiful demoiselle, intelligent and good, chaste and pious?

And even though, in the intimacy of her being, someone laughed at her—sometimes not wanting to believe that she was sincere, sometimes threatening her with the supreme disillusionment—she strove ardently toward that virtue, toward that health, toward that redemption: cherishing her daughter.

She dared not believe entirely that she would cherish her, but she wanted it so much that she almost believed it. In sum, the journey that she was making was already proof that she was not indifferent in regard to that child. If nothing were summoning her, why would she have set forth? She did not confess that the prospect of some respite in her terrors was the sole reason that attracted her.

"Carola! Carola!"

In truth, that name was not as unpleasant as it had appeared to her once. Magalo had not been wrong to . . .

Magalo! She repudiated that memory, reproached herself for having thought of that whore. It was not a matter of Magalo! Between Magalo and Carola there was nothing in common. It was truly absurd and culpable to have mingled two such different people in the same thought. Carola must be so candid, so ignorant of everything that is evil: a kind of little angel in the uniform of a convent pupil. To adore that young soul, still celestial: what a religious charm, what a forgetfulness of all sin!

Sophor felt a constriction of the heart as the train pulled away after a station. She recalled that she had once made another journey full of a hope more plausible than the present one, the journey toward Emmeline; as soon as she had arrived she had encountered the most abject of disappointments. But it would have been stupid to assimilate the evil desire that had drawn her toward her friend—it had been justly punished, that desire—and the honest design that was guiding her toward her daughter. This time, she merited not being disappointed. Providence had been right, previously, to humiliate her; it would be wrong, today, if it refused her the sacred felicity for which she was ambitious.

Sophor criticized herself almost as much for having thought about Emmeline as she had just now for having evoked Magalo. It was necessary to occupy herself with Carola, and Carola alone. She imagined her very modest, tall, slightly pale, with chestnut hair. The dear child's voice must be infinitely soft, but clear, without too tender an intonation, a voice accustomed to singing canticles.

What would they do, after having embraced? They would leave straight away; Sophor would not leave her daughter in the convent. People recounted that young girls in dormitories sometimes have amities for one another that are too tender, and acquire bad habits. Sophor shivered; she had been wrong to leave

Carola in the cloister. The dread that her daughter might not be as ingenuous as the youngest saints tormented her cruelly.

She changed her train of thought; she would not imagine anything sad, deleterious to her dream; she returned to her project of a prompt departure. Certainly, they would not go to Paris. Oh, no, not to Paris! A frisson ran through her at the idea that her child might lodge in the frightful house where so many women . . . never! They would make a long voyage to England or Italy. Carola would be delighted by all the beautiful things that she would see. They would be adorable, the words she found to express the naiveties of her surprise and her imagination.

Oh my God, what if I don't love her!

Sophor drove away that alarm. She would love her. She would love her, because Carola must be worthy of affection, and, above all, because a mother ought to love her daughter. That was natural. Increasingly, Madame d'Hermelinge persuaded herself that the interest of her repose, of her soothed conscience, had nothing to do with her attraction toward the unknown child; decidedly, she believed that she was only obeying a very dear and very noble duty, and she already found the quietude of a kind of redemption in the conviction of her disinterest.

Then, after the long voyage, when they returned to France, they would live in Auteuil or Versailles, in a slightly isolated house of bourgeois aspect. They would be very tranquil, the two of them. They would make music together, take turns to read aloud. However, Sophor did not know whether she would permit her daughter to read. For young women, all books are bad, even the most chaste, because they excite in young souls a concern for the unknown, for the unreal, and it is necessary not to be romantic. No music either; the bad angels, the tempting spirits, floated in the wave of sounds; it is the mysterious beat of their wings that provides rhythm to melodies.

Instead of reading, instead of playing nocturnes or sonatas, they would work. Carola must have been rather poorly edu-cated in that provincial convent; Sophor would recommence her daughter's education. She would relearn in order to teach her history and the sciences. No masters, no mistresses—why did she shiver at that word?—she alone would be her child's instructress. The professors that one pays do their duty, nothing more; it is fortunate when they do not inculcate evil thoughts in their pupils. Above all, Carola must never remain alone with the domestics; a young girl hears a vile word, does not understand it, thinks about it, and ends up understanding it, strangely.

Afterwards, when Carola was twenty—not sooner—a man would arrive, very honest, very sound in mind and heart, and he would marry her. What would become of Sophor then? Well, she would live with the young wife and the young husband. How far away they would be from all villainy, all anguish! How good it would be to be happy together, with little boys and little girls no bigger than this—now she was interested even in the youngest infancy!—and in order to spend the summer they would have a property in the country, far from Paris, where they would dine at dusk in the arbor. No more suffering, no more languor! No longer to be an object of horror and disgust to oneself! To be a mother, a grandmother; the little ones, at dessert, would climb on to her legs and sit down on her knees.

It was via a long, silent, almost deserted avenue of plane trees that the old heavy fiacre into which Sophor climbed on leaving the station took her toward the convent. It was still light, before dusk, but there were almost no passers-by: on a bench, a very old woman, her head unsteady, who must remain all day where she was put, until a maidservant came to fetch her at dinner time; further away, a retired officer, his moustache gray and his nose red, smoking an extinct pipe, making patterns in the gravel with the tip of his cane between his parted legs—and not a sound, except, in the distance, beyond the fields, the whistle of a locomotive, or the faint barking of a dog in the direction of the town.

That peace, that scarcity of life, did not displease Sophor, filling her with silence and solitude, putting a décor into her heart appropriate to the imminent appearance of a calm and reserved child, who scarcely speaks, with lowered eyes.

It was a great square façade of blackened stones, that of the cloister of the Dames de la Salutation. On the wood of the high door, the hammer, in falling back, made a profound sound of heaviness in the hollow like that which one hears when one drops a rock on to previously volcanic soil. Behind an iron trellis, the eyes of the *soeur tourière* were like little dead flames. And when Madame d'Hermelinge, after naming herself and saying that she was expected—she had announced her visit by telegram—had entered beneath the cold and bleak porch that extended along a courtyard, she had the impression of penetrating into a vast tomb in which slumber is eternalized, softly taciturn.

It was at that moment that she perceived something so pleasant, to which, for several hours, without having paid any attention to it, she must have owed a repose, a calming of all her aguish: she could no longer hear the Laughter in her ear and could no longer smell the Odor emanating from her, as if something or someone mocking and nauseating that she carried within her had slipped away, was no longer there. There was throughout her entire being a disappearance of anxiety: what the possessed must experience after exorcism.

The *soeur tourière* introduced her into the parloir, saying: "Madame la Supérieure will come, with Mademoiselle d'Hermelinge."

Sophor remained alone, sitting in front of a grille in the room with bare walls. She waited, she hoped. With regard to that grille she was like a prisoner waiting for a signal that a distant bell is about to give: a signal of joy or despair . . . of joy, surely, of tranquil and reassuring joy.

It was not behind the grille that Mademoiselle d'Hermelinge appeared; a door opened and, almost pushed by a blue and white nun, a young woman entered, her head turned away, her arms alongside her body.

"This is your mother," said the Superior. "Embrace her."

The child dared not come any closer, dared not look at the visitor, and, out of weakness or an instinct of respect, fell to her knees, and then, with her hands beneath her chin, she started to say a prayer.

Well, why did Sophor not open her arms to her, not clasp her, crying: "My daughter!" She had hoped for that abrupt surge of tenderness. She did not budge, observing her.

She did not find her very pretty. Not ugly, however. Rather tall, with a long upper body, and thin, pale, with red patches under her eyes. Mademoiselle d'Hermelinge resembled somewhat those girls raised by the charity of communities that one encounters on walks. And Sophor was no more moved than on the day when she had stared at the newborn presented by the midwife. What? Was she forever incapable of knowing maternal love? Would no tenderness ever awaken in her for the being to whom she had given birth?

Oh, what prevented her from being moved was the presence of the nun and the coldness of that room, and also the timidity of Carola, who ought to have thrown her arms around her. So she resolved to go away immediately.

She excused herself for such a brief stay, offered the pretext of having to return to Paris without delay, the time of the express train; a few moments later—she had not even given them time to pack the child's trunk—she climbed back into the fiacre with her daughter and gave the coachman the order to return to the station very quickly.

❋

As soon as they were alone in the carriage she seized Carola's hands and looked her in the eyes, searching for a flame at which something within her would ignite.

The girl was very troubled, not knowing what to say or to do, turning toward the street and stammering a few words that even she could not hear. Seeing her mother like this, suddenly, when one has never seen her; quitting the convent to go she knew not where, with an unknown person—that was frightening! But it was also very pleasant to have a maman, who finally shows herself, who takes you away . . .

Suddenly, she leaned her head toward Sophor's shoulder, and burst into brief sobs, which resembled little cries of joy. Then she started to chatter, girlishly, weeping with pleasure. Oh, how glad she was! She had thought that everything was finished for her, that she would never be taken out of that cloister, where everyone was so good to her, but where she was so bored. Then, truly, she would be like the other demoiselles? She would no longer resemble the orphans, the abandoned? How good it must be no longer to be alone! "Maman! Maman!" And her father, would she see him too? Yes? Soon? What joy! But she said, above all: "Maman." That word, which she had never said, seemed to her so charming to pronounce that she repeated it at every opportunity, at every minute. Yes, doubtless she had good friends who would be very sad at her departure; she would go to see them from time to time. But a classmate is not a maman. There are little mothers in the convent who are only bigger friends, not veritable mamans. Oh, God, to be the daughter of a beautiful woman who cajoles you, who kisses you, who tells you that she loves you, that must be better than paradise.

In the midst of that chatter, Carola, with slender fingers, blew her mother kisses at close range, which, still timid, she dared not give her on her lips.

Those tender, ingenuous delicacies insinuated themselves into Madame d'Hermelinge like a cheerful freshness, like an early morning awakening that brightens, reassures and amuses; it was something like the twittering of little birds, which comes into the bedroom, after bad nights, through the luminous crack in the shutters. It was very lively and very sweet.

Sophor had not experienced, since Carola's appearance, the surge of tenderness for which she had wished, but there was nothing extraordinary in that; it is only in novels and in dramas that the passions have that suddenness; and then, she did not have the habit of being a mother, she had not spent her life waiting for the minute when she would find her lost daughter again; it was therefore natural that her maternity had not burst forth in sobs and cries of joy, and the gradual nature of that affection was perhaps a sign that it would be more profound and more durable.

Yes, very profound and very durable, and delightful too.

While her daughter talked to her, she felt within her blooms of benevolence, and ease; for hours she had not had an evil thought. To tell the truth, she did not find her daughter very similar to the young girl she had imagined; a little silly, Carola did not always say the words that would have been veritably moving. But that awkwardness implied a candor that made her more lovable. Sophor no longer regretted that her daughter was scarcely pretty. In being almost ugly, with her excessively pale complexion and her patches of redness, and her lips that were not rosy enough, she seemed more virginal, more filial. Too much beauty would not have revealed her as pure; her disgrace was like one modesty more.

Sophor had not yet kissed her, had only touched her hands momentarily, but she felt certain that she would soon love that little girl entirely, and that she would truly be a mother, with calm tenderness, with no memory of the vain agitations of old.

The express train had just left when they arrived at the station. Fortunately, there was another train for Paris at twenty past midnight. An omnibus train. No matter, they would take it. Only, what were they going to do for some four hours?

"What if we go back to the Dames de la Salutation?" said Carola.

It was much simpler to go into one of the hostelries near the railway, to rest there while awaiting the time of the departure. They would go to an inn that had a good enough appearance and ask for a room.

Because of so much emotion, the girl was so tired that scarcely had they gone in than she fell into an armchair. She also had a desire to sleep, because it was the hour when one went to bed in the convent.

"Yes, yes," said Madame d'Hermelinge, "sleep. I'll wake you up when it's time."

And, semi-recumbent in the large armchair, the drowsy Carola had a good and charming smile on her lips at the thought of going to sleep there, away from the convent, so close to her maman.

Sophor, under the shade of a lamp, still wearing her hat and mantle, with her elbows on the table, contemplated her daughter.

She felt happy, and also proud, because of her victory over herself. So Urbain Glaris had been right! Maternal love can chase away evil hauntings, triumph over dolors and false desires. That love, she only knew partially as yet, but what she experienced in it was like a promise that she would experience it entirely. Already she was no longer thinking about anything but Carola, no longer remembering sins and remorse. Very different from what she had been prior to today. A duty to fulfill, that was what occupied her. She imagined a life full of calm and mildness. Veritably, she was appeased. And she was saved. A long series of placid days—like the avenue of plane trees by which she had one toward the convent—opened up before her, silent and deserted, interminable . . .

She was still looking at the sleeper, smiling.

She had been wrong just now not to find her pretty. Her hair, chestnut indeed, put such a soft shadow over the narrow forehead. There was a blue transparency in the bulge of the lowered eyelids. The mouth was a little too wide, but between the thin lips the teeth were neatly arranged and very white, bright to the point of seeming diaphanous. And beneath the schoolgirl's bodice, the slow movement of breasts revealed the recent puberty . . .

348

Sophor shivered. She thought she had heard the little noise in her ear, like a laugh . . .

No, no, she was looking at her daughter, she would take her away, the two of them would be happy; the things of old were as if they had never been. Well, it was not here that the temptress would dare to mock her. She was defeated, the demoness! Sophor thought about the big, bourgeois house in a suburb, where she would live alone with her daughter for a long time, a very long time, and so peacefully.

Carola, entirely asleep, turned over in the armchair. She was having some dream that oppressed her, fatigued her. She was breathing with an apparent unease. Instinctively, with a groping hand, without waking up, she unfastened the top of her bodice. A little bright flesh appeared under the chin, a smooth whiteness sliding toward the young virgin breasts, and Sophor—while the laughter sounded more distinctly in her ear—leaned forward under the lamp, gazing at that pale whiteness, sniffing, with flared nostrils, a recognized perfume, all the sweeter for coming from a fresh flower . . .

Mercy! She stood up, took her head in her hands, ran out of the room, went downstairs, found herself in darkness, in solitude, and she went away, went away, and would never retrace her steps, because it was frightful, what she had just sensed in that room up there, because she was monstrous, incurably! Oh, how hideous it was! Near that child, exquisitely pure, near that child, not even pretty, and who was her daughter—her daughter! supreme crime! extrahuman infamy!—she had had the diabolical thought that threw her toward so many detested creatures.

Not desire, no; it was a long time ago that desire had died in her; but the inveterate habit survived the covetousness, obliged her to recommence the evil. She could not avoid being filthy. To tell the truth, she would not have suspected that she could be to this degree. This, truly, was too much. That such an abomination was possible was astonishing!

With a snigger, she complimented herself on her ignominy. And to think that she did not have the courage to smash her skull there, against the wall, under that street-lamp! She ran alongside the houses, stopped momentarily in order to draw breath, started running again, and would have liked to be able to run faster, to be far away from everything, to be far away from herself, above all. Alas, one cannot drop one's villainies on the road, like the debris of a staved-in barrel; wherever she went she would carry her vice and her terrors with her.

Certainly, abject as she judged herself, she hoped that she would never have been weak enough to yield to the temptation that had assailed her just now; weak, and cowardly, and defeated, she would have found a residue of will-power to refuse the abject sin, in order not to look at her daughter with the eyes of a lover. But no matter, the crime that she would not have carried out, she had conceived. The sacrilegious idea had insinuated itself into her momentarily; and, even if, once expelled, it never came back, the mere fact of having had it forbade Sophor maternal familiarities. To take Carola away, to live with her, to listen to her, to take pleasure in seeing her smile, was forbidden to her. She would not be able to kiss her daughter without remembering that she had thought of a more ardent embrace; her mouth on the child's forehead would not distract her from the preoccupation of a mouth so close by.

How she hated herself! How she pitied herself too! And soon, she dared not even seek comfort any longer in the conviction that she would remain effectively innocent. Did she truly have the right, after so many lax capitulations, to believe in the firmness of her honest design? In spite of the sincerity of her present resolution, could she affirm to herself that that resolution would never weaken? Oh, what an abominable thing if, some evening, in the tranquil house at Auteuil or Versailles, awakened by the necessity of evil, she slid, in the shadows of the corridor, breathlessly, her hands extended, toward the room where, in a bed of muslin and modesty, Carola was asleep . . .

Execrable accomplishment of destiny! She could not attempt maternity without risking incest—oh, to what frightful incest as yet unimagined! Her supreme resource of salvation would be for her an opportunity for further crime, further shame, a more irremediable damnation. And she understood fully what it had made of her.

She had sat down, as if dropped, on a boundary marker near a coaching entrance. With one knee between her joined hands, she gazed at the pavement without seeing it, with fixed and empty eyes. One might have thought that she was no longer alive. She was thinking, however, so dolorously!

She had been there, immobile, for more than an hour, when a clock chimed in the tenebrous silence. Sophor stood up. She seemed calm, as if she had made a resolution. She looked around. She divined, in the shadows, the avenue of plane trees leading toward the railway station. She started walking, without excessive haste, with a firm tread, like someone who knows where they are going and will arrive, in spite of any obstacle.

※

In the room, Carola was still asleep. Without touching her, pronouncing her name, Sophor woke her up. She stood by the window, a long way from the armchair. She added: "It's time, come along."

The child got up, hastily, and offered her forehead, but Sophor said: "We don't have any time to lose, let's go."

They left the hotel, traversed a square, and after having bought tickets, went into the waiting room. They did not exchange a word.

Surprised and frightened by her mother's cold, almost sinister attitude, Carola dared not speak to her; she isolated herself in an apprehension, her eyes lowered. And during the journey, there was the same silence. Sitting some distance from Carola, Madame d'Hermelinge, her forehead against the window, gazed at the night. Sometimes, under the light of the little lamp, she consulted the railway timetable; then she returned to her corner and stayed there, attentive to the darkness.

The schoolgirl had the impression that something sad and bad was happening, that it was better not to budge, to keep quiet. If she had approached, affectionately, if she had spoken, she would doubtless have been repelled by a harsh gesture, a chilling word. For one second—for they closed again immediately—she saw her mother's eyes; she shivered.

Meanwhile, the nocturnal hours went by. Shortly before dawn, Madame and Mademoiselle d'Hermelinge got down from the carriage, sat on a wooden bench under an awning, and waited. Then they boarded another train. Carola had the intuition that they were no longer going where they had initially intended to go, that her mother had changed her mind, had modified their itinerary.

When day dawned, she could no longer see Madame d'Hermelinge's face; the latter had lowered her thick veil, which gave her a mask of lace. What was behind that mask? The child imagined a very pale face, with staring, frightening eyes. Because of the morning, because of her fear, she was cold. She enveloped herself entirely in her mantle, and pretended to sleep.

At about ten o'clock in the morning, the train slowed down. An employee shouted: "Gemmilly!"

"We've arrived," said Madame d'Hermelinge.

They traversed the platform and the station. On the threshold of the inn, a stout, red-faced woman with an enormous belly was awaiting travelers. They went into a ground-floor room, followed by the innkeeper, whose sandals resonated on the floor tiles.

Madame d'Hermelinge asked for writing materials, traced a few lines, and sealed the envelope. Then, after saying to the hostess: "I'll be back in a minute," she made a sign to the child to follow her, and went out. All that was accomplished with neither haste nor slowness, with the precision of a rite.

They began to go up a sunlit road, florid with fallen flowers, between a double row of acacias stirred by the breeze; at the summit stood a house of pink brick, with a façade scaled by wild vines and climbing ivy.

Sophor stopped half way up. She said to Carola: "You see that house up there? That's where you're going, and that's where you're going to live, with your father. Here's a letter for him."

"Oh! Maman?" said Carola, holding out her hands.

"No, I can't go with you. Adieu."

"But Maman, all alone . . ."

"Don't be afraid; there's no one on the road, and in that house you'll be well received. Go on, I want you to."

She had not lifted her veil. She was speaking as if from very far away through the obscure lace. The child bowed her head, took the letter and continued going up the hill.

Motionless, Sophor, utterly somber in the midst of the gaiety of the morning and the flowers, watched her draw away.

The child sometimes looked round, hoping for a gesture that would call her back or signify: "I'm coming too." Nothing. She continued going up. She arrived at the gate. She pulled the iron bell-cord; there was a clear, joyful, tinkling sound, which Sophor heard; which entered into her heart like twenty slight and rapid wounds. And the gate was opened by a maidservant.

After a final glance toward her mother, Carola disappeared.

What was disappearing, what was going into Baron d'Hermelinge's house, into the familial dwelling, into the honesty and peace of the hearth, was Sophor's last hope.

She waited for a long time. Carola did not reappear. She had been welcomed.

Then Baronne Sophor d'Hermelinge retraced her steps, without a backward glance, took the train to Paris, and returned to the irremissible . . .

EPILOGUE

It is finished, she no longer resists; long vanquished, she now is a submissive slave; she indulges in vice without pleasure, with the punishment of rare truces, accepts captivity in evil without the hope of escape. She no longer tries even to want to die. And those who see her are astonished by her, and alarmed by her. Between the toque that hides all her hair and the firm collar that grips her neck, her face is wan, with round, bloodshot eyes devoid of lashes and eyebrows. She looks straight ahead; it seems that she does not see anything, but that she has just witnessed some terrible spectacle. Her immobility is that of a stupefaction in which a residue of fear is perpetuated. Her features, which are certainly convulsed by fear, retain the distention of a grimace in the pale and dead peace in which they are fixed; the rectitude of her entire pose, also, is a petrified frisson. One must remain thus after having contemplated Medusa. It prompts the idea of the aftermath of something horrible, of the minute that follows a sin—it is that minute, eternalized, that must be Hell—and, made up, she seems like the mummy of remorse.

To tell the truth, under the scorn and the hatred, she still retains and appearance of pride. Imperturbable, haughty, authorized, one might say, Baronne Sophor d'Hermelinge, in her sinister fixity, in her pallor of a poorly resuscitated corpse, resembles the white empress of some macabre Lesbos. But when no one is observing her, when she has returned to the house that sinister legends decry, when she is alone, then she is pitiful. Now her eyelids flutter over bleak irises, in spasms like sobs, and in her round eyes, devoid of lashes and eyebrows, fathomed by a transparency of emptiness a little while ago, in her wide eyes, shadows rise up, flow, descend and rise again like the clouds of mud that expend in disturbed water; and she considers, in panic terror . . . what?

That gaze is the gaze of Macbeth toward the empty armchair occupied by a spectral absence.

Then, suddenly, with a desperate sideways movement of the head, she puts her hands to her ears, as if to prevent herself from hearing. There is no one in the room except her, nor any sound; what, then, does her hearing perceive? Is it in her ears that it is born, that it persists, that it is obstinate, the doubtless terrible sound?—for she shivers in her entirety, spasmodically, stammering words that beg for pity; and, previously rigid, her face—the forehead, the cheeks, the lips—goes from pale to livid, from livid to earthen, stretches, elongates, weaken into a pasty and viscously fluid laxity; one might think her a mummy that is running to putrefaction.

Never has a human face expressed with more perfect hideousness the discouragement of having lived, the confession of an irremediable agony. Oh, what self-disgust, what cancerous remorse can be residing in that woman and eating her away for her to resemble, before death, the cadaver of a creature buried alive that has just been exhumed, not yet a skeleton?

At times she extends one of her hands toward a chest of drawers placed not far from her; her gesture is that of a drowning person trying to take possession of a piece of wreckage, but she does not complete the gesture, as if in the inanity of all hope, as if in the certainty of the impossibility of salvation; she must know that even to attempt salvation will only exasperate the anguish of her disaster, since merely having the intention adds to the fear of her sinister face—yes, adds to the fear again.

However, suddenly changing her mind, with the long combated decision of a starving man about to steal a loaf of bread, she leaps toward the chest of drawers, opens one of them, seizes a small gilded bottle and a nacre case, in which, when the lid is raised, a long, thin instrument of metal and crystal appears, which terminates in a needle—a Pravaz syringe—and the Baronne fills it with the morphine contained in the bottle. Then, her skirt lifted above the garter, she immediately finds on her skin, near the base of the thigh, the customary place, a gray and black callus as large as a sou, raised up, similar to the scaly ridges of a horse. The slightly puffy dry crust of that wound of sorts is hideous against the pale cream silk of the skin, amid the ruffles of batiste and valenciennes, alongside the pink ribbon that tightens the black stocking.

The hollow needle of the syringe, held between her thumb and the middle finger, has penetrated the flesh, enlarging the circle of the callus with a pin-prick; and by means of the light, adroit pressure of a single fingernail, that of the index finger, the liquid spreads under the dermis, insinuating itself, radiating like a warmth, reaching in the gliding descend the palms of the hands and the soles of the feet, and climbing again, squeezing the heart in passing with a familiar caress, which signifies: "You know, it's me," infiltrating all the way to the brain—the calm eyelids are no longer beating, the eyes, still wide open, are moistened by a liquid light—and enabling to blossom under the cranium a development of luminous and slow reveries in which the bogged-down mind drifts, as if in the hammock of a sunlit siesta.

Then—for the regal and merciful poison pours out its largesse very rapidly into those accustomed to imploring it, like a god in haste to grant the prayers of his worshipers—there is an infinite bliss without the reproach of any duty, a disdain for everything that is not the present moment, perhaps a minute, perhaps an eternity, the melting of all bitterness in a languorous mildness, the ignorance of yesterday and tomorrow, life arrested at the exquisite moment of forever, peace, forgetfulness, divine annihilation.

The face of Baronne Sophor d'Hermelinge—reminiscent of those singular faded, frayed flowers, relics of a dead spring, which, steeped in a mixture, resume the smiling splendor of old former middays—opens and expands, blissfully radiant. For a long time, a very long time, as if not living, with the visible ecstasy of a deceased person dreaming of paradise, she remains in that delectable inertia . . .

But now she agitates, feebly at first, at the same time as an expression of discomfort deforms the calm of her smile; and her two hands, which rise up and beat the air, unconsciously desirous, one might think, like a sleeper, of driving away a fly, removing from the ears the importunity of a contact or a sound. Doubtless she does not succeed, for she agitates more violently, her limbs extended and then drawn back, and then opened wide; then, her head between her closed fists, she gets up with a single bound, and, her eyes bulging, her features contorting as if in demoniac or hysterical tics, with white foam on her lips, she starts running around the room.

As she flees—for, without quitting the room, she gives the impression of fleeing—she looks behind her, at the carpet, as if some invisible swarm of creatures were pursuing her, in order to bite her or crawl up her legs. That flight does not stop, going from one wall to the other, avoiding the mirrors; and now, Baronne Sophor d'Hermelinge utters the long howls of a beaten dog or a wolf baying at the moon.

Oh, what howls! And suddenly, in a more lacerating clamor that is followed by silence, she collapses, her forehead toward the fireplace. There, she writhes, rolling over twice, seizes the brass of the grate between her teeth and bites it, a more abundant drool on her lips.

Anyone who saw her would hesitate to bring her help, so hideous and formidable does she appear in that crisis; and during the rare calms, when the upheaval of her entire being is appeased, when the palpitation of her breast and abdomen relents, she has in her round, iron-gray, staring eyes, devoid of lashes or eyebrows, the bleak void of definitive despair.

And such will be her life, until the day that will see her—aging, her soul extinct, it will seem, in hebetude, and her body bound in inertia—become, for the perfect accomplishment of an atavistic fatality or the triumph of the Demonic temptress, similar to the haggard idiots who sit with their hands under their chins in the courtyard of the Salpêtrière: a lamentable exemplar of Neurosis or Possession, her face fat and livid under sparse gray wisps, she will drool the nausea of dirty kisses.

But total unconsciousness will not be accorded to her! Always, with no possible flight, she will believe that she sees swarming, and climbing over her, like an assault of vermin, the ant-hive of her former sins; and it is in vain that she will want to take refuge in blind and deaf imbecility, for a sound, in order to keep her soul awake, will be ringing in her ear: a strange and detestable sound, the persistent symptom of a hereditary disease, or the frightful laughter of Mephistophela.

AFTERWORD

Some Observations on the Ambiguities and Paradoxes in *Mephistophela.*

Mephistophela is a novel about diabolical possession by a demoness of lust, a demoness who tortures her victim relentlessly, robbing her of everything that makes life worth living, and not allowing her any respite or release, including death. In the meantime, it torments her with the idea—the absurd idea—that people who are less intensely victimized by the particular form of lust by which she is afflicted can easily find happiness by conforming to the norms laid down, arbitrarily, by the society in which they live. The demoness in question is perhaps the most thoroughgoing ever imagined in a work of fiction, who eventually contrives a more thorough damnation for its victim than any of her many rivals. But does she really exist, or is she merely an illusion?

In a novel, of course, demons can exist; all that is required is for the narrative voice to state that they do; in a novel, anything can exist, because the narrative voice is omnipotent within the fictitious world of the text. So the demoness is real if the narrative voice says that she is. But does it? Sometimes yes and sometimes only maybe; the narrative voice teases, often holding out the provocative suggestion that it might only be joking, or speaking metaphorically, or even mistaken in its interpretations. The narrative voice is, in that regard at least, a deceptive, hypocritical flirt. So how is the reader supposed to deduce what is "really happening" within the fictitious world of the story? Perhaps he or she is not supposed to deduce it, or to be able to deduce it, but simply required to make up his or her own mind. Perhaps the narrative voice is itself a kind of demon or demoness, a parent of lies, an adversary of logic.

But let us attempt logic, and if it fails, we shall still remain free to make our choice as to what to think.

What seems to be indubitable is that Sophor receives her affliction of lust by heredity; whether it is a demon or disease, it is a continuation of the hereditary "possession" of the Tchercelews. It is worth bearing in mind, however, that heredity is a combination, that Sophor had a mother as well as a father, and that her mother was, in a sense, even more corrupt than her father, obtaining the accused sperm that fertilizes her womb by means of a strange rape. But Madame Luberti is an anomaly within the plot; not only does the early development of her corruption seem devoid of any external explanation, but its eventual terminus seems to be in frank contradiction to assertions made elsewhere in the story, guiding her to seek a simulation of bourgeois respectability that is ruled elsewhere to be flatly impossible, not merely for Sophor but for anyone tainted with Sin, whether the latter is conceived in Biblical terms or those of Urban Glaris' cynicism. She is a paradox. Perhaps Sophor inherits her paradoxicality. Either way, her existence in the universe of the story renders more problematic the question of Sophor's inheritance, and its alleged inevitability.

If Madame Luberti is paradoxical and problematic within the story's schema, how much more so is poor Magalo, who, without being possessed, anticipates the same strange loss of affect that Sophor will later suffer, and which Madame Luberti has apparently already suffered, losing the capacity to feel desire by virtue of the mysterious annihilation called "ennui." Can we believe that ennui can really do what the narrative voice credits it with the ability to do, in close collaboration with Remorse? More specifically, can the narrative voice's assertion that Magalo has come to hate her own sexuality and identity, and only seeks out Sophor, in the end, in order to preach a sermon to her on the alleged evil of her existence, and to provide a prophecy of sorts as to what awaits Sophor if she cannot heed the warning, be believed? All of that seems frankly absurd: an absurdity at least confused, and perhaps confounded, by the peculiar allegation that, before delivering her last sermon, Magalo has died and returned to life.

In the real world, we would not believe anyone who made such a statement, but in a novel, characters really can die and come back to life, because all that is necessary for that to happen in the story is for the narrative voice to say that it has. If the narrative voice tells us that the character concerned has gone to Heaven or Hell in the interim, then that is where they have gone, but in Magalo's case there is no such explicit statement, and Magalo's assertion that she has become a kind of angel seems lacking in sincerity as well as plausibility. In fact, while dead, or apparently dead, she has only vanished into the darkness of the narrative voice, and whatever she brings back, no matter what she might say about it, has originated there. In Magalo's case, surely, what she brings back is lies, mockeries and hypocrisies—unsurprisingly, those being the narrative voice's main stocks-in-trade in this particular fictional universe. Just as much a victim as Sophor, but a straightforward victim of the narrative voice rather than a surrogate demoness, she is not responsible for her act of treachery, and is entirely to be pitied rather than scorned for her apparent moral failure

Magalo's fall is all the more tragic and poignant because, in her brief period of triumph, when she teaches Sophor the elements of lesbian sexual technique, she also hints, and is almost allowed to spell out, the reason why the narrative voice—her deadly enemy and persecutor—is so scared of the very idea of lesbian sexual intercourse that it feels compelled to declare it dirty, abominable and forbidden by divine law, and also to go to the loathsome extreme of making Magalo declare it too. Magalo has previously explained to Sophor that the inability to induce female orgasm is actually commonplace among men, many of whom, for all their much-vaunted virility, cannot succeed in giving women the sexual satisfaction that other women can contrive, and many of whom, even if they are capable, are often unwilling to do so.

Men, of course, have generally lied about that frequent incapacity and similarly frequent disinclination, and narrative voices, including female ones, have very often collaborated in that denial. Sigmund Freud came to their aid at the end of the nineteenth century by inventing a hypothetical "vaginal orgasm" allegedly much superior to the "clitoral orgasm," which only men and machines could provide, but conscientious empirical investigation eventually proved it to be imaginary. Catulle Mendès and his readers only knew about the folklore that the pseudoscientific myth in question was devised to support, and such terminology was still unmentionable in 1889, so it is unsurprising that the narrative voice of *Mephistophela* tacitly finds the notion of the uniqueness of the clitoral orgasm, if not actually unthinkable, at least utterly terrible. On the other hand, it appears to know full well that, in terms of sexual performance and the giving of sexual satisfaction to women, a skilled lesbian like Sophor can, if the expression can be forgiven, knock men into a cocked hat.

That, in essence, is why the narrative voice feels compelled to consider Sophor to be a demon-led monster, and to condemn her, in revenge, to the worst damnation imaginable: she can turn women on and can afford them a satisfaction that many men, much of the time, either cannot, or do not care to, provide. That is not a thought that masculine vanity can easily tolerate; indeed, it is the ultimate horror of macho pride, and that horror is the key to the paradoxicality of the strange fictional universe of *Mephistophela* and of its stupid, stunted, deceptive demiurge, the sadistic torturer who subjects the innocent Sophor to every cruelty, ignominy and martyrdom that its admittedly-limited imagination can devise.

So, yes, *Mephistophela* is a novel about demonic possession, in the fictitious universe of which demonic possession is quite real—but behind all the teasing and hypocrisy, beyond all the calculated ambiguity, the possessor in question is not the demoness who laughs at Sophor and torments her; she is merely an agent, a mask, and a narrative device, like Sophor herself. The real demon, the real Father of Lies, is the narrative voice.

The reader is, of course, perfectly free to sympathize with that voice, and agree with what it contends. But what would that make the reader?

—Brian Stableford

3/174/P